An Award-Winning Literary Career...

From the start of her writing career, Joyce Carol Oates has earned high literary awards, among them a Guggenheim Fellowship, the Richard and Hinda Rosenthal Foundation Award of the National Institute of Arts and Letters and, in 1975, the Lotos Club Award of Merit. For her novel *Them* she won the National Book Award in 1970. Her novel *Do With Me What You Will* was a major selection of the Literary Guild of America and *The Assassins* and *Childwold* were both Featured Alternates of that book club.

Ms. Oates was a First Prize winner of the O. Henry Awards and her work has been included for many years in the *O. Henry Prize Stories*. In connection with these awards, she was selected for a Special Award for Continuing Achievement.

Ms. Oates is Professor of English at the University of Windsor.

Fawcett Crest Books
by Joyce Carol Oates:

THE ASSASSINS

BY THE NORTH GATE

CHILDWOLD

DO WITH ME WHAT YOU WILL

EXPENSIVE PEOPLE

A GARDEN OF EARTHLY DELIGHTS

THE GODDESS AND OTHER WOMEN

MARRIAGE AND INFIDELITIES

NIGHT-SIDE

NEW HEAVEN, NEW EARTH

THE POISONED KISS

THEM

UPON THE SWEEPING FLOOD

THE WHEEL OF LOVE

WITH SHUDDERING FALL

WONDERLAND

LOVE AND ITS DERANGEMENTS (poems)

WHERE ARE YOU GOING, WHERE HAVE YOU
    BEEN?

Night-Side

stories by
Joyce Carol Oates

Fawcett Crest • *New York*

NIGHT-SIDE

THIS BOOK CONTAINS THE COMPLETE TEXT OF THE ORIGINAL HARDCOVER EDITION.

Published by Fawcett Crest Books, a unit of CBS Publications, the Consumer Publishing Division of CBS Inc., by arrangement with The Vanguard Press, Inc.

ISBN: 0-449-24206-4

Printed in the United States of America

First Fawcett Crest printing: January 1980

10 9 8 7 6 5 4 3 2 1

for
Ruth and John Reed

Acknowledgments

The stories in this collection have appeared previously in the following magazines, often with different titles and in slightly different forms: *Atlantic Monthly, Exile, Fiction International, Harpers Magazine, Hudson Review, Iowa Review, Kansas Quarterly, Mademoiselle, Ontario Review, Tales, Tri-Quarterly, Viva, Yale Review, Chicago Review, Queen's Quarterly,* and *Fiddlehead.* "The Blessing" appeared as *Sparrow* 45. "Daisy" appeared in a special limited edition published by Black Sparrow Press, 1977. To all these acknowledgment and thanks are due.

Contents

Night -Side

TO GLORIA WHELAN

6 February 1887. Quincy, Massachusetts. Montague House.

Disturbing experience at Mrs. A————'s home yesterday evening. Few theatrics—comfortable though rather pathetically shabby surroundings—an only mildly sinister atmosphere (especially in contrast to the Walpurgis Night presented by that shameless charlatan in Portsmouth: the Dwarf Eustace who presumed to introduce me to Swedenborg himself, under the erroneous impression that I am a member of the Church of the New Jerusalem—*I!*) Nevertheless I came away disturbed, and my conversation with Dr. Moore afterward, at dinner, though dispassionate and even, at times, a bit flippant, did not settle my mind. Perry Moore is of course a hearty materialist, an Aristotelian-Spencerian with a love of good food and drink, and an appreciation of the more nonsensical vagaries of life; when in his company I tend to support that general view, as I do at the University as well—for there is a terrific pull in my nature toward the gregarious that I cannot resist. (That I do not wish to resist.) Once I am alone with my thoughts, however, I am accursed with doubts about my own position and nothing seems more precarious than my intellectual "convictions."

The more hardened members of our Society, like Perry Moore, are apt to put the issue bluntly: Is Mrs. A————of Quincy a conscious or unconscious fraud? The conscious frauds are relatively easy to deal with; once discovered, they prefer to erase themselves from further consideration. The unconscious frauds are not, in a sense, "frauds" at all. It would certainly be difficult to prove criminal intention. Mrs. A——, for instance, does not accept money or gifts so far as we have been able to determine, and both Perry Moore and I noted her courteous but firm refusal of the Judge's offer to send her and her husband (presumably ailing?) on holiday to England in the spring. She is a mild, self-effacing, rather stocky woman in her mid-fifties who wears her hair parted in the center, like several of my maiden aunts, and whose sole item of adornment was an old-fashioned cameo brooch; her black dress had the appearance of having been homemade, though it was attractive enough, and freshly ironed. According to the Society's records she has been a practicing medium now for six years. Yet she lives, still, in an undistinguished section of Quincy, in a neighborhood of modest frame dwellings. The A——s' house is in fairly good condition, especially considering the damage routinely done by our winters, and the only room we saw, the parlor, is quite ordinary, with overstuffed chairs and the usual cushions and a monstrous horsehair sofa and, of course, the oaken table; the atmosphere would have been so conventional as to have seemed disappointing had not Mrs. A—— made an attempt to brighten it, or perhaps to give it a glamourously occult air, by hanging certain watercolors about the room. (She claims that the watercolors were "done" by one of her contact spirits, a young Iroquois girl who died in the seventeen seventies of smallpox. They are touchingly garish—mandalas and triangles and stylized eyeballs and even a transparent Cosmic Man with Indian-black hair.)

At last night's sitting there were only three persons in addition to Mrs. A——. Judge T—— of the New York State Supreme Court (now retired); Dr. Moore; and I, Jarvis Williams. Dr. Moore and I came out from Cambridge under the aegis of the Society for Psychical Research in order to make a preliminary study of the kind of mediumship Mrs. A—— affects. We did not bring a stenographer along this time though Mrs. A—— indicated her willingness to have the sitting transcribed; she struck me as being rather warmly cooperative, and even interested in our formal procedures, though Perry Moore remarked afterward at dinner that she had struck him as "noticeably reluctant." She was, however, flustered at the start of the séance and for a while it seemed as if we and the Judge might have made the trip for nothing. (She kept waving her plump hands about like an embarrassed hostess, apologizing for the fact that the spirits were evidently in a "perverse uncommunicative mood tonight.")

She did go into trance eventually, however. The four of us were seated about the heavy round table from approximately 6:50 P.M. to 9 P.M. For nearly forty-five minutes Mrs. A—— made abortive attempts to contact her Chief Communicator and then slipped abruptly into trance (dramatically, in fact: her eyes rolled back in her head in a manner that alarmed me at first), and a personality named Webley appeared. "Webley's" voice appeared to be coming from several directions during the course of the sitting. At all times it was at least three yards from Mrs. A——; despite the semi-dark of the parlor I believe I could see the woman's mouth and throat clearly enough, and I could not detect any obvious signs of ventriloquism. (Perry Moore, who is more experienced than I in psychical research, and rather more casual about the whole phenomenon, claims he has witnessed feats of ventriloquism that would make poor Mrs. A—— look quite shabby in comparison.) "Webley's" voice was raw, singsong, peculiarly disturbing. At times it was shrill and at other times so faint as to be nearly inaudible. Something brattish about it. Exasperating. "Webley" took care to pronounce his final g's in a self-conscious manner, quite unlike Mrs. A——. (Which could be, of course, a deliberate ploy.)

This Webley is one of Mrs. A——'s most frequent manifesting spirits, though he is not the most reliable. Her Chief Communicator is a Scots patriarch who lived "in the time of Merlin" and who is evidently very wise; unfortunately he did not choose to appear yesterday evening. Instead, Webley presided. He is supposed to have died some seventy-five years ago at the age of nineteen in a house just up the street from the A——s'. He was either a butcher's helper or an apprentice tailor. He died in a fire—or by a "slow dreadful crippling disease"—or beneath a horse's hooves, in a freakish accident; during the course of the sitting he alluded self-pityingly to his death but seemed to have forgotten the exact details. At the very end of the evening he addressed me directly as Dr. Williams of Harvard University, saying that since I had influential friends in Boston I could help him with his career—it turned out he had written hundreds of songs and poems and parables but none had been published;

would I please find a publisher for his work? Life had treated him so unfairly. His talent—his genius—had been lost to humanity. I had it within my power to help him, he claimed, was I not *obliged* to help him...? He then sang one of his songs, which sounded to me like an old ballad; many of the words were so shrill as to be unintelligible, but he sang it just the same, repeating the verses in a haphazard order:

> *This ae nighte, this ae nighte,*
>   *—Every nighte and alle,*
> *Fire and fleet and candle-lighte,*
>   *And Christe receive thy saule.*
> *When thou from hence away art past,*
>   *—Every nighte and alle,*
> *To Whinny-muir thou com'st at last:*
>   *And Christe receive thy saule.*
>
> *From Brig o' Dread when thou may'st pass,*
>   *—Every nighte and alle,*
> *The whinnes sall prick thee to the bare bane:*
>   *And Christe receive thy saule.*

The elderly Judge T—— had come up from New York City in order, as he earnestly put it, to "speak directly to his deceased wife as he was never able to do while she was living"; but Webley treated the old gentleman in a high-handed, cavalier manner, as if the occasion were not at all serious. He kept saying, "Who is there tonight? *Who* is there? Let them introduce themselves again—I don't *like* strangers! I tell you I don't *like* strangers!" Though Mrs. A—— had informed us beforehand that we would witness no physical phenomena, there were, from time to time, glimmerings of light in the darkened room, hardly more than the tiny pulsations of light made by fireflies; and both Perry Moore and I felt the table vibrating beneath our fingers. At about the time when Webley gave way to the spirit of Judge T——'s wife, the temperature in the room seemed to drop suddenly and I remember being gripped by a sensation of panic—but it lasted only an instant and I was soon myself again. (Dr. Moore claimed not to have noticed any drop in temperature and Judge T—— was so rattled after the sitting that it would have been pointless to question him.)

The séance proper was similar to others I have attended. A spirit—or a voice—laid claim to being the late Mrs. T———; this spirit addressed the survivor in a peculiarly intense, urgent manner, so that it was rather embarrassing to be present. Judge T——— was soon weeping. His deeply creased face glistened with tears like a child's.

"Why Darrie! *Darrie!* Don't cry! Oh don't cry!" the spirit said. "No one is dead, Darrie. There is no death. No death! . . . Can you hear me, Darrie? Why are you so frightened? So upset? No need, Darrie, no need! Grandfather and Lucy and I are together here—happy together. Darrie, look up! Be brave, my dear! My poor frightened dear! We never knew each other, did we? My poor dear! My love! . . . I saw you in a great transparent house, a great burning house; poor Darrie, they told me you were ill, you were weak with fever; all the rooms of the house were aflame and the staircase was burnt to cinders, but there were figures walking up and down, Darrie, great numbers of them, and you were among them, dear, stumbling in your fright—so clumsy! Look up, dear, and shade your eyes, and you will see me. Grandfather helped me—did you know? Did I call out his name at the end? My dear, my darling, it all happened so quickly—we never knew each other, did we? Don't be hard on Annie! Don't be cruel! Darrie? Why are you crying?" And gradually the spirit voice grew fainter; or perhaps something went wrong and the channels of communication were no longer clear. There were repetitions, garbled phrases, meaningless queries of "Dear? Dear?" that the Judge's replies did not seem to placate. The spirit spoke of her gravesite, and of a trip to Italy taken many years before, and of a dead or unborn baby, and again of Annie—evidently Judge T———'s daughter; but the jumble of words did not always make sense and it was a great relief when Mrs. A———suddenly woke from her trance.

Judge T——— rose from the table, greatly agitated. He wanted to call the spirit back; he had not asked her certain crucial questions; he had been overcome by emotion and had found it difficult to speak, to interrupt the spirit's monologue. But Mrs. A——— (who looked shockingly tired) told him the spirit would not return again that night and they must not make any attempt to call it back.

"The other world obeys its own laws," Mrs. A——— said in her small, rather reedy voice.

We left Mrs. A———'s home shortly after 9:00 P.M. I was too exhausted; I had not realized how absorbed I had been in the proceedings.

Judge T——— is also staying at Montague House, but he was too upset after the sitting to join us for dinner. He assured us, though, that the spirit was authentic—the voice had been his wife's, he was certain of it, he would stake his life on it. She had never called him "Darrie" during her lifetime, wasn't it odd that she called him "Darrie" now?—and was so concerned for him, so loving?—and concerned for their daughter as well? He was very moved. He had a great deal to think about. (Yes, he'd had a fever some weeks ago—a severe attack of bronchitis and a fever; in fact, he had not completely recovered.) What was extraordinary about the entire experience was the wisdom revealed: There is no death.

There is no death.

Dr. Moore and I dined heartily on roast crown of lamb, spring potatoes with peas, and buttered cabbage. We were served two kinds of bread—German rye and sour-cream rolls; the hotel's butter was superb; the wine excellent; the dessert—crepes with cream and toasted almonds—looked marvelous, though I had not any appetite for it. Dr. Moore was ravenously hungry. He talked as he ate, often punctuating his remarks with rich bursts of laughter. It was his opinion, of course, that the medium was a fraud—and not a very skillful fraud, either. In his fifteen years of amateur, intermittent investigations he had encountered far more skillful mediums. Even the notorious Eustace with his levitating tables and hobgoblin chimes and shrieks was cleverer than Mrs. A———; one knew of course that Eustace was a cheat, but one was hard pressed to explain his method. Whereas Mrs. A—— was quite transparent.

Dr. Moore spoke for some time in his amiable, dogmatic way. He ordered brandy for both of us, though it was nearly midnight when we finished our dinner and I was anxious to get to bed. (I hoped to rise early and work on a lecture dealing with Kant's approach to the problem of Free Will, which I would be delivering in a few days.) But Dr. Moore enjoyed talking and seemed to have been invigorated by our experience at Mrs. A———'s.

At the age of forty-three Perry Moore is only four years my senior, but he has the air, in my presence at least, of being considerably older. He is a second cousin of my mother, a very successful physician with a bachelor's flat and office in Louisburg Square; his failure to marry, or his refusal, is one of Boston's perennial mysteries. Everyone agrees that he is learned, witty, charming, and extraordinarily intelligent. Striking rather than conventionally handsome, with a dark, lustrous beard and darkly bright eyes, he is an excellent amateur violinist, an enthusiastic sailor, and a lover of literature—his favorite writers are Fielding, Shakespeare, Horace, and Dante. He is, of course, the perfect investigator in spiritualist matters since he is detached from the phenomena he observes and yet he is indefatigably curious; he has a positive love, a mania, for facts. Like the true scientist he seeks facts that, assembled, may possibly give rise to hypotheses: he does not set out with a hypothesis in mind, like a sort of basket into which certain facts may be tossed, helter-skelter, while others are conveniently ignored. In all things he is an empiricist who accepts nothing on faith.

"If the woman is a fraud, then," I say hesitantly, "you believe she is a self-deluded fraud? And her spirits' information is gained by means of telepathy?"

"Telepathy indeed. There can be no other explanation," Dr. Moore says emphatically. "By some means not yet known to science . . . by some uncanny means she suppresses her conscious personality . . . and thereby releases other, secondary personalities that have the power of seizing upon others' thoughts and memories. It's done in a way not understood by science at the present time. But it will be understood eventually. Our investigations into the unconscious powers of the human mind are just beginning; we're on the threshold, really, of a new era."

"So she simply picks out of her clients' minds whatever they want to hear," I say slowly. "And from time to time she can even tease them a little—insult them, even: she can unloose a creature like that obnoxious Webley upon a person like Judge T—— without fear of being discovered. Telepathy. . . . Yes, that would explain a great deal. Very nearly everything we witnessed tonight."

"*Everything*, I should say," Dr. Moore says.

In the coach returning to Cambridge I set aside Kant and my lecture notes and read Sir Thomas Browne: *Light that makes all things seen, makes some things invisible. The greatest mystery of Religion is expressed by adumbration.*

19 March 1887. Cambridge. 11 P.M.

Walked ten miles this evening; must clear cobwebs from mind.

Unhealthy atmosphere. Claustrophobic. Last night's sitting in Quincy—a most unpleasant experience.

(Did not tell my wife what happened. Why is she so curious about the Spirit World?—about Perry Moore?)

My body craves more violent physical activity. In the summer, thank God, I will be able to swim in the ocean: the most strenuous and challenging of exercises.

Jotting down notes re the Quincy experience:

I. Fraud

Mrs. A——, possibly with accomplices, conspires to deceive: she does research into her clients' lives beforehand, possibly bribes servants. She is either a very skillful ventriloquist or works with someone who is. (Husband? Son? The husband is a retired cabinet-maker said to be in poor health; possibly consumptive. The son, married, lives in Waterbury.)

Her stated wish to avoid publicity and her declining of payment may simply be ploys; she may intend to make a great deal of money at some future time.

(Possibility of blackmail?—might be likely in cases similar to Perry Moore's.)

II. Non-fraud

Naturalistic

1. Telepathy. She reads minds of clients.
2. "Multiple personality" of medium. Aspects of her own buried psyche are released as her conscious personality is suppressed. These secondary beings are in mysterious rapport with the "secondary" personalities of the clients.

Spiritualistic

1. The controls are genuine communicators, intermediaries between our world and the world of the dead. These spirits give way to other spirits, who then speak through the medium; or

2. These spirits *influence* the medium, who relays their messages using her own vocabulary. Their personalities are then filtered through and limited by hers.
3. The spirits are not those of the deceased; they are perverse, willful spirits. (Perhaps demons? But there are no demons.)

III. Alternative hypothesis

Madness: the medium is mad, the clients are mad, even the detached, rationalist investigators are mad.

Yesterday evening at Mrs. A———'s home, the second sitting Perry Moore and I observed together, along with Miss Bradley, a stenographer from the Society, and two legitimate clients—a Brookline widow, Mrs. P———, and her daughter Clara, a handsome young woman in her early twenties. Mrs. A——— exactly as she appeared to us in February; possibly a little stouter. Wore black dress and cameo brooch. Served Lapsang Tea, tiny sandwiches, and biscuits when we arrived shortly after 6 P.M. Seemed quite friendly to Perry, Miss Bradley, and me; fussed over us, like any hostess; chattered a bit about the cold spell. Mrs. P——— and her daughter arrived at six-thirty and the sitting began shortly thereafter.

Jarring from the very first. A babble of spirit voices. Mrs. A——— in trance; head flung back, mouth gaping, eyes rolled upward. Queer. Unnerving. I glanced at Dr. Moore but he seemed unperturbed, as always. The widow and her daughter, however, looked as frightened as I felt.

Why are we here, sitting around this table?

What do we believe we will discover?

What are the risks we face...?

"Webley" appeared and disappeared in a matter of minutes. His shrill, raw, aggrieved voice was supplanted by that of a creature of indeterminate sex who babbled in Gaelic. This creature in turn was supplanted by a hoarse German, a man who identified himself as Felix; he spoke a curiously ungrammatical German. For some minutes he and two or three other spirits quarreled. (Each declared himself Mrs. A———'s Chief Communicator for the evening.) Small lights flickered in the semi-dark of the parlor and the table quivered beneath my fingers and I felt, or believed I felt, something brushing against me, touching the back of my head. I shuddered violently but

regained my composure at once. An unidentified voice
proclaimed in English that the Spirit of our Age was Mars: there
would be a catastrophic war shortly and most of the world's
population would be destroyed. All atheists would be destroyed.
Mrs. A—— shook her head from side to side as if trying to
wake. Webley appeared, crying "Hello? Hello? I can't see
anyone! Who is there? Who has called me?" but was again
supplanted by another spirit who shouted long strings of words
in a foreign language. [Note: I discovered a few days later that
this language was Walachian, a Romanian dialect. Of course Mrs.
A——, whose ancestors are English, could not possibly have
known Walachian, and I rather doubt that the woman has even
heard of the Walachian people.]

The sitting continued in this chaotic way for some minutes.
Mrs. P—— must have been quite disappointed, since she had
wanted to be put in contact with her deceased husband. (She
needed advice on whether or not to sell certain pieces of
property.) Spirits babbled freely in English, German, Gaelic,
French, even in Latin, and at one point Dr. Moore queried a spirit
in Greek, but the spirit retreated at once as if not equal to Dr.
Moore's wit. The atmosphere was alarming but at the same time
rather manic; almost jocular. I found myself suppressing
laughter. Something touched the back of my head and I shivered
violently and broke into perspiration, but the experience was not
altogether unpleasant; it would be very difficult for me to
characterize it.

And then—

And then, suddenly, everything changed. There was complete calm. A spirit voice spoke gently out of a corner of the room
addressing Perry Moore by his first name in a slow, tentative,
groping way. "Perry? Perry . . . ?" Dr. Moore jerked about in his
seat. He was astonished; I could see by his expression that the
voice belonged to someone he knew.

"Perry . . . ? This is Brandon. I've waited so long for you, Perry,
how could you be so selfish? I forgave you. Long ago. You
couldn't help your cruelty and I couldn't help my innocence.
Perry? My glasses have been broken—I can't see. I've been afraid
for so long, Perry, please have mercy on me! I can't bear it any
longer. I didn't *know* what it would be like. There are crowds of
people here, but we can't see one another, we don't know one
another, we're strangers, there is a universe of strangers—I can't
see anyone clearly—I've been lost for twenty years, Perry, I've

been waiting for you for twenty years! You don't dare turn away again, Perry! Not again! Not after so long!"

Dr. Moore stumbled to his feet, knocking his chair aside.

"No—Is it—I don't believe—"

"Perry? Perry? Don't abandon me again, Perry! Not again!"

"What is this?" Dr. Moore cried.

He was on his feet now; Mrs. A—— woke from her trance with a groan. The women from Brookline were very upset and I must admit that I was in a mild state of terror, my shirt and my underclothes drenched with perspiration.

The sitting was over. It was only seven-thirty.

"Brandon?" Dr. Moore cried. "Wait. Where are—? Brandon? Can you hear me? Where are you? Why did you do it, Brandon? Wait! Don't leave! Can't anyone call him back— Can't anyone help me—"

Mrs. A—— rose unsteadily. She tried to take Dr. Moore's hands in hers but he was too agitated.

"I heard only the very last words," she said. "They're always that way—so confused, so broken—the poor things— Oh, what a pity! It wasn't murder, was it? Not murder! Suicide—? I believe suicide is even worse for them! The poor broken things, they wake in the other world and are utterly, utterly lost—they have no guides, you see—no help in crossing over— They are completely alone for eternity—"

"Can't you call him back?" Dr. Moore asked wildly. He was peering into a corner of the parlor, slightly stooped, his face distorted as if he were staring into the sun. "Can't someone help me?...Brandon? Are you here? Are you here somewhere? For God's sake can't someone help!"

"Dr. Moore, please, the spirits are gone—the sitting is over for tonight—"

"You foolish old woman, leave me alone! Can't you see I—I—I must not lose him— Call him back, will you? I insist! I insist!"

"Dr. Moore, please—You mustn't shout—"

"I said call him back! At once! *Call him back!*"

Then he burst into tears. He stumbled against the table and hid his face in his hands and wept like a child; he wept as if his heart had been broken.

And so today I have been reliving the séance. Taking notes, trying to determine what happened. A brisk windy walk of ten miles. Head buzzing with ideas. Fraud? Deceit? Telepathy? Madness?

What a spectacle! Dr. Perry Moore calling after a spirit, begging it to return—and then crying, afterward, in front of four astonished witnesses.

Dr. Perry Moore of all people.

My dilemma: whether I should report last night's incident to Dr. Rowe, the president of the Society, or whether I should say nothing about it and request that Miss Bradley say nothing. It would be tragic if Perry's professional reputation were to be damaged by a single evening's misadventure; and before long all of Boston would be talking.

In his present state, however, he is likely to tell everyone about it himself.

At Montague House the poor man was unable to sleep. He would have kept me up all night had I had the stamina to endure his excitement.

There *are* spirits! There have always been spirits!

His entire life up to the present time has been misspent!

And of course, most important of all—there is no death!

He paced about my hotel room, pulling at his beard nervously. At times there were tears in his eyes. He seemed to want a response of some kind from me but whenever I started to speak he interrupted; he was not really listening.

"Now at last I know. I can't undo my knowledge," he said in a queer hoarse voice. "Amazing, isn't it, after so many years . . . so many wasted years. . . . Ignorance has been my lot, darkness . . . and a hideous complacency. My God, when I consider my deluded smugness! I am so ashamed, so ashamed. All along people like Mrs. A——— have been in contact with a world of such power . . . and people like me have been toiling in ignorance, accumulating material achievements, expending our energies in idiotic transient things. . . . But all that is changed now. Now I know. I *know*. There is no death, as the Spiritualists have always told us."

"But, Perry, don't you think—Isn't it possible that—"

"I *know*," he said quietly. "It's as clear to me as if I had crossed over into that other world myself. Poor Brandon! He's no older now than he was *then*. The poor boy, the poor tragic soul! To think that he's still living after so many years. . . . Extraordinary. . . . It makes my head spin," he said slowly. For a moment he stood without speaking. He pulled at his beard, then absently touched his lips with his fingers, then wiped at his eyes. He seemed to have forgotten me. When he spoke again his voice was hollow, rather ghastly. He sounded drugged. "I . . . I had been thinking of him as . . . as dead, you know. As dead. Twenty years. Dead. And now, tonight, to be forced to realize that . . . that he isn't dead after all. . . . It was laudanum he took. I found him. His rooms on the third floor of Weld Hall. I found him, I had no real idea, none at all, not until I read the note . . . and of course I destroyed the note . . . I had to, you see: for his sake. For his sake more than mine. It was because he realized there could be no . . . no hope. . . . Yet he called me cruel! You heard him, Jarvis, didn't you? Cruel! I suppose I was. Was I? I don't know what to think. I must talk with him again. I . . . I don't know what to . . . what to think. I. . . ."

"You look awfully tired, Perry. It might be a good idea to go to bed," I said weakly.

". . . recognized his voice at once. Oh at once: no doubt. None. What a revelation! And my life so misspent. . . . Treating people's *bodies*. Absurd. I know now that nothing matters except that other world . . . nothing matters except our dead, our beloved dead . . . who are *not dead*. What a colossal revelation. . . . ! Why, it will change the entire course of history. It will alter men's minds throughout the world. You were there, Jarvis, so you understand. You were a witness. . . ."

"But—"

"You'll bear witness to the truth of what I am saying?"

He stared at me, smiling. His eyes were bright and threaded with blood.

I tried to explain to him as courteously and sympathetically as possible that his experience at Mrs. A———'s was not substantially different from the experiences many people have had at séances. "And always in the past psychical researchers have taken the position—"

"You were *there*," he said angrily. "You heard Brandon's voice as clearly as I did. Don't deny it!"

"—have taken the position that—that the phenomenon can be partly explained by the telepathic powers of the medium—"

"That was Brandon's *voice*," Perry said. "I felt his presence, I tell you! *His*. Mrs. A——— had nothing to do with it—nothing at all. I feel as if . . . as if I could call Brandon back by myself. . . . I feel his presence even now. Close about me. He isn't dead, you see; no one is dead, there's a universe of . . . of people who are not dead. . . . Parents, grandparents, sisters, brothers, everyone . . . everyone. . . . How can you deny, Jarvis, the evidence of your own senses? You were there with me tonight and you know as well as I do. . . ."

"Perry, I don't *know*. I did hear a voice, yes, but we've heard voices before at other sittings, haven't we? There are always voices. There are always 'spirits.' The Society has taken the position that the spirits could be real, of course, but that there are other hypotheses that are perhaps more likely—"

"Other hypotheses indeed!" Perry said irritably. "You're like a man with his eyes shut tight who refuses to open them out of sheer cowardice. Like the cardinals refusing to look through Galileo's telescope! And you have pretensions of being a man of learning, of science. . . . Why, we've got to destroy all the records we've made so far; they're a slander on the world of the spirits. Thank God we didn't file a report yet on Mrs. A———! It would be so embarrassing to be forced to call it back. . . ."

"Perry, please. Don't be angry. I want only to remind you of the fact that we've been present at other sittings, haven't we?—and we've witnessed others responding emotionally to certain phenomena. Judge T———, for instance. He was convinced he'd spoken with his wife. But you must remember, don't you, that you and I were not at all convinced . . . ? It seemed to us more likely that Mrs. A——— is able, through extrasensory powers we don't quite understand, to read the minds of her clients, and then to project certain voices out into the room so that it sounds as if they are coming from other people. . . . You even said, Perry, that she wasn't a very skillful ventriloquist. You said—"

"What does it matter what, in my ignorance, I said?" he cried. "Isn't it enough that I've been humiliated? That my entire life has been turned about? Must you insult me as well—sitting there so smugly and insulting *me*? I think I can make claim to being someone whom you might respect."

And so I assured him that I did respect him. And he walked about the room, wiping at his eyes, greatly agitated. He spoke again of his friend, Brandon Gould, and of his own ignorance, and of the important mission we must undertake to inform men and women of the true state of affairs. I tried to talk with him, to reason with him, but it was hopeless. He scarcely listened to me.

". . . must inform the world . . . crucial truth. . . . There is no death, you see. Never was. Changes civilization, changes the course of history. Jarvis?" he said groggily. "You see? *There is no death.*"

25 March 1887. Cambridge.

Disquieting rumors re Perry Moore. Heard today at the University that one of Dr. Moore's patients (a brother-in-law of Dean Barker) was extremely offended by his behavior during a consultation last week. Talk of his having been drunk—which I find incredible. If the poor man appeared to be excitable and not his customary self, it was not because he was *drunk*, surely.

Another far-fetched tale told me by my wife, who heard it from her sister Maude: Perry Moore went to church (St. Aidan's Episcopal Church on Mount Street) for the first time in a decade, sat alone, began muttering and laughing during the sermon, and finally got to his feet and walked out, creating quite a stir. *What delusions! What delusions!*—he was said to have muttered.

I fear for the poor man's sanity.

31 March 1887. Cambridge 4 A.M.

Sleepless night. Dreamed of swimming ... swimming in the ocean ... enjoying myself as usual when suddenly the water turns thick ... turns to mud. Hideous! Indescribably awful. I was swimming nude in the ocean, by moonlight, I believe, ecstatically happy, entirely alone, when the water turned to mud.... Vile, disgusting mud; faintly warm; sucking at my body. Legs, thighs, torso, arms. Horrible. Woke in terror. Drenched with perspiration: pajamas wet. One of the most frightening nightmares of my adulthood.

A message from Perry Moore came yesterday just before dinner. Would I like to join him in visiting Mrs. A—— sometime soon, in early April perhaps, on a noninvestigative basis ... ? He is uncertain now of the morality of our "investigating" Mrs. A—— or any other medium.

4 April 1887. Cambridge.

Spent the afternoon from two to five at William James's home on Irving Street, talking with Professor James of the inexplicable phenomenon of consciousness. He is robust as always, rather irreverent, supremely confident in a way I find enviable; rather like Perry Moore before his conversion. (Extraordinary eyes—so piercing, quick, playful; a graying beard liberally threaded with white; close-cropped graying hair; a large, curving, impressive forehead; a manner intelligent and graceful and at the same time rough-edged, as if he anticipates or perhaps even hopes for recalcitration in his listeners.) We both find conclusive the ideas set forth in Binét's *Alterations of Personality* ... unsettling as these ideas may be to the rationalist position. James speaks of a *peculiarity* in the constitution of human nature: that is, the fact that we inhabit not only our ego-consciousness but a wide field of psychological experience (most clearly represented by the phenomenon of memory, which no one can adequately explain) over which we have no control whatsoever. In fact, we are not generally aware of this field of consciousness.

We inhabit a lighted sphere, then; and about us is a vast penumbra of memories, reflections, feelings, and stray uncoordinated thoughts that "belong" to us theoretically, but that do not seem to be part of our conscious identity. (I was too timid to ask Professor James whether it might be the case that we do not inevitably own these aspects of the personality—that such phenomena belong as much to the objective world as to our subjective selves.) It is quite possible that there is an element of some indeterminate kind: oceanic, timeless, and living, against which the individual being constructs temporary barriers as part of an ongoing process of unique, particularized survival; like the ocean itself, which appears to separate islands that are in fact not "islands" at all, but aspects of the earth firmly joined together below the surface of the water. Our lives, then, resemble these islands.... All this is no more than a possibility, Professor James and I agreed.

James is acquainted, of course, with Perry Moore. But he declined to speak on the subject of the poor man's increasingly eccentric behavior when I alluded to it. (It may be that he knows even more about the situation than I do—he enjoys a multitude of acquaintances in Cambridge and Boston.) I brought our conversation round several times to the possibility of the *naturalness* of the conversion experience in terms of the individual's evolution of self, no matter how his family, his colleagues, and society in general viewed it, and Professor James appeared to agree; at least he did not emphatically disagree. He maintains a healthy skepticism, of course, regarding Spiritualist claims, and all evangelical and enthusiastic religious movements, though he is, at the same time, a highly articulate foe of the "rationalist" position and he believes that psychical research of the kind some of us are attempting will eventually unearth riches—revealing aspects of the human psyche otherwise closed to our scrutiny.

"The fearful thing," James said, "is that we are at all times vulnerable to incursions from the 'other side' of the personality.... We cannot determine the nature of the total personality simply because much of it, perhaps most, is hidden from us.... When we are invaded, then, we are overwhelmed and surrender immediately. Emotionally charged intuitions, hunches, guesses, even ideas may be the least aggressive of these incursions; but there are visual and auditory hallucinations, and forms of automatic behavior not controlled by the conscious mind.... Ah, you're thinking I am simply describing insanity?"

I stared at him, quite surprised.

"No. Not at all. Not at all," I said at once.

Reading through my grandfather's journals, begun in East Anglia many years before my birth. Another world then. Another language, now lost to us. *Man is sinful by nature. God's justice takes precedence over His mercy.* The dogma of Original Sin: something brutish about the innocence of that belief. And yet consoling....

Fearful of sleep since my dreams are so troubled now. The voices of impudent spirits (Immanuel Kant himself come to chide me for having made too much of his categories—!), stray shouts and whispers I cannot decipher, the faces of my own beloved dead hovering near, like carnival masks, insubstantial and possibly fraudulent. Impatient with my wife, who questions me too closely on these personal matters; annoyed from time to time, in the evenings especially, by the silliness of the children. (The eldest is twelve now and should know better.) Dreading to receive another lengthy letter—sermon, really—from Perry Moore re his "new position," and yet perversely hoping one will come soon.

I must know.

(Must know *what*...?)

I must know.

10 April 1887. Boston St. Aidan's Episcopal Church.

Funeral service this morning for Perry Moore; dead at forty-three.

17 April 1887. Seven Hills, New Hampshire.

A weekend retreat. No talk. No need to think.

Visiting with a former associate, author of numerous books. Cartesian specialist. Elderly. Partly deaf. Extraordinarily kind to me. (Did not ask about the Department or about my work.) Intensely interested in animal behavior now, in observation primarily; fascinated with the phenomenon of hibernation.

He leaves me alone for hours. He sees something in my face I cannot see myself.

The old consolations of a cruel but just God: ludicrous today.

In the nineteenth century we live free of God. We live in the illusion of freedom-of-God.

Dozing off in the guest room of this old farmhouse and then waking abruptly. *Is someone here? Is someone here?* My voice queer, hushed, childlike. *Please: is someone here?*

Silence.

Query: Is the penumbra outside consciousness all that was ever meant by "God"?

Query: Is inevitability all that was ever meant by "God"?

God—the body of fate we inhabit, then; no more and no less.

God pulled Perry down into the body of fate: into Himself. (Or Itself.) As Professor James might say, Dr. Moore was "vulnerable" to an assault from the other side.

At any rate he is dead. They buried him last Saturday.

25 April 1887. Cambridge.

Shelves of books. The sanctity of books. Kant, Plato, Schopenhauer, Descartes, Hume, Hegel, Spinoza. The others. All. Nietzsche, Spencer, Leibnitz (on whom I did a torturous Master's thesis). Plotinus. Swedenborg. *The Transactions of the American Society for Psychical Research.* Voltaire. Locke.

Rousseau. And Berkeley: the good Bishop adrift in a dream.

An etching by Halbrech above my desk, The Thames 1801. Water too black. Inky-black. Thick with mud . . . ? Filthy water in any case.

Perry's essay, forty-five scribbled pages. "The Challenge of the Future." Given to me several weeks ago by Dr. Rowe, who feared rejecting it for the *Transactions* but could not, of course, accept it. I can read only a few pages at a time, then push it aside, too moved to continue. Frightened also.

The man had gone insane.

Died insane.

Personality broken: broken bits of intellect.

His argument passionate and disjointed, with no pretense of objectivity. Where some weeks ago he had taken the stand that it was immoral to investigate the Spirit World, now he took the stand that it was imperative we do so. We are on the brink of a new age . . . new knowledge of the universe . . . comparable to the stormy transitional period between the Ptolemaic and the Copernican theories of the universe. . . . More experiments required. Money. Donations. Subsidies by private institutions. All psychological research must be channeled into a systematic study of the Spirit World and the ways by which we can communicate with that world. Mediums like Mrs. A——— must be brought to centers of learning like Harvard and treated with the respect their genius deserves. Their value to civilization is, after all, beyond estimation. They must be rescued from arduous and routine lives where their genius is drained off into vulgar pursuits . . . they must be rescued from a clientele that is mainly concerned with being put into contact with deceased relatives for utterly trivial, self-serving reasons. Men of learning must realize the gravity of the situation. Otherwise we will fail, we will stagger beneath the burden, we will be defeated, ignobly, and it will remain for the twentieth century to discover the existence of the Spirit Universe that surrounds the Material Universe, and to determine the exact ways by which one world is related to another.

Perry Moore died of a stroke on the eighth of April; died instantaneously on the steps of the Bedford Club shortly after 2 P.M. Passers-by saw a very excited, red-faced gentleman with an open collar push his way through a small gathering at the top of the steps—and then suddenly fall, as if shot down.

In death he looked like quite another person: his features sharp, the nose especially pointed. Hardly the handsome Perry Moore everyone had known.

He had come to a meeting of the Society, though it was suggested by Dr. Rowe and by others (including myself) that he stay away. Of course he came to argue. To present his "new position." To insult the other members. (He was contemptuous of a rather poorly organized paper on the medium Miss E——— of Salem, a young woman who works with objects like rings, articles of clothing, locks of hair, et cetera; and quite angry with the evidence presented by a young geologist that would seem to discredit, once and for all, the claims of Eustace of Portsmouth. He interrupted a third paper, calling the reader a "bigot" and an "ignorant fool.")

Fortunately the incident did not find its way into any of the papers. The press, misunderstanding (deliberately and maliciously) the Society's attitude toward Spiritualism, delights in ridiculing our efforts.

There were respectful obituaries. A fine eulogy prepared by Reverend Tyler of St. Aidan's. Other tributes. *A tragic loss....Mourned by all who knew him....* (I stammered and could not speak. I cannot speak of him, of it, even now. Am I mourning, am I aggrieved? Or merely shocked? Terrified?) Relatives and friends and associates glossed over his behavior these past few months and settled upon an earlier Perry Moore, eminently sane, a distinguished physician and man of letters. I did not disagree, I merely acquiesced; I could not make any claim to have really known the man.

And so he has died, and so he is dead....

Shortly after the funeral I went away to New Hampshire for a few days. But I can barely remember that period of time now. I sleep poorly, I yearn for summer, for a drastic change of climate, of scene. It was unwise for me to take up the responsibility of psychical research, fascinated though I am by it; my classes and lectures at the University demand most of my energy.

How quickly he died, and so young: so relatively young.

No history of high blood pressure, it is said.

At the end he was arguing with everyone, however. His personality had completely changed. He was rude, impetuous, even rather profane; even poorly groomed. (Rising to challenge the first of the papers, he revealed a shirtfront that appeared to be stained.) Some claimed he had been drinking all along, for years. Was it possible . . . ? (He had clearly enjoyed the wine and brandy in Quincy that evening, but I would not have said he was intemperate.) Rumors, fanciful tales, outright lies, slander. . . . It is painful, the vulnerability death brings.

Bigots, he called us. Ignorant fools. Unbelievers—atheists— traitors to the Spirit World—heretics. Heretics! I believe he looked directly at me as he pushed his way out of the meeting room: his eyes glaring, his face dangerously flushed, no recognition in his stare.

After his death, it is said, books continue to arrive at his home from England and Europe. He spent a small fortune on obscure, out-of-print volumes—commentaries on the Kabbala, on Plotinus, medieval alchemical texts, books on astrology, witchcraft, the metaphysics of death. Occult cosmologies. Egyptian, Indian, and Chinese "wisdom." Blake, Swedenborg, Cozad. *The Tibetan Book of the Dead.* Datsky's *Lunar Mysteries.* His estate is in chaos because he left not one but several wills, the most recent made out only a day before his death, merely a few lines scribbled on scrap paper, without witnesses. The family will contest, of course. Since in this will he left his money and property to an obscure woman living in Quincy, Massachusetts, and since he was obviously not in his right mind at the time, they would be foolish indeed not to contest.

Days have passed since his sudden death. Days continue to pass. At times I am seized by a sort of quick, cold panic; at other times I am inclined to think the entire situation has been exaggerated. In one mood I vow to myself that I will never again pursue psychical research because it is simply too dangerous. In another mood I vow I will never again pursue it because it is a waste of time and my own work, my own career, must come first.

Heretics, he called us. Looking straight at me.

Still, he was mad. And is not to be blamed for the vagaries of madness.

19 June 1887. Boston.

Luncheon with Dr. Rowe, Miss Madeleine van der Post, young Lucas Matthewson; turned over my personal records and notes re the mediums Dr. Moore and I visited. (Destroyed jottings of a private nature.) Miss van der Post and Matthewson will be taking over my responsibilities. Both are young, quick-witted, alert, with a certain ironic play about their features; rather like Dr. Moore in his prime. Matthewson is a former seminary student now teaching physics at the Boston University. They questioned me about Perry Moore, but I avoided answering frankly. Asked if we were close, I said *No.* Asked if I had heard a bizarre tale making the rounds of Boston salons—that a spirit claiming to be Perry Moore has intruded upon a number of séances in the area—I said honestly that I had not; and I did not care to hear about it.

Spinoza: *I will analyze the actions and appetites of men as if it were a question of lines, of planes, and of solids.*

It is in this direction, I believe, that we must move. Away from the phantasmal, the vaporous, the unclear; toward lines, planes, and solids.

Sanity.

8 July 1887. Mount Desert Island, Maine.

Very early this morning, before dawn, dreamed of Perry Moore: a babbling gesticulating spirit, bearded, bright-eyed, obviously mad. Jarvis? Jarvis? Don't deny me! he cried. I am so...so bereft....

Paralyzed, I faced him: neither awake nor asleep. His words were not really *words* so much as unvoiced thoughts. I heard them in my own voice; a terrible raw itching at the back of my throat yearned to articulate the man's grief.

Perry?

You don't dare deny me! Not now!

He drew near and I could not escape. The dream shifted, lost its clarity. Someone was shouting at me. Very angry, he was, and baffled—as if drunk—or ill—or injured.

Perry? I can't hear you—

—our dinner at Montague House, do you remember? Lamb, it was. And crepes with almond for dessert. You remember! You remember! You can't deny me! We are both nonbelievers then, both abysmally ignorant—you can't deny me!

(I was mute with fear or with cunning.)

—that idiot Rowe, how humiliated he will be! All of them! All of you! The entire rationalist bias, the—the conspiracy of—of fools—bigots— In a few years— In a few short years— Jarvis, where are you? Why can't I see you? Where have you gone?— My eyes can't focus: will someone help me? I seem to have lost my way. Who is here? Who am I talking with? You remember me, don't you?

(He brushed near me, blinking helplessly. His mouth was a hole torn into his pale ravaged flesh.)

Where are you? Where is everyone? I thought it would be crowded here but—but there's no one—I am forgetting so much! My name—what was my name? Can't see. Can't remember. Something very important—something very important I must accomplish—can't remember— Why is there no God? No one here? No one in control? We drift this way and that way, we come to no rest, there are no landmarks—no way of judging—everything is confused—disjointed— Is someone listening? Would you read to me, please? Would you read to me?—anything!—that speech of Hamlet's—*To be or not*—a sonnet of Shakespeare's—any sonnet, anything— *That time of year thou may in me behold*—is that it?—is that how it begins? *Bare ruin'd choirs where the sweet birds once sang.* How does it go? Won't you tell me? I'm lost—there's nothing here to see, to touch—isn't anyone listening? I thought there was someone nearby, a friend: isn't anyone here?

(I stood paralyzed, mute with caution: he passed by.)

—*When in the chronicle of wasted time*—*the wide world dreaming of things to come*—is anyone listening?—can anyone help?—I am forgetting so much—my name, my life—my life's work—to penetrate the mysteries—the veil—to do justice to the universe of—of what—what had I intended?—am I in my place of repose now, have I come home? Why is it so empty here? Why is no one in control? My eyes—my head—mind broken and blown about—slivers—shards—annihilating all that's made to a—a green thought—a green shade—Shakespeare? Plato? Pascal? Will someone read me Pascal again? I seem to have lost my way—I am being blown about— Jarvis, was it? My dear young friend Jarvis? But I've forgotten your last name—I've forgotten so much—

(I wanted to reach out to touch him—but could not move, could not wake. The back of my throat ached with sorrow. Silent! Silent! I could not utter a word.)

—my papers, my journal—twenty years—a key somewhere hidden—where?—ah yes: the bottom drawer of my desk—do you hear?—my desk—house—Louisburg Square—the key is hidden there—wrapped in a linen handkerchief—the strongbox is—the locked box is—hidden—my brother Edward's house—attic—trunk—steamer trunk—initials R. W. M.—Father's trunk, you see—strongbox hidden inside—my secret journals—life's work—physical and spiritual wisdom—must not be lost—are you listening?—is anyone listening? I am forgetting so much, my mind is in shreds—but if you could locate the journal and read it to me—if you could salvage it—me—I would be so very grateful—I would forgive you anything, all of you— Is anyone there? Jarvis? Brandon? No one?—My journal, my soul: will you salvage it? Will—

(He stumbled away and I was alone again.)

Perry—?

But it was too late: I awoke drenched with perspiration.

Nightmare.
Must forget.

Best to rise early, before the others. Mount Desert Island lovely in July. Our lodge on a hill above the beach. No spirits here: wind from the northeast, perpetual fresh air, perpetual waves. Best to rise early and run along the beach and plunge into the chilly water.

Clear the cobwebs from one's mind.

How beautiful the sky, the ocean, the sunrise!

No spirits here on Mount Desert Island. Swimming: skillful exertion of arms and legs. Head turned this way, that way. Eyes half shut. The surprise of the cold rough waves. One yearns almost to slip out of one's human skin at such times . . . ! Crude blatant beauty of Maine. Ocean. Muscular exertion of body. How alive I am, how living, how invulnerable; what a triumph in my every breath. . . .

Everything slips from my mind except the present moment. I am living, I am alive, I am immortal. Must not weaken: must not sink. Drowning? No. Impossible. Life is the only reality. It is not extinction that awaits but a hideous dreamlike state, a perpetual groping, blundering—far worse than extinction—incomprehensible: so it is life we must cling to, arm over arm, swimming, conquering the element that sustains us.

Jarvis? someone cried. *Please hear me—*

How exquisite life is, the turbulent joy of life contained in flesh! I heard nothing except the triumphant waves splashing about me. I swam for nearly an hour. Was reluctant to come ashore for breakfast, though our breakfasts are always pleasant rowdy sessions: my wife and my brother's wife and our seven children thrown together for the month of July. Three boys, four girls: noise, bustle, health, no shadows, no spirits. No time to think. Again and again I shall emerge from the surf, face and hair and body streaming water, exhausted but jubilant, triumphant. Again and again the children will call out to me, excited, from the dayside of the world that they inhabit.

I will not investigate Dr. Moore's strongbox and his secret journal; I will not even think about doing so. The wind blows words away. The surf is hypnotic. I will not remember this morning's dream once I sit down to breakfast with the family. I will not clutch my wife's wrist and say *We must not die! We dare not die!*—for that would only frighten and offend her.

Jarvis? she is calling at this very moment.

And I say *Yes—? Yes, I'll be there at once.*

The Widows

Why was she drawn to the telephone?—it was not ringing. She found herself walking out of her way, through the narrow hall, where the telephone was kept on a small pedestal table beneath the stairs. Even during the day it was dark in this part of the house; there were not many windows and she didn't want to waste money on electricity. She knew the passageway so well that she moved through it with the stiff, alert confidence of the blind. Why bother with a telephone? She meant to have it disconnected.

Sometimes it did ring. And she listened to it, bitterly. She might be in the kitchen, at the table: a small cleared-off space at one corner of the table, *her* space. She ate there, absentmindedly, quickly, while she read. If the telephone rang, she listened to it with a kind of respectful distaste: a call could be only a disappointment or an insult. Or a wrong number. It was strange, it might even have been exhilarating—she would have to think about the possibilities—the fact that no one in the world, no one at all, could have anything valuable to tell her.

Yet she found herself wandering along the passageway, distracted and vaguely expectant. As if she were about to receive an important call. When the telephone call had come from the hospital, some months before, of course she had not expected it—she might have been expecting a call from someone else, in

34

fact, a house painter with his estimate of what it would cost them to have this shabby little house repainted—so she had answered it easily enough, neither eager nor terrified. Now she drifted near the phone and stood there, in the dark. If it rang, she had the option of answering or not answering: that was freedom. Her mother, her in-laws, anyone who cared to communicate with her could write to her—if they liked—if they imagined that anything they might say would mean much to her. She might even reply eventually.

One evening in late August she went to the telephone, and, as she approached it, it began to ring. She smiled. She smiled knowingly. For a few moments she resisted; then she picked up the receiver. She said nothing. She hoped it might be a wrong number so that she could replace the receiver gently, in the middle of a stranger's query. But it was someone who called her by name, a woman, a woman people had wanted her to meet—another young widow—and before Beatrice could cut her off, the woman was suggesting that they meet for lunch sometime. Was she free? Would she be interested?

"Why are you telephoning me?" Beatrice stammered. "Why—what is it— Why are you harassing me?"

The woman paused. Then she began again, in a rather warm, aggressive voice, apologizing for bothering Beatrice— explaining that friends of friends had suggested she call— Manitock was such a small city, as Beatrice knew, of course people talked about one another constantly. And they were saying that Beatrice was not looking well; that she had resigned her teaching job; someone had even said she was—

Beatrice interrupted. She said calmly: "Who are these people? I don't know these people. I don't know you. You're a stranger—why are you telephoning me? Haven't you anyone else to telephone tonight? There's no connection between us. This is insulting. It's degrading. If people worry about me, it isn't me they are worrying about—is it?—I'm onto their games! If they want to worry about me, let them discover what it is in themselves they are afraid of. Where is the fear? It isn't in me; it's in all of you. The thought of death isn't in me, it's never in me; it's in the rest of you. If—please don't interrupt. Mrs. Greaney—if you have nothing else to do but gossip about me and clack your teeth about me if Manitock is really so impoverished, that's unfortunate, but it's hardly my fault, is it? Good night."

She dropped the receiver into place. She began to sob,

pounding at her thighs and belly with her fists, not knowing what she did. The sobs were dry, hoarse; like laughter. She took the receiver off the hook so that the woman could not call her back.

She whispered: *Let me alone! Let him die! . . . Let me die!*

A few days later someone approached her, someone's wife, evidently a woman Beatrice had known in her former life—she had been *Mrs. Kern* in that life—and began reproving her, gently scolding her, for what she had said to Moira Greaney. The woman was middle-aged, maternal. Perhaps she had a right to speak to Beatrice and even to suggest that a misdeed, a crime of some kind, had been committed. "Why, what did I say?" Beatrice asked. "Did I say something? What did I say? I don't remember. Were you listening in on an extension?—are you someone I'm supposed to know?"

It was the drug that asked these questions, the aftermath of a drug—barbiturates, because of her insomnia—and not Beatrice herself. Beatrice was angry. The drug altered her voice, made it sound confused and innocent. She might have been lost in a foreign city instead of standing helpless in the Village Pharmacy, staring at a woman whose name she could not recall. Fortunately, the woman did not touch her. That might have meant she was really Beatrice's mother, a few pounds heavier, disguised crudely as a blond. Beatrice herself was angry, outraged, but the sounds she made were really quite childlike. So many short, abrupt, baffled questions—surely she was innocent of any crime, and must be forgiven.

Innocent. Always so innocent. She no longer knew whether her extraordinary innocence was genuine, as much a part of her as her small, frail body, or whether it was a form of savage irony. Had she been less intelligent, her open-eyed bewilderment, her ceaseless questioning, might have been genuine. But she was too intelligent. Some part of her had developed too shrewdly, like a head that has grown out of the drowsy earth and can now gaze down upon it—a head on a long stalk—an eerie drunken-swaying stalk of a neck! But Wallace had not judged her so harshly. He had forbidden her to judge herself in those censorious terms. Now he was dead; now the dates of his death and of his funeral were retreating, day by day, pages back on the calendar, so she had the freedom to say whatever she liked about herself. Other people talked about her, other people stated their opinions.

Whispering. Worrying. Gleefully "worrying." She had the freedom to judge herself however she liked, as cruelly as she wished; she wanted no pity, not even from herself. But she could not quite imagine herself. *Beatrice Kern.* Before her marriage she had been *Beatrice Egleston*, but she finished with that. That was done.... She could not analyze herself thoroughly enough, could not be certain that she understood the nature of the being she evidently inhabited. A face, a body. Yes. Fine. As usual. If the insides are secrets no one especially cares to know, the outside can at least be contemplated: that was the basis of life. But—what are the visions a mirror offers? The mirror is too friendly, demoniacally friendly, always distorting reality in order to give us back our own expectations. Always lying, always slanting, muffling....

So Beatrice did not know if she was that young woman whom everyone pitied, and who seemed pitiful indeed. A young wife who had lost her husband. *Lost her husband.* Other people lost gloves, books, tickets; or they lost at a game of cards. But Beatrice had lost her husband, which was tragic or freakish, depending. Across town was the *other widow*, who had also "lost" her husband, months before Wallace's death. A coincidence, in such a small town...among so small a circle of acquaintances. Two young widows, in their late twenties. Inevitable, hideous, that they should rush together, should embrace each other, should weep together while the rest of the community watched with solemn approval....

Beatrice wandered around the house, a rented single-bedroom frame house not far from the University, murmuring to herself—not arguing, not angry—only befuddled. Sometimes she wept. Sometimes no tears came, only that dry wracking sob, a kind of chuckle. She taunted herself with the thought that perhaps she was weeping, mourning, because of the role she had to play—people were spying on her, demanding tears. She was a widow, childless. She was deathly, like all widows; she must acknowledge it.

She wondered when it would be concluded—when her husband would really die.

"Do you ever imagine—he might be trying to contact you?"
"No."
"Do you ever—do you— Would you want it, would you want him to communicate with you, if it were possible?"

"You're insane."

"*But would you want it?*"

"Want what? What are you saying?"

"—want *it*—"

"What is *it?* What kind of a joke is this? You're teasing me, you're trying to drive me crazy—you're crazy yourself and want me to become like you—"

"No. You can't become like me. You have to be yourself—you can only become yourself."

She was frightened of the other widow. Though she went out rarely—no more than three or four times in an entire week—she seemed to meet Moira Greaney all the time. But they were not friends, not even acquaintances. They knew each other only by sight. Manitock was not really so small, but it seemed small: once a mill town, a factory town built upon the banks of a river in upstate New Hampshire, now a university town in which everyone connected with the University knew everyone else. And most of them lived in town, in the radius of a few miles, because the mountains were so steep, the foothills so unfriendly, the only houses or farms available outside Manitock were very poor. Some were hardly more than shanties. The University itself was losing money. Beatrice had resigned her part-time position, teaching art history in night school, and no one had tried to argue her into keeping it. Possibly she would have been dismissed anyway—except for the embarrassing fact that she was the wife of a man who had died suddenly, in an automobile accident. The other widow was not so poor as Beatrice . . . not even childless, exactly, because her husband had a son somewhere, from his first marriage. *Do you wish you had had a baby? No. Yes. Were you waiting . . . ? Yes, we were waiting. Do you regret it now? . . .* She regretted nothing. She had very few emotions, no more than two or three. They narrowed, they expanded. They narrowed again. She took a book out of the town library, an income-tax guide, and saw that Moira Greaney had taken it out before her—the name printed in small block letters, in green ink.

She hiked out to the cemetery, north of town. It had an older section, for the natives; the newer section looked cheap, with tombstones and markers of polished stone, slick and neat. The old gravestones were battered, gray, some of the very old ones even encrusted with bird droppings—entirely natural, proper. What could be said about the newer graves, the newer deaths?—the younger people? A shame they died, that was about all. Beatrice considered the marker on her husband's grave adequate. It was adequate. She had already forgotten its price—it had been the least expensive of those markers currently available—and she could never remember what it was made of, perhaps granite.... The Greaney grave was nearby, slightly uphill from the Kern grave. Better drainage. A better location. The stone was fairly large, must have been costly, but its front was black-gleaming and highly polished—so that it looked too prosperous for this place. It looked hearty, smug. There were potted geraniums around it and Beatrice detested geraniums and she taunted herself with the possibility of kicking them over ... and hearing a cry ... turning to see Mrs. Greaney running at her, running up the incline to her. *Why, you're a murderer!—only pretending to be in mourning!*

More sanely, she considered the ugly possibility of meeting the woman out here, in the cemetery. There was only one entrance, one way out. It could happen.... Once, on a Sunday, she lingered in the vicinity of her husband's and Mr. Greaney's graves, as if waiting. But no one came along.

That was in September. By November, she had given in.

"I am the catastrophe, the ugly disaster," Beatrice laughed. "My husband died in an accident. An eighteen-year-old boy ran into him broadside, he hit the driver's side of our car—going over seventy miles an hour, they said—running a four-way stop. The boy died and so did my husband. Instantly, they said. How did they know? With what authority do people say such things? ...*Instantly. So he didn't suffer. It isn't much of a consolation, Mrs. Kern, but....* When people see me now, they think of disaster. The impact of one car on another, seventy miles an hour, the noise, the smashed metal, the way bodies must be ruined, so strangely, being only flesh.... They dread seeing me because what happened to my husband could happen to them, and it's an insult. They can't control it ... it's a betrayal of their civilized lives ... of sanity itself. My face reminds them of the closed casket. Their imaginations run wild, they're sickened, excited, they rush forward to pity me, but they wish I had died in the accident along with him. This place is too small to absorb me.... I remind them of something demonic, that goes against their God. Because they do have versions of God, their own kind of God, having to do with their brains, their reason. Their careers.

All that is godly to them, because they have to worship something and so they worship themselves. But it can be changed in a few seconds. I don't blame them for hating me."

"They don't hate you. They're just a little frightened of you," Moira said. She was two years older than Beatrice, twenty-nine, but she looked younger—that wide, frank, freckled face, those blue eyes that protruded slightly, charmingly, as if everything fascinated her. She stared. She stared at Beatrice. Her stare came first, then her slow, friendly smile. Was she pleased? Always. Curious? Always. "Nobody hates you, Beatrice," she said. "...It's what I represent they really fear. It isn't so bad now, because he's been dead quite a while, but while he was dying, the last six weeks especially, I walked around like a criminal, I pitied people who happened to see me, because they were genuinely frightened of me.... That long, slow, protracted death...eighteen months of it...he wasn't as young as your husband, but he was too young to die, only forty-four, and whenever anyone saw me I knew he wanted to duck away, to hide. And the strained, absurd conversations!—their eyes grabbing at me, hoping I wouldn't say anything obscene. They dreaded the very word *cancer*. They dreaded me.... But now that he's dead, people can see I'm still alive. I'm not a leper, I'm not contaminated with his disease. After all, death isn't contagious."

"Isn't it?" Beatrice said.

She was getting drunk. Her voice was wild, unpredictable.... She had noticed a mirror in the foyer, by a coat rack; she went to observe herself in this new role. But what was there to say?—whether "Beatrice" was an attractive woman or whether she was obscene, ugly, contaminated by death, she could not judge. Her skin was pale. But it was always pale, especially when she was tired. Her hair was dark, almost black. She had not bothered to remove the several silvery hairs she had discovered one morning, but no one noticed anyway. A delicate woman, hardly more than a girl. Her eyes were slanted or gave the appearance of being so, especially when she was intense or suspicious. Very dark eyes. But their expression was usually dreamy, inward, contemplative, as if she were engrossed with images inside her head.

Moira's face hovered near hers in the mirror. But Moira was careful to stand some distance from Beatrice, not touching her. She was a tall woman—at least five feet nine—with broad shoulders, a wide, clear forehead, and ash-blond hair that stuck out around her head in clumps of curls. Sometimes her hair was frizzy, messy. At other times it was striking; Beatrice had seen her on the street occasionally, and had noticed how other people glanced at her, especially men. Her manner was brisk, hearty, almost oppressively healthy. "Nobody hates us, Beatrice. You shouldn't allow yourself to think that," she said. There was a subtle edge to her voice, as if the two of them had been quarreling off and on all their lives.

Beatrice had telephoned the Greaney woman one night in November.

Unable to sleep, she had wandered downstairs, barefoot, thinking that she would sit in the kitchen for the rest of the night. She would be quite safe there. Walls painted a very light yellow, a refrigerator that hummed and rattled, linoleum tile of orange and brown. Warm colors. At her usual place, her feet primly up on the chair, arms around her knees. Like a child. She could sit there until dawn. It was well known that consciousness alters with daylight. She had faith in that. . . . From a distance she heard the dry, heaving sobs. She heard her own voice, lifting in a question. *But when will it not be mad, so that I can return to it?* She closed her eyes. Listened. It was her own voice, cheerful and witty. Evidently time had passed. There was some confusion. When the sleeping pill did not work, confusion followed: like a storm at every window, while you are trying heroically to close one window. Resist? Give in? . . . She heard her own voice and the voices of others. She realized they were at a party. Of course. One of the many parties she had attended. She and her husband they had many friends, especially when they were in graduate school in Boston. Sitting in one another's apartments, late into the night. Talking. Arguing. Rarely getting drunk, because the value of their being together lay in their conversations.

Some of them, men and women both, had been daring, iconoclastic. Some had taken other roles: Beatrice herself had always sounded fairly conservative. All this was conversation. Personalities expressed in talk, in words. There was a kind of psychological chastity to it, harmless. Of course none of them had known this at the time. How energetically they had discussed all things, even the topics that dismayed their parents—even the forbidden things, the taboos. Sexual behavior. Sexual promiscuity. Deviance. The possibility of divorce. Of death. Of

madness. Of suicide. Quite calmly, fearlessly, they had assumed
the world was mad anyway. What did it matter?—governments,
social programs, philosophical principles. They knew everything. They knew everything in essence, if not in detail. And they
were totally unmoved, undismayed, as if anything that might be
expressed in words was already rendered quaint, its power to
wound thwarted. It was even the fashion, for a while, not to
know very much, to avoid reading newspapers. A young man, a
close friend of Wallace's, had encouraged Beatrice to do
graduate work involving a Maine artist of the nineteenth century
and to turn her back on the "madness" of the contemporary
world. Beatrice had replied wittily that the world has always
been mad: one crisis after another, wars and the preludes to war,
treaties, peace pacts, agreements, and then war again. How
could he expect her, or anyone, to hide until the world returned
to normal? It would never return to what he considered normal.
In fact it was normal at the present time; it was always normal.
And when would it not be mad, so that she could safely return to
it?

Anyway, she had said, she had no interest in dead men.

She remembered this conversation. Horrible, that she should
both recall it from the outside, as if she had been a third person
observing the scene, and animate it, give life to her own words.
She was not ashamed of herself, she was terrified. There was
nothing for her to claim; nowhere to retreat to. She realized that
she might possibly not survive. She had no interest in the dead
and yet she had nothing else, no one else, except a dead man
whose features were already unclear, his voice dubious and
vague, his love for her in all probability based upon a
misunderstanding of her nature, which she had deliberately
cultivated.

"I want...I don't want...I...I'm not going to..."

It was very late, nearly three o'clock in the morning, when she
telephoned Moira Greaney.

Moira's husband had disappeared long before his death.
Whoever remained had put up a struggle of some kind, assisted
by the hospital staff, and he was now buried in the Manitock
cemetery; she should sell the house on Fort Street, people
advised, and return to her own life. But he was buried nearby.
How could she leave? She had been very happy with him and
was very happy now. No, she would not betray him. She paused

before the windows of the local tourist agencies, staring at brightly colored advertisements for travel. *Fly Away to India. Africa the Golden Continent.* No, she would not betray him, not again.

"Really. *Really.* Is that true."

"Is that *really* true."

She stared at people, absorbed their remarks, marveling with a vague note of protest at the most ordinary of disclosures. She could not help herself. An intensity of interest in other people, an exaggerated respect for whatever they said or did, had characterized her almost since childhood. Because she was big-boned, her shoulders quite wide for a woman, people expected her to be ungainly, but in fact she was graceful; she had the effortless grace of the natural athlete. Her feet were rather large. Her hands were large also, but she filed her nails carefully and even polished them, and wore a number of rings that she changed from day to day, except for her wedding ring. *How pretty Moira is!* people sometimes said, as if surprised. Seeing her at close range, they were often surprised. *How pretty your wife is!* people had told her husband, meaning to flatter him.

He liked her with her hair tied up behind. Or in blouses with frilly, fussy collars and cuffs. Or in those outfits she had pieced together, years before, from secondhand shops: crushed-velvet skirts, furred vests, shoes with odd heels and straps, felt hats shaped like buckets or shovels. She was taller than her husband, a golden-glowing girl with a daughterly manner, both robust and shy. It had been years since she had played on girls' hockey and basketball teams, yet her husband often alluded to her skill at sports; he complimented her, embarrassed her, as if to explain to her—however obliquely—why she was not maternal and should not take that risk. She told Beatrice about the humiliating visits of the son, her husband's boy, up from New York City for weekends; she had told no one else, had never dared complain, because of course people would have told Edgar. Everyone in Manitock was his friend. Everyone was loyal to him. He was respected, admired, possibly because he looked so much older than he was—in his early forties he had lost most of his hair except for a few blond-white strands that floated about his head like a halo or an aura, and his face was furrowed, the indentations around his mouth both severe and kindly. He looked like a man who has suffered. He looked like a man who fully expects to suffer. His son was totally unlike him, but he seemed to love the boy very much, whenever he remembered him. So Moira had tried to love the boy too.

"I even practiced basketball shots with him," Moira told Beatrice. Her tone was lightly sardonic. "There was a playground a few blocks away with a basketball hoop, so we trudged over there and practiced shots while my husband worked. . . . We didn't talk at all. He had nothing to say to me. He wasn't friendly to anyone; he wasn't even boyish. I couldn't remember him now if I met him on the street. He wouldn't know me; he rarely looked at me." The wife, the other Mrs. Greaney, had fattened the boy up, so that at the age of eleven he was thirty pounds overweight, a sullen child who admired athletes and hunters. He had no interest in his father's work—never looked through the encyclopedias and world books and almanacs his father owned. He confided in Moira only once, begging her to talk his father into buying him an air rifle. He wanted to hunt in the field behind his father's house, a hilly area that was partly wooded, where starlings and grackles and cardinals and blue jays and occasionally even pheasants might be found. He carried around with him, folded many times, full-color advertisements from *Boy's Life* that he showed Moira, displays of handsome air rifles. He could not have a gun in the city, could not hunt or kill in the city. His eyes glistened, with pain or desire, as he spoke to Moira. She had told him it was hopeless. If she even brought up the subject to his father, which she would not, his father would be angry at them both; it was hopeless. So he had turned away from her and had not seemed to like her much after that.

"I didn't hate him," Moira said. "I have never hated anyone. . . . I felt him hating me, but I didn't hate him. Instead I forgot him. After the funeral, I forgot him. I'm forgetting everything. Sometimes I think . . . I halfway think that my husband didn't have any children, that the child he had was *me*. I was his child. I wasn't his daughter, necessarily, but his child. He was twelve years older than I was; he ended his marriage for me, in order to marry me, because I loved him so much. He loved me too. But he realized how much I loved him, how I needed him; so he ended his marriage with that other woman. He . . ."

"He loved you very much," Beatrice interrupted. "Obviously he loved you very much. My husband would never have married me, he would never even have noticed me, if he had already been married . . ."

"No, he did it out of kindness, out of charity," Moira said. "I loved him so much it made him feel guilty. I was only twenty-two. . . . He gave up living in the city, all his friends there and his position at the University, to move up here to Manitock, where everyone admired him but didn't know him . . . and he was contemptuous of nearly everyone here, because of course he couldn't talk to them. But he never accused me, he never blamed me. He was a wonderful man."

Beatrice tried to remember Edgar Greaney: she could recall only one rather large gathering. Greaney in a wing chair by a fireplace, surrounded by younger men, and the wife, Moira, sitting with other wives, a woman with ash-blond hair who might have been pretty, even beautiful, had she not smiled so persistently. Greaney was a small man with a dapper, brusque manner; his skin was pitted, perhaps from acne or smallpox, but this did not detract from his good looks. In a way he was ugly, in another way quite charming. Beatrice had disliked him at once—she noted how everyone stood at attention around him, stiff and silent, respectful, while he explained something, speaking in a logical, precise way, developing a statement to its inevitable conclusion. Not only would no one dare interrupt, but the possibility of an interruption was grotesque. Edgar Greaney was the author of a number of books, both introductory and advanced, on the subject of logical positivism . . . he had been brought to Manitock as chairman of the philosophy department. Beatrice had liked the man's certainty, she had liked his slightly British accent, believing him to be a European who had spent time in England and was now trying, with some success, to speak American English. She had even admired, in a way, his method of bringing an evidently abstract argument to a powerful, emotional conclusion that surprised his listeners, but she had no interest in meeting him; his crossed leg, his twitching foot, the explosive laughter he seemed to force in others, had annoyed her. *I can see the thoughts rising in your mind*, he had said to someone playfully. A joke, yet a serious joke.

"I loved him so much," Moira said. "I don't want to forget him."

Beatrice confessed to Moira. She confessed her jealousy, her envy. For months she had seen Moira at a distance, had dreaded her, had been bitterly envious of her. But why? Because Moira had been a widow five months before Beatrice and had always been so healthy, so intelligent about her fate. No one pitied her.

No one worried about her. "There was an outfit you wore last summer, yellow trousers and a striped pullover shirt, like a sailor's shirt, that made me think ... Forgive me," Beatrice said, "but it made me think that you couldn't possibly be a widow. Not like me."

"People wanted us to meet, did you know that?" Moira said. "I drove by your house a few times, though it was out of my way, thinking that if you were out in the yard.... I must say that everything you wore, even the expression on your face, did seem to indicate you were a widow. Or an older woman. Like some of the mill-workers' wives or mothers, those older Italian women who like to dress in black. I envied you, that you could disguise yourself like that. Sometimes you seemed almost dowdy, almost ugly, did you know that? You looked so pale, almost greenish white. You looked sick. But you did it deliberately. That was courageous, really; you went down into the grave with him. I was afraid to do that. I thought I might not return again."

Beatrice was offended. *Went down into the grave with him.* What was the woman talking about, was she crazy? ... But Beatrice pretended not to mind, she even laughed. They were having coffee together at Beatrice's one afternoon, and her hand shook so that coffee spilled into her saucer, but she did not mind.

"Cancer of the throat," Moira said without hesitation. "Didn't you know?"

"I didn't know, not specifically...."

"Yes, it was strange how at first everyone seemed to know," Moira said in her amused, sardonic voice, though her expression showed that she blamed no one, "at least all our friends knew. All his friends. He went to Boston for treatments, he came back, and for a while the news seemed to be optimistic; or he lied a little. People were anxious about him. They cornered me, telephoned me when he was at school, wanted to know how he was. But as time passed they no longer asked. There's a moment at the very start of a conversation when the person you've just met asks how you are, how things are with you, and this moment was almost intolerable—I could see the question in the person's mind, I could see it there almost before he could—"

"How strange," Beatrice said.

"—and I could also see the instant in which the person realized he must not ask that question. So—there was nothing to be asked, no question, except a clumsy substitute. But I pretended to notice othing, I filled in the gaps in conversations; after all, I was an ndependent, healthy person, not at all sick; I didn't even get a ad cold last spring when everyone was sick with the flu, do you emember?— Yes, it was cancer of the throat. The preliminary months were the worst in a way, since there was some hope. Afterward, when there was no hope..."

She began to cry. She cried openly, almost irritably, like a child.

"...people came to visit him in the hospital, but I could tell hey dreaded the visits. They were terrified and bored at the same time. Because he wouldn't talk. He didn't even seem to be istening. If I was there I had to talk in his place...I felt as if my oul were being drained out of me in all those spurts of conversation, trying to make other people feel halfway at ease. There was one awful visit when an associate of his ..when...the man had come alone, without his wife, and he was so miserable, so naively miserable, he believed he had to stay until visiting hours were over at seven, so he was there an hour and a half...ashen-faced....He kept staring at me, directing question to me, and I kept replying and asking him questions, an hour and a half of it, and so pointless...."

Beatrice was moved by the woman's tears. And the sound of her voice, which was no longer well-modulated, but had the unashamed, undignified whine, the ugly unmusical noise, of angry grief. Beatrice was panicked that she might begin to cry as well. And they would be united involuntarily by their tears—like young girls, like children, like sisters. She stared at Moira, whose face was contracted almost like an infant's, and was upset that Moira should allow herself to appear so ugly.

"Don't do that!—Your face, you'll ruin your face!" Beatrice cried.

By January, the two of them were so obviously friends, so often seen together in Manitock, that when people invited either of them to parties and dinners, they always added, as if incidentally, that the other was also being invited. But Beatrice always declined. She was gracious, but she declined. She wanted no part of social life; for years she had hated it without ever comprehending the depth of her hatred, always imagining it was a particular evening, a particular set of people, that had disappointed her. But no: it was the commotion and strain of social life itself. Especially, she had come to dislike the ritual remarks women made to one another, even in the presence of men—always complimenting one another on their clothes, their hair, their physical appearance. They did not know how insulting such remarks were to her, as if she were to be continually assessed from the outside, as an aesthetic phenomenon; they did not sense how, unconsciously, they were setting one another up for the routine, perfunctory admiration of men, which was always slightly contemptuous. And of course she was frightened of their pity. When someone said that it was good she had a teaching job—teaching was so absorbing, wasn't it—she had replied angrily that she no longer had the job. She had quit. And why was it "good," why might anyone imagine it was "good" for her to have something to absorb her?

That time, Moira had interrupted, had gracefully intervened. Like an older sister. She had turned the conversation onto something else, while Beatrice stood, smarting, angry and remorseful at the same time, knowing herself a stranger to all these people. . . . Like an older, wiser, more worldly sister, Moira seemed to precede her; she might have made the social events tolerable, but Beatrice thought it better to withdraw. She knew that people were not to blame, that they meant only well; she knew it was selfish of her to dislike them. So she declined invitations. But when the telephone rang, she was no longer worried—most of the time it was Moira.

"People ask about you," Moira reported. "Men ask about you."

Beatrice laughed. "You're lying."

"I'm not lying; I never lie."

"They ask about you, not me. They crowd around you, not me. . . . I have no interest in men."

"Still, they ask about you."

"I don't want to hear it," Beatrice said.

"I've had to decline invitations from certain people," Moira said slowly, ". . . men I knew in the past . . . I mean, men I was very friendly with. . . . Before Edgar's death, I mean."

Beatrice wondered what she meant. But she did not ask: the subject of men sickened her. She was still a young woman, only a few months from her twenty-eighth birthday, but she felt aged, soured by too much experience. She and Wallace had been married only five years. But it seemed much longer—more than half her lifetime. He had drawn her spirit out of her and into him, partly, and then he had been killed, one ordinary afternoon. It was as if her right arm had been yanked off. And now she walked around, her arm gone at the socket, bloodless, a scar healing over it, and people asked her cheerfully about how things were going, wasn't it good to be teaching, shouldn't she get out more, shouldn't she have more interests? Even Moira hinted that she should go out. The two of them could go out together, Moira laughed, so men could approach them both, openly....

"And then what?" Beatrice asked.

"Then we could explain how we don't need them," Moira said.

"It was worse for you, the fact that he died so slowly," Beatrice said.

"...no, I think it was worse for you. You weren't prepared for it. You had the worst shock."

"But you had to endure him changing. His personality must have changed."

"Yes, it changed. He changed. The man who died wasn't the same man I knew," Moira said. "So in fact it was easier for me....I mean, people seem to die a while before their actual deaths, their physical deaths. It was the same way with my father. They seem to leave themselves. Do you know what I mean? I don't know if I believe in a soul, a soul detachable from the body, but the personality seems to leave...or disappear...and someone else is there, left behind. It's very strange. About the third week before he actually died, my husband seemed to leave. He even said good-by to me....I mean, in a way, in a way I can't explain....You don't understand! I can see that you don't understand and I'm frightening you. I meant only to tell you that I think you had the worst of it, a sudden death. You're very brave."

Beatrice remembered the night she had gone mad. She thought of it that way, as madness. Hearing the voice of a former self, hearing her party voice, her social self, going on and on and on so happily and witlessly about the tragic madness of the world, which could not, of course, have any effect upon an intelligent person....And then the terror, the utter, blank, deathly terror. She had experienced a sensation that was indescribable. There were no words for it, nothing. Yet, stammering her anguish over the phone to Moira, to a stranger whom she believed she disliked, she managed to say it was like the empty silence after the *click* of an automatic phonograph, when the last record has been played and the machine neatly shuts itself off.

"You haven't gone mad," Moira said gently. "You didn't go mad. It's just the shock of it, of his death. It was so much worse for you because he died instantly."

Beatrice pressed her fingertips against her eyes. No, she could not allow her friend to be so generous. No. They argued late into the night, in voices that grew strident at times; at other times, quite tender. "No, I think it must have been more torturous for you, because he died so slowly...."

Beatrice would never forget how Moira had come to her house. Three in the morning, awakened by the telephone, able to recognize Beatrice's voice in spite of the hysteria...without hesitating she had put on ski pants and a sweater, slid her bare feet into boots, snatched a parka from wherever she had tossed it the day before...trudged through the brittle snow to her car...driven all the way across town on the desolate, icy streets, to Beatrice. She had even known where Beatrice lived.

Beatrice wept that anyone should be so generous. She knew she herself was not that generous. Something had been left out of her soul, perhaps. Again and again she thanked Moira. And she could not resist saying: "Would I have done that much for you? Or for anyone? ...Of course not."

"Certainly you would," Moira said warmly.

"Then you don't know me," Beatrice said.

"I know you very well!" Moira laughed. "I know you in a way you don't know yourself.... Yes, it's possible," she said seriously, "in fact, my husband always claimed to know me in a way I didn't know myself. Because he could sense what I was as a possibility, while I only knew myself from the inside, in terms of what I was."

"Your husband was a genius," Beatrice said. "I always admired him...."

"Yes, everyone admired him," Moira said. "...Did you like his voice, his accent?"

"Was he European?"

"Born in Columbus, Ohio," Moira laughed. "His parents were from Warsaw; they were Jews, they escaped just before the war. They lived in New York for a while; evidently they were very poor; then somehow ended up in Columbus—I don't know the details because Edgar didn't tell me. Of course his name was another name. It wasn't Edgar Greaney. He changed it when he went to England, he was a Rhodes scholar at Oxford . . . so in a way, yes, you could say he was European," Moira said thoughtfully. "Yes. But obliquely. He was always around the corner from where anyone stood . . . and if you turned the corner, he'd duck around another corner."

Beatrice looked away. She hoped that Moira would say nothing further.

". . . toward the end he even spoke in Yiddish," Moira said. "I didn't know what on earth he was saying. I didn't know it was a language—any language—I did't know the sounds of it. Somehow it came back to him, words and phrases. Names. Prayers. I can't be certain, but I think they were prayers, mixed in with other words. English, Polish, Yiddish, German, even French . . . I sat there by his bedside and experienced these sounds, these various struggling sounds, and I came to know what language adds up to. Then, at the very end, he couldn't speak at all. I think he was at peace then; he'd managed to say what he wanted to say, so he was at peace. . . . He was a genius, yes," Moira said dreamily, "but that had nothing to do with his death."

"I don't think we should talk about these things," Beatrice said.

"No," said Moira. "But we will."

They fell into each other's lives as if, all along, they had known about each other. Parallel lives, parallel habits. Both woke early, around dawn, and could not get back to sleep. In the kitchen at seven, making coffee, Beatrice felt no dismay when the telephone rang. If it did not ring by seven-thirty, she went to call Moira.

They shopped together. They had lunch at one of the three or four good restaurants in town—were seen together as late as two-thirty in the afternoon in the dining room of the Ethan Allen Inn, discussing something that must have been of vital importance to each. Moira with her ash-blond hair, her turtle-neck sweaters, her tweed skirts and leather boots . . . Beatrice small, dark, so unaware of her surroundings that she sometimes raised her voice in an incredulous whine, like a child. They evidently argued a great deal. Then Moira would laugh, husky-voiced, totally at ease. . . . In the ski shop adjacent to Manitock's only department store, a man who had known

Wallace Kern fairly well tried to have a conversation with them, but it seemed to him that Beatrice was not even listening and that the Greaney woman, whom he did not know, was simply waiting for him to go away, aggressively gracious, nodding before he even finished what he had to say. Moira evidently was going skiing; she was trying to talk Beatrice into going along, up into Canada, into the Laurentians. But Beatrice was silent, even a little sullen. "It would be good for her, wouldn't it," Moira said to the man, "to get away from Manitock for a few days...? And nothing could happen. She wouldn't have to ski, not even the beginners' slopes, if she didn't want to."

The man agreed. He said clumsily that it would be good for Beatrice.

"Why should I want what's good for me?" Beatrice asked him, smiling. "Is that what you want for yourself—only what's good for you?"

Yet when Moira had a dinner party in the big, Victorian-Gothic house on Fort Street—built by one of the mill-owners at the turn of the century—Beatrice was not there. Someone asked about her and Moira explained gravely that Mrs. Kern wasn't well, that she regretted very much having to miss the party—since she liked the other guests—she enjoyed small parties and serious, intelligent conversations. But she wasn't well.

Moira telephoned her from her bedroom upstairs while the party was still going on; she told Beatrice that everyone missed her and was asking about her and, yes, she had to admit that Beatrice was right: these people were too busy, too distracting, they talked loudly and tried to joke, even about matters that were not funny—like the University's financial problems—Beatrice had made the correct decision to stay away. Even though it was almost rude of her.

"Rude? Why is it rude?" Beatrice cried. "...Did I hear you right? *Rude?*"

"Isn't it? Deliberately rude?"

They argued for several minutes. Moira was whispering angrily. She wanted to know what Beatrice was doing—was she in bed? No? Then she wasn't ill; it had been a lie. But Beatrice protested, saying she had never claimed to be ill. What was going on? Ill? When? She had simply refused to come to the party because other people made her nervous. even people she liked; she could not endure their forced cheerfulness. Moira paused, then said that Beatrice's husband had been a very extroverted person, hadn't he—he had enjoyed parties? Beatrice did not reply; she might have been trying to remember. "I can see him in my mind's eye," Moira said. "He had brown curly hair . . . he was tall . . . he laughed a great deal, didn't he? . . . he liked to drink, didn't he? And . . . and . . . And his eyes were heavy-lidded, he was handsome, his mouth was . . . he was. . . . You're at home tonight thinking about him, aren't you? Aren't you?"

"He didn't like to drink," Beatrice said. "No more than anyone else. He—"

"He might have been let go at the University, did you know that?" Moira said. "There were rumors. Of course it wouldn't have had to do with his professional competence—but the budget is being cut back— Did you know that? Did he tell you?"

"He told me everything," Beatrice said.

"Did he tell you that?"

"He kept nothing from me!" Beatrice said.

She hung up.

When Moira telephoned her back, she let the phone ring.

"How many weeks has it been?" Moira asked.

"Weeks? I think in terms of months," Beatrice said, ashamed.

"I think you loved him more than I loved my husband. I get that impression."

"No. No, really. I loved my husband very much, but . . . but I don't think I'm as mature a person as you; I don't think I'm capable of love in the way you are."

They sat together in the dining room of Moira's house; Beatrice had come over for dinner at six and it was now eight-thirty. They were finishing a bottle of wine.

"I envy you," Beatrice said, "because he was so much older than you. He taught you so much. He even taught you how to die. . . . Wally was too young, he left me too young. He was just a boy. It was said about him . . . this is a secret, Moira, I know you won't tell anyone . . . it was said about him that he was immature, in spite of being so intelligent. Yes, I actually saw it, the word *immature*. The chairman of his department called me in one day, meaning to be kind, and was very sweet to me . . . praised Wallace . . . told me how the entire department was grief-stricken, and many students . . . because he was very popular with students, especially underclassmen. And the chairman actually showed me the files he and the Dean kept on Wallace, meaning only to be kind...a very sweet, nervous man...and though most of the comments on the forms were very good, excellent, I happened to notice that word *immature* down in the left-hand corner of the page." She began to laugh. "He may have tried to cover it with his thumb, I don't know, but in any case I saw it.... Isn't that funny?"

Moira seized her wrist to make her stop. She never allowed Beatrice to laugh in that dry, self-mocking way; she found it intolerable. "But you never betrayed your husband. Did you? You were never unfaithful to him, were you? So you did love him more than I loved my husband, regardless of whether some ignorant sons of bitches labeled him 'immature'...You were faithful; you were never unfaithful. You're better than I am."

"I don't want to hear about it," Beatrice said.

"I don't want to talk about it. I won't talk about it," Moira said.

One day in February the telephone rang very early, a few minutes after six in the morning. Moira wanted to know if Beatrice had had disturbing dreams. Beatrice had confided in her, as she had never confided in anyone else, that she sometimes suffered from extraordinarily ugly dreams. "What are they? What did you dream? Maybe you should tell me," Moira said.

"They're degrading. I can't talk about them."

Moira said nothing for several seconds. Then, hurt, she mumbled something about the fact that she slept without dreams: blunt and big and healthy as a horse, she was. A clumsy, ugly creature.

"That's ridiculous," Beatrice said sleepily. "You're not ugly. You're not clumsy."

"Sometimes Edgar said I was clumsy. And my mind...my imagination...he said it was crude. That's why I don't dream. I would welcome even nightmares, I'd be happy to share your nightmares. That would be better than nothing."

"When were you unfaithful to your husband?" Beatrice asked.

"When he was dying."

"Did you tell him?"

"Tell him! No, of course not....And you were never unfaithful to Wallace?"

"Never."

"And now...?"

"What do you mean, *and now?*"

"Are you still faithful to him?"

"... last night I dreamed that someone was trying to get into bed with me, he'd climbed through the window.... I was paralyzed with fear, I was sick with fear, I tried to scream because I knew I was sleeping and I had to wake up, I had to escape...."

"Yes?" Moira said sharply. "Why are you telling me this? Was the man your husband, is that it?"

"I think—I think— Yes, I think it was my husband."

For a moment Moira was silent. Then she said sullenly, "I thought that might be happening. With you. I don't dream, myself, but I sense dreams elsewhere... I sense *your* dreams. ... And so, Beatrice, did you allow him in your bed?"

Beatrice murmured something unintelligible. She was very embarrassed.

"I want to know," Moira said. "Did you allow him in? Did he actually—?"

"I woke up terrified," Beatrice said. "I told you: I was sick with fear."

"All right, Beatrice," Moira said slowly. "But would you have allowed him in your bed if you'd known who he was? I mean to say—did you know, at the time, that the man was your husband?—or did you think it was a stranger, an intruder?"

"It happened too quickly," Beatrice said. "I had no time to think. All I knew was that someone had crawled through the open window and was trying to get into bed with me, moaning, making a hideous moaning noise, as if he were pleading with me, trying to pronounce my name—and I was terrified, I began to scream in my sleep, and somehow—somehow I managed to wake up. And I was very grateful to know that I'd been sleeping. And that I was alone."

Moira was silent for a long, strained moment. Then she said simply, strangely, "Yes."

THE MANITOCK MILL
Manitock, New Hampshire

This 3-story gristmill was built by Dawdon Cody and Robertson Wesley Turner and began operation in 1854. Restored in 1956, the mill is open to the public. One set of original millstones still exists and the six turbines are still in operation.

The inauguration of the mill in 1854 was marred by a tragic accident. The bride of the co-owner, R. W. Turner, was accidentally killed in the machinery.

Beatrice read the plaque and immediately turned away. She did not approve of the prose style. She was alone, out for a long walk, the mill was not open this late in the afternoon, she had no interest in seeing it or in anything else. Moira was not with her. But she was talking to Moira, under her breath, muttering. "Loathsome. Disgusting. . . . No one of them will ever . . . not with me, not again. Never. No man. . . . No one."

". . . he did something terrible once. Terrible. You won't tell anyone? . . . We had seen his son off at the airport, and on the way back, at the entrance to the expressway . . . well, there was a girl in a Volkswagen just ahead of him, going rather slowly, because there was so much traffic out on the expressway. And . . . and evidently he was angry about something or just impatient, because he honked his horn a number of times, furiously, and forced the girl out onto the expressway. Because she was just a girl, a frightened girl, and not certain about driving. And a truck rammed her from behind, and . . . and he didn't stop but just pulled out around the wreck and sped home . . . he forbade me ever to speak of it. He was upset, yes, and guilty and remorseful, and sick about what he had done . . . but he forbade me ever to speak of it."

". . . but you loved him, of course?"

"Didn't you? . . . love *your* husband?"

Beatrice felt illness coming gradually upon her, as if from a distance: the way light sometimes moved across the late-winter hills, patches of inexplicable sunlight that appeared . . . and disappeared . . . and appeared again while she held her breath. The exact route this sunshine would take could not be predicted, but it moved with a strange blithe certainty, as if it had happened innumerable times in the past. She could feel the sickness in her throat and in her bowels. And in her head: a quick darting piercing pain. She lay in bed, propped up with pillows. Was she, now, going to die? Was this the beginning of death? How little it seemed to matter . . . ! She read books of a kind one reads in bed, mildly sick. Too weakened to be alarmed. She read poetry for hours and could not always judge—were such lines exquisitely beautiful, or were they terrifying?

> *Such consciousness seemed but accidents,*
> *Relapses from the one interior life*
> *In which all beings live with god, themselves*

Are god, existing in the mighty whole
As indistinguishable as the cloudless east
Is from the cloudless west, when all
The hemisphere is one cerulean blue.

She wanted to read these lines aloud to another person. To Moira. Her voice would shake, her absurd terror would be exposed, yet she wanted to match her emotions with another person's—for how could she know, being so sick now, so weak, what was terror and what was awe? What was beauty?

In the end she did not read the lines to Moira. She closed the book, put it aside. It was beautiful, yes, but inhuman. Earlier in her life, when she had known so little, she might have rejoiced in the poet's massive vision, assuming—smugly, and wrongly—that it was a vision one might easily appropriate. And perhaps later in her life, near its completion, she might approach such a vision without any fear at all. But now: no. It wasn't possible. Not now, not yet.

Instead she craved an art that defined limits, a human, humble, sane art, unashamed of turning away from the void, unashamed of celebrating what was human and therefore scaled-down; an art of what was possible, what must be embraced.

"As you probably know, I nursed my husband for months. I was his nurse. He didn't want anyone else and I didn't want anyone else around him. It wasn't easy, in fact I dreaded it at first... I dreaded not only him but myself in that role, I was afraid something irrevocable might happen to me. After a while, though, I came to almost like it, to feel fulfilled by nursing him. I'm ashamed of that now. I can hardly believe it. Then, near the end, when he was very sick, I dreaded it again and resented it, I think, and I was very, very unhappy. I was ashamed of that too.... But what do these emotions matter? We do what we must do. He died. Whether I was ashamed or not, happy or unhappy, the poor man died.... But *you're* not going to."

"Of course I'm not," Beatrice said softly. "You've been so generous, Moira, coming over here so often, fixing meals for me... I'm not really sick. Not really. You must be neglecting your own life, aren't you?"

Moira gazed down at herself contemplatively. She took in the length of her body: that day she was wearing a cable-stitched ski sweater and faded blue jeans. So tall, so confident!—Beatrice had always admired women like Moira. Moira said strangely, "How can I be neglecting my own life? This *is* my life here. We inhabit our own lives constantly."

". . . he did like parties, yes, and he liked to drink. He couldn't seem to control it. The color of his skin actually changed, it got pink, rosy, flushed . . . and he would start to laugh over nothing . . . he liked to be happy, he liked to laugh. It was a mistake for him to come here, to this place; it wasn't right for him. . . . The accident wasn't his fault, but I was told he had been drinking; he had a bottle in the glove compartment and it flew out and was smashed and the smell of it was everywhere . . . so I believed, I tried to believe, that it was just that, the smell of liquor, they were going by. I've never told anyone. . . . He was hardly more than a boy, really. He wasn't an adult. You would have liked him so much, he could make anyone laugh once he got going. He could even make me laugh. . . . But most of the time I don't see anything amusing in the world."

"There isn't anything amusing in the world. It's in your head."

". . . I mean the world in itself," Beatrice said uncertainly.

". . . in your head. The world is. The world," Moira said, as if imitating someone else, ". . . is in your head. The world is your idea."

"But I can't alter it."

"Why not?"

"Don't frighten me," Beatrice said. "It must be the pills, but I can't seem to understand you."

"We understand everything," Moira said. She had brought Beatrice some soup and tea on a tray; she squatted at the bedside. Her hair had been brushed carelessly and sprang out in all directions. "We know and foresee and remember simultaneously."

Beatrice shuddered.

"The past is gone, but the future is gone too—it's inaccessible. It's completed and inaccessible. Today is February twenty-seventh; we can talk about the past and the future today; we can talk about our dead husbands or we could talk about ourselves; we could make plans for leaving this part of the world together . . . or even singly . . . escaping together or singly. But it doesn't matter because everything has already happened. That's why you feel like a corpse: in a sense you're already dead."

"I don't feel dead," Beatrice said.

"Nobody ever does," Moira laughed.

"I don't know what you mean," Beatrice said.

"Would you get married again?"

"And have him die again?"

"But they have to die! It's what must happen."

"It won't happen again," Beatrice whispered.

Moira's eyes were blue, that cerulean blue. She told Beatrice it did not matter in the slightest, she would not hold it against Beatrice that Edgar had not seemed attractive to her. "He was a bastard. He would have hurt you," Moira said.

"I did admire him...."

"He hadn't time for women, really. I don't know why he fell in love with me. It would have upset me terribly if that man had taken advantage of you.... No, he wasn't right for you. He may have appeared to be a genius, but...but wasn't quite human; he'd forget about his own son for weeks at a time. Yes, you were right to avoid him."

"...I was afraid of him," Beatrice said.

"Yes, and you should have been. He would have hurt you. You're not as tough as I am....I am tough, I'm strong. Don't underestimate me. He always underestimated me because he didn't know how to value women.... You were afraid of him, then? But you admired him?"

"Yes. Yes."

"But nothing came of it."

"Nothing came of it...."

"You didn't ever see him in private?"

"No."

"So nothing came of it.... And now he's dead. I should sell the house; it's my property. This house is rented, isn't it? We could move back to Boston. We could move all the way out to San Francisco. Would you like that? When you're well again?"

"I'm not sick," Beatrice said. "It's just a cold."

"People think you're ill; they say the most absurd things about you," Moira said. "They do nothing but gossip. We have to leave, don't we? Either together or each of us singly....I'll have to leave him there, in the cemetery. I'll have to leave everyone and so will you.... No, you're not sick; you look a little pale and you've lost weight, but there's nothing wrong with you."

"I'm afraid to leave," Beatrice said.

"Do you still dream about him?"

"Yes. No. I dream about many things."

"What did you dream last night?"

Beatrice shook her head, as if not wanting to remember.

"Was he trying to get back to you, trying to...?"

"No," Beatrice said. "It was someone else. I think it was you...but then it was a stranger...it was you, Moira, but also someone else, a stranger. You were pushing me out somewhere, out onto a highway. It was so noisy, the traffic and horns and people screaming and...and I was terrified...."

Moira seized her wrist and shook it. "What do you mean?"

"...I don't mean anything," Beatrice said. "The dream doesn't mean anything....But it was so vivid."

"It was only a dream, it doesn't mean anything," Moira laughed. "In fact, I forbid it to mean anything."

"I don't want to go to Boston," Beatrice said. "Or to San Francisco either. I'm afraid...."

"I can forbid that too," Moira said.

"Who was your lover, here in Manitock?"

"It isn't important. It doesn't matter. I never see him."

"Who was he?"

It was late March now: they had hiked out to the cemetery. The earth was moist, the wind chilly and fragrant; miles away, in the mountains, sunlight and shadow moved restlessly together, apart, together. Beatrice was frightened of the cemetery, but she had come out anyway. She dreaded the little marker—*Kern*—and there was something about the *Greaney* stone, that highly polished black rock, that made her uneasy. Yet she had walked the two miles just the same. And now she felt invigorated.

"...people came to visit him at the hospital..." Moira was saying slowly. "...especially on Sundays...and...and it was such a horror for them, and so boring, that....Well, a friend of Edgar's came one day without his wife, and I felt so sorry for him because he was miserable....In the elevator going down, I started to cry and he.....So it happened. But it isn't important."

"And he what?"

"He comforted me. I comforted him too, in a way, because he was frightened of what was happening to my husband, and...and so it happened. But it isn't important. It has no meaning."

"You saw the man again, though?"

"A few times."

Beatrice looked at Moira wonderingly.

"I didn't know what I was doing exactly," Moira said. "I was very upset and so was he and.... But it's over now. I never see him now."

"He was married, your lover? Who was he?"

"It isn't important."

"Was he...my husband?" Beatrice asked.

Her eyes filled suddenly with tears. She had been angry all along, without knowing it; and now her body pulsed with excitement. Moira stared at her, utterly amazed. There were faint lines on her forehead, her skin looked bleached out, the ash-blond hair was coarse as a horse's mane...yet she was an attractive woman, certainly; Wallace would have been drawn to her. Beatrice tried to smile.

"*Your husband?*" Moira whispered.

"Was it? You can tell me. You can admit it."

"Beatrice, are you joking?"

"Was it—?"

"Of course not."

"But why do you look so guilty?"

"...I didn't even know your husband, Beatrice. Edgar didn't know him. The four of us weren't friends, were we, we didn't know one another, did we...? It was someone else, someone you don't know. It doesn't matter."

Beatrice was trembling. "But I can see the two of you together, you and my husband. I can see you. Yes, it's like something I've already dreamed, something that has already happened....Were you happy with your lover while your husband was dying?"

Moira turned away. "Weren't you happy, at least occasionally?"

"No."

"Moira—"

"Frankly, no!"

"Why don't you say *yes?*" Beatrice said.

Moira looked at her, frowning. Then she laughed. "All right. *Yes.*"

"So you were happy betraying your husband?"

"If you insist."

"And it was my husband...?"

"Beatrice, please. You're frightening me. You look so strange . . . you're not going to be sick again, are you? Of course it wasn't—"

"He was going to die anyway in a few months. But he didn't know it. Why shouldn't he have loved you? Why shouldn't the two of you have been happy? . . . He liked life, he liked laughter, I wasn't right for him. Obviously he fell in love with you and I don't blame him."

She was shouting. Moira backed away.

"I don't blame him! I don't blame either of you!"

"Beatrice, please," Moira said. "The man was someone you don't even know—you and Wallace didn't know him—and it didn't matter, we never loved each other—"

"I don't believe that," Beatrice said.

"We never—"

"No. I know Wallace too well. I know *you*." She pressed her hands against her face. The wind must have drawn tears out of her; her cheeks were wet. "Don't you deny it, Moira . . . don't you deny him . . . he was going to die anyway and why shouldn't he have been happy . . . why would it have mattered? . . . I don't mind. I don't mind."

"Beatrice, it wasn't your—"

"I don't mind!"

She turned away. *Don't you deny it . . . don't you resist. . . .*

Moira said nothing; she simply stood there. Then she said softly, "I knew you would understand, Beatrice, all along. It was your husband, yes."

Beatrice saw that her friend's expression had changed; the tension was gone, the guilt gone.

They walked back to town in silence. It was a wild, windy day.

Eventually, both women left Manitock. Beatrice got a job in the public-school system in Albany, New York, teaching part-time in junior high, and enrolled in a graduate program in art history at the State University there. Moira, after selling her house, moved to San Francisco where she bought into a small bookstore. On an impulse Beatrice sent her a note one day: *Thank you, Moira.* Months passed. When she received a reply on a stiff oatmeal-colored piece of paper, she had nearly forgotten about the note she had sent. *You're welcome, Beatrice,* Moira had said. And that was all.

Lover

No longer young?... Must remind himself of his age: thirty-seven. That was not exactly young. But when he had time to study his face in the mirror he was always shocked, subtly, by how relatively youthful he did appear, in spite of.... Of course, the men in his family hardly seemed to age: his father had been energetic up until the very last week of his life. Tony had his father's gentle good looks: his dark, heavy eyebrows; his pained, distracted courtesy. *Yes...? Of course I'm listening.*

A woman whose face was a soft, lined, infinitely lined glove: like a glove that has been crushed and let to fall. Aged. Elderly. Out of that pale, softly wrinkled face her eyes peered at him with an intensity that was painful. *Doctor, please. Doctor...?* Tugging at his sleeve. Trying to pull him down to her where she lay; trying to pull herself up, up from the pillows. Her clawing fingers. His wrist. *You are too young to know.... You don't understand.* It was necessary that he extricate her fingers one by one. Gently. With courtesy. The woman's voice was nearly gone now, he heard only a whisper. In fact he did not always hear the words, but he supposed he knew what they were: he had heard them so often from her. The woman's body was nearly gone now: one hundred and fifty pounds some months ago, now sixty-five pounds. Yet she had that timid, desperate strength. Pulling at him, begging him. *Doctor, let me die. Tony...?*

The Huron Nursing Home: the daily and weekly and monthly records, the monthly insurance payments, the nurses, the Director who had been a friend of Tony's father. All were real, all were public. He was a public man. Thursdays at the Home, the other days at the hospital and in his office, in white, a public man. *You are too young to know*, the woman accused him, but it was a lie. He knew everything. And he was not young.

Ah, lovely! At first, from the air, London had looked like any other city. And the crowds at the airport were like crowds at any airport. And the long ride in, the heavy traffic, the unmistakably gritty taste of the air, the dizzying, swarming sea of people at the very center of the city: Leicester Square, Piccadilly. But nearing their hotel Tony began to realize how quiet it was. The traffic noises faded to a nervous, energetic hum, a constant hum, well within the range of what one could tolerate. The air seemed to lighten: a long stretch of park, the damp fresh chill of spring. Suddenly he was happy to be here. It was lovely here, he would be happy here.

Mina had been saying for months: *You're so different now, so distracted all the time. You don't listen to me....* His mother criticized him affectionately, pulling at his wrist as only she had a right to pull: *Must take a vacation this spring, Tony, don't wait until August; you must take two weeks off and escape....* She had always been jealous of Tony's father, hadn't she? And jealous of his patients and his success? But that was natural, wasn't it? And Tony tried not to mind her siding with Mina: his father had minded this sort of thing, had too often lost his temper. "Oh, isn't it lovely!... Hyde Park," Mina was saying. "Aren't you happy to be here? It's so lovely here, look at all the daffodils and jonquils and tulips." Mina was leaning against the window as if she were slightly drunk.

"Happy," Tony murmured, unpacking. He took his things out with care; Mina had folded them and packed them with care. "Happy.... Very happy, yes. Happy."

Such tall windows: floor to ceiling. Yet they were impractically narrow, hardly more than a foot across. Strips of glass, green-tinted. Tony counted nine windows in the room and wondered what the point of it was. Must be very expensive. And the room was oddly shaped, one wall shorter than the others, so that he had the illusion of being inside a distorted cube, an artwork that was a playful trick on the senses. The hotel was a

ube, an elegant cylinder. The room was soundproof. Mina stood
at the window, pointing fourteen stories below to the bright red
double-decker buses and the stately black taxis that moved in
countless lanes, streaming to the right, streaming to the left, a
continual motion that was fascinating. And silent, unlike the
traffic of Wisconsin Avenue.

"I don't want you to think of it while we're here," Mina said.

Her back was to him, but he smiled in her direction. "Yes,
that's right," he said.

No need for him to stoop as he knotted his tie, since the bureau
mirror was immense. Tony was over six feet three; his
dark-brown hair stuck out from his head stiffly, so thick it looked
as if he could not comb it, only brush it out; his shoulders were
wide. Yet his size was easily accommodated by the mirror and
the long, highly polished mahogany dresser. The bed caught his
eye: almost as wide as it was long. Accommodations for
Americans, for giants.

"Why are we staying here?" he asked. "Why aren't we staying
at a. . . ." But he had let her do all the arranging. She and the very
helpful man at the travel agency in Bethesda. The tickets, the
reservations, the countless details worked out by Jessamyn
Carlson, the checks signed by Jessamyn in her neat, graceful
handwriting. She was dressing in a corner of the room, out of his
vision. Fortunately, she had not heard his question; he must have
spoken too softly. So he said: "It seems to be very quiet here. The
room is very attractive; it's like an American hotel."

When he glanced toward Mina he was surprised to see his own
reflection; one of the mirrored closet doors was open, shielding
her as she changed her clothes. His blue-gray suit looked good.
Possibly he was tired, his complexion a little yellowish; he hated
to travel. But the suit was attractive. Bought for this trip,
especially for this trip, his first suit in two years . . . *you'll need
something light and yet warm, no matter that it's supposed to be
spring there, that crocuses started to bloom back in early March;
England is always cold, always cold.* . . . Mina leaned around to
smile at him. What had he said? She stood in a lacy white slip, her
hands busy with her hair, pinning it up. Fast-moving little hands,
the fingernails polished a very light pink, so subtly lacquered
Tony could not always tell they were lacquered. She was a very
pretty woman, with her silvery-blond hair and pale blue eyes and
her smile. Barefoot, she was much shorter than he. Like a young
girl, a child. But why did she wear white?—it reminded him of

the paper smocks, those throwaway paper smocks patients wor
for examinations. The smocks were a single size, large, wit
enormous armholes and a string to tie around the waist....

Death is a privilege! he had wanted to shout at the old woma;

But Mina was not begging him for death, not even for on
more quarter of a gram of morphine; she was not tempting him t
commit murder for her sake. Instead, she was listing the events c
their stay here in London. But one thing was disappointing; th
travel agent back home hadn't gotten them very good seats for
certain play.

"We can get to the theater early," Tony heard himself saying
"And if someone has turned in his tickets, then ... then .... W
can do that."

What good was it to have money if you never spend you
money? Money too was a privilege. Spending it, being happ
with it, was a privilege. Two years since he'd bought a new sui
and his shoes were run-over at the heels; Mina nagged hir
laughed at him, argued with him.... This vacation could be
second honeymoon, she said. Tony agreed. He sat with her on th
upper level of one of the buses, listening to her excited chatter a
she read from a guidebook ... reading names of parks and street
and buildings and statues ... famous names, immortal names
Here, immortality was everywhere.

"So many people," Tony murmured.

Crowds along Oxford Street. A plunging stream of shoppers
tourists. Incredible, so many people.... Yet an occasional square
glimpsed from the main road, looked almost deserted.

"Aren't you sorry you haven't traveled more?—you'r
thirty-seven years old!" Mina said, squeezing his hand. She wa
only a few years younger than he, but it had always been
tradition between them that she was much younger: girlish
sweet, sometimes audacious. He loved her very much and hope
he might learn from her.

It was difficult to carry on a conversation now that they wer
studying the menus.

Enormous ivory placards. The names of the dishes in French
in flowery script. *The White Elephant:* an exclusive private clul
on Curzon Street. Only a two-minute walk from the hotel, n
need for a taxi.... Their hosts were explaining things to them
Mina was listening attentively, but Tony's mind wandered. H

had waited for Mina to shower, had been standing at one of the windows gazing down at the traffic, had found himself thinking that the value of travel might be a secret no one voiced: the realization that so many people existed, thousands upon thousands of people existed, quite unrelated to one another, unaware of one another, lives that scurried among lives without touching them ... and so it was liberating, wasn't it, to see how little one's own life mattered? ... how little one's own life obsession mattered? And it was true, as Mina so often said, that people who had money might as well spend it. Money too was a privilege.

He was happy enough to be here, in this handsome dining room, studying this complicated menu. Their hosts were friends of friends. A connection through Mina's brother-in-law, who worked in Washington with someone else's brother-in-law, something to do with the London-based subsidiary of a pharmaceutical company: not necessary for Tony to remember the exact relationships, but he should try to remember generally who was who, who was American and who was English. ... Odd, the New York accent of the man beside Mina, a handsome forty-year-old in a stylish suit, sideburns halfway down his cheeks. Tony listened to what was being said. Explanations of English holidays, bank holidays, indifference of workers to work and income and the old enticements of the materialistic culture ... the terror that cynics had never considered of the possibility that God had retreated into Material for most people, into cars and television sets and semi-detached houses in the suburbs, and now the scornful intellectuals had done their work: now Material itself was losing its divinity. And could total chaos be far behind? ... Laughing over their cocktails and caviar and pâté. Tony leaned forward. He wanted to ask whether that was really true? ... whether it had been offered as a serious remark, or only as part of the conversation? ... but already the subject was changed, already they had not so much backed away from it as leaped over it.

One of them asked Mina about their plans: which required her listing the plays and tours and museums and galleries once again. Flushed with joy, she was, hardly more than a girl after all. Blond and American and eager to live, eager for life to be made tempting to her. She was from Charleston, South Carolina, and in the company of strangers her soft, gracious, utterly charming accent reasserted itself without her knowledge. Tony felt a little jealous that she should be so happy with other people and so unhappy with him and not even know it.

During dinner Tony's mind wandered and he could not call it back. One of the men in their party reminded him of a patient of his who had died not long ago. Fifty years old, a wealthy broker, a sportsman with hundreds of acres in the Smokies, articulate about his own dying: witnessing with a kind of irritated awe the blemishes that covered his body and would not fade, the scales and itchy patches that gradually merged, scraggy scabby patches of reddened flesh gone mad, wild, turned against the person who inhabited it. Was that death, was it that simple? Of course. Tony had been embarrassed for so long, he'd stumbled and reddened, as embarrassed as his father, but what good did it do to always resist? . . . so many of them died anyway. Died. And not all of them seemed to mind. The dying man smoked cigars and lay propped up in his expensive bed and spoke to Tony of the phenomenon of dying. Evidently he had begun to die, he explained, the day he lost all interest in his disease; like most educated people, he had taken an obsessional interest in "his" disease, had become rather a specialist in it (a rare kind of bone cancer). But one day that interest left him. He saw that "his" disease did not matter; it wasn't disease that mattered, only the balance of power between life and death . . . the shift of power and allegiance to the other side, to death, that was the beginning of dying. *I felt it with relief, that shift.*

One of the women asked Tony a question. He answered. He must have done well because she smiled, laughed, was obviously pleased with him. She was the wife of the man with the sideburns. Behind her the paneled wall gleamed, her perfect honey-blond hair was reflected in it; and behind her image, beyond it, the amiable blur that must have been Tony's face. All was well. Tony found himself in the conversation without having anything to say, but that did not matter, not in the slightest. What had anyone to say? These healthy trivial people, strangers who turned out to be friends: what did they have to say? They praised the dishes, or complained about them. They commented on the wine. And was that James Mason seated at a nearby table? . . . or someone who resembled him? . . . and how long would the Carlsons be in London, or had they already asked that question? Tony heard himself laughing. He must have been happy to be with them, though not so happy as his wife was; it was like being with their friends in Bethesda or Georgetown or Chevy Chase, people turned out to be familiar, brothers and sisters, alluding to the same subject and eating the same food, as long as their allegiance was to this visible, handsome, costly world. . . . But how could they eat so much? Tony was amazed. Amazed at himself as well. It must have been because they were celebrating something important. They had to snatch at the food, had to snatch at whatever they were celebrating, not wanting it to end. Cocktails and hors d'oeuvres and appetizers and the courses that followed one another in an important sequence and then the after-dinner drinks and the after-dinner conversation. . . . Jesus, so much food. So much of it wasted. Tony wanted to jump up and leave and get back to the hospital. He could shower there. Could change his clothes there. And. . . .

The food must have been ornamental; he was missing the point of it. He was too literal. Not enough imagination. Without appetite he ate, as they ate without appetite. Tony's problem, Mina said, was that he never enjoyed anything; why couldn't he enjoy life as others did? . . . He made an effort, he brought his spirit back to the table and listened to what was being said, trying to hide his discomfort. They must not miss Speakers' Corner at Hyde Park—did they know about that?—was it in the guidebook? There they could hear the most extraordinary speeches, sincere people and obvious madmen, and fascinating people in the crowds, really fascinating. If you're interested in eccentrics. In abnormal psychology. *Will I, won't I, will I, won't I,* Tony heard himself thinking, while he agreed that he was interested in such things; he was interested in everything, that was why he and Mina had come, wasn't it? A small drunken voice, taunting him. *I think I will, I think I won't, I think I will.* And the old woman's face appeared in his mind's eye, begging him to leave these people, to fight his way past them, to release her from her agony. Tony half shut his eyes. He was smiling. His lips were smiling. *Will I, won't I, will I.*

One of the women was telling an anecdote about an attempt made on the life of the Queen some months before, and Tony's eyes filled with tears and he thought in a panic *Jesus Christ, what if I start to cry, what if I ruin this evening like all the others?* but there was no danger of that, the anecdote was really a joke, it resolved itself in laughter and all was well.

"You want to go home, don't you?"
"Of course not."

"You're not happy here, you want to go home. . . . You hate me. You're not happy with me."

"I'm very happy. I don't want to go home."

"You're always thinking of. . . ."

"No."

They went to famous immortal sites and yet time did not pass. The present could not be dislodged. The Tower of London: Americans tramping happily in the drizzle, taking pictures, crowding one another on the narrow, poorly lit stone staircases, calling to the ravens. . . . *Look at the crows! Look at the crows!* a young father cried. His children were delighted. They went to the British Museum where, grateful for Mina's awed silence, Tony gave himself up to *Will I, won't I, will I, won't I.* He had explained to that woman that he was not preventing her death. He did not stand in the way of her death. Not he. How was it his fault that, once she was hospitalized in that place, he could not cross any boundary established by the law? . . . could not cross any boundary? . . . he was sick with shame and terror, not knowing what to do. And yet: had her life evaporated to the point at which it was no more than a bubbling phosphorescence he could not have abandoned it, could not have given it up. . . . He was frightened, excited. He walked Mina through the enormous drafty rooms and kissed her when they were hidden for a moment by a marble wall.

Yet time did not move: only three calendar days had passed.

In the Kensington Gardens Mina slipped her arm through his and accused him of being in love with another woman. Did she know the woman? . . . was it the wife of one of his friends? Was it a patient of his? Tony laughed, she was so endearing, so absurd. On the gravel path he kissed her.

"Have you every seen parks so very green?" they asked each other.

Mina was happy. Tony was happy, but he began to sweat through his clothes, though the restaurants and theaters and museums were ill-heated, possibly not heated at all. At odd, unaccountable times he thought of his office, thought of the lights out and the shade drawn, *Dr. Carlson, M.D.* in gold leaf on the door, the waiting room empty and *Réalité* and *Today's Health* and *Scientific American* and *Newsweek* and *Medic-World News* in their proper places in the magazine rack, everything in its place, silent, undisturbed, dustless. He thought of the hospital. He thought of the Huron Nursing Home. . . . Mina spoke wistfully of going to visit a cousin of her mother's, a spinster who lived in Highgate, but Tony did not reply, did not argue. In the end she went alone: he saw her off at the Underground near their hotel and they said good-by bravely, as if they might never meet again.

Of course they met again, and though it was much later it seemed to Tony that time had not passed at all. He had wandered beneath the pavement, studying the crowds in the subway, his hands in the pockets of his raincoat . . . a man with nothing to do, absolutely nothing to do. An observer, a stroller. A witness. A tourist. As soon as Mina was gone he began to notice, uneasily, how dirty it was down here. The corridors were depressing, especially a very long, poorly lit one he wandered into by mistake, having misread a sign. He had intended to walk up to the Marble Arch but had turned at the wrong place and found himself in a parking garage; huge, hideous place, smelling of exhaust. A man was sprawled at Tony's feet, humming to himself. Drunk. Sick. The corridor was puddled: some of it water, some of it urine. At the intersection with the main corridor an aged woman derelict sat beside her bundle of clothing or food, her hands folded, eyes shut, her expression peaceful. People streamed past her. . . . Not far away three guitar-playing beggars, all Americans, singing happily to the crowds that ignored them; a girl in blue jeans and a bright yellow blouse rattled a tambourine that was also a kind of tin cup. It was quite cold down here. People hurried by, up toward Marble Arch or back in the other direction, not wanting to linger. Tony gave the girl in the yellow blouse a pound note, but she did not seem to notice. She smiled vacuously toward him, nodding in time with the lively, thumping music. He wondered what the hell she was doing here and what the point of it was . . . but it was something to tell Mina about, at least. She could not accuse him of having nothing to say to her.

"What were you reading there in that old book? . . . you missed what the guide was saying about. . . ."

"About Indian customs," Tony said. "A Jesuit's journal . . . seventeenth century . . . North America."

She waited and he did not continue.

"What was so interesting about the book?" she asked.

He was light-headed from all the walking that day, from the

miles of pavement and the crowds. Vague, blundering. He began
to tell her, as they sat in this charming French restaurant in
Mayfair, holding hands, began to tell his wife about a way of
Indian torture . . . Indians torturing Indians . . . the pulverizing of
the body's organs one by one and the necessity, the sacred
necessity, of preserving the life of that body until the very. . . .

She drew her hand away.

"You sicken me," she whispered. "You disgust me."

He pretended not to have heard and she did not repeat her
words.

Rather small, cramped seats. Tony yawned. Familiar faces all
around him: other tourists. The commotion five minutes before
the ballet began was exciting; even Tony felt some interest,
yawning after his heavy dinner. Mina seemed to be reading the
program, studying it. She wore her glasses. In the theater were
women with bright, smiling, expectant faces, all wonderfully
dressed, their hair wonderfully prepared. That was what they
did with their splendid good health. The men were smiling too.
But some were sleepy after their heavy dinners. A few of them
red-faced, sluggish, uncomfortable. Hypertension, heart attack;
Tony glanced at them and past them, not wanting anyone to
catch his eye. Why are we here, what are we doing here? . . . But
this was absurd: everyone wanted to be here. Obviously,
everyone wanted to be here.

The music was delicate, enticing. The girl was shy . . . the boy
bold. The perfection of their movements charmed Tony: bodies,
arms and legs, faces that were intelligent, feet that seemed to
possess their own thought. Tony was fascinated by the stylized
motions of power there on the stage: the male dancer now lifting
the girl above him as if redeeming her with his strength. She was
very pretty. He was very handsome. And those muscular
shoulders, those powerfully muscular legs . . . to think of the
power locked in them! . . . Then another dancer entered, another
woman. Tony's heart lurched. He realized this was only a dance,
only an illusion. Images chasing one another in a pretense of
being alive, bodies that mocked ordinary bodies with a supreme
godly irrelevant strength, while the audience stared and smiled.
The second girl had the face of a girl he had examined a few
months ago, and when she entered the dance he seemed to lose
the illusion before him in an instant. His mind shifted from the
stage because it was not real. He wanted to cry out, wanted to

protest, nothing could interest him except what was real, nothing could excite his passion....

The dancer was tall; her black hair whipped about; lovely muscular legs, absolutely certain of each movement, each note... absolutely certain of the dance. It turned out that this second girl was the important one, not the first. The man's interest shifted. The dance shifted.... Tony was watching the second girl and thinking of the other girl, of his patient, and he sank into an erotic daze, making no effort to concentrate on the dance or to avoid his memory of that day at the hospital, which he had very nearly forgotten. Of course he had forgotten it. He forgot, forgot everything; he had to.... But the music and the black-haired dancer brought it back and he felt his yearning spread out everywhere in him, not concentrated in any part of his body. It was everywhere in him. It could not be discharged; it could come to no climax. It was everywhere. In the brain. At the back of the throat, that dryness that could turn into a stabbing ache.... In his lips, in his eyes. In the upper part of his body, in his chest, where the lungs yearned to take in air as fully and fiercely as possible, the violence of muscles never fully exercised, taking their pleasure. Jesus, how he wanted... how badly he wanted.... But he didn't know what it was; he could not get it into an image, not into a single image. *Beautiful young schizo*, they had said. Brought in by police, found wandering in a railroad yard, clothing ripped, bare-legged though it was about twenty degrees that day, mumbling something about being raped, by a black man who said he would return to twist her head off if she told police... *beautiful schizophrenic* they had said *though pretty battered at the moment*.

Intermission. Tony woke to applause. His desire mocked him: his spirit had swollen to the point of anguish, and now everyone was applauding, the dancers were taking their bows, he was sweating inside his clothes and Mina was saying things he must reply to, must respect. In the seat before him was a young German woman. Harsh-voiced, hair that was too blond, hand-clapping that sounded violent, hollow, out of proportion to whatever had happened on stage. His yearning was being mocked, his tender excited memories were being clapped out of existence.... He joined in the clapping. He agreed with what Mina had said. With part of his mind he had actually been watching the ballet; he had been watching it. He had been listening to the music. With part of his brain he had concentrated on the dance, and it was not a lie, his applause, his willingness to join in the tumult of clapping. It was certainly pleasant to be here, it was a privilege to be here, and in a way he was grateful to be so suddenly awakened.

. . . Drinks in the lobby? . . . Ice cream? . . . Cigarettes?

Tony thought it touching that adults would eat ice cream out of little cardboard containers, with wooden spoons. Like children they were, eating with those wooden spoons. And so soon after their enormous dinners. . . . Boxes of candy. Hard candies, mints. . . . Would you like some, Mina? No. Thank you, no. Ice cream? cigarettes? a drink in the lobby? She countered by asking if he was enjoying the dance and when he said he was enjoying it, yes, very much, she turned away, offended by the sound of his voice. That he should not try harder to convince her! . . . that he should lie so unconvincingly!

They had not made love for so long now, the worry of it had become abstract, philosophical.

Sometimes she took on the burden of being at fault, not out of kindness but out of malice: she detested him. Sometimes he took on the burden, when he was genuinely tired or when he had had to leave the dining room during dinner because something that had happened that day returned to upset him. He loved her, he did not blame her for the rage she insisted she did not feel, and of course she loved him too: otherwise what was the point? The last several times they had made love Tony had had to convince himself that it was necessary, it was a sacred necessity, and as far as he knew she believed him . . . she seemed to believe him. He was not to blame that images rushed into his head. Was he? Nor was Mina to blame that her warm eager body and her loving words seemed to fade, to become abstract and unconvincing. How am I to blame, she once sobbed, tell me how am I to blame . . . is it someone else, do you love someone else, what has happened and how am I to blame . . . ?

They looked through the program together. They read the notes, commented on the dancers, studied the glossy advertisements, decided upon a restaurant in this very block where after-the-show suppers were a specialty.

"I'm enjoying this very much," Tony said.

And indeed he was eager for the dance to begin. The intermission was far too long. He got up to stretch his legs, made his way nervously through the crowds, returned to his seat and still there was a wait. A woman beside Mina turned out to be from South Carolina and the two of them were talking in warm, enthusiastic voices. So interesting here in London! . . . so unusual in so many ways!

The second ballet was by a contemporary composer named Fuhr and it was harsh, jarring, deliberately unrhythmic. Tony looked from one dancer to another to another, not knowing what would happen. The dancers seemed to pace and lunge . . . the black-haired girl appeared, her face grotesquely white, the features penciled in, the mouth too red. The male dancer circled her. His movements showed passion, but passion restrained by the structure of the music. . . . And his face was heavily made up, like the girl's. Was it a parody? Was it serious, a serious monstrosity? Tony judged from the restlessness of the audience that they simply did not know: they hadn't the right cues, they didn't know how to react. A sickening sense of chaos, of unbalance. . . . The music swerved this way, the dancers that way. *Will I or won't I? Will any of us?* Then there was a complicated turn and a spontaneous burst of applause from a few perceptive people in the audience, followed by a larger wave of applause. Tony seemed to catch the ballerina's joy as she felt the applause; she must have glanced out, a half-second, her exaggerated dark gaze acknowledging the audience . . . and Tony smiled, relieved and disappointed as the illusion broke for him, once again, and he was conscious of himself sitting in a cramped seat, perspiring, watching a contorted and very clever modern dance he did not understand.

Beautiful? No. Why did they always exaggerate? So few people were beautiful, what was the point of demanding beauty? In fact, beauty now bored him. He was thirty-seven years old and hungry for other things, not beauty; the illusion of beauty could not hold his attention for long. . . . The male dancer was like one of the guitar-playing boys in the underground tunnel, though more attractive. A very comely, handsome face, carefully made up, stylized, unreal. And his strength was not real; it was a convention. It was art. He guided the girl not by the power of his own spirit but by the power of the music and the power the audience gave him. He was the male dancer; he must be strong. His power was theatrical, stylized, coolly beautiful in its precision, and yet it was simply play . . . that quickening of the music, that outburst of percussion, suggested how the entire ballet was a cruel playfulness, a kind of abstract code. Gradually the audience caught on, gradually it began to respond to this code. The dance was one of asexual, graceful bodies that hinted at the dilemma of life in the flesh, without evoking it. Those thighs were muscular beneath the dead-white tights, and surely the bodies were sweating inside the strenuous caprice of the music, but it was not visible to the audience; therefore it did not exist. Tony crossed his legs. He uncrossed them, with difficulty. So uncomfortable in here. . . . On stage the dancers labored in an art that subdued the instincts by deadening them, by denying their existence. It was only a performance, Tony thought irritably. For him it was a parenthetical interlude, but for the people around him, for Mina, it seemed to be much more: the intensification of their lives.

How he pities them! . . . sad, ordinary people. Their passion had to be danced out for them, on stage. Otherwise they lost it.

Twenty years old, she was. But not beautiful. Why did they always exaggerate? Naked beneath the paper smock, her bare feet stuck in straw sandals, hugging herself, shivering. Not beautiful. Her skin was blemished, her forehead too broad and rather bumpy, as if the bone were uneven; her teeth were discolored. But the eyes were attractive. Except for the shifting, the ceaseless evasion of her gaze, swinging to the ceiling and into the corners of the room and down to her long pale skinny feet. Dark red hair would have been attractive, no doubt, if it had been washed. But it was greasy and hung about her face in snarled strands. Twenty years old. Dragged off the street and raped, she said. Could identify her attacker, she said. She spoke to Tony in a peculiar detached drawl. She would not look at him, but looked everywhere else. He wondered if she were really sane and only pretending to be insane. . . . She was obedient enough when he took her blood pressure, not resisting. She stared at the far corner of the room. For some reason he didn't feel afraid of her; he believed she was no crazier than anyone else. *Beautiful young schizophrenic!* . . . And her legs hairy, unshaven. Her armpits unshaven. Fingernails broken, filthy.

Then he asked her to step into the lavatory; he handed her a container, for a urine specimen.

No.

She turned away, hugging herself. She was evidently embarrassed.

. He offered her the container and she pushed it away with her elbow.

He explained what the procedure was. She must be examined—didn't she want to be helped? And he must make several tests, several more tests . . . must try to determine what had happened to her . . . see if there were live spermatozoa . . . it was emergency-room procedure.

She seemed to be listening, though she wouldn't look at him. He thought again that she wasn't crazy, only aping the mannerisms of crazy people: muttering to herself, turned away from him. Stop this! Stop! Go into the lavatory and get the sample for me and lie down on the table so I can examine you and all will be complete. . . . Then he had an idea. He told her he'd wait in the corridor. When she was finished in the lavatory she could come back into the examining room and lie down and prepare for the rest of the examination. How was that? . . . More privacy for her.

So he went into the corridor. There were two orderlies by the drinking fountain, yawning and stretching. . . . She's crazy, isn't she? She wasn't raped, was she? Like hell she was raped! . . . she must be lying. It didn't look like rape, her legs and belly weren't bruised, she must be lying. Tony waited until he supposed she was ready for him. He went back into the examining room and there she stood, in the paper smock, her hands clenched before her. She was staring at the floor. . . . He happened to notice the container with the urine specimen, partly hidden behind a filing cabinet. She had hidden it there out of modesty.

Tony thanked her.

And now for the examination: he saw at once that she wasn't bruised. But that might not mean anything. . . . He asked her to put her feet in the stirrups and slide down to his end of the table, but she couldn't seem to do it. She whimpered. She lay still and obedient, and then tensed up at once, as soon as he touched her. . . . He asked her to please relax, to cooperate. He had to complete the examination, had to get a smear. But she couldn't lie still. Tony tried to explain the procedure to her, but she didn't seem to be listening. So he called the attendants in and asked them to hold her down. A third attendant came along. Tony worked as quickly as possible. He felt light-headed, almost faint, that this girl should resist the examination and force him to hurt her; but this often happened, it couldn't be helped. He had to make four tests, it was for her own good, she had claimed to be raped . . . the police would want as much evidence as they could get. . . . She squirmed and whimpered, but he got the smear. Jamming his fingers up inside her: testing quickly for lumps, for any disorder. Quickly, deftly, and it was over and she had not even screamed.

That didn't hurt, did it?

She was relaxed now. She seemed to go dead.

That didn't hurt, did it? Tony asked conversationally.

They let her go. She lay for a moment without moving, then rose to a sitting position at the end of the table. How she panted! . . . like an animal. He could smell the stench of panic about her. But he had won, without really hurting her. He had completed the examination and would send the specimens to the laboratory and. . . .

He was taking off the rubber gloves when she attacked. She must have thrown herself off the table sideways—must have lifted herself by the sheer strength of her arms—jumping sideways at him, halfway onto his back, her hands around his throat. She was screaming now. Her screams came from every direction. She had grabbed Dr. Carlson by the throat and was somehow crawling up his back, literally climbing up his back. He fell heavily against the metal shelves. She was screaming and pounding his head against the floor. . . .

Mina was sobbing.

"There must be someone else. Another woman."

". . . no."

"Someone else. Someone else. Someone you love. . . ."

"For Christ's sake, no."

". . . and you don't love me."

"No. Can't you sleep?"

"Sleep. Can't I sleep," Mina laughed. They lay side by side in the enormous bed. The room was soundproof, nearly: from time to time they could hear a siren passing on Park Lane, but even that wailing noise was indistinct. Or maybe there were no sirens. Maybe the noises, faint and teasing, were from inside the hotel itself. Or maybe they were imagining it all. Tony sometimes heard his wife sobbing at a distance. But when he confronted her she was bitter and dry-eyed and waiting ironically to be loved. ". . . So we'll leave a week early; we'll leave tomorrow afternoon, to please you. To get you back home to your work. Your life."

"I don't want to leave early," Tony said weakly.

She required so little!...only to be held in his arms, to be comforted. And so he comforted her. She wanted to be loved: it was what she deserved as his wife. So he must love her. He must make love to her. Sobbing, her breath scanty as a child's, she lay in his arms and pressed her damp face against his...his wife of eleven years...so sweet, so anguished, so helpless and aggressive....Of course she was innocent; she was not to blame. She was one of those who danced in the background, who could not rush forward and demand the audience's attention. She was his wife and required rituals appropriate to that role. *You don't love me. You love someone else. Please don't lie....* She begged him to lie. His mind gave him images, flashes of the past: not bodies so much as entire scenes, experiences in which he and the other person were wedded, impersonally, irrevocably. *Tony...? Do you love me?* The dying old woman: except she was not old, really. The disease had aged her. Sixty-four and she looked twenty years older, clutching at his hand, at his wrist, begging....He was not guilty of her life or of her dying, but he would mourn anyway afterward, alone where no one would discover him: of course he was guilty, he was always guilty. He was their physician, he belonged to them and they to him. He was always guilty. He was theirs. They were wed to one another, irrevocably, and no other marriage, no earthly marriage, could compete with that marriage. No other passion could compete with it....The girl stinking of sickness, of panic, squirming on the examination table while he perspired over her, guilty, excited, nearly faint with the enormity of what she was forcing him to do, almost against his own will: What ordinary woman could match her? There were none, none like her. He knew none like her. Dark red hair, dirty, sullen, lusterless...and her eyes lusterless except at the moment he entered her....

The yearning was everywhere in him now. An ache, a wistful bewildered ache: that he might inhale so deeply, so wildly, that everything yet unknown to him, unknown to man, every secret, every terror, every adventure of the finite world, could be realized in one ecstasy....Still, a woman spoke to him, called him by name. Her voice was small, terrible. *You do love me?...Me?*

He loved them—all of them—*All of you.* Yes.

The Snowstorm

At the back of her mind, shadowy there, yet crazed and whirling like a blizzard, shapeless, terrifying, ordinary, the number grew—the faces, the bodies, sometimes nameless; sometimes there were names without specific faces attached to them, but memories just the same, equally powerful. She had lost count.

One of them had compared her to his wife. He had meant to flatter her; perhaps he had imagined, at that time, that he loved her and must flatter her. *You are so much more.... You are always so much more....* She had been very hurt, angered to the point of tears. She had told him: *I don't want to be compared to anyone else.*

The day of the snowstorm, the first heavy snowfall of the year, a girl sat across the desk from Claire, sniffing, weeping.

"I hate myself...I don't know what the point of it all is...what is the point...I'm failing three courses, I telephoned home last night to Rochester the first time in a week, I was so scared and ashamed and...and what I told you about before, that I thought I was pregnant...you know...well, I didn't know how I could be but I...I think that I kind of...at the back of my mind I kind of hoped I would be, you know, I mean not on purpose, but I had this strange sensation that it should be true, I would deserve it to be true...and then I would have the abortion, you know, I even have the two hundred dollars for it to be done right . . . and . . . and then I would be punished for it, does that make any sense?"

Claire did not say *It makes exquisite sense!*

Claire must have nodded. You hid your anguish, your dread; you nod to encourage them, but gently.

". . . I would be punished for it. Maybe I could start over again then."

A mane of dark red hair. Eyes painted, especially the upper lids—a silvery turquoise. Shells, seashells, that beautiful satin-glimmering mixture of colors. . . . An exotic coat: looked like goatskin, rimmed with fluffy white fur that might have been imitation fur. Quite long, fell to mid-calf, to the tops of tightly laced black leather boots. Expensive boots. Nervous hands, the constant movement of that hand holding the cigarette—back and forth, back and forth to her pale chewed-at mouth, filling Claire's office with smoke and sorrow. Claire tried not to cough at the smoke, tried not to show her impatience with that sorrow. She had heard so much of this before, so much of this!—and all the girls seemed to smoke. They were all pretty, like this girl, though not always so exotically dressed. They all said: ". . . I hate myself, I don't know what the hell is going on . . . it isn't this guy now, he was very sweet when I thought maybe I was, you know, pregnant . . . as I told you . . . it isn't this guy but the next one that I can already guess will take his place . . . because I lose interest in them once, once I, once we. . . . I didn't use to, in the beginning; now I do. . . . No, they don't know about any of this at home, certainly not, that would kill them. You're the only one I told, and one girl friend, and, uh, the boy . . . I told him about it. My mind just goes on and on. You probably think I'm crazy."

Staring from under those inverted seashells: *Am I? What am I? Will you help me . . . ?*

Claire tried to explain something. You must use words, that was the difficulty. The puzzle. You must use words, but what will be explained, what will be communicated, cannot be in the form of words.

She had been helping people with their lives now for many years; for centuries. She was new at this particular place, but the tears, the anxiety, the crumpled tissue, were familiar, almost reassuring. You reassured them: you reassured whoever was present.

". . . yes, yes, I can understand that. I can understand that. But I just can't seem to stop myself in my imagination . . . it's my imagination. It isn't anything to do with my body or with being in love, Mrs. Dougherty—Mrs.?—Miss?—it isn't anything to do with that. My mind, my thinking, is just restless and already leaping on to the next guy no matter who it is . . . no matter if . . . if I even like them, or like the one I'm going with at the time or not. . . . No, there isn't any quarrel or anything like that. No big deal. I mean, that just doesn't enter into it. I'm always nice I guess as far as I can judge . . . but with each of them there's always that point where you lose interest, do you know what I mean? . . . and it seems to come faster and faster this year, I'm only nineteen, and . . . probably I shouldn't tell you this because you'll think I'm crazy . . . wouldn't blame you . . . but it must be maybe twenty or twenty-five guys or maybe more by now . . . most of them up here, the last two years, and some back in Rochester, where I went to high school. Sometimes I just want to die, I think I might as well die—what's the point of it all—and I'm failing half my courses though I started the year out so excited; I was very excited about my courses in September and would just never have believed that I'd be in here talking to you and it isn't even Christmas recess yet . . . you're awful nice to listen to all this . . . I don't have anybody to talk to that knows anything . . . I think sometimes I'm just going to jump off the bridge or something, I feel so low, then the hell of it is I sort of forget and go for three-four days feeling just fine . . . then it swings back to the other again . . . I can't make any sense of myself or of anything."

Someone had painted the face on her. She was not sure who had done it—perhaps it had been herself. She was inventive, whimsical, she did surprising things. But it might have been someone else, whom she had never met. There was a passport photograph of her that, like the passport photograph of her husband, had been crudely stamped over in indelible official blue ink, so that you could not see the alterations in the photographed face and would not become alarmed. She had never dared study that picture. Somehow it had not looked adequately painted over, the face, and she shied away from it the way you shy away from mistaken things, misprints in the newspaper that slide from *The President has ordered* to *Yje Lfdxicwet jsf ueswews* without any warning.

Once in a snowstorm all the paint wore off: tears or melting snowflakes or the wind wore it off, and she had been surprised at her own exposed face: fifteen or sixteen years old at the time, back in Iowa or Colorado or wherever she told people she was from, staring at herself in the mirror of a cigarette machine in a bus station somewhere...the face all her own again, windblown, roughened, even the lipstick gnawed off. She had looked exactly the way she looked to herself. The change had seemed minimal, almost disappointing. She had wanted to disguise herself, fussing in the near-dark of the bedroom she had shared with her sister, couldn't use the bathroom for very long because other people wanted to use it, there was only that one bathroom in the house and six people living there...fussed to disguise herself but succeeded, perhaps, only in fooling herself into thinking she was disguised, hidden. In that snowstorm, the school buses delayed, the roads so dangerous, she had been away from home for so long that every disguise of hers, every meager defense, had been lost. But she soon forgot that blizzard. She made every effort to forget her past, especially her girlhood.

In this new storm she did not think of that blizzard of many years ago. If she had happened to think of it, she would have pushed the memory aside, back into the shadowy tumbled recesses of her mind, where everything ended up eventually; like a cellar where things are thrown promiscuously, with no care for their value.

She might have denied the relevancy of that earlier snowstorm. She might have thought *Each storm we endure is the first*.

She was not alarmed, only disturbed, when she couldn't get her car out of the parking lot—couldn't back it out of the space she was in. The lot was icy and there was slush on top of the ice; the back wheels of her car spun, would not take hold. The noise of the engine, the noise of the spinning, were a little sickening. Motion that hungered to be physical—to be free—yet was held back; the horror of being buried alive; a news story she had read the other evening, not wanting to read it, but fascinated: a grave dug up somewhere outside Rome, a woman apparently buried alive some decades ago, the inside of the coffin clawed at, the body contorted in its struggle....

There was no one here, in this city that was new to her, whom she could telephone; no one she cared to telephone.

Three people ahead of her, a straggly half dozen behind her, when she saw that the bus was filled; the bus driver was about to close the door. She must have looked stricken, her expression more painful than the others, because it was Claire he seemed to address, yelling *Sorry! No more room!*

One of the boys tried to push his way on.

But the driver refused to close the door; would not start the bus.

The boy jumped off, swearing.

Another bus with the same destination passed, not bothering to swing in to the curb. Claire could see that it, too, was filled—people jammed in, standing, lurching and swaying against one another as the bus slid on the icy street.

Traffic moved slowly, cautiously. The snowfall was wet and deceptively beautiful; it melted, hardened to ice, made the surfaces of visible things slick, wetly gleaming, dangerous. Suddenly the late afternoon of an ordinary day in December became a time of sinister festivity; games had to be played with machines, sliding and skidding on what had been the street. Claire felt the excitement. She was shivering slightly but had not really noticed the cold. *It began when...it seemed to begin when...the bus driver shouted out at me....*

At another bus stop, on a parallel-running street, a long line of people were already waiting. Most of them were students. One of them, hatless, her long shiny hair now covered with snow, reminded Claire of the girl who had taken up so much of her time that afternoon—an hour and a half, and very little accomplished—and Claire hoped it would not be the girl; she didn't care to see her again so soon.

No, someone else. The coat was different.

A boy in a sheepskin coat, his nose running like a child's, told Claire that the next bus wouldn't be along for ten or fifteen minutes; maybe longer, since they were running behind schedule.

"The bastards lie to you. They say there's one right behind them, a five-minute wait, so you stand out here freezing," he said. He spoke to Claire as if they were acquaintances, as if they were the same age or the same sex. He didn't have any boots on, only sneakers; he wiped at his nose with the sleeve of his coat.

Claire decided to return to the parking lot to try again.

There was an atmosphere of slyness, of festivity; not a single game that was being played but a number of games, uncoordinated, improvised, set into motion by the snowfall that had seemed so lovely earlier that day, before noon. The temperature had not been low—had been around the freezing point—so that big flakes fell and melted and were covered by more flakes. Then, in patches, everything turned to ice. The really cold, harsh wind was the one that swept down from the northeast, over the lake, along the river. It froze everything it touched: Claire felt one side of her face grow numb, though she had only a quarter of a mile or less to walk, crossing one corner of the campus.

It seemed to begin when....Sorry. No more room.

But that was illogical; a lie. Nothing began at any point. She could not have said with any assurance that her life had really begun with her own birth; somehow that seemed too limited, too narrow a theory. One of her lovers, a biochemist, a man she had not paid much attention to at the time, had told her that it was probable that everything—all of life—everything—was born of a single cell, born of lightning and methane. Hence all the radii fled backward, in the mind's eye, to a single point, a single astonished explosion; no individual could claim any separate beginning. She had not appreciated that man at the time. He had been crowded out of her life by someone else, whom she later detested....Now she could hardly remember either of them.

That was untrue: she could remember well enough. But she had no interest in remembering.

Better to forget. Let it pass by, pass away. She was too intelligent to hold onto anything, even memories; too intelligent to make any claims on anyone else....No end to her intelligence! It swirled about her feet, inviting her to fall and crack her head on the bumpy ice. Inviting her to climb back into that trap, that car.

She tried again, and still the back wheels spun. She was calm, knowing that eventually she would get home; everything would work out, as it always did. She had been hysterical no more than two or three times in her life. It did no good, accomplished nothing. Eventually she would get home. Everyone would get home. Already the sidewalks and streets were emptying out: stalled cars abandoned at the curbs, a squad car's flashing red light, slow-falling, endless flakes seeming to turn, to turn at angles, in the various shifting lights. Most of the students were residents, lived on campus, in those high-rise buildings of poured gray concrete....Claire wished for the first time that she had rented an apartment nearby, instead of seven miles away.

You aren't happy. You aren't happy with your attitude.

She had tried to explain to the girl: *Behavior is neutral, the life patterns you explore are neutral; it's your attitude toward your behavior that is giving you trouble.* The girl began nodding, though it was obvious she didn't understand. Claire had learned to speak rather quickly, since everyone agreed with her anyway; before she said more than a few words people here were already nodding. Claire tried to explain that the girl was unhappy because she was evidently judging herself according to standards of morality or behavior that belonged to another culture, to another generation... but she herself did not belong to that way of life—did she?—and so she was judging herself according to inappropriate standards.... Did she understand? Yes?

The girl wiped her eyes carefully with a tissue, the lower parts of her eyes. Even so, the mascara streaked. She looked at Claire, soiled and baffled, the face of a twelve-year-old. *Could you repeat what you said?* she asked shyly.

They enter your life, weeping and guilty, wanting only to be kicked. When you tell them that nothing is wrong, there is no sin and consequently can be no punishment, their wars are with themselves only—mental confusions, deceptions—they feel the loss as children do, not even understanding what you say. Claire wanted to scream at some of them. Standards...morality...patterns of interpersonal relationships...socio-psychological stress...adaptations to new environments...restrict/nonrestrictive structures.... She knew the words well. She believed in them.

Then I didn't do wrong? the girl asked. *Then...?*

There were about a dozen cars left in the parking lot, evidently abandoned for the day. Claire watched someone drive out—cautiously, painfully—windshield wipers slashing back and forth like propellers—the driver hunched forward in order to see better—bare hands grasping the steering wheel— For a while it looked as if he might not make it, the ice and slush were so bad, but finally he got to the gate. He unrolled his window as Claire watched; he inserted the small plastic card; the gate-pole remained immobile, as if frozen in place; then it struggled free and lifted, and the driver made his way out.... Claire watched his rear lights through the haze of falling snow.

Logs bordered the parking lot. You could step over them, but you could not drive over them. Never. An enormous log, partly hidden by a snowdrift, blocked Claire's car. It was probably no more than a foot high, but it was like a wall, an ancient wall, heaped with snow that had been around for centuries.... She was on a mountain road, alone. A tree had fallen across the road, blocking her path. It would be night soon; snow was falling madly, blowing into the headlights of her car, rushing at her with the illusion of terrific speed as if she were being propelled forward herself and not sitting quite still, too intelligent to be angry or to weep, like the girls who came to her daily for help. They wanted someone to punish them, but she, Claire, would not punish them; they must find someone else to trap them and kick at them and destroy them, she would not; she could only tell them gently how they were free, how everyone was free, utterly free.... The interior of the car was cold, and smelled of leather. She turned off the ignition.

Where was the sky? The sky had broken into thousands upon thousands of bits.

In which direction was her home? Anywhere. Everywhere.

She made her way back to the building in which she worked. Fortunately the front doors were still unlocked; otherwise she would have to fumble with her keys. One side of her face was numb.

Her office was on the second floor. She always used the stairs, never the elevator. There was something gritty and melancholy about this building when no one was in it—one of the older buildings, constructed just after the war, without the slick, windowless precision of the more modern buildings, but rather run-down, dirty. The floors were stained and the walls marred, as if furniture carried through the corridors had been banged against them.

She did not sit at her desk, did not unbutton her coat, but dialed a taxicab company. Busy signal. She dialed another: also busy. She put the receiver back, waited, and then tried again. Still busy.... Now she remembered: the night before, in a dream, she had seemed to see herself, Claire, standing like this, alone, dialing a telephone.... Had she really dreamed it? She couldn't remember. She couldn't be sure. There had been something wrong with the dream, some alteration of the air—the atmosphere darker and more highly charged than usual—that must have been caused by the storm outside. She tried again, one number after another, until finally someone answered rather rudely: *Yes? Yes?* It would be an hour before a cab could get there; did she want to wait? She told the man yes, of course. She had no other way of getting home. Maybe it would be an hour, maybe more. All their cabs were busy, he said, and half the cars didn't have snow tires on yet. She told him she would be waiting, told him the address again and asked him to repeat it.

Okay, lady, we'll see what we can do.

One day someone had telephoned her, here in this office. She had picked up the phone and immediately someone said *Do you remember me? Don't you remember me?* and she could hear the crackling distance between them and the pauses in his breath, the way he cleared his throat, a noise familiar to her and yet bewildering—what had she to do with this man, or with anyone?—why had he telephoned her after so many months? He had not mattered to her. She had not mattered to him. She had forgotten him, really. She would have supposed that he had forgotten her. Why not? Why? He sounded drunk over the phone, telephoning long distance, *Don't you remember me, Claire?* as if they were lovers or friends or acquaintances, as if they had anything to say to each other. Afterward she tried to summon back his face. Unremarkable. Unhandsome. A hazel-eyed frankness . . . a small scar, healed so that it seemed no more than a deep indentation in his flesh, just above one of his eyebrows. A faunish face, but a body that was thickset and rather ungainly. No, she didn't remember him.

She stood at the single window in her office, looking out. A few boys walked by below, sliding on the ice, clowning around. One wore a wool cap pulled down low, onto his forehead; reminded her of a boy, a retarded boy, who had lived a mile away from her grandparents' home, out West. The storm was still quite fierce. Wind from the north, northeast, blowing across the lake . . . howling across the choppy gray-green waves. . . . For a while that day, when the snow began to fall, everything had seemed lovely, enchanted. Patches of blue in the sky. Patches of sunlight. Claire was new to this climate, had not lived this far north before, though she had lived in semi-mountainous land; she knew how dangerous a sudden storm could be. Yet it had not seemed serious to her, because she was just outside a city. In fact the city had grown out to include the University. There were buses, taxicabs, many people around; there was no danger, absolutely no danger. . . .

The first half hour went by slowly. For some reason she did

not care to unbutton her coat; it was cold in her office. The thermostat had been turned down by one of the custodians to conserve fuel. She was shivering. Seemed worse in here than outside; must be her imagination; she was awfully tired suddenly; had not eaten since noon.... What if the cab didn't come? Not much traffic on the street. This was a side street, rather narrow; there were parked cars on both sides, snow covering them in awkward humps; possibly the taxi could not make its way through.... How beautiful it looked out there! An evergreen tree bent to one side, snow piled on its limbs...snowflakes swirling in the streetlights, which had just come on...the wide, paved walk bumpy, irregular, icy, with an eerie tessellated appearance.... But what if the taxi couldn't get through that street? What would she do? What if they forgot about her? *Okay, lady, we'll see what we can do.*

It struck her that the man had probably not bothered to write down her address. What did he care? He didn't care. He had been rude, harassed, in a hurry. What did he care? All the cabs were busy tonight, everyone was making money tonight; it would be a matter of complete indifference to them whether Claire got home or not.

A telephone was ringing somewhere, in one of the other offices. That was absurd. No one was there, no one would answer. The telephone rang and rang and rang and finally stopped.

Claire remembered a small emergency she had endured, with her husband. They had driven to Vermont to visit his family; had not been in his parents' house an hour when his father had had a heart attack—it had seemed to be a heart attack—or extremely painful indigestion—an attack of some kind. The fuss, the terror! The strange sense of guilt! Her husband's father had been, like her husband, a tough, defiant man, with a permanently flushed face, a look of being windburned. She had disliked the father at first; it had taken several years for her to learn to dislike the son. In all, they were married five years. A gaping hole in her life, the years from twenty-one to twenty-six, best forgotten. He was not one of the men who bothered her afterward. She had imagined she would need another man, a lover, someone from the outside, to release her from her marriage—a stranger who could step in and change everything—but she had needed no one, really. There had been a lover, there had been two lovers. She had already stopped loving her husband, but enough emotion remained, enough tension remained between them, for her to want to hurt him as badly as possible. *Adultery. Adulterous.* Grounds for divorce, if nothing else. Pragmatic. Wise. Thoughtful. She had always been an intelligent woman and marriage made her keener, more shrewd. Afterward she cut her hair so that it fell about her face like a cap, a small shining dark blond helmet, showing the tips of her ears. She rarely wore jewelry, but when she did, it was made of gold—plain earrings, a chunky handcrafted necklace, the thick, carved wedding band now shifted to her right hand, shades of gold or imitation-gold that made her face seem to glow with health, her greenish-gray eyes alert. She had a look of perpetual keenness; it would be difficult to imagine her alarmed or even startled.

She was not alarmed now, only rather tired. At six o'clock she went out front, afraid of missing the cab. It was much colder, but the wind had died down. A kind of enchantment over everything, in spite of the patternless heaps and mounds and blossoms of white, the surprising rawness of certain things—part of an oak tree left entirely bare, the bark showing dim, exposed—and three blocks away, on Mercer Avenue, a flashing blue light from a snowplow, disturbing the silence with its agitation. She was watching the snowplow as it clumsily turned onto this street; it looked like a creature out of mythology, a mixture of species, which you might interpret as playful or nightmarish, depending upon what it did to you. She watched it for several seconds before it occurred to her that the taxi could not get past that truck if the taxi were to arrive now. She felt a jab of panic.

What if words break free of their order, what if the syntactical structures cannot contain them? She stared at the snowplow, at the intersection that seemed so far away. Probably she should wait inside, just inside the doors where it was warmer; but she felt under a kind of enchantment, a paralysis of the will. One thing about a snowstorm that had always impressed her was that it had no past and no future. It was a continuous present. Motion that speeded up or turned sluggish, depending upon the wind...a galaxy of bits, parts, fragments, clumps...an essential silence. The shapes of natural things were always exaggerated, given new contours. Gravity seemed to shift. All was freakish and restful to the eye. Absentmindedly she tried to open the door behind her. It wouldn't open; it had locked automatically. This did not matter, since she had a key. But she had lost interest in going back inside. She was fascinated, watching to see if the cab would turn in from Mercer—it was time for the cab to have arrived—the focus of her attention, of her entire life, narrowed to that intersection, that sluggish noisy snowplow, the possibility of a car's headlights turning in—

But the snowplow passed.

Time passed.

The snowplow made its way beyond her, down the street and out of sight, and no taxi came. She was not irritated until she saw what time it was; she had wasted a great deal of time. *Okay, lady we'll see what....* Her anger changed into a kind of stubborn satisfaction. She had known all along that the cab would not arrive, that the man hadn't bothered taking down the address, that it was a mistake to depend upon anyone. Her mother had depended upon too many people. Claire herself had made a few mistakes, which she now regretted bitterly; but she would not make them again.

By the time she walked out to Mercer she felt better, almost exhilarated. The air was thin, clear, razor-fresh. She was dressed warmly—her single heavy coat, with a fur lining; boots that were also lined—except for her gloves, which were made of leather, fashionable but too thin. It must have been very cold: her smallest fingers began to go numb. She had to keep her hands in her pockets.

So many options lay before her, she felt almost dizzy with the choices she had. Ahead was a drugstore. She could go inside to get warm; she could telephone another cab company. If she wanted, she could telephone someone from the depart-ment.... She went inside. A fluorescent-lit *Cunningham's*, obviously just renovated, stark and new, the usual tile floor ... she had stopped in here a few times in the past. For some reason had not liked it. Only one other customer, a man in a checked jacket, like a hunting jacket, and unbuckled boots, talking with the pharmacist. Claire went to the row of telephone booths. The first was out of order. She hesitated at the second booth, wondering if there was much point in telephoning another cab company. Even if they told her the truth, it was obvious that their cars were tied up for the evening; she would have to wait here for hours. It was degrading.... Another possibility was returning to her car. She considered this: the staff parking lot, the gate-pole lowered, perhaps frozen, the abandoned cars, like her own now covered with snow. No good. Hopeless. Her mistake had been to rent an apartment so far from the University. Other people lived nearer. Other people were now at home, safe. They would be wondering about whether the school might cancel classes the next day; otherwise, they no longer worried about the storm.

She could telephone someone in the department. But she shied away from asking people for help . . . she had moved here, to this city, in order to escape an involvement that had begun casually enough, freely enough, but had grown increasingly degrading and uncontrollable, and . . . and she did not want to become involved with anyone again; not for a long while. And the people she knew might not welcome a call from her. After all, she was a stranger, new to the department. Why should they do anything for her? Claire was not like a friend of hers, a woman in her early thirties who, having chosen not to marry at one point in her life, having chosen to lead a life uncontaminated by old-fashioned emotions, at the same time suffered bouts of loneliness and tried to blame others for not befriending her, for not having enough time for her—seeking friends, always new friends, close friends, sisterly friends. Claire could understand the woman well enough. She could even sympathize with her. But. . . . It did no good, to break through to one kind of freedom only to lose it again in other dependencies, making other demands upon people. . . . Claire was restlessly flipping through the telephone directory, not aware of what she was doing. Who could she telephone? Who did she want to telephone? There was the departmental chairman, a man named Nicholas Benton . . . bald, a mustache, a habit of smiling and nodding, no matter what was said to him, gaze distracted, vague, a brisk handshake, an odor of tobacco and. . . . He had hired Claire himself; kept making references to his wife, who wanted to meet Claire, who was trying to determine a good time when they were all free so that Claire could meet someone . . . meet friends of theirs who . . . an evening together, dinner and . . . conversation and. . . . It was the usual thing: promises vaguely made, no date ever set, Claire herself uninterested, though forced to pretend she was. *Alone. But lonely? Lonely? Alone—lone—lonely? No? Yes?* Whose business was it? It was no one's business.

Claire let the directory fall shut. She felt slightly angered, as if Mr. Benton had personally insulted her.

"Can I help you? Is something wrong?"

Claire told the pharmacist there was nothing wrong.

The man in the red-and-black checked jacket asked her if her car was stuck?—like his? He was waiting for a tow truck. Claire was moved by their interest in her, but for some reason did not care to talk; she told them that nothing was wrong, her car wasn't stuck, no, she lived nearby and there was nothing wrong. She turned the collar of her coat up, preparing to leave. The man in the jacket muttered something about the weather—wouldn't be surprised if the entire city was paralyzed—everything stopped—big trucks out on the highway were being abandoned, and the airport was shut down, and he'd been waiting over an hour for a tow truck, his car was broken down on a side street and practically covered with a mountain of snow—a goddam snowplow came by and buried it—

She hurried out, as if there were something she had to concentrate on, something she must discover. That pleasant exchange of words, of complaints!—no, she didn't want that. She didn't want any help.

She lived several miles to the north of the downtown area. She walked along Mercer in that direction, her hands stuck in her pockets. It was fairly busy here, considering the weather. Stores were closed, of course, but a few restaurants were open—a tavern—even a billiard hall. A pizza take-out restaurant: a tiny place, grimy steamy window, empty except for the girl in attendance, who stood behind the counter in a white outfit, staring out at the snow as if she were hypnotized. Cars moved along slowly in both directions. A taxi—a Yellow Cab—passed Claire, heading toward the University. Claire wondered— Was it the one she had telephoned so long ago? She wondered—should she try to signal it? But too late. It was past. Anyway, she did not much care. She had the vague idea that she'd walk along this street for a while, maybe catch a bus at one of the stops. Certainly the buses must be running. There were people around, hurrying from place to place. A bus stopped across the street, a number of people got off, tramped away. This stretch was certainly not deserted.... Someone was calling to her. *Hey? Hey there?*

A car had pulled up alongside the curb. The window was rolled halfway down. A young man was asking her something—a carful of young men—asking her if she was stuck, if she wanted a ride?—but Claire smiled quickly and told them no, no thank you, no, she lived just around the corner, and— The boy said

something further, laughed, rolled up the window, and the car
sped away. Claire hadn't heard his words. Her face burned,
though she had not heard his words.

... There was somewhere she must get to. She felt the need,
the pressure. People said to one another *I think I'll go home now.
Are you going home? Where does he make his home...?* The
word was *home.* The other words revolved around it. Yet it had
no meaning in itself. It had no meaning at all. Claire had been
thinking vaguely for hours now that she must get *home;* one of
the departmental secretaries had suggested that she leave a little
early, others were leaving early, in order to get *home* safely.
Where do you make your home? Your home is...? Her apartment
was on the eighth floor of a high-rise building out near the river.
Everything in it was new. The too-thin walls, the white plaster,
the drapes and the carpets and the built-in kitchen nook.... It
was so new that it had the power to disorient her when she
entered it. She always seemed to be stepping into a stranger's
apartment, fitting a key that did not belong to her into a lock not
hers, opening a door not hers to open, stepping into an empty,
absolutely silent apartment in which someone else lived,
invisibly. *I must get home. It's time for me to be home.* The
apartment building was bitterly resented in the neighborhood,
which was a residential neighborhood of older brick houses;
Claire gathered that its construction had been angrily opposed.
But the zoning laws had been altered. The building had been
built. Was that her fault? She'd been hundreds of miles away,
totally innocent. Was it her fault that there were no other
apartments in the city that seemed quite right, that she had
somehow ended up renting that one, not even liking it, in fact
disliking it for reasons she could not determine? How was that
her fault? ... Out back, in the untended yard, in what had been a
garden, were quite a few trees, even a willow tree. And an old
apple tree. A birdhouse had been hung in the apple tree, a small
russet-painted house; it turned in the wind, half-turned, turned
back again in the wind.... But no: Claire was confusing things.
The weedy garden had belonged to a house she'd rented a few
years ago, in another city. The apple tree ... the birdhouse ... the
flocks of sparrows and juncos and mourning doves Claire had
tried to feed, pitying them because of the cold. That belonged to
another time in her life.

It grew windier: she had to go over a bridge. Below were
railroad tracks. On the other side of the bridge Mercer Avenue

suddenly became rather dark—no so many lights—row houses, older homes, the edge of a slum. Claire hesitated. She could still catch a bus along here. There was a bus stop just ahead. Deserted. Very windy. She could wait for the bus here, except the wind made her ears ache. Also, she would have to catch another bus downtown, since the Mercer Avenue bus did not go out into her neighborhood. It might be better, after all, to call a cab. . . . On the other hand, she was hungry. She should probably have had something to eat in one of those restaurants behind her. They were small and unattractive; but she should probably get something to eat. . . . At the same time she knew she would never go back across the bridge. She had wasted enough time already. If she walked back toward the University, she might as well return to her office and stay there . . . she could stay there all night. It was a matter of indifference to her, really. What did she care? She felt uncomfortable in her apartment anyway. Why had she rented it? Why had that girl with the red brown hair been so upset? Smoking so nervously, sniffing, crying. . . . Claire had wanted to shake her by the shoulders. Stop! Stop it! It was degrading, such behavior. It was an insult to one's intelligence.

And that boy shouting at her—the window rolled down, the carful of them jeering at her, half-drunk, cruising around with nothing better to do—insulting, degrading. She was not afraid of them. She was not afraid to walk along here, even in the dark. Heated by anger, by a kind of stubborn excitement, she had nearly forgotten the cold. She felt it as if from a distance—as if she were far inside her own skin, hiding there, quite in control of her limbs, in control of everything she did, yet far from the surface, safe. Cunning. They would not get her. They would not even understand her. One of them said, baffled, hurt: *I don't understand.* . . . But why had he thought he might understand? How did he dare think he might understand her? She had allowed one or two people to know her, too well. She had loved them. Probably. Yes, probably she had loved them. It had made no difference; she had always been alone, she would always be alone, except: now she was more careful, far more careful. *Promiscuity. Promiscuous.* Someone had written her a letter, using those words. Her husband? Yes, but not the same one. But she had been married only that one time. . . . Still, there had been another man, a kind of "husband," and . . . and afterward . . . and he had not loved her well enough, he had disappointed her; men had always disappointed her, then turned against her...accusing, angry, pretending to be baffled by her behavior....He had written her an incoherent letter. She had ripped it up, thrown it away. Such melodrama! Such emotions! She had vowed she would never feel them again. Never. Her mother's listless humiliating tears mixed with Claire's memory of her own tears; the sound of women crying was always the same. Why did they cry, since it did no good?—since it was expected of them? *Promise. Promiscuous*. She had looked the word up in the dictionary, on an impulse. It was a harmless word, a neutral word. *Without discrimination. Without restriction*. She had been scornful of making choices, of choosing men, as if they were important enough to be chosen with any care. A stream...a series of faces, bodies, names...what did they matter to her as individuals? They did not matter. A *heterogeneous mixture*. In that way she revenged herself upon them all, back to and including her husband, who had disappointed her by being so weak. She revenged herself upon him and the others by leveling them all: one mass, one squirming swirling undifferentiated mass of human beings, without names, without value. She even revenged herself upon men she had yet to meet—deflating them in advance, making certain they would get no real power over her.

No one would ever get any power over her.

At least she did not lie to herself the way others did. She knew they lied. They lied to themselves and to one another, using a common language of lies, the most ordinary words used as lies, a kind of code of lies. Lies. It was maddening, how people lied. She was twenty-six years old, slapped awake. He had betrayed her by not being what she had imagined, what she had married; he had cried in her arms like a child; she came to detest him, that he should be so weak. In the beginning they made a show of seeming so strong, so superior. She was twenty-eight, twenty-nine years old. Beginning to know in advance the lies that would be used to manipulate her. Beginning to anticipate every move....*From a small town in western Iowa, near the Missouri River. Yes. No. Mother, grandparents. Sister. Brothers. A big family, yes. Father? Of course I had a father; didn't you, didn't everyone?* She was thirty years old and it wearied her to tell and retell the circumstances of her childhood. She would rather have forgotten. She had forgotten. But intimacy demanded answers to questions; answers to questions assured further intimacy, lies feeding lies, a wheel spinning out of control; she lied to them and they lied to her and she lied prettily to them and they slyly to her and she lied cleverly cynically shrewdly to them and they clumsily to her, and.... *From a small town in eastern Colorado, near the———River.* Sisters brothers grandparents mother tornados farm poverty father killed in the war?—killed in a farm accident, a tractor overturning?—killed out on the highway? Sometimes she would make up a fake name for the river. Any name. They listened, nodded, believed her. She could tell them anything because they were not truly listening. They lied, even as they smiled and kissed her, stroked her, seemed to be memorizing whatever she was telling them. *The Platte River. The Hays River. World War II—in the Philippines. No, in Italy. Outside Rome, buried outside Rome.* How old was she? Thirty-two, thirty-three. Thirty-five. Married how many times?

Any number. Anything. A storm of numbers, a storm of words, of people. What did it matter? It did not matter. They lied to her; they had always lied to her, to women. She would not make the mistake her mother made, crying over a man, half-crazy over a man. But she had made the mistake, a few times. But.... But she had been too intelligent to really make it; even while she wept, wanting to die, her intelligence had stood apart from her, pitying her, scornful of her, waiting for the emotional madness to pass. It always did.

Not many cars now. She had given up waiting for the bus. Too excited, too overwrought to stand there by the bus stop, stupidly. A bus would be along soon and, if she turned to see it in time, she could probably hail it out on the street . . . could force the driver to stop. If it mattered that much. She was tired, but at the same time she did not feel like waiting for a bus, exposed there on the curb, the wind tearing at her hair. The buses smelled of wet wool, of people, of rubber boots, of exhaust. She hated them. She was nervous, jammed into a bus, standing with the others . . . staggering, lurching as the bus started and stopped . . . everyone jammed in together, Claire among them, enduring it. She was not far from the downtown area, was she? A mile or two? How far was it? She kept mixing this city up with the others. . . . Not a very large city, but sprawled out, the downtown area consisting only of a few blocks. . . . She could get a room at a hotel: yes. There were hotels not far away. She was certain she remembered them . . . remembered one, at least. She could get a room for the night. She had money, enough money. Once, in

London, her purse had been stolen in the Underground ... she had goten off a subway in a great crowd of people, at Piccadilly Circus, and suddenly her purse was gone, snatched from her, and. . . . And it was gone: just gone. She had been panicked, really panicked. Worse than that, she had been sickened by her own helplessness. Her money and her identification and her passport snatched from her so quickly; she had turned to see the boy ducking under someone's arm—darting away—lost in the mob of people— Helpless, she had started after him. Helpless. Numb. Trapped.

She turned her collar up higher around her face. She wondered what time it was. She wondered what would happen to her—would anything happen? Tomorrow morning, would she be back at the University, in her office? Or would the University be closed for the day? She would listen to news bulletins tonight and in the morning, of course. Once she got home she would take a hot bath; would eat, would try to relax. Once she got home safe, she would be very grateful for her decision not to telephone anyone—Mr. Benton above all. She felt distaste, almost shame, at the thought of it—herself in the drugstore, so weak, undecided. Once you asked anyone for help you were in his power; it was nearly a law of nature. People were sometimes generous, sometimes not. Sometimes they were kind, sometimes not. It really did not matter which they were, what they were. *I don't have any ill-feeling toward you*, she had explained to someone, years ago. *I don't have any feelings toward you at all.*

But she was tired: maybe she should have gone back, across the bridge.

If only the back wheels had not spun so ignobly. . . . And that enormous log. . . .

Her husband had wept, like a boy. She had wanted to push him away. No, she hadn't married a man for that, not for that, not for such weakness. Let other women cradle them in their arms, let them forgive, let them delude themselves with what they called love. Claire knew it was a lie, one of the word-lies. . . . *You must remember me. Don't you remember . . .?* She wanted to scream—Why should she remember? Who were they that she should remember any of them?

Now the landscape looked suddenly familiar: a closed-down gas station, a streetlight. She was walking at a good pace, though not so fast as before. She was getting very tired. Arguments in her head, her own voice arguing back and forth, so tiring, infuriating. Something about the scene was familiar. Had she driven this way before, had she walked this way before? . . . Had she dreamed about this corner, the boarded-up gas station, the drifts of snow high around the gas pumps, the creaking *Sunoco* sign nearly hidden by falling snow? She might have dreamed it. Must have dreamed it. An abandoned car on the street here—yes—that too was somehow familiar. Across the way, a viaduct. What was that, a school?—it looked like a school. Someone's blinding headlights, ferocity of snowflakes illuminated for long moments as she stared, then the car was past, the snowflakes not so brilliant; she was alone.

She seemed to see herself from a distance. Seemed to remember herself. A woman hunched over, against the wind; the coat, the boots, the bowed head; crossing the street exactly at this point, at this moment. How strange it was that she should feel herself merge into that dream-woman, giving life to her, pumping life through her exhausted limbs! She foresaw that something would happen. Something must happen. As always. Downtown was far away, as the woman would discover at the top of the next hill—that hill just ahead. She would see more row houses. More snow. Miles of snow. Turning to look back, she would not see a bus—only the shiny, hard-packed snow and ice of the street. She would think, suddenly—

—a mistake?—

—And not long afterward someone would cruise by, slowing to keep pace with her, someone would ask if her car had stalled—if she wanted a ride somewhere— She would hear words; she would hear some words. Muffled because of the rolled-up window. He would be alone, the driver. She would not quite hear what he said. Probably he would ask if she wanted a ride—*Hey, you want a ride?* Probably. She foresaw that this would happen, she seemed to see the car, herself on the sidewalk just beyond the darkened gas station; she seemed to know that, without even checking to see who the driver was, she would run to the car and open the door, eagerly, gratefully. . . .

I don't like to be compared to anyone else.
And he would say:
And I don't either.

The Translation

What were the words for *woman, man, love, freedom, fate?*—in
this strange land where the architecture and the countryside and
the sea with its dark choppy waters and the very air itself seemed
to Oliver totally foreign, unearthly? He must have fallen in love
with the woman at once, after fifteen minutes' conversation.
Such perversity was unlike him. He had loved a woman twenty
years before; had perhaps loved two or even three women in his
lifetime; but had never fallen in love, had never been *in love*; such
melodramatic passion was not his style. He had only spoken with
her for fifteen minutes at the most, and not directly: through the
translator assigned to him. He did not know her at all. Yet, that
night, he dreamed of rescuing her.

"I am struck and impressed," he said politely, addressing the
young woman introduced to him as a music teacher at the high
school and a musician—a violist—herself, "with the marvelous
old buildings here . . . the church that is on the same street as my
hotel . . . yes? . . . you know it? . . . and with the beauty of the
parks, the trees and flowers, everything so well-tended, and the
manner of the people I have encountered . . . they are friendly but
not effusive; they appear so very . . . so very healthy," he said,
hearing his voice falter, realizing that he was being condescend-
ing; as if it surprised him, the fact that people in this legendary,
long-suffering nation were not very different from people

anywhere. But his translator translated the speech and the young woman appeared to agree, nodding, smiling as if to encourage him. Thank God, he had not offended her. "I am very grateful to have been allowed a visa," he said. "I have never visited a country that has struck me in such a way . . . an immediate sense of, of . . . how shall I put it . . . of something like nostalgia . . . do you know the expression, the meaning? . . . nostalgia . . . emotion for something once possessed but now lost, perhaps not now even accessible through memory. . . ."

If he was making a fool of himself with this speech, and by so urgently staring at the woman, Alisa, the others did not appear to notice; they listened intently, even greedily, as Oliver's young translator repeated his words, hardly pausing for breath. He was a remarkable young man, probably in his early twenties, and Oliver had the idea that the translator's presence and evident good will toward him were freeing his tongue, giving him a measure of happiness for the first time since he had left the United States. For the first time, really, in many years. It was marvelous, magical, to utter his thoughts aloud and to hear, then, their instantaneous translation into a foreign language—to sit with his translator at his left hand, watching the effect of his words upon his listeners' faces as they were translated. An eerie, uncanny experience . . . unsettling and yet exciting in a way Oliver could not have explained. He had not liked the idea of relying upon a translator; one of his failings, one of the disappointments of his life, had always been a certain shyness or coolness in his character, which it was evidently his fate not to alter, and he had supposed that travel into a country as foreign as this one, and as formally antagonistic to the United States, would be especially difficult since he knew nothing of the language. But in fact the translator was like a younger brother to him, like a son. There was an intimacy between them and a pleasurable freedom, even an unembarrassed lyricism in Oliver's remarks that he could not possibly have anticipated.

Of course his mood was partly attributable to the cognac and to the close, crowded, overheated room in which the reception was being held and to his immediate attraction for the dusky-haired, solemn young woman with the name he could not pronounce—*Alisa* was as close as he could come to it; he would have to ask the translator to write it out for him when they returned to the hotel. It would not last, his mood of gaiety. But for the present moment he was very happy, merely to hear these people speak their language, a melodic play of explosive consonants and throaty vowels; it hardly mattered that his translator could manage to translate only a fraction of what was being said. Oliver was happy, almost euphoric. He was intoxicated. He had to restrain himself from taking one of Alisa's delicate hands in his own and squeezing it, to show how taken he was by her. *I know you are suffering in this prison-state of yours,* he wanted to whisper to her, *and I want, I want to do something for you...want to rescue you, save you, change your life....*

The Director of the Lexicographic Institute was asking him a courteous, convoluted question about the current state of culture in his own nation, and everyone listened, frowning as if with anxiety, while, with one part of his mind, Oliver made several statements. His translator took them up at once, transformed them into those eerie, exquisite sounds; the Director nodded gravely, emphatically; the others nodded; it seemed to be about what they had anticipated. One of the men, white-haired, diminutive, asked something in a quavering voice, and Oliver's translator hesitated before repeating it. "Dr. Crlejevec is curious to know—is it true that your visual artists have become artists merely of the void—that is, of death—they are exclusively morbid, they have turned their backs on life?" The translator blushed, not quite meeting Oliver's gaze, as if he were embarrassed by the question. But the question did not annoy Oliver. Not in the least. He disliked much of contemporary art anyway and welcomed the opportunity to express his feelings warmly, knowing what he said would endear him to these people. It pleased him most of all that Alisa listened so closely. Her long, nervous fingers toyed with a cameo brooch she wore at her throat; her gray eyes were fixed upon his face. "Art moves in a certain tendril-like manner...in many directions, though at a single point in history one direction is usually stressed and acclaimed...like the evolutionary gropings of nature, to my way of thinking. Do you see? The contemporary pathway is but a tendril, a feeler, an experimental gesture...because it is obsessed with death and the void and the annihilation of self it will necessarily die...it pronounces its own death sentence."

The words were translated; the effect was instantaneous; Oliver's pronouncement seemed to meet with approval. The Director, however, posed another question. He was a huge man in his fifties, with a ruddy, beefy face and rather coarse features, though his voice seemed to Oliver quite cultured. "...But in the meantime, does it not do damage? . . . to the unformed, that is, to the young, the susceptible . . . does it not do irreparable damage, such deathly art?"

Oliver's high spirits could not be diminished. He only pretended to be thinking seriously before he answered, "Not at all! In my part of the world, 'serious' art is ignored by the masses; the unformed, the young, the susceptible are hardly aware of its existence!"

He had expected his listeners to laugh. But they did not laugh. The young woman murmured something, shaking her head. Oliver's translator said to him, "She says she is shocked . . . unless, of course, you are joking."

The conversation shifted. Oliver was taken to other groups of people, was introduced by his translator, was made to feel important, honored. From time to time he glanced back at the young woman—when he saw her preparing to leave, he was stricken; he wanted to tell his translator to stop her, but of course that would have been indecorous. *I want to do something for you. Anything. I want.* . . . But it would have been indecorous.

"She is a fine person, very hard-working, very trustworthy," Liebert was saying slowly. "Not my friend or even acquaintance, but my sister's . . . my older sister, who was her classmate. She is a very accomplished violist, participated in a festival last spring in Moscow, but also a very fine teacher here, very hard-working, very serious."

"Is she married?" Oliver asked.

They were being driven in a shiny black taxicab along an avenue of trees in blossom—acacia, lime—past buildings of all sizes, some very old, some disconcertingly new, of glass and poured concrete and steel, and from time to time the buildings fell back and a monument appeared, sudden, grandiose, rather pompous—not very old either, Oliver noted. Postwar.

"There is some difficulty, yes," the translator said, "with the husband . . . and with the father as well. But I do not know, really. I am not an acquaintance of hers, as I said. She lives her life, I live mine. We meet a few times a year, at gatherings like the one last night . . . she too does translations, though not into English. Into Italian and German exclusively."

"Then she is married? You mentioned a husband . . . ?"

Liebert looked out the window, as if embarrassed by Oliver's interest. He was not unwilling to talk about the young woman, but not willing either. For the first time in their three days' acquaintance, Oliver felt the young man's stubborn nature. "They have not been together in one place for many years, as I understand it," he said. "The husband, not an acquaintance of my own, is some years older than she . . . a doctor, I believe . . . a research specialist in an area I know nothing of. He is in another city. He has been in another city, and Alisa in this city, for many years."

"I'm sorry to hear that," Oliver said sincerely. "She struck me as sweet, vulnerable . . . possibly a little lonely? I don't like to think that she may be unhappy."

Liebert shrugged his shoulders.

"Unhappy, so?" he murmured.

They drove through a square and Oliver's attention was drawn to an immense portrait of a man's face: a poster three stories high.

"Amazing!" he said without irony.

"It is not amazing, it is ordinary life," Liebert said. "We live here."

". . . She isn't unhappy then? No more than most?"

"There is not the—what is the word?—the compulsion to analyze such things, such states of mind," Liebert said with a vague air of reproach. "It is enough to complete the day—working hard, carrying out one's obligations. You understand? Leisure would only result in morbid self-scrutiny and the void, the infatuation with the void, which is your fate."

"My fate?" Oliver said. "Not mine. Don't confuse me with anyone else."

Liebert mumbled an apology.

They drove on in silence for a few minutes. They were approaching a hilly area north of the city; in the near distance were mountains of a peculiar magenta color, partly obscured by mist. Oliver still felt that uncharacteristic euphoria, as if he were in a dream, a kind of paradise, and on all sides miracles ringed him in. He had not been prepared for the physical beauty of this place, or for the liveliness of its people. And his translator, Liebert, was quite a surprise. He spoke English with very little accent, clear-voiced, boyish, attentive to Oliver's every hesitation or expression of curiosity, exactly as if he could read Oliver's thoughts. He evidently took it as his solemn duty to make Oliver comfortable in every way. His manner was both shy and composed, childlike and remarkably mature. He had a sweet, melancholy, shadowed face with a thick head of dark curly hair and a widow's peak above a narrow forehead; his cheekbones were Slavic; his complexion was pale but with a faint rosy cast to it, as if the blood hummed warmly close beneath the skin. Large brown eyes, a long nose, ears too large for his slender face... something about him put Oliver in mind of a nocturnal animal, quick, furtive, naturally given to silence. In general he had an ascetic appearance. No doubt he was very poor, in his ill-fitting tweed suit and scuffed brown shoes, his hair crudely cut, so short that it emphasized the thinness of his neck and the prominence of his Adam's apple. Not handsome, perhaps, but attractive in his own way. Oliver liked him very much.

"If you would like, perhaps another meeting could be arranged," he said softly. "That is, it would not be impossible."

"Another meeting? With her?"

"If you would like," Liebert said.

Love: loss of equilibrium. Imbalance. Something fundamental to one's being, an almost physical certainty of self, is violated. Oliver had loved women in the past and he had felt, even, this distressing physical urgency, this anxiety, before; but it had never blossomed so quickly, based on so little evidence. The night of the reception at the Institute he had slept poorly, rehearsing in his sleep certain phrases he would say to Alisa, pleading with her, begging her. For what? And why? She was a striking woman, perhaps not beautiful; it was natural that he might be attracted to her, though his experiences with women in recent years had been disappointing. But the intensity of his feeling worried him. It was exactly as if something foreign to his nature had infiltrated his system, had found him vulnerable, had shot his temperature up by several degrees. And he rejoiced in it, despite his worry and an obscure sense of shame. He really rejoiced in it. He woke, poured himself some of the sweet-tasting brandy he had left on his night table, lay back upon the goose-feather pillows, and thought of her. Was it possible he could see her again? Under what pretext? He was leaving in four days. Possibly he could extend his visit. Possibly not.

He recalled her bony, broad cheekbones, the severity of her gaze, her rather startled smile. A stranger. One of many strangers. In this phase of his life, Oliver thought, he met only strangers; he had no wish to see people he knew.

I love you. I want... what do I want? ... I want to know more about you.

A mistake, but he could not resist pouring more brandy into

the glass. It tasted like sweet, heavy syrup at first and then, after a few seconds, like pure alcohol, blistering, acidic. One wished to obliterate the strong taste with the sweet—the impulse was to sip a little more.

According to his clock in its small leather traveling case it was three-fifteen.

I want . . . what do I want? he murmured aloud.

Liebert translated for Oliver: "She says that the 'extravagance' you speak of in Androv's chronicles . . . and in our literature generally . . . is understood here as exaggeration . . . metaphors? . . . metaphors, yes, for interior states. But we ourselves, we are not extravagant in our living."

"Of course I only know Androv's work in translation," Oliver said quickly. "It reads awkwardly, rather like Dreiser? . . . do you know the name, the novelist? . . . one of our distinguished American novelists, no longer so popular as he once was. . . . I was enormously impressed with the stubbornness, the resiliency, the audacity of Androv's characters, and despite his technique of exaggeration they seemed to me very lifelike." He paused, in order to give Liebert the opportunity to translate. He was breathing quickly, watching Alisa's face. They were having a drink in the hotel lounge, a dim, quiet place where morose potted plants of a type Oliver did not recognize grew more than six feet high, drooping over the half dozen marble tables. Oliver was able to see his own reflection in a mirror across the room; the mirror looked smoky, webbed as if with a spider's web; his own face hovered there indistinct and pale. His constant, rather nervous smile was not visible.

In the subdued light of the hotel lounge Alisa seemed to him more beautiful than before. Her dark hair was drawn back and fastened in an attractive French twist; it was not done carelessly into a bun or a knot, the way many local women wore their hair; it shone with good health. She wore a white blouse and, again, the old-fashioned cameo brooch, and a hip-length sweater of some coarse dark wool, and a nondescript skirt that fell well below her knees. Her eyes were slightly slanted, almond-shaped, dark, glistening; her cheekbones, like Liebert's were prominent. Oliver guessed her to be about thirty-five, a little older than he had thought. But striking—very striking. Every movement of hers charmed him. Her mixture of shyness and composure, her quick contralto voice, her habit of glancing from Oliver to Liebert to

Oliver again, almost flirtatiously—he knew he was staring rudely at her, but he could not look away.

"She says—Of course we have a reputation for audacity; how else could we have survived? The blend of humor and morbidity...the bizarre tall tales...'deaths and weddings,' if you are familiar with the allusion?...no?...she is referring to the third volume of *The Peasants*," Liebert murmured. Oliver nodded as if he were following all this. In fact he had lost track of the conversation; the woman fascinated him; he was vexed with the thought that he had seen her somewhere before, had in some way known her before.... And he had read only the first two volumes of Androv's massive work. "From the early fifteenth century, as you know, most of the country has been under foreign dominion...the most harsh, the Turks...centuries of oppression...between 1941 and 1945 alone there were two million of us murdered.... Without the 'extravagance' and even the mania of high spirits, how could we have survived?"

"I know, I understand, I am deeply sympathetic," Oliver said at once.

He could not relax, though he had had two drinks that afternoon. Something was urgent, crucial—he must not fail—but he could not quite comprehend what he must do. An American traveler, not really a tourist, prominent enough in his own country to merit the designation of "cultural emissary"—the State Department's term, not his own—he heard his own accent and his own predictable words with a kind of revulsion, as if, here, in this strange, charming country, the personality he had created for himself over a forty-three-year period were simply inadequate: shallow, superficial, hypocritical. He had not suffered. He could pretend knowledge and sympathy, but of course he was an impostor; he had not suffered except in the most ordinary of ways—an early, failed marriage; a satisfactory but not very exciting profession; the stray, undefined disappointments of early middle age. He listened to the woman's low, beautifully modulated voice, and to his translator's voice; he observed their perfect manners, their rather shabby clothing, and judged himself inferior. He hoped they would not notice. Liebert, who had spent so many patient hours with him, must sense by now his own natural superiority; must have some awareness of the irony of their relative positions. Oliver hoped the young man would not resent him, would not turn bitterly against him before the visit came to a conclusion. It seemed to him an ugly fact of life: that he, Oliver, had money, had a certain measure of prestige, however lightly he valued it, and had, most of all, complete freedom to travel anywhere he wished. The vast earth was his—as much of it as he cared to explore. Other cultures, other ways of life were open to his investigation. Even the past was his, for he could visit places of antiquity, could assemble countless books and valuable objects, could pursue any interest of his to its culmination. As the editor and publisher of a distinguished magazine, which featured essays on international culture, with as little emphasis as possible upon politics, Oliver was welcome nearly anywhere; he knew several languages— French, German, Italian, Spanish—and if he did not know a country's language a skillful interpreter was assigned to him and there was rarely any difficulty. Though he was accustomed to think of himself as colorless, as a failure—as a young man he had wanted to be a poet and a playwright—it was nevertheless true that he was a public success, and that he had a certain amount of power. Alisa and Liebert, however, were powerless; in a sense they were prisoners.

Of course they proclaimed their great satisfaction with postwar events. The Nazis had been driven back, another world power had come to their aid, the government under which they now lived was as close to perfection as one might wish. Compared to their tumultuous, miserable past, how sunny their present seemed!—of course they were happy. But they were prisoners just the same. They could not leave their country. It might even be the case that they could not leave this particular city without good cause. Oliver happened to know that nearly one-third of the population was involved, on one level or another, in espionage—neighbors reporting on neighbors, relatives on relatives, students on teachers, teachers on supervisors, friends on friends. It was a way of life. As Liebert had said the other day, it was nothing other than ordinary life for them.

Oliver knew. He knew. The two of them were fortunate just to have jobs that weren't manual; they were fortunate to be as free as they were, talking with an American. He believed he could gauge their fate in the abstract, in the collective, no matter that the two were really strangers to him. He knew and he did sympathize and, in spite of his better judgment, he wished he could help them.

At dusk they walked three abreast along the sparsely lit boulevard, the main street of the city; Oliver was to be taken to a workingman's café; he was tired of the hotel food, the expensive dinners. They spoke now of the new buildings that were being erected, south of the city, along the sea-cliff; they told Oliver that he must take time to visit one of the excavations farther to the south—he would see Roman ornaments, coins, grave toys, statuary. "Alisa says—the evidence of other centuries and other civilizations is so close to us," Liebert murmured, "we are unable to place too much emphasis upon the individual, the ephemeral. Do you see? I have often thought along those lines myself."

"Yes, I suppose so—I suppose that's right," Oliver said slowly.

Alisa said something to him, looking up at him. Liebert, on his right side, translated at once: "Future generations are as certain as the past—there is a continuity—there is a progress, an evolution. It is clear, it is scientifically demonstrable."

"Is it?" Oliver said, for a moment wondering if it might be so. "Yes—that's possible—I'm sure that's possible."

Liebert translated his words and Alisa laughed.

"Why is she laughing? What did you say?" Oliver asked, smiling.

"I said—only what you said. I translated your words faithfully," Liebert said rather primly.

"She has such a ready, sweet laugh," Oliver said. "She's so charming, so unconscious of herself.... Ask her, Liebert, where she's from ... where she went to school ... where she lives ... and what her life is like."

"All that?" Liebert asked. "So much!"

"But we have all evening, don't we?" Oliver said plaintively. "... All night?"

That day he had been a guest at the District Commissioner's home, for a two-hour luncheon. He had been driven to the village where the poet Hisjak had been born. Along with another guest of honor, an Italian novelist, he had been shown precious documents—the totally illegible manuscripts of an unknown writer, unknown at least to Oliver—kept in a safe in a museum. The first two evenings of his visit had been spent at endless dinners. He had witnessed a troupe of youthful dancers in rehearsal; he had admired the many statues of heroes placed about the city; he had marveled over the Byzantine domes, the towers and vaulting roofs and fountains. But his hours with Alisa and Liebert were by far the most enjoyable; he knew he would never forget them.

They ate a thick, greasy stew of coarse beef and vegetables, and many slices of whole-grain bread and butter, and drank two bottles of wine, of a dry, tart nature, quite unfamiliar to Oliver. The three of them sat at a corner table in an utterly unimpressive restaurant; it was crude and brightly lit and noisy as an American diner. At first the other patrons took notice of them, but as time passed and the restaurant grew noisier they were able to speak without being overheard. Oliver was very happy. He felt strangely free, like a child. The food was delicious; he kept complimenting them, and asking Liebert to tell the waitress, and even to tell the cook; the bread, especially, seemed extraordinary—he insisted that he had never tasted bread so good. "How can I leave? Where can I go from here?" he said jokingly. They were served small, flaky tarts for dessert, and Oliver ate his in two or three bites, though he was no longer hungry and the oversweet taste, apricots and brandy and raw dark sugar, was not really to his liking.

"You are all so wonderful..." he said.

Alisa sat across from him, Liebert sat to his left. The table was too small for their many dishes and glasses and silverware. They laughed together like old friends, easily, intimately. Alisa showed her gums as she laughed—no self-consciousness about her—utterly natural, direct. Her eyes narrowed to slits and opened wide again, sparkling. The wine had brought a flush to her cheeks. Liebert too was expansive, robust. He no longer played the role of the impoverished, obsequious student. Sometimes he spoke to Oliver without feeling the necessity to translate his English for Alisa; sometimes he and Alisa exchanged remarks, and though Oliver did not know what they were saying, or why they laughed so merrily, he joined them in their laughter. Most of the time, however, Liebert translated back and forth from Oliver to Alisa, from Alisa to Oliver, rapidly, easily, always with genuine interest. Oliver liked the rhythm that was established: like a game, like a piece of music, like the bantering of love. Oliver's words in English translated into Alisa's language, Alisa's words translated into Oliver's language, magically. Surely it was magic. Oliver asked Alisa about her background, about the village she had grown up in; he asked her about her parents; about her work. It turned out that her father had been a teacher also, a music teacher at one of the colleges—"very distinguished and well loved"—but he had become ill, there was no treatment available, he had wanted to return to his home district to die. Oliver listened sympathetically. There was more to it, he supposed, there was something further about it . . . but he could not inquire. And what about the husband? But he could not inquire; he did not dare.

"You are all so remarkably free of bitterness," he said.

Liebert translated. Alisa replied. Liebert hesitated before saying: "Why should we be bitter? We live with complexity. You wish simplicity in your life . . . good divided sharply from evil, love divided from hate . . . beauty from ugliness. We have always been different. We live with complexity; we would not recognize the world otherwise."

Oliver was staring at Alisa. "Did you really say that?" he asked.

"Of course she said that. Those words exactly," Liebert murmured.

"She's so . . . she's so very . . . I find her so very charming," Oliver said weakly. "Please don't translate! Please. Do you see? It's just that I find her so. . . . I admire her without reservation," he said, squeezing Liebert's arm. "I find it difficult to reply to her. Central Europe is baffling to me; I expected to be meeting quite different kinds of people; your closed border, your wartime consciousness that seems never to lift, your reputation for . . . for certain inexplicable. . . ." Both Liebert and Alisa were watching him, expressionless. He fell silent. Absurdly, he had been about to speak of the innumerable arrests and imprisonments, even of the tortures reported in the West, but it seemed to him now that perhaps these reports were lies. He did not know what to believe.

"Freedom and constraint cannot be sharply divided, the one from the other," Liebert said coldly. "Freedom is a relative thing. It is relative to the context, to the humanity to serves . . . shelters. For instance, your great American cities, they are so famed, they are 'free'; you would boast citizens can come and go as they wish . . . each in his automobile—isn't that so? But, in fact, we know that your people are terrified of being hurt by one another. They are terrified of being killed by their fellow citizens. In this way," Liebert said, smiling, "in this way it must be judged that the nature of freedom is not so simple. But it is always political."

"There's a difference between self-imposed restrictions and . . . and the restrictions of a state like yours," Oliver said, obscurely hurt, blinking. He had no interest in defending his nation. He did not care about it at all, not at the moment. "But perhaps you are correct, the issue is always political, even when it is baffling and obscure. . . . In America we have too much freedom and the individual is free to hurt others, this is an excess of...am I speaking too quickly?...this is an excess rather than...But I don't wish to talk of such things," he said softly. "Not tonight. It is more important, our being together. Do you agree? Yes? Ask Alisa—does she agree?"

They agreed. They laughed together like old friends.

"Alisa says—We must live our lives in the interstices of the political state," Liebert said slyly, "like sparrows who make their nests on window ledges or street lamps. They are happy there until the happiness stops. We are happy, until it stops. But perhaps it will not stop for many years—who can predict? Political oppression is no more a disaster than an accident on the highway or a fatal disease or being born crippled—"

"Disaster is disaster," Oliver said thickly. "What do we care? There isn't time. I must leave in a few days....I admire you both so very, very much. You're noble, you're brave, you're attractive...she is beautiful, isn't she?...beautiful! I've never met anyone so intelligent and beautiful at the same time, so vivacious, good-natured....Will you tell her that? Please?"

Liebert turned to her and spoke. She lowered her head, fussed with her hair, reddened slightly, frowned. A long moment passed. She glanced shyly at Oliver. Seeing the desperation in his eyes, she managed to smile.

"Thank you," Oliver whispered. "Thank you both so very much."

Something was stinging him.

Bedbugs?

His arms were curiously leaden; he could not move; he could not rake his nails against his sides, his abdomen, his buttocks, his back. He groaned but did not wake. The stinging became a single sweeping flame that covered his body, burned fiercely into his eyes.

"Alisa?" he said. "Are you here? Are you hiding?"

He was in the Old City, the City of Stone. Much of it had been leveled during the war, but there were ancient buildings—fortresses, inns, cathedrals. The weight of time. The weight of the spirit. On all sides voices were chattering in that exquisite, teasing language he could not decipher. They were mocking him, jeering at him. They knew him very well. He was to be led to their shrine, where a miracle would be performed. The holy saint of Toskinjevec, patron saint of lepers, epileptics, the crippled and the insane and the fanatic. . . . He was being hurried along the cobblestone streets. There were heavy oak doors with iron hinges; there were rusted latches and locks; walls slime-green with mold, beginning to crumble. Footsteps rang and echoed. Liebert held his hand, murmured words of comfort, stroked his head. He wanted only to obey. "Where is she? Is she already there?" he whispered. Liebert told him to be still—he must not speak! Someone was following them. Someone wished to hurt them. Oliver saw, in a panic, the greenish-copper steeple of an old church; he could take refuge in its ruins; no one would find them there. The main part of the building had been reduced to rubble. A wall remained and on this wall were posters of the great President—charmingly candid shots that showed the man with one of his children, and in a peasant's costume, and with a rifle raised to his shoulder, one eye squinted shut, and on the ledge above a waterfall, his arm raised in a salute to the crowd gathered below. Oliver hurried. Someone would stand guard for them—one of the men he had seen in the restaurant, had seen without really considering; a young black-haired man who had been playing chess with a friend, and who had not glanced up a single time at Oliver and his friends. But now he would stand guard. Now he was to be trusted.

They descended into a cellar. Everywhere there were slabs of stone, broken plasterboard, broken glass. Weeds grew abundantly in the cracks. "Hurry," Liebert urged, dragging him forward. Then Oliver was with her, clutching at her. By a miracle they were together. He kissed her desperately, recklessly. She pretended to resist. "No, there isn't time, there isn't enough time," he begged, "no, don't stop me. . . ." She went limp; she put her arms around his neck; they struggled together, panting, while the young translator urged them on, anxious, a little annoyed. Oliver's entire body stung. Waves of heat swept over him and broke into tiny bits so that he groaned aloud. He wanted her so violently, he was so hungry for her, for her or for something. . . . "How can I bring you with me?" he said. "I love you, I won't surrender you." She spoke in short melodic phrases. He could not understand. Now she too was anxious, clutching at him, pressing herself against him. Oliver could not bear it. He was going mad. Then, out of the corner of his eye, he happened to see someone watching them. The police! . . . But no, it was a poorly dressed old man, a cripple, peering at them from behind a broken wall. He was deformed: his legs were mere stumps.

Oliver stared, in a panic. He could not believe what he saw. Behind the old man were two or three others, half crawling, pushing themselves along through the debris by the exertions of their arms, their legs cut off at the thigh. They were bearded, wide-eyed, gaping, moronic. He understood that they were moronic. Oliver tried to lead Alisa away, but she resisted. Evidently the men were from a nearby hospital and were harmless. They had been arrested in an abortive uprising of some sort, years before, and punished in ways fitting their audacity; but now they were harmless, harmless....

His sexual desire died at once. The dream died at once.

He could not sleep. The dream had left him terrified and nauseous.

During the past few years life had thinned out for Oliver. It had become insubstantial, unreal, too spontaneous to have much value. Mere details, pieces, ugly tiny bits. Nothing was connected and nothing made sense. Was this "life"?—an idle pointless flow? He had watched it, knowing that one must be attentive, one must be responsible. But he had not really believed in it. There was no internal necessity, no order, only that jarring spontaneity, a world of slivers and teasing fragments. Ugly and illusory.

Here, however, things seemed different. He could breathe here. There were travelers who could not accept the reality of the countries they visited, and who yearned, homesick, for their own country, for their own language; but Oliver was not one of them. He would not have cared—not for a moment!—if the past were eradicated, his home country destroyed and erased from history.

He poured brandy into a glass, his fingers steady.

"Would I mourn...? Never."

The dream had frightened him, but it was fading now. It was not important. He had had too much to eat, too much to drink. His emotional state was unnatural. Love was an imbalance: he was temporarily out of control. But he would be all right. He had faith in himself.

The woman lived in a one-room apartment, Liebert had informed him. She shared it with another teacher at the high school, a woman. Should Oliver wish to visit her there—how could it be arranged? She could not come to the hotel. That was out of the question. Liebert had muttered something about the possibility of the other woman going to visit her family ... though this would involve some expenses ... she would need money. It would be awkward, but it could be arranged. If so, then Alisa would be alone and Oliver would be welcome to visit her. There might be danger, still. Or was there no danger? Oliver really did not know.

"And what of her husband?" Oliver had asked hesitantly.

"Ah—there is no risk. The man is in a hospital at Kanleža, in the mountains ... he is receiving treatment for emotional maladjustment ... a very sad case. Very sad. It is tragic, but he is no risk; do not worry about him," Liebert said softly.

They looked at each other for a moment. Oliver warmed, reddened. He did not know if he was terribly ashamed or simply excited.

"I love her," he whispered. "I can't help it."

Liebert might not have heard, he had spoken so softly. But he did not ask Oliver to repeat his words.

"How much money would the woman need?" Oliver asked helplessly.

They had been here, in this room. The money had changed hands and Liebert had gone and Oliver had undressed at once, exhausted from the evening, from all the eating and drinking and talking. He had wanted only to sleep. His fate was decided, he would meet Alisa the following day, he would extend his visit for another week perhaps, in order to see her every day; but now he must sleep, he was sick with exhaustion. And so he had slept. But dreams disturbed him: in them he was trying to speak, trying to make himself understood, while strangers mocked and jeered. The last dream, of Alisa and the deformed old men, was the most violent of all, a nightmare of the sort he had not had for years. When he woke, he felt debased, poisoned. It was as if a poison of some sort had spread throughout his body.

He sat up, leafing through a guidebook in English, until dawn.

"But I don't understand. Where is Mr. Liebert?"

His new translator was a stout, perspiring man in his fifties, no more than five feet four inches tall. He wore a shiny black suit with a vest and oversized buttons, of black plastic. Baldness had enlarged his round face. His eyebrows were snarled and craggy, his lips pale, rubbery. With a shrug of his shoulders he dismissed Liebert. "Who knows? There was important business. Back home, called away. Not your concern."

He smiled. Oliver stared, thinking: He's a nightmare. He's from a nightmare. But the man was real, the bright chilly

morning was real, Oliver's dismay and alarm were real. He tried
to protest, saying that he had liked Liebert very much, the two of
them had understood each other very well; but the new translator
merely smiled stupidly, as before. "I am your escort now and
your translator," he repeated.

Oliver made several telephone calls, but there was nothing to
be done.

"I do not have the acquaintance of Mr. Liebert," the new
translator said as they walked out together. One eyelid
descended in a wink. "But there is no lack of sympathy. It is all
the same.—A nice day, isn't it? That is acacia tree in blossom; is
lovely, eh? Every spring."

The man's accent was guttural. Oliver could not believe his
bad luck. He walked in a trance, thinking of Alisa, of
Liebert—Liebert, who had been so charming, so quick. It did not
seem possible that this had happened.

That day he saw the posters of his dream. He saw a tarnished
coppery-green steeple rising above a ruined church. He saw, in
the distance, long, low, curiously narrow strips of cloud or mist
rising from the sea, reaching into the lower part of the city.
Beside him, the squat, perspiring man chattered in babyish
English, translated signs and menus, kept asking Oliver in his
mechanical chirping voice, "It is nice, eh? Spring day. Good
luck." From time to time he winked at Oliver as if there were a
joke between them.

Oliver shuddered.

The city looked different. There was too much traffic—buses,
motorbikes, vans of one kind or another—and from the newer
section of the city, where a number of one-story factories had
been built, there came invisible clouds of poison. The sky was
mottled; though it was May fifteenth, it was really quite cold.

"Where is Liebert?" Oliver asked, more than once. "He and I
were friends . . . we understood each other. . . ."

They went to a folk museum where they joined another small
group. Oliver tried to concentrate. He smiled, he was courteous
as always, he made every effort to be civil. But the banalities!—
the idiotic lies! His translator repeated what was said in a thick,
dull voice, passing no judgment—as Liebert would have done,
slyly—and Oliver was forced to reply, to say something. He
stammered, he heard his voice proclaiming the most asinine
things—bald, blunt compliments, flattery. Seven or eight men in
a group for an endless luncheon, exchanging banalities,

hypocritical praise, chatter about the weather and the blossoming trees and the National Ballet. The food was too rich, and when Oliver's came to him it was already lukewarm. The butter was unsalted and tasteless. One of the men, a fat, pompous official, exactly like an official in a political cartoon, smoked a cigar and the smoke drifted into Oliver's face. He tried to bring up the subject of his first translator but was met with uncomprehending stares. Afterward he was taken, for some reason, to the offices of the Ministry of Agriculture; he was introduced to the editor of a series of agricultural pamphlets; it was difficult for him to make sense of what was being said. Some of these people spoke English as well as his translator, and he had the idea that others merely pretended not to know English. There was a great deal of chatter. He thought of Alisa and felt suddenly exhausted. He would never get to her now—it was impossible. Beside him the fat sweating man kept close watch. What was being said?—words. He leaned against a gritty windowsill, staring absently out at the innumerable rooftops, the ugly chimneys and water tanks, the banal towers. He remembered the poison of his dream and could taste it in the air now; the air of this city was remarkably polluted.

"You are tired now? Too much visit? You rest, eh?"

"Yes."

"You leave soon, it was said? Day after tomorrow?"

"Yes. I think so."

There were streetcars and factory whistles. Automobile horns. In the street someone stared rudely at him. Oliver wondered what these people saw—a tall, sandy-haired man in his early forties, distracted, haggard, rather vain in his expensive clothes? They looked at his clothes, not at him. At his shoes. They did not see him at all; they had no use for him.

"You are maybe sick...?"

"A little. I think. Yes."

"Ah!" he said, in a parody of sympathy. "You go to room, rest. Afterward perk up. Afterward there is plan for evening—yes? All set?"

"Evening? I thought this evening was free—"

The man winked. "She is friend—old friend. Sympathizes you."

"I don't understand," Oliver stammered.

"All understand. All sympathize one another," the man said cheerfully.

"Is wealthy? Own several automobiles? What about house—houses? Parents are living? How many brothers and sisters? Is married, has children? How many? Names?"

The three of them sat together, not in Alisa's room but in another café. Oliver was paying for their drinks. He was paying for everything. The woman's curt, rude questions were being put to him in clusters and he managed to answer, as succinctly as possible, trying not to show his despair. When his translator repeated Oliver's answers, Alisa nodded emphatically, always the same way, her eyes bright, deliberately widened. Wisps of hair had come loose about her forehead; it annoyed Oliver that she did not brush them away. She was a little drunk, her laughter was jarring, she showed her gums when she laughed—he could hardly bear to watch her.

"Say like our country very much? Good. New place going up—there is new company, Volkswagen—many new jobs. When you come back, another year, lots new things. You are friendly, always welcome. Very nice. Good to know...."

The conversation seemed to rattle on without Oliver's intervention. He heard his voice, heard certain simple-minded replies. Alisa and the fat man laughed merrily. They were having a fine time. Oliver drank because he had nothing else to do; whenever he glanced at his watch, the others looked at it also, with childish, open avarice. Time did not pass. He dreaded any mention of the room, of the alleged roommate who had left town, but he had the idea that if he refused to mention it, the others would not mention it either. They were having too good a time drinking. They murmured to each other in their own language and broke into peals of laughter, and other patrons, taking notice, grinned as if sharing their good spirits.

"Is nice place? All along here, this street. Yes? Close to hotel. All close. She says—Is wife of yours pretty? Young? Is not jealous, you on long trip, take airplane? Any picture of wife? Babies?"

"No wife," Oliver said wearily. "No babies."

"No—? Is not married?"

"Is not," Oliver said.

"Not *love*? Not once?"

"Not," he said.

The two of them exchanged incredulous looks. Then they laughed again and Oliver sat, silent, while their laughter washed about him.

Being driven to the airport he saw, on the street, a dark-haired cyclist pedaling energetically—a young long-nosed handsome boy in a pullover sweater—Liebert—his heart sang: *Liebert*. But of course it was not Liebert. It was a stranger, a boy of about seventeen, no one Oliver knew. Then, again, at the airport he saw him. Again it was Liebert. A mechanic in coveralls, glimpsed in a doorway, solemn, dark-eyed with a pronounced widow's peak and prominent cheekbones: Liebert. He wanted to push his way through the crowd to him. To his translator. He wanted to touch him again, wanted to squeeze his hands, his arm. But of course the young man was a stranger—his gaze was dull, his mouth slack. Oliver stared at him just the same. His plane was loading; it was time for him to leave, yet he stood there, paralyzed.

"What will I do for the rest of my life ... ?" he called to the boy.

The Dungeon

—Unable to wake up this morning. Dream-haunted. The muscular intensity of dreams, straining of heart, organs. Eyes. Yet without the release of visions. And never any color—do others lie, bragging that they dream in color? The images are black-white-gray. Recently there have been no images. M—— praised me for my ability to distinguish between subtleties of color, teased me about being tone-deaf in regard to music (which I am not), yet the dreams are vaporous and disappointing. Unable to wake for hours. Most of the day. Headache. E—— is so sweet—reminds me of my sister as she *should have been* & of course was not.

—Went for a long walk to clear my head. Demons, small leaping jokes of demons, can't be taken seriously. Golcando Blvd.— grotesquely named—buses, trucks, cars, renovation, mess, dust, dirt, people. Things blowing this way, that way. Look of desolation beneath all the activity. Smells in the air, promiscuous, swirling gaily together, as the sun came out taking everyone by surprise. Nevertheless, breathed in pollution & grime & even a blast of foul perfume from some creature striding past me, middle-aged but face painted like a mannequin's, a bad joke. A high-school boy in tight rust-colored trousers, pedaling his bike past me slowly, very slowly. Stranger. Cigarette stuck in his mouth, hair bursting out all over his head, somehow seemed part black. Looked at me so strangely!—seemed to know me. But impossible.

E——— the sister of my soul. Unmistakable. Put her hands on my forehead today, to ease the headache, small cool delicate hands, incredible. So sweet, so playful. Intelligent. Not like S——— and the disgusting G———. But dare not sketch her for fear the *Forbidden* would creep into it...& she would guess at once.

—Sly hideous twist the pen takes, sketching any subject I know to to be innocent. Can manage horrors like S——— and his pal G——— but not the others. Nature no risk: total abandonment to beauty. Trees, birds, landscapes. Creatures both natural & mythological. But a girl like E——— is defaced, brutalized, broken, by the cancerous urge in me.

—Cannot deny the intensity of the pleasure. The Secret. The costumes, scenarios, dialogue. Irony glimpsed only on one side—mine. Always in control. I respect her—never doubt that!—but can't deny the fits of giggling that sometimes overtake me afterward. Cruel, even crude. Hideous thought that I might end up in a few years like that ugly old P——— cracking dirty jokes about an ex-wife some of us have our doubts ever existed. No, I must be more careful. She is truly a match for me: our conversations, our laughter, the eager darting movement of our imaginations when we are together. Of course she is not talented, as I suppose I am. Yet in her way she is gifted. Just the tone of her voice, her green-gray eyes, her manner of lightly touching my arm as if to call me back to "reality"...not wanting people in the park or other customers in Rinaldi's to overhear. Voice shrill, laughter shrill. Must guard against excitement....A true gift such women possess; "artistic arrangement of life" a phrase I think I read somewhere. Can't remember. She wants to understand me but will not invade me like the others. Sunshine: her hair. (Though it is brown, not very unusual. But always clean.) Sunshine: dispelling of demons. Intimacy always a danger. Intimacy/hell/intimacy/hell. Could possibly make love to her thinking of M——— or (say) the boy with the kinky reddish hair on the bicycle...but sickening to think of. What if. What if an attack of laughter. Hysterical giggling. And. Afterward. Such shame, disgust. She would not laugh of course but might be wounded for life: cannot exaggerate the dangers of intimacy, on my side or hers. The Secret between us. My secret, not hers. Our friendship—nearly a year now—on my footing, never hers. Can't deny what others have known before me, the pleasure of secrecy, taking of risks.

—With D—— etc. last night, unable to wake this morning till after ten; already at work; sick headache, dryness of mouth, throat. But no fever. Temperature normal. D—— so bitter, speaks of having been blackmailed by some idiot, but (in my opinion) it all happened years ago, not connected with his position here in town. Teaches juniors, seniors. Advises Drama Club. Tenure. I'm envious of him & impatient with his continual bitterness. Rehashing of past. What's the point of it? Of course, he is over 40 (how much over 40 is his secret) and I am a decade younger, maybe fifteen years younger. Will never turn into that. Hag's face, lines around mouth, eyes. Grotesque mustache: trying to be 25 years old & misses by a mile.... Yet my pen-and-ink portrait of him is endearing. Delighted that it should please even him. & did not mind the CASH. Of course I am talented & of course misused at the agency but refuse to be bitter like the others. S—— lavish, flattery and money. I deserve both but don't expect everyone to recognize me...in no hurry...can't demand fame overnight. Would I want fame anyway???? Maybe not. With S——'s $100 bought her that $35 book of Toulouse-Lautrec's work, dear Henri, perhaps should not have risked it with her but genuinely thought she would like it. Did not think as usual. She seemed grateful enough, thanking me, surprised, said she'd received only a few cards from home & a predictable present from her mother, certainly did not expect anything from me—"But aren't you saving for a trip to Europe"—remembers so much about me, amazing—so sweet—unlike D—— who calls me by the names of strangers and is vile. His image with me till early afternoon, tried to vomit in the first-floor lavatory where no one from the office might drop in, dry heaving gasps, not so easy to do on an empty stomach. Mind over matter?????? Not with "Farrell van Buren"!

—A complete day wasted. Idiotic trendy "collage" for MacKenzie's Diary, if you please. Cherubs, grinning teenagers, trophies. An "avant-garde" look to it. Haha. Looking forward to layout for the Hilton & Trader Vic's, at least some precedent to work from *and resist*. . . . Could send out my Invisible Soldiers to hack up a few of these bastards, smart-assed paunchy hags bossing me around. Someday things will be different. (Of course must bow to Reality Principle. "Farrell van Buren" will never be recognized in this armpit of a town. "Maiden of the Great Lakes"—cannot be parodied, such jokes.)

—Took her to Rinaldi's. Fascinating, her ability to switch from gossip at work—her anecdotes about that employer of hers are first-rate satire, could she only draw or sketch!—an eye for detail like Hogarth's—not exaggerating—to remarks of a higher nature ("There are times when you ask yourself who has been here before you—as if someone else preceded you, everywhere—and you were the shadow this person threw"). I had trout stuffed with shrimp, pasta on the side, she had ordinary baked lasagna; shared an immense tossed salad in one of those wooden bowls. Red napkins, red tablecloth. Flickering light from the candles on the wall. Could talk with her for hours, hypotized. Sometimes it is not even her but someone else. She laughs so easily, would never hurt me . . . never pinch me, the way my sister did. . . . And my mother's raw-red arms, roughened elbows. Not her fault that she had to work so hard. Whose fault? My father's? . . . Died one weekend in a hospital, bleeding ulcers, just bled to death & nobody's fault, but my mother blamed him, of course; the insurance was so meager; could have been worse I suppose. . . . Told her about such things & she about things in her Past. (She's 26 years old & "still Catholic" & must be intimidated by me, to feel she should apologize—not that I would mock her tho' my own faith is long vanquished.) One unpleasant note: three men in a booth on the other side, drunk, giggling, one of them in a bright yellow jersey & his head somehow shaved, anything to attract attention, & when we left she stared at them, could see her expression go cold, hard. Coarsen. In the parking lot I made some small joke, nothing important, referring to a movie that'd been playing at the Capitol—across the street—for 6 months now & she misunderstood & thought I referred to those men. Made a face. Small pale prim. "Well I pity them" or words to that effect.

—Bled to death. It gushed out of any available hole, I suppose. Mouth, nose. Ears? Out through the bowels? It's lifeblood, precious but cheap. If you give blood, they store it in sacks, drain it out of you. I was too young to help my father. Wouldn't have mattered. But then!—he was an ignorant bastard, so weak helpless & stupid, the insurance premiums all screwed up like that.... Wasted an evening doodling, drawing. "Farrell van Buren" bleeding to death from various pores. Why do I maintain the fiction of that name? (My real name is ———). Rhymes with Farrell anyway. If I were to show her these notebooks.... If something happened to me they'd be found here in my apartment & confiscated & possibly sent to my mother with the rest of my belongings. Not that she'd read them anyway. Probably can't read, except newspapers. My sister, married to that smart-ass doctor. "Your brother-in-law has bought into a practice in Bar Harbor isn't that wonderful" blah blah. Stared at me first time we met, Thanksgiving, my sister pretending to be proud of me ("Had a show of his own at one of the galleries only twenty years old"), his handshake quick and almost cringing. *He knew.* But said nothing or so I assume. The filthy son of a bitch, to avoid me like that.... Some doctor, imagine what he tells his patients, makes me want to puke. Argument with my sister, argument with my mother. Nothing goes right. In Rinaldi's I went to help her with her coat, imagined she shrank from me, her shoulder sloping away. Well I pity pity pity.

—Drove to Point Garry. Lighthouse, blacksmith's shop, phony little boutiques. "Open air artists' mart" a laugh.... Met A——— and his friend N———; hadn't seen since last winter. (???) Looking good. Little red Fiat, A——— must have gotten promoted, looked tan, healthy. His friend claimed to be a sculptor but shut up fast when he learned I was an artist. Out late. Talked me into staying overnight. Forget name of motel. A dump: smelled of sewage.... Reddened nostrils a giveaway, will recognize in future, not my world at all. What if raided, arrested. What if arrested for possession of. & she would learn of it & the agency & my life blotted out.

—Never again.

—Pretty good chance for a one-man exhibit at the Cooperative; showed that big gal, Lucy, my "Dungeon of the Flesh" series & was absurdly pleased, her reaction. I intend to show Eleanora this journal & will not blot out her name from now on. If the drawings are exhibited she will certainly see them & the shapes there on the wall may argue eloquently for me; if not, the notebooks should explain. I have faith in her. I have faith in you, Eleanora....Told her about "dungeon" experience but was afraid to come out with the truth. We talked & talked. She is shy but at the same time surprises me—a roll of her eyes, a grin, dimpled cheek, like those high-school girls in the coffee shop at noon, can't always predict her. But won't blot out the name from now on. Eleanora?...Here is the quotation behind the series of pen & ink drawings, so hard to explain to one who stands firmly in the day:

> O dear children, look in what a dungeon we are lying, in what lodging we are, for we have been captured by the spirit of the outward world; it is our life, for it nourishes and brings us up, it rules in our marrow and bones, in our flesh and blood, it has made our flesh earthly, and now death has us.
>
> —Jacob Boehme

—Long-distance call from B——, three in the morning, hysterical as usual. Eighteen months since we talked last. Same tone, same high-pitched querulous voice. Demanding. Accusing. Or is it a pose—the "controlled hysteria" meant to reveal the depths of his soul? Everyone has turned against him. Friendless now. Enemies—"perverts." Someone left a note for him at work, in his mailbox, simply the word *Queer* in red ink. The possibility that his psychotherapist at the clinic is keeping secret records & will blackmail him. (When he taught for the U.S. Army, in the Orient, the same terrors plagued him: the G.I. students in his composition class taking notes on him, on his behavior; the army base psychiatrist turning his records over to the Army and to the director of the overseas program.) Sick—sick—sick. Sick. Expecting me to sympathize with him—console him—join him in obscene curses against the "enemy."

—After that call, could not sleep the rest of the night. My fate? Our fate? I am swimming through a tunnel of filth, holding my head high, my mouth shut, grim. Terrified. To be "liberated" like B——; is that all I can hope for? "Liberation"? Mania of the repressed breaking free into consciousness?—yammering, sniveling, boasting, whimpering now in public? One of my worst nights. Then at work that thick-calved pimply beast hung over my workbench, friend of a friend of Eleanor's. What is her game???? Chewing gum, a woman in her thirties. Ugh. The ring of my friend's hysteria in my ears all day—only dispelled when I telephoned Eleanor—thank God for her sweet light manner—the saving grace of unserious conversation. Relief just to hear the girl's voice. No edge to it. None of that "knowing," *I despise those who know me.* My secrets are life itself, the breath of life.... Do you wish to know the artist?—take yourself to the artist's dungeon! Eleanora does not know me & I map the future for both of us. But if the drawings are exhibited. But. *O dear children* etc....

—My bright green sleeveless sweater. Green & white silk shirt. & the white blazer, for the hell of it. The good trousers with that reliable crease. Eleanora playing "little wife," greeting me in the vestibule, hair pinned up somehow behind, ringlets around her ears...smelling of perfume but very very sweet perfume, not offensive like the others. The old lady on the first floor with the cats peeking out at us; thinks I am E's lover, eh? Old bitch! Yellow-faced old bitch! It stinks of cats, passing her door. But Eleanora likes her, calls her "Miss Lawrence," feels sorry for her because she's a widow. (I could tell her a thing or two about widows.) She wore a paisley dress, aqua and green; shoes with buckles. The dinner was lukewarm but delicious—poached fillet of sole—some kind of French sauce—grapes (???) in it. & whipped potatoes. Must have remembered my mentioning them & angel food cake with apricot sauce poured over it, hours of work, Eleanora so flushed & pleased.... I squeezed her hand. Very happy, excited. The wine went to my head. *(Should not drink.)* Fascinated with her hair—light brown, bangs over her forehead, those curly ringlets, other curls arranged in back. How do they do it? My sister's coarse red hair, like twine. Dyed. To mock the bitch I bought a $7.98 synthetic wig at the drugstore, bright red, almost a match for hers; jammed it on my head & put on her Easter coat & waddled into the dining room shaking my hips & the nasty thing could not see herself but only screamed at me, at *me*. & my mother also. Without imagination, without humanity. Eleanora got a little drunk, unused even to sweet red wine, giggling about some nuns at her school, how the girls were warned against sitting on boys' laps for fear of getting pregnant. "In trouble." Could I believe it. Could anyone believe it. Such rot, such craziness. I told her the nuns ought to have been stripped—their heads shaved—made to march naked in the streets, the nasty things. So nasty, nasty. A nun in our school, with the odors of her body trailing her; shameless.

—My sister thought she was *Beau-ti-ful*!

Married The Doctor (only a GP) & bought the most laughable mock-Tudor house on the country-club drive (of course). Never had me over to admire their carefully "weathered" oaken beams, eh? I was only in the dungeon overnight, in fact only six hours. A single telephone call & bond arranged & the informing officer frightened with a suit for false arrest tho' nothing came of any of it. They push us a little, we push back. There is a wildness in me never explored, not even in my dreams.

—Tomorrow I will show Eleanora my notebooks.... Have you read this far yet???? "Judge not lest ye be judged."

—I love you.

—Decided to show her the notebooks next week. The one-man show fallen through: Cooperative can't make April's mortgage payments. Lucy a *genuinely nice woman*.... So few of them. Without the pressure of the show felt invigorated, did a half dozen sketches on Saturday, one of them (modest self-portrait!) the best likeness I've ever done. Hair floppy, forehead just right, my pug nose—which I hate—and the slight cleft of my chin & even the slope of my shoulders, which I guess I must live with. One of Eleanora's front teeth slightly crooked. Brownish stains on the bottom teeth— is that tartar? (Says she drinks a lot of tea.) Nobody's perfect. Arranged in my room are the two dozen drawings...some of them rather graphic...sleepy young men, athletic young men lazy & muscular & cruel-eyed...& one of the boy who passed me on the street, hardly more than a glimpse of him & I captured his essence. Such mysteries in the street.... Long languorous limbs, hairy bodies, smooth bodies, eyes risky because so deep, so detailed. The eyes in my faces threaten to sink back into the skull, someone once said. Scholarship. Prizes. Promising. Next week will show Eleanora the notebooks, maybe ask to wait while she reads them—reads this—I have tickets for the University Players on the other side of town for Thursday evening, perhaps a good time. Good as any.

—Eleanora's face bobbing close to mine. The bangs, the baby skin, the mascara on the eyes; the arched eyebrows; the sly wink. *She knows.* I crouch before her as if before a mirror, adjusting the wig on my head. Damn thing, why is it so slippery? But with bangs it's easier to fix, you can hide half your face practically. Is that why women wear their hair in their faces, to hide them? Haha. I made up my face to mirror hers, not much of a trick to it, except the eye-liner is hard to manage. Dangerous, so close to the eye. My hand jerked with hatred for the face I was creating, I was trembling with disgust for it & myself but how else to show her what it's worth, her cute little personality? Wiggling her bottom. *Beau-ti-ful.* In the dream I began shouting & crying & when I woke it was the middle of the night & raining out, sleeting out, & I was all alone. Very upset. Heart going like crazy. They say you can die in such a state of sleep—they say that old men die of heart attacks in such a state—possibly infants die too, crib deaths, so-called "mysterious deaths" where the heart stops. *Jesus was I frightened!* ... Turned on the light, went to my workbench, hand shook so that ink spilled, but I doodled & drew till I was calmed down again. Drawing her face & my own & the faces of the others. That slight coarseness around her mouth. . . .

—A luncheon today, junior staff & even some of the girls. I wasn't invited. At the Red Fox. I'm positive there was a luncheon. Certain people are out to get me—envious of me—whispering about me. The gum-chewing witch in the pants suits; she'd better watch out. Who wishes to understand me had better watch out. S——— dropping by & I wouldn't let him in. Told him I couldn't trust myself, had dreams of bashing in his skull (yes! little gentle Daryl can be melodramatic too! like everyone else!) & calling the police & putting an end to it. The End. . . . Thursday, I'll let her read the notebooks. We'll see. I won't judge her ahead of time. I won't judge her/you. Nor will I plan ahead. My cruelty cannot be planned—has not been given enough freedom. How do I know what I will do? The *Forbidden* guards me too closely.

—Friday, I am writing this in the reference room of the state university library—drove 150 miles this morning—called in sick at work could barely disguise the contempt in my voice (*I will not endure* a life of conjured-up "truth" for the sake of fools &

half-witted tramps)—got in the car & pressed down the gas
pedal & waited to see where it would take me, what the hell
would happen, & got the old bitch up to 100 mph occasionally,
which isn't bad for an eight-year-old car with half the fenders
rusted off. Law-abiding little Daryl with the pug nose & eyes
that brim too readily with tears & the *precocious* talent that
brought him at the age of thirty to such acclaim & fame &
MONEY!!!! Because I was law-abiding & wept for mercy & had
no record whatsoever not even a traffic ticket (I do believe the
judge sneered at me, because I was so "innocent") they deemed
me worthy of returning to Reality that morning & graced me
with $500 bail; not so fortunate the other creatures hauled in the
night before. One of them with nose broken... bleeding &
laughing... hideous.

—What has this to do with Eleanora/Eleanor?

—Refrain of "I don't understand" & strained little smile & "I just
don't understand" & "You're frightening me; it's late" & a toss of
her cute little head & pleading smile & charming crooked teeth &
nervous playing with the pearls she wore (imitation). Brought
along a few of the drawings, in the portfolio; left them in the car
during the play; couldn't concentrate on the play except to try to
laugh when the audience did ("What's wonderful about you is
your sense of humor—you laugh so easily at things—") tho' what
is amusing about Brecht, about the disasters accumulating
offstage & in history & even the audience is beyond me. Still, you
must laugh. ("You seem a little sad tonight or subdued." "You're
not so funny anymore." "What's wrong?"—stray idiot comments
from an ex-friend, after the Saturday night lockup of five years
ago & constant memory.) Dragged the portfolio up to her room.
She wanted to see the drawings first, I wanted her to read the
Notebooks first, almost a childish tug-of-war, *for Jesus Christ's
sake don't do this to me!*—actually shouted at her. I am not crazy
but am being forced that way. I am not a pervert & not even a
radical & not out to change the world & tho' they laughed at me
for my Constant Guilt & Sense of the Unclean, why should I
care?—having my talent & my own soul & intellectual/spiritual
preoccupations to sustain me. Am a classicist, almost. Yet am
forced each day of my life to enter into moronic melodramas—
skits vulgar & pornographic in a spiritual sense—tug-of-war with
portfolio—mix-up with tickets (bought weeks ago yet wouldn't

you know—our seats not together; the usual story of my life)—the Cooperative evidently bankrupt & worse (rumors of theft by committee members) & on & on. Shouted. Tears of anger (?) or despair.... Gave in to her whims, showed her the drawings. Silence. Silence.... Eleanora frowning like a schoolgirl & frightened to death & slack-mouthed (actually!), you wouldn't know she was a woman of twenty-six, even with a sheltered life or whatever she claims (probably hypocritically), pretense of virginity & "not getting" certain jokes or puns.... Then the Notebooks, but I doubt she read them...skimmed them...silent, her pretty face gone stupid, frowning, blinking, the hypocrisy of looking for art in what I was offering her. Yes, yes, I am an artist or might have been—maybe will be yet—I'm not defeated yet—but offer myself too—offer myself for interpretation & possibly even affection & love or at least friendship—must have someone to talk to, to talk with; the other is not enough. It is friendship I crave FRIENDSHIP HUMANITY CIVILIZATION & my life clogged with enemies & the tunnel gushing sewage higher & higher & I must swim through it without drowning. There are beasts with tufts of fur on shoulders & chests & stomachs, broad grinning tanned faces, leering at us from the covers of newsstand magazines—nothing intimidates them or disgusts them—certain of my own drawings perhaps perpetuate this myth—lie—illusion—dream. Embarrassed little Eleanor one of the safe soulless tidy ones, little bitch, aren't you Eleanor, are you reading this far Eleanor, so prudently withdrawing your "friendship" from me as if I DID NOT EXIST any longer. One minute we are friends (& you hoped perhaps for an engagement ring, I suppose—to show your envious pop-eyed friends), the next minute we are ex-friends. How simple, how neat. But you won't get away with it. The perusal of a half-dozen pen-and-ink drawings. No more than two or three minutes. And afterward everything changed, changed irreparably.

—Tried to see it as art, did you? Aesthetic reaction. Yes of course it is art—is meant to be, at least—but it is also LIFE & SORROW & INARTICULATE YEARNING out of the dungeon—where you daylight people never go—"They're very interesting. They're very well done.... I don't quite understand them."

—("Why are you so upset, aren't they friends of yours? I mean, don't you all share the same interests?—hobbies? Why should you mind getting insulted by the police, pushed around a little to terrify you into catatonia, why should you mind actually being *arrested*...? Dragged to the lockup with your friends, reduced to a quivering mass of fear-flesh, weeping before the judge, why should you mind, isn't it part of your subculture, why should *you* be offended, of all people? Aren't you an artist? Can't you probably use these adventures for your art?") Freaks perverts queers broken-nosed dying alcoholics pitted faces rheumy eyes the insult of being thrown in among them & fainting in their stink.... Yet an acquaintance said why should you mind, why so upset, aren't they...friends of yours...& anyway can't you exploit such pain for your art....

—Shall I murder you all?

—What an enormous room, this reference room. Row after row of long tables...row after row after row.... Lamp-desks at the tables, at about the height of one's head, the effect being (visually) to cut off the heads of others in the room. Freakish. Trick of the eye. Students are jammed in this place as always: the revolutions of the 60's must have failed: media-hype, perhaps. Anyway here they are. Here we all are. Students taking notes vacantly contentedly. I am the only creature in the room writing so quickly—perspiring—hand aching with the violence of the words in me. Others are sleepy, lazy, idiotically content, taking notes on note-cards...professors' assignments...pointless, harmless...decade after decade...& here they are, still, in the same ceremony. A boy in a university sweat shirt across from my seat, sprawling, sniffing (no Kleenex), docile, eating a tangerine. The tart sharp smell of it is distracting. The boy is taking notes in green ink, red ink, & blue ink. Must be different subjects, topics. Unshaven, a little coarse but fairly attractive (except for the perpetual sniffing & wiping of his nose on his fingers). If he glances at me I will glance away. I am nervous, heated, too exhilarated...glasses sliding down my nose...perspiration must show on my face. Why did I come here? A mistake. Pressed the accelerator down as far as it would go...half hoping for...concrete pillars, the median divider, side-swiping one of those diesel trucks.... But no. No. I am not going to kill myself. That would be your victory, Eleanor.

—In this room of dizzying space I will calculate the future. Our future. Eleanor, it will not be that easy to forget *me*. There are many marriages & not simply the one you aspire to. Wise people know this fact but simple-minded secretaries ("I'm an executive secretary!"—oh my) do not. I foresee the friend of a friend of a friend transmitting secrets...across town....I foresee your inability to keep a secret & a corresponding intensity in their plots against me...deliberate "misunderstandings" in the office..."didn't you get the memo about the luncheon/conference" etc., etc. Insult to my intelligence, such trashy tricks. They have happened before. I have resigned jobs before. BUT I WILL NOT CONTINUE TO DO SO. That would be your victory.

—I did not judge you ahead of time. I was fair, absolutely fair. Now the *Forbidden* slips easily into my consciousness, teasing & prickling my skull. Shall I send my Invisible Army over to maul & rape you as in your girlhood fantasies you decided (Real Men! Soldiers! Masculine 100%)...or should I keep my distance in amused pity, knowing myself superior to you in every way...refusing to be hurt by you & your kind...or should I mail you certain drawings of Eleanora which I attempted in all good faith but which reveal you in your twisted hideous deformity, hidden from the outside world. Or. If. And. (Could buy a cheap wig with curls & idiot bangs & a paisley sack-dress & witches' shoes with brass knuckles. Could clump over to your place & bang on the door & give you a good look at yourself. Could surprise you at work in the same costume...face made up to resemble yours including the grotesque eye paint & the rosebud mouth...& shame you before the entire office. Do you see yourself? Bitch!)

—You failed me. Like all women. Might have 'saved'—baptized—me. But no: too selfish.

—The boy in the sweat shirt has left, I was writing so furiously I hardly noticed. The odor of citrus fruit remains. I am alone, and so free! Exhilarated now....My mouth is watering.

Famine Country

When Mrs. Cody, who had never done anyone harm in her
lifetime, and had never wished anyone ill, saw her son Ronnie,
twenty years old, so emaciated that he made her think of a
gigantic spider, his eyes yellowed and his complexion liverish
and mottled, she said, "He's going to die on us," and Mr. Cody
said at once, angrily, "Don't be ridiculous, Edith. Don't be
stupid." But fortunately Ronnie had not heard anything.

When Ronnie was discharged from the hospital, he shook
hands all around. He carried himself cautiously, like an
eighty-year-old man, taking his leave of the other patients,
blowing pert, formal kisses at the nurses. He promised in his high,
thin, curiously remote voice that he would be back soon to visit
with them all; he hoped they would not forget him too quickly.

He was polite to Mr. and Mrs. Cody. He did not quite
acknowledge them, but he did not ignore them either. For one
brief, warm moment he looked Mrs. Cody full in the face and his
lips twitched, as if he were going to smile, so she knew he was
recovering and everything would be fine again. He insisted upon
carrying his own suitcase though. He held it in both arms against
his scrawny chest, as if he feared someone might snatch it away
from him. At first Mrs. Cody did not recognize the suitcase. She
had never seen it before. Then she recognized it: a plaid canvas

zip-around bag she and Mr. Cody had given Ronnie two years before. He had been going to enter college in the fall, so the bag was a good practical present, and attractive too. It had cost $59.98 and was supposed to be washable, but Mrs. Cody doubted that.

"I can carry that for you, Ronnie," Mr. Cody said.

"Oh no you can't," Ronnie said mildly.

Mr. Cody drove the two hundred eighty-five miles back home, along the expressways, without saying much. Mrs. Cody believed he might be hurt by his son's rudeness. Or perhaps he was frightened. Ronnie had insisted upon sitting between them in the front seat of the car, like a little boy. He was docile, sweet, no trouble at all. He sat almost motionless for the entire trip. He was no danger. His hair was strawlike and scentless. It looked like synthetic hair; the ends were brittle. His skin was parchment-colored and did not resemble any skin Mrs. Cody recognized; it looked as if it had been left out in the rain and then baked by the sun. Were his eyes going to remain yellow or would they return to normal, a boy's normal eyes, bright and gleaming and healthy?—Mrs. Cody wondered. They were such lovely eyes, thickly lashed, hazel-brown-bronze with tiny flecks of green. Her own eyes filled with tears, but she did not dare turn to him or fuss over him. That would have upset both Ronnie and his father.

Enormous rattling trucks passed Mr. Cody from time to time. He drove exactly at the speed limit—55 mph—and once the trucks passed him and eased over into the right-hand lane, they slowed to about 50 mph. So Mr. Cody was forced to pass them. He put on his turn signal and moved out into the left-hand lane, pressing hard on the accelerator. His car was hardly a year old and quite handsome and it held the road well, but Mr. Cody was no longer an aggressive driver and he dreaded the expressways and the big trucks and the high speeds. When he passed a truck he reverted to a speed of about 55 mph and a few minutes later the truck would move out into the left-hand lane and bear close upon him, making his car shudder; and after a short, tense space of time the truck would pass him and move over into the right-hand lane . . . and then it would begin to slow again, gradually, until it was going about 50 mph and Mr. Cody would be forced to pass it. Once he made a noise like a sob, but neither Mrs. Cody nor Ronnie acknowledged it.

"Remember how anxious you were to learn to drive,

Ronnie?—how anxious you were to get your driver's license?"
Mrs. Cody said.

Ronnie sat silently, as if he had not heard.

"Don't you remember—'" Mrs. Cody said, shocked.

"I don't drive now," Ronnie said.

"You don't? But you have a driver's license, don't you?"

He sat in silence, as if he had not heard her question or did not
know how to answer it.

Ronnie lay in his brother's bed and listened to rain drumming
on the roof. He lay peacefully, unable to sleep. He did not care to
sleep. His dreams were of two types: one was the God-dream,
which was terrifying and exhausting, and the other was the
student-dream, which was banal and exhausting. The student-
dream was quite common. Many of his friends had it. They filed
into examination halls and took their seats in long rows and tried
to write examinations though they could not comprehend the
questions, or had lost their pens, or had failed to attend classes all
semester. Sometimes they were in their underwear, sometimes
they were naked. If they required glasses, it often happened that
their glasses were misplaced and they could not see to read the
questions. Ronnie's dream was of an examination in chemistry or
Russian, given in one of the old buildings on campus. He turned
the test pages hoping for a question he could answer, but the
symbols and equations and Cyrillic letters were indecipherable
and he woke, sweating, whimpering aloud. When he regained his
senses, he was all right. He realized the dream could not possibly
be his. It must have belonged to someone else, to another student;
Ronnie had not been registered for courses in chemistry or
Russian.

"Are you all right, Ronnie?" his mother cried through the
door.

He lay stiffly, trying not to hear.

"Ronnie?—did you cry out? I thought I heard—"

When she began rattling the doorknob, he said: "Stop. Please.
Don't. There's nobody here. There's nothing. It isn't important."

"Ronnie—?"

"There's nothing! Nothing!" he whispered.

The Codys lived on the river in a residential area north of a
great American city. They lived in a fine old stone house built in
the eighteen eighties, with turrets and gables and fancy

stonework. There were a number of similar houses in the neighborhood, but theirs was one of the two or three most impressive of all. They were very proud of their house and made nervous, coy jokes about it, complaining of the heating bills and the wiring that would have to be replaced soon. They never complained, however, of the view of the river, which was magnificent.

Mr. Cody took several days off from work. He wanted to be with his son as much as possible. One day he and Mrs. Cody and Ronnie went down to the river, through their hilly, rather wild backyard; it was a fine April day, still cold but sunny and fresh. "Isn't it lovely here?" Mr. Cody said. He was embarrassed. It was not that beauty itself embarrassed him; but he was uneasy in the presence of others, observing beauty. There was so little to say.

"It's so lovely," Mrs. Cody said, looking around. She wore a white wool cardigan sweater and had to hug herself, the air was so chilly.

Ronnie had found a dead turtle on the beach. It was quite large—a compact, muddy monster—lying dead on its stomach, absolutely motionless. The waves must have washed it ashore. Ronnie bent over it, frowning. His manner was gentle, even reverent.

"Now that Albert's gone, you can have his room. You always liked his room better than yours. "You can use his desk and his books and his hi-fi," Mr. Cody said. He had to raise his voice, to be heard over the waves. 'You can do your schoolwork. You can complete your courses and pass your year."

Ronnie was bent over the turtle, now prodding it with a forefinger.

"I talked to the Dean of Men," Mr. Cody said. "We came to an understanding."

"That was last semester, last fall," Mrs. Cody whispered.

"What?" Mr. Cody said, cupping his ear.

Ronnie's pale hair blew languidly in the wind. He was staring at the dead turtle; his profile was peaked, harsh. From the side he looked like a sickly old man, not a boy of twenty.

"Don't contradict me in front of my son," Mr. Cody said, reddening.

"This turtle had appeared to me in a dream, just before I left the hospital," Ronnie said. When he spoke, his lips moved slowly and thickly. Words appeared to cause him pain. "This turtle—I recognized it at once. The Turtle-God. I was walking through a substance like mud in my dream and I couldn't keep my balance and I was going to fall, I knew I would fall and it would get in my mouth, you know, and smother me, and it was filthy too, horrible filth...and then I did start to fall and I grabbed hold of something and it was this turtle. It was God in the shape of a turtle—the Turtle-God. That woke me to reality. When I start to forget that God is everywhere, when I start to be frightened again, God appears to me in a dream and teaches me the right pathway again and I'm all right. I know I'm saved and I'm all right. That's why the turtle was washed ashore here, for all of us to see."

"Feel that breeze," Mr. Cody said loudly. "Isn't it fresh? Isn't it wonderful?"

"When you're on the right pathway," Ronnie said, "there is no pain. It's incredible. It's incredible, that realization. Everything pivots upon it and everything is illuminated by it.—Whenever I forget, God is washed ashore at my feet."

Mr. Cody was calling their attention to a small flock of geese high above the river. They were flying north once again. "Isn't it wonderful to see such things?" he said. "I wonder if they're Canada geese."

Mrs. Cody pretended to be watching the geese but she was really staring at her son. His narrow, bony shoulders—the dry snarled hair that blew about his wasted face! She loved him but did not dare touch him. He would draw away from her. He would blink rapidly at her, as if not knowing who she was. *You'll have to wash your hands if you've been touching that dead thing,* she thought, and was dismayed at her thought.

"Isn't this world wonderful? Isn't nature wonderful?" Mr. Cody cried, as if he had been challenged. "It's worth every penny it costs, in my opinion."

"... In those years Mozart continued to create delightful, joyous works of music, despite the misery of his life. Even when he knew he was dying, he did not indulge in self-pity; he created beautiful, immortal works of music. It is inspiring to realize that..."

Ronnie turned off the radio.

"God has nothing to do with man," he said.

"I'm afraid of him," Barbara said.

"Of your own brother? Don't talk like that."

"He's crazy and I'm afraid of him," Barbara said.

"It breaks my heart," Mrs. Cody said, "to hear you talk that way."

"He walks around at night. I locked my door and put a chair in front of it last night. I heard him prowling around. He went outside, I think, down to the river. He was alone, but I could hear voices."

"He's resting," Mrs. Cody said weakly. "He's mending. He's going to get his health back and return to college in the fall; we think it would be best for him to transfer to the state university.—What do you mean, voices? How could you hear *voices?*"

"He's nobody I know now," Barbara said thoughtfully. She was fifteen years old and wore glasses with shell-pink frames and cultivated a throaty, dramatic manner. "The acid must have rearranged his chromosomes, like they warn. Or damaged his brain tissue. Or maybe it was the—what-was-it—the poison stuff, the strychnine...? He isn't Ronnie now."

"Barbara, he needs out help," Mrs. Cody said. "Our love."

"What am I supposed to tell my friends?" Barbara said.

Mrs. Cody remained in her bathroom as long as possible. She dreaded Mr. Cody's dark, brooding expression, that bruised look about the eyes. She knew he was accusing her silently. She knew he was preparing a case against her, rehearsing an argument. But what had she done wrong?

If she had brought up the children differently, Mrs. Cody thought, things would have gone wrong in different ways.

There were three children in this family: Albert, Ronnie, Barbara. Three complex human beings had been channeled into the universe by way of Mr. and Mrs. Cody. They could not be retracted. They could not even be reinterpreted. All I ever wanted for my children was happiness, Mrs. Cody said bitterly to the mirror. Was that so wrong? Was that a sin?

The mirror surprised her. It held an attractive face that was far younger than Mrs. Cody knew herself to be. The woman in the mirror was in her early forties but rather girlish, pretty. The woman who stood before the mirror, however, was far, far older—centuries old. The pinkened face in the mirror had nothing to do with the grayish, sour face she wore.

Mrs. Cody touched her face. She ran a forefinger along her cheek, beneath her eye.

I'm deceiving everyone, she thought. But it isn't intentional.

Several months before Ronnie's hospitalization, Barbara called for her parents to hurry into the family room. There was something on television they should see, she cried.

Mr. Cody was ahead of Mrs. Cody and by the time she got there, he was already switching the channel. He seemed rather angry.

"What was it? What—?" Mrs. Cody asked, smiling. She often smiled when she was confused.

"A man selling vacuum cleaners who looked just like Daddy," Barbara said, snorting with laughter. "Just *like* Daddy."

Mr. Cody stood watching the television screen, his hands on his thighs. He was fifty years old, no more than ten pounds overweight, and very attractive. Mrs. Cody had always thought him very attractive. Now he stood before the television set, flushed with anger, pretending to watch the tail end of a news story or a documentary. Barbara was still giggling. As a jeep approached the crest of a sand dune Mr. Cody turned off the set with a violent gesture.

He faced Mrs. Cody and Barbara and said: "I may appear to you to be a man in a commercial. I don't mind. I really don't mind. However I appear to you, you'll have to live with it; I know myself from the inside and I'm always somewhere else. Even when I say things that belong on television, I'm just saying them because you expect them of me—I don't believe them one bit, not one bit."

He left and Mrs. Cody and her daughter stared at each other, frightened.

"What do you suppose . . . ? Did you understand what he . . . ?" Mrs. Cody whispered.

I would hate everyone, Barbara wrote in her diary, except I don't know who they are. They don't tell me.

Mr. and Mrs. Cody lay in their darkened bedroom, in their twin beds. They heard someone prowling through the house, footsteps light and cautious and graceful. Once there was the sound of broken glass, probably from the kitchen. Another time, the sound of their wrought-iron terrace furniture being moved about. They listened, lying stiffly awake. Most of the time, however, there was nothing to hear except the wind and the waves and the night birds.

"He's mourning that girl," Mrs. Cody said.

"He doesn't even know she's dead."

"They said he wasn't suicidal any longer and I believe them. He's eating again a little."

Mr. Cody made a grunting sound. He lay on his back, arms at his sides. Sometimes he and Mrs. Cody slept in the same bed, sometimes she held him in her arms for a brief period. But he perspired so much and, after he fell asleep, he was so twitchy and restless, Mrs. Cody could not relax and would lie awake for hours. She loved him but, lying awake, she came to resent him and was afraid she would hate him. So they slept in twin beds. The arrangement was working quite well. But when Mrs. Cody spoke to her husband she addressed the dark, the air, and could not always be certain he had heard her or even that he was in the same room with her.

"...in Riverdale, it was, last year...that man who heard a prowler downstairs and shot at him, from the top of the stairs...a shotgun, I think...wasn't it!...and it turned out to be his own son," Mr. Cody said quietly. "Not a prowler but his own son. *His own son.*"

"My God, yes, I remember that," Mrs. Cody said. "Such a tragedy..."

"*His own son.* Imagine having to live with that for the rest of your life."

One Sunday they drove fifty miles up the coast to Hank's Anchor Inn, which was near a famous lighthouse. The lighthouse was no longer in operation, but it had been preserved as a historical monument. "Do you remember climbing up all those stairs, to the very top?" Mr. Cody asked Ronnie. "You were only ten years old and you had to climb to the very top. Maybe eleven years old."

Ronnie wore a dark-blue shirt with a white collar; his hair was brushed flat against his head and caught up at the nape of his neck in a rubber band. His cheekbones protruded. Hunched over his plate, he looked insubstantial, almost waiflike. Mrs. Cody observed him covertly and had to fight down her impulse to touch him, to make him eat. She knew he was going to die.

"Everything smells of fish here," Barbara said. "That glinting stuff out on the pier, like sequins—do you suppose those are fish scales?"

"This is a fine place," Mr. Cody said. "You have to book

reservations two weeks in advance."

"It's a wonderful place and this is a wonderful table," Mrs. Cody said. "The view couldn't be finer."

Ronnie pushed his food around on his plate with a look of genuine regret.

"You're not even trying to eat," Mrs. Cody whispered.

"Yes, I'm trying," Ronnie said.

"You're not even trying."

They talked of other things. They talked about the surprisingly cool weather and about the people who lived next door—the Sewalls, who were evidently going to get a divorce but were still living in the same house—and they talked about members of the family, Ronnie's and Barbara's aunts and uncles and cousins. They talked about Albert, who was studying Business Administration at Cornell. He was in a two-year Master's degree program and had another year to go.

Ronnie crossed his knife and fork over his plate. He sat with his eyes closed, as if praying.

"Ronnie—?" Mrs. Cody said.

"It's useless," he said.

"What? What's useless?"

"Useless. Worthless. There's no need for us—we're like flies—like lice," Ronnie said.

"Who's like lice?" Mr. Cody said. "Who are you talking about?"

"People my age. People like Albie. There's no place for us out there—you don't want us—we don't want you—the only place is inside, deep inside."

He opened his eyes and began to speak quite cheerfully, as if he were entirely detached from his words. Mrs. Cody could not follow him, but he seemed to be speaking of something that made sense—the unemployment problem, the large numbers of college graduates without jobs. Mr. Cody said there were many positions available to those who were qualified. He said that a good man always found a job—throughout history, at any time, a good man always found a job.

"Six miles beneath the surface of the ocean," Ronnie said, "it's perpetual night and everything is silent and the creatures there are blind, all mouths and teeth and jaws, all eating—eating one another. It never stops. Their appetites never stop. They eat and digest and are eaten and are digested and they're blind, so they never see what they eat and they never see what glides over to them, to eat them. That's God too. I try to realize that, but sometimes I'm afraid. That's God too, all mouth and intestines, with bumps where eyes didn't grow out. Where can a good man find a job, six miles beneath the surface of the ocean?" Ronnie giggled.

"That isn't funny," Mr. Cody said. "I don't find that in the least amusing."

"He's crazy," Barbara said. Her fork clattered onto her plate.

"Do you think we wanted children?" Mr. Cody said quietly. "Do you? Even if we did, your mother and me, we didn't necessarily want *you*. That's something your generation can't comprehend."

"I don't think we should talk like this," Mrs. Cody said. "This is such a wonderful place and the hostess gave us such a wonderful table, with a view of the river and the lighthouse and the boats...."

"It's true, Edith. But their generation can't comprehend it. We didn't necessarily want *them*. And if we had it to do over again...."

"God directed you," Ronnie said. "You had no choice. Today we're sitting here together and you think we're related, but we're only related through God. God directed everything and when God takes away the spirit...then we're gone, and there's no relationship either. It's gone. It's all over."

"I wish we wouldn't talk about these things," Mrs. Cody said. "We'll only regret it afterward."

"You tried to direct me personally," Ronnie said, "and that was a sin. Maybe you're beginning to realize that now. You tried to take God's place, but God is a jealous God—now we're beginning to learn! All of us!—You tried to create me in your own image and you failed and now you want me dead, but God has other plans," he said excitedly.

"Want you dead...?" Mrs. Cody said. "How can you talk like that?"

"There's a lawn mower outside, a power mower," Ronnie said. "I can't make myself understood. My head is starting to ache."

"It's a boat on the river," Barbara said. "It isn't a lawn mower."

"It's too loud," Ronnie said.

"It's going away, dear," Mrs. Cody said. "It's already past."

"We'd better leave," Mr. Cody said.

"Nobody wants you dead, Ronnie, how can you say such things?" Mrs. Cody said.

"God's plans involve us but have nothing to do with us," Ronnie said in a high, strained voice. People at a nearby table were watching. "Trying to communicate that simple truth to you is making my head ache.... It's hopeless."

"Not so loud, please," Mr. Cody said. "Please."

"I fell into God by accident, like falling into a swamp or a bog or quicksand," Ronnie said, "and God enveloped me and gave me new life, and I don't know who you people are. I really don't. I try to be polite but it's a strain and then when you spy on me and try to make me eat—it's hopeless. I don't think it's going to work."

"I'll get the check," Mr. Cody said. He stood. "That's our waiter over there.—Why don't you and Barbara take him out, Edith?—take him out of here—"

"God wants nothing from man," Ronnie said shrilly. "God doesn't even know who man is. It's all a delusion—you're all a delusion, don't you know?—nothing is real but God. If I believe in God, I can't believe in you. Not for one minute! Not for one second!" Boyish suddenly, as if given spirit by his own breathless words, he made feinting gestures at them, his bony fists clenched. He held his right fist close to his body and led with his left, his right shoulder lowered, his head ducked cunningly. He grinned. He made a *Pzzzssst!* noise out of the corner of his mouth, like a cartoon character. "Nothing happens without God. I can't read a single line in a single book. I can't recognize my own face in the mirror. I can't pick up a fork, can't swallow a mouthful, if God's spirit isn't in it. You see? Eh? Staring at me as if I'm crazy when *you* are the crazy ones, you! All of you!—I don't even know who you are," he said, tiring suddenly. His voice went flat and cold.

Next door the Sewall children were squabbling. Mrs. Cody closed the kitchen window on that side of the house. For years Mr. and Mrs. Sewall had argued with each other and the Codys had often overheard them, embarrassed at their neighbors' rage, and rather intrigued by it. It was a pity, they said, that river-front property was so narrow, and that their neighbors' homes on either side were so close. One day, years before, Mrs. Cody had stood trembling at an upstairs window, behind closed Venetian blinds, hearing Mrs. Sewall scream obscenities at Mr. Sewall. She had known such words existed, of course, but she had never heard anyone use them like that—shouted in a kind of jubilant, crazy rage, innocent and inhuman.

Now Mrs. Sewall had moved out and Mr. Sewall, who was with an insurance company in the city, was gone all day, and when the children came home from school they were often noisy. This afternoon they were down at the beach, shouting. Mrs. Cody tried not to listen, but the harsh cries reached her anyway. What were they doing?—what was wrong? She stepped out onto the terrace and saw a sight that froze her: her son Ronnie was down there with them, grappling with one of the boys, shouting. It was his high, frenzied voice she had been hearing.

She ran toward the river, calling his name. She nearly fell, running stiffly, clumsily; one of her straw shoes came off.

"Ronnie! Ronnie! No! Stop! Don't hurt him! No! Please!"

When she got to the river, to the small sandy beach, the children had fled and only Ronnie remained, panting. Mrs. Cody and Ronnie were both panting. "They were—they were trying to— Trying to smash its shell," Ronnie said, pointing at the dead turtle. Mrs. Cody stared at the ugly thing, astonished. Was it still here? Why hadn't the waves washed it out again? Why hadn't someone buried it?

Ronnie began to sob. Mrs. Cody led him back to the house, walking with her arm around his waist. She made no reference to the turtle at all, nor did she speak of the Sewall children and the fact that Ronnie had seized the ten-year-old by the shoulder and had been shaking him violently, murderously.

"The other day you ate some apricot yogurt, do you remember," she said, "and you said you liked it . . . it had a gentle taste . . . do you remember? Will you have some now? I went out especially this morning to buy some."

"They wanted to smash its shell," Ronnie said faintly. "Its lovely shell. They had rocks, they were hitting it and kicking it. . . ."

"Apricot yogurt?" Mrs. Cody said, "Please?"

"I didn't hear God's voice. I really didn't," Ronnie said slowly. "But something came over me and I heard my own voice and I thought it best to stop him . . . to kill him, maybe. I don't know. It wasn't clear."

"But you aren't going to do it again," Mrs. Cody said.

Ronnie shook his head. His eyelids fluttered.

"No events repeat themselves," he said. "Everything is singular, unique. I'm myself and you're you. God connects us. But we're different and the things we do are different and nothing can be repeated in the universe. That's a law of the universe."

"Then you aren't going to do it again, to that boy?—or to any other boy?"

He spooned the yogurt into his mouth, holding the spoon in his fist, like a small child.

Sometimes Mr. Cody cut the lawn himself, and sometimes he hired a neighborhood boy. In the past Albie and Ronnie had often done the lawn, but now circumstances were altered, and Mr. Cody seemed to like the exercise. He spent most of Saturday on the lawn, raking and mowing and trimming, and Mrs. Cody, watching him covertly from one of the upstairs windows, often saw his mouth move as he worked. She wondered if he was arguing with someone or if, like herself, he sang when he believed himself alone. And if he sang, what did he sing? Ah, she would have liked to know! It would have meant so much to her to know!

He was out there pushing the power mower, a golfing cap on his stiff gray hair, his shoulders rather hunched. Yes, he was talking to himself. Grimacing. Talking or singing. "I like to sing songs from *Oklahoma!* or *South Pacific* or *An American in Paris*," Mrs. Cody said to him from the second floor of the house. She pressed her warm forehead against the glass. "I sing when I do the vacuuming and the dishes if there's no one to hear me and ridicule me, and of course I always sing in the car when I'm alone."

She woke from a light sleep to hear footsteps on the stairs. Her heart was pounding. It was terrible, that pounding. "Ronnie?" she whispered.

Mr. Cody was asleep in the other bed. His breathing was deep, strained, laborious. Mrs. Cody lay awake, horribly awake, and listened to the almost-imperceptible creaking of the stairs. He was going downstairs, slowly. Very slowly. She lay wide awake listening to the footsteps and imagining at the bottom of the stairs a vast dark substance, muddy, liquid, into which her son would sink. His feet, his calves, his thighs, his abdomen, his torso, his skinny shoulders, his neck and the lower part of his face and last of all his eyes, his eyes, and his white-blond dead hair floating up behind for a long moment....

She rose and slipped on her dressing gown and went downstairs.

"Ronnie? Ronnie?"

He was kneeling by one of the living-room windows. The window was immense, overlooking the backyard and the river and the moonlit sky, but Ronnie did not appear to be looking outside. He was simply kneeling there, in the darkened living room. He was naked.

"Ronnie... ?" she whispered.

He said nothing. His eyes were shut tight and his hands were pressed against his mouth. He was no one she knew—no one at all. She could not have said his age, could not really have guessed his race. A sensation of anger swept over her, a flash of physical heat; she wanted to grab hold of his ugly hair and shake him viciously.

"Ronnie? Why are you here? What are you doing?" she whispered. "This is sick, Ronnie. You know it's sick. You promised you would try to... would try to be well... would try to.... Didn't you promise? Wasn't that you? Someone promised something," she said, her voice a low soft wail, "*someone promised me something....*"

"Pray with me, Mother," he said.

He had not opened his eyes. He spoke through his fingers.

"This is sick, this is ridiculous," Mrs. Cody said. "You're breaking my heart...."

"Pray with me. Kneel with me."

"You let that girl die and now you've come here, to destroy us," she whispered. "You don't even know she's dead. You don't care. It could have been me—it could have been me, swallowing some poison of yours, swallowing some poison of your father's, and then forgotten! You were unconscious and you let her die; the two of you were in that filthy place for days, and now you don't even remember—"

"I remember," Ronnie said. He took his hands away from his face; he looked up at her, wincing. "Of course I remember. How could I forget?"

"Did you love her? Do you miss her? Is that why—?"

"You're so tall, standing there," he said. "Kneel with me."

"I don't want to kneel," Mrs. Cody said. "You're breaking my heart; you won't get well and strong; you're dragging us all down with you—Why should I kneel? I have no reason to kneel. I don't know what this is—what you're doing—I hate it—I hate it! No, I won't kneel. I'm not going to kneel."

"Pray with me. Then you'll understand."

"I'm not going to pray with you!" Mrs. Cody laughed. "You're crazy! I don't want to be crazy like you!"

"The two of us were there, Mother, with God," Ronnie said calmly. "Suddenly we were there. We went together. We were in a corridor or a tunnel and I remember thinking it was cold there, Susan would get cold—I wanted to give her what I was wearing, but I couldn't, you know, I couldn't do anything with my hands; they were transparent. No skin and bones. Nothing. We went to the place where God was, all dark, and Susan pulled away from me, she pulled away like a child; suddenly she was impatient and I lost her—I couldn't get her back. I knew she was gone then. I knew she wouldn't return with me. —It got so I could see everywhere, could see throughout the entire universe, and God was all around me, breathing in and out of me, and everything came to a halt, everything was perfect. Susan stepped away. She was impatient. She did that sometimes out on the street if she saw someone she wanted to talk to or if there was a store window she wanted to look into—she'd just pull away from me, wouldn't even say anything. I knew God was going to swallow her up and I wanted to be with her. I wanted God myself; it was worse than wanting sex, you know?—every part of my body, every cell of my body, was yearning for it—yearning to explode into God. But it wasn't my time," he said.

"I wish you wouldn't talk like that," Mrs. Cody said. "It's sick."

"She went into God. I couldn't bring her back. No one could. I don't feel guilty. We're all going into God, hour by hour. At night most of all. At night—can't you feel it? Now? You'd better kneel, Mother. You'd better prepare yourself for God."

He seized her wrist and began tugging at it.

"I'm not going to kneel; I'm not going to do any such crazy thing," Mrs. Cody said, laughing. She was frightened and confused. Her mouth stretched wide, grinning. "If you think—If—You're sick, you're crazy—let me go—you want to be sick, deliberately sick—"

He pulled at her and suddenly she was off-balance, about to fall. She sank to her knees. She gasped. He had hurt her wrist and she whimpered with the pain and, as if alarmed at what he had done, Ronnie released her; and she scrambled to her feet again, clumsily, panting. She felt her face stretched out of shape, grinning. "What are you doing! Murderer! Horrible—ugly— Never, never—never—*Never*—"

"I pity you, Mother," he said coldly.

Next morning she took a shovel from the garage and went down to the beach and buried the turtle herself. She should have asked Mr. Cody to do it, but for some reason she had hesitated, not wanting to bring up the subject. So she buried it herself, holding her breath against the stench, muttering. *All I ever wanted for them was happiness; that doesn't seem too much to ask, does it—?* It was an ugly task, one she would remember with revulsion, but at least she did it. That was something, at least.

Bloodstains

● He sat. He turned to see that he was sharing the bench with a young mother who did not glance around at him. The park they were in was a small noisy island around which traffic moved in a continual stream. Aged, listless men sat on other benches—a few women shoppers, pausing to rest, their eyes eagle-bright and their gloved fingers tugging at the straps of shoes or at hemlines—a few children, urchins from the tenement homes a few blocks off this wide main street. Great untidy flocks of pigeons rose and settled again and rose, startled, scattering. Lawrence Pryor looked at everything keenly. He knew he was out of place here; he had come down from his office because his eleven-o'clock appointment had canceled out; he was free for half an hour. The only place to sit had been beside this pretty young mother, who held her baby up to her face and who took no interest at all in the pigeons or the chattering children or Lawrence himself. He was sitting in a patch of sunlight that fell upon him through the narrow channel between two tall buildings, as if singling him out for a blessing.

All these women shoppers! He watched them cross quickly to the island, and quickly over to the other curb, for they rarely had the time to sit and rest. They were in a hurry. Because of them, hurrying across the street, traffic was backed up waiting to make right-hand turns. Out of the crowd of shoppers he saw a blond woman appear, walking briskly and confidently. She hurried against a red light, and a horn sounded. How American she was, how well-dressed and sure of herself! Lawrence found himself staring at her, imagining the face that might reveal itself to him if he were to approach her—startled and elegant and composed, seeing by his face that he was no danger to her, no danger.

She did not cross the little park but took the sidewalk that led around it. Avoiding the bench-sitters and the pigeons. Lawrence was disappointed. And then, watching her, he saw that the woman was familiar—her brisk, impatient walk, her trim blue coat—and, indeed, he knew her well; the woman was his own wife! He tapped his jaw with the tips of his fingers in a gesture of amused surprise. Of course! Beverly! As if acting out embarrassment for an audience, he smiled up toward the sky . . . and when he looked back, his wife was already hurrying across the street, moving bravely against the light while buses and taxicabs pressed forward.

He got to his feet to follow her. But an extraordinarily tall man got in front of him, walking quickly, and then a small crowd of women shoppers, everyone hurrying now that the light had turned green. Something held Lawrence back. The tall man was hurrying as if to catch up with Beverly. He was strangely tall, freakishly tall, with silver-gray hair that was bunched around his head in tight little curls, like grapes. He wore a dark coat and, on the back of his neck, there was a vivid red birthmark, a stain in the shape of a finger. The shoppers moved forward, in front of Lawrence, and the tall man and Lawrence's wife moved into the distance. All this motion made Lawrence feel slightly dizzy.

The legend about him was his fanaticism about work: Beverly complained of this, she worried about it, she was proud of it. He was a doctor and his patients were sacred to him. And so he had better not run after his wife, because she would be alarmed to see him out on the street at this time of day and because it might be ten or fifteen minutes before he could get away again. She might want him to have lunch with her. She might want him to go into stores with her. Better to stay behind, to stay hidden. So he watched her disappear—his wife hurrying into the midst of the city—and he sat down again, feeling oddly pleased and excited. He felt as if something secret had been revealed to him.

Beside him the young woman was leaning her face to her child, whispering. She had a pale, angular face, illuminated by love, or by the child's reflecting face, or by the narrow patch of sunlight that was moving slowly from Lawrence and onto her. Women, seen like this, were gifts to men.

He considered smiling at her. But no, that might be a mistake—this was not a city in which people smiled freely at one another.

● Herb Altman came into the office, striding forward with his head slightly lowered. Bald, but only forty-five. He had a portly, arrogant body and his clothes were always jaunty—today he wore a bright yellow necktie that jumped in Lawrence's vision.

Shaking hands.

"How are you?"

"Not well. I can't sleep. I never sleep, you know that," Altman said.

He sat and began to talk. His voice was urgent and demanding. As he spoke he shook his head so that his cheeks shivered. Altman's wife, Connie, was a friend of Lawrence's wife. It seemed to Lawrence that the women in their circle were all close friends; in a way they blended into one another. The husbands too seemed to blend into one another. Many of them had several lives, but lives were somehow shared. They lived in one dimension but turned up in other dimensions—downtown late in the afternoon or in downriver suburbs. Their expensive homes and automobiles and boats could not quite contain them. Too much energy. Urgent, clicking demanding words. While Altman talked angrily about his insomnia and switched onto the complaints of his wife and then onto the complaints of his girl, Lawrence again saw his wife in the distance of his imagination, a dream he had dreamed while awake, moving freely and happily along the sidewalk of this massive city.

What mystery was in her, this woman he had lived with for so long? They had one child, a daughter. They had known each other for two decades. And yet, seeing her like that, Lawrence had been struck by the mystery of her separateness, her being....

Altman said in a furious whisper, "I'm going to have her followed!"

"Your wife?"

"Evie. *Evelyn.* Twenty-five years old, a baby, and she tells me the plans she dreams up! She wants me to marry her next year!"

The numerals of Lawrence's watch were greenish-white, glowing up out of a dark face. They were supposed to glow in the dark, but they glowed in the light as well.

"All right," Altman said, seeing Lawrence look at his watch, "so I'm wasting your time. So. Check my heart, my blackened lungs, tap me on the back to see if I have echoes inside, to see what's hollowed out—I'm a sick man, we both know that. Here I am."

In the end Lawrence did as he always did: refilling Altman's prescription for barbiturates. It was for six refills and Altman would be back again in a few weeks.

At the door Altman paused dramatically. His white shirtfront bulged. "Why do they keep after me?" he said. "Larry, what is it? Why are they always after me? I can't sleep at night. I'm planning a trip in my mind, but when I get up I can't remember it—I don't sleep but I don't remember what I think about— Why are they always after me, those women? What are they doing to me?"

● Lawrence and his wife and daughter lived a few blocks from the lake in a brick home that had been painted white. The house glowed in the air of twilight. It had the ghostly weightless look of something at the bottom of a lake, made perfect. It was a place in which Lawrence might sleep soundly, as he had never slept in his parents' oversized, combative home in Philadelphia. No more of that life! He had blocked out even the memory of that life.

Behind him in the city were his patients and the unhappy memories of his patients. Ten, sometimes twelve hours of ailments—the shame of being sick, of being weak, of uttering words better left unsaid. Office hours were worse than hospital hours. During the day Lawrence's hand turned shaky and reluctant, writing out so many prescriptions, smiling with his prescribed smile, a forty-year-old face that was in danger of wearing out. His patients had too many faces. They were blotched or sullen or impatient or, like Altman's, familiar but eerily distant, demanding something Lawrence could not give and could not understand.

Many of the ailments were imaginary. They existed, yes, but they were imaginary; how to cure them?

The telephone was ringing as he entered his home. He had the idea that it had been ringing for some time. When he went to answer it, in the kitchen, it stopped ringing and he stood with his hand out, a few inches above the receiver, listening to the silence of the house.

● His mother is coming to visit, due the next morning on the nine-thirty flight from Philadelphia.

Beverly and Edie are going out again; they get in each other's way by the closet. Edie, fourteen years old and taller than her mother, sticks her arms angrily into her coat. The coat is khaki-colored and lined with fake wool, years old; Edie will not give it up in spite of her mother's pleas. Lawrence stands with the evening newspaper, watching them. It is six-thirty. "Do you have to go out now?" he says.

"I forgot to get new towels. I wanted to get new towels for your mother, I can't let her use those old ones," Beverly says.

"New towels? You're going out now for new towels?"

"Everything is old. It isn't *good enough for her.*"

Beverly's jaws are hardening. Her eyes are bright, alert, restless. Edie is shiny-faced and almost pretty, but always in a hurry, always bumping into things. It is obvious to Lawrence that his wife and daughter have been arguing about something. Edie knocks against a chair in the foyer and screws up her face. "God!" she winces.

"Did you go shopping downtown today?" Lawrence asks his wife.

She is frowning into her purse, looking for something. "No."

"I thought I saw you."

"Saw me? When?"

"A little before noon."

She stares at him, closing her purse. There is a cold, bright look around her eyes, a look Lawrence cannot understand. Then she smiles. "Oh yes, I was downtown ... I just drove down and back, looking for some things I couldn't get out here.... I've been running around all day. I had to pick Edie up at school and take her to the dentist and now ... now I have to go out again."

"You're making too much out of it. My mother doesn't expect you to fuss over her."

She shakes her head and avoids his eye. He thinks of the tall, silver-haired man with the birthmark, hurrying along after her as if to catch up with her.

● His mother. The airport. They have met his mother like this many times and each time they say the same things; it seems that the same crowds are at the airport. His mother begins at once to tell him about the news at home and she will continue to tell him of funerals and weddings, births, illnesses, surgery, unpleasant surprises, all the way home, though she has written him about these things in her weekly letters.

"Oh, look at this!" she says in disgust.

She holds up her hands for them to see her white gloves, which are soiled and even stained with something that looks like rust or blood, a very faint red-brown color.

"I'll wash them out for you, Mother," Beverly says at once.

"Traveling is so dirty. Filthy," Lawrence's mother says.

He recalls her having said that before.

While his mother and his wife talk, Lawrence drives in silence. He is happy that his mother is visiting them. She comes often, several times a year. Lawrence has the idea that she blames him for having left Philadelphia and come to this city of strangers where he has no relatives. The letters they write to each other do not seem to express them. Beneath his neat, typed lines, and beneath her slanted lines in their lavender ink, there seems to be another dimension, a submerged feeling or memory, that the two of them can only hint at but cannot express.

They are approaching Lawrence's home. "I like that house," his mother says flatly, as she always does. This seems to settle something. Lawrence and Beverly both feel relieved.

The old family home had been white also. Now Lawrence's mother lives in an apartment favored by other widows, but for decades of her life she lived in a house the size of a municipal building. In his dreams Lawrence sometimes climbs the stairway to the third floor, which had been closed off, to look through the stacks of his father's old medical journals, as he did when he was a child. There were bundles of journals. Small towers. He had spent many hours looking through them, fascinated.

● His mother's presence in his house, his own house, makes Lawrence feel a little displaced. It seems to him that time is confused. His own age is uncertain. But he is a good host to his mother; he makes an effort to be gallant. After dinner that night they look through snapshots—another ritual. The snapshots are passed around. Then, leaning toward him, in a sudden stiff motion that makes him realize how his mother is corseted—his wife, also, her body slim and deft but smoothly hard to the touch—she hands him a photograph that had been taken years ago. That photograph again! It is Lawrence, Larry Jr., sitting on a spotted pony at some forgotten fair, a rented pony, Lawrence's dark hair combed down onto his forehead in a way that makes him look like a moron, his stare startled and vacuous, his mouth too timid to smile. Lawrence stares at the photograph. Why does his mother treasure it so much? Why does she always bring it along with the more recent snapshots, as if she doesn't remember she has shown it to him on her last visit?

"Look at that, isn't that darling? A darling boy?" she says stubbornly.

Lawrence stares down at his own face, which is blank and stark in the photograph. It was a face that might have become anything. Any personality might have inhabited it. It was so blank, that face—anything could inhabit it.

He stands suddenly. His mother and his wife stare at him in alarm.

"Larry? What's wrong?" Beverly says.

He passes his hand over his eyes. He sits down again.

"Nothing."

"Did you hear something—?"

"No. Nothing."

● Two evenings later he is driving home when a car veers out around him, passing him with its horn blaring. The car is filled with kids—boys and girls—and he thinks he sees Edie in with them. His heart jumps. But he cannot be sure.

When he gets home, it is nearly dark. His mother kisses him on the side of the face. She is powdery and yet hard, a precise, stubborn little woman. What do they talk about all day, women? His mother and his wife? They are telling him now about what they have done today. Their chatter is like music, rising in snatches about them, airy and incomplete. It never quite completes itself; it has to continue.

"Is Edie home yet?" he says.

"No, not yet," says Beverly.

"Where is she?"

"She had something after school—choir practice—"

"All this time?"

"No, not all this time. She's probably at someone's house. She'll be home in a few minutes."

"But you don't know where she is?"

"Not exactly. What's wrong? Why are you so angry?"

"I'm not angry."

When she comes in he will find out nothing from her. Nothing.

She will move her body jerkily through the kitchen and to the front closet, she will take off her coat, she will sit slouching at dinner and stare down into her plate, or stare dutifully up at him, and he will find out nothing about her, nothing. His heart pounds angrily. Once Beverly had said of Edie, "She has all that stuff on her face, but you should see her neck—she never washes. Oh, she's hopeless—what can I do?"

What can they do?

● His mother asks him about his day. Did he work hard? Is he tired?

He answers her vaguely, listening for Edie to come in. But when she does come in, he will find out nothing from her. His mother switches to another topic—complaints about one of his aunts—and he can't follow her. He is thinking of Edie, then he is thinking of his wife. Then he finds himself thinking of one of his patients, Connie Altman. She had wept in his office that morning. "I need something to help me sleep at night. I lie awake thinking. Then in the morning I can't remember what I was thinking about. I'm so nervous, my heart pounds, can you give me something stronger to help me sleep? Everything is running out...."

This had puzzled him. "What do you mean, everything is running out?"

"There isn't any point. I don't see it. We are all running out, people our age, things are running out of us...draining out of us....I will have to live out my life in this body...."

She was a woman of beauty, very small, with childish wrists and ankles. But her face had begun to harden in the last few years.

"I need something to help me sleep. Please. I know that in the other room *he* is awake, he can't sleep either, it drives me crazy! I prefer the nights he stays out. At least he isn't in the house, lying awake like me, I don't care who he's with....I need something to help me sleep, please. I can't stand my thoughts all night long."

● His daughter's room. Saturday afternoon. The house is empty for a few hours and he may walk through it, anywhere, because it is his house and all the rooms are his, his property.

Edie's room is piled with clothes, schoolbooks, shoes, junk. Two of the three dressers are pulled out. The top of the dresser is cluttered. Lawrence's reflection moves into the mirror and he looks at himself in surprise—is that really him, Dr. Pryor? He is disappointed. He is even rather alarmed. The man reflected there in the smudged mirror bears little resemblance to the image of himself he carries with him in his imagination; it does not even resemble the man of recent snapshots. He stares, frankly bewildered. Why does his shirt appear to be rumpled when he put it on fresh only that morning—why is his face sallow, lined, why do his hands appear to be strangely empty, loose at his sides? For a moment he doubts that the man in the mirror is really Dr. Pryor. He doubts the necessity of his continuing to exist in that body, waking each morning to that particular face and body, out of all the multitudes of human beings. Is existence itself an illusion, he thinks. He smiles. In the mirror the sallow-skinned man smiles with him as if mocking him. No: perhaps he is sympathetic, perhaps he is in agreement.

Is existence an illusion? A commonplace illusion.

He wakes from his trance and goes quickly to his daughter's dresser. Must not hesitate. Must move swiftly, confidently. He tugs at the first drawer: a jumble of stockings, black tights, bright red tights, knee-length woollen socks of various colors and designs; filmy, gauzy things tangled together; some stiffly new as if just taken from packages, some rather soiled, thrown into the drawer in a heap. A spool of black thread rolls noisily about. Lawrence is about to close the drawer when he remembers that it wasn't closed, it was open a few inches. Good. Good he remembered. He pulls out the second drawer, which sticks; he tugs at it and it nearly falls out; he exclaims in vexation. Here there are underclothes of various colors that release an air of freshness—clean from the laundry; but they too are rudely jumbled together.

Lawrence has never come into his daughter's room alone. Never. He would not violate her privacy; he would not dare anger her. But being here this afternoon, so close to her, so strangely intimate with her, he feels oddly pleased. She is very real to him at this moment. She might be standing close behind him, about to break into one of her breathless greetings—"Hi, Friend!" has been a maddeningly frequent greeting of hers this past month; perhaps it is in common usage among children her age—she might be about to hum into his ear one of her slangy, banal, mysterious little tunes.

He finds himself looking through the silky underclothes.

Things stick together; there is the crackle of minor electricity. He holds up a half-slip of mint green with tiny white bows on it. Pretty. It is very pretty. Probably a birthday or Christmas gift from her mother, probably not something she would have bought for herself. He wants to rub it against his face. Very carefully he folds it and puts it back, and discovers a book hidden against the side of the drawer—a journal, a diary—is it a diary?—but he's disappointed to see that it isn't a diary: instead it is a small hardcover book, *Edgar Cayce and the Miracle of Reincarnation*.

He does no more than leaf through the book, irritated. What trash. How dare such books be published and sold. One sentence especially angers him: *Modern medical science has lagged shamefully behind. . . .* He snaps the book shut and eases it back into its hiding place. And now a kind of despair weakens him, he doesn't know quite why. He touches the green slip again, and a very silky—satiny?—pair of panties, pale blue with an elastic band. He tries to see his daughter's face but she eludes him. Oh Father, she might say, drawling, oh Daddy. For God's sake! This afternoon she is at the shopping mall with her girl friends. What do you do there all day? he asks, and she shrugs her shoulders and says, Go through the stores and buy a few things and sit around, and meet people, you know; have a few Cokes; sit around and meet people and have a good time. Is there anything wrong with that?

It is a mystery, his having a daughter. He cannot quite comprehend it. He looks through the drawer farther, this sense of despair rising strongly in him. . . . Rolled up in a ball, stuck back in a corner of the drawer, are a pair of white underpants. He picks them up. They have several bloodstains on them, thick and stiff, almost caked. He stares. Why bloodstains? Why here? For a moment he feels nothing, he thinks nothing. He is not even surprised. Then it occurs to him that his daughter was ashamed to put these soiled underpants in the wash, that she had meant to wash them herself but had forgotten, and weeks, maybe months have gone by . . . the blood grown old and hard, the stains impossible to get out . . . she has forgotten about them . . . balled up, rolled up and stuck in the corner of the drawer, forgotten. . . .

● His mother is talking with some friends of theirs who have dropped in. An ordinary Sunday afternoon. Beverly is handing

drinks around. In the mirror above the fireplace his mother's
bluish-white hair bobs weightlessly. On the mantel, long white
candlesticks in holders of silver, the wicks perfectly white, never
burnt. What are they talking about so earnestly? Lawrence tries
to listen. Beverly is chiding him gently for working so hard—it's a
familiar pattern, almost a tune, the words of his mother to his
father years ago—and he nods, smiles, he is Dr. Pryor, who works
hard. The fact is that he has done nothing all day except sit in his
study, at his desk, leafing through medical journals. He has not
been able to concentrate on anything.

Ted Albrecht, a friend of many years, is talking in his usual
fanciful manner. He is a stockbroker but thinks of himself as a
social critic. A short man, with glasses and lively eyebrows, he is
considered a friend of Lawrence's, and his wife is a friend of
Beverly's. They have known each other for some time, which is
why they are friends. They always meet at parties, in someone's
living room, with groups of other people close about them.

Ted says, "I guarantee you, disaster is on its way for this
nation!"

Lawrence has not been able to concentrate on the conversation. He thinks that he may not be able to endure this minute, this
very, minute.

Voices ring around him. It is a ring of concentric rings, a ring
of voices and breaths and bright glances, circling him. Like
music, the voices do not come to rest. They pause shrilly; they
pause in expectation. Lawrence accepts a drink from his wife, a
woman whose face looks oddly brittle. The ice cubes in his glass
make him think of the Arctic—pure crystal, pure colorless ice
and air, where no germs survive. It is impossible, this minute.
Impossible. Impossible to stand with these people. He does not
know what is wrong and yet he understands that it has become
impossible, that his body is being pushed to the breaking point,
that to contain himself—his physicalness, his being—would take
the strength of a wrestler, a man not himself.

The minute expands slowly. Nothing happens.

● Again, the airport. The reversal of the meeting last Monday:
now she is going home. The airliner will draw up into it a certain
number of people, Lawrence's mother among them, and then it
will be gone. Now there is a rush of words. Things to be said. His
mother complains bitterly of one of his aunts—he nods in

agreement, embarrassed that she should say these things in front of Beverly—he nods yes, yes, he will agree to anything. "What could she know? She was never married!" Lawrence's mother says, twisting her mouth. Of Lawrence's father, who died in a boating accident when Lawrence was eighteen, she does not ever speak, exactly; she speaks of other misfortunes and disasters, glibly, routinely, with petulant jerks of her stiff little body. Lawrence's father died on the lake, alone. He drowned, alone. The boat must have capsized and he had drowned, alone, with no one to witness the death or to explain it.

Lawrence's mother begins to cry. She will back off from them, crying, and then at a certain point she will stop crying, collecting herself, and she will promise to telephone them as soon as she lands in Philadelphia. The visit is concluded.

● Though it was a weekday evening, they went to Dorothy Clair's art gallery, where a young sculptor was having an opening. Dorothy Clair was a widow some years older than the Pryors, a wealthy woman on the periphery of their social group. It was a champagne opening. Lawrence and his wife were separated, drawn into different groups; Lawrence was not really taking part in the conversation, but he appeared enthusiastic. The champagne went to his head. His mother had stayed with them for seven days, seven nights; the visit had gone well, everything was over. Good. It was a weekday evening, but they had gone out as if to reward themselves.

Next to Lawrence there was a piece of sculpture—a single column of metal, with sharp edges. It looked dangerous. A woman seemed about to back into it and Lawrence wondered if he should warn her. He could see his own reflection in its surface, blotchy and comic. All the pieces of sculpture were metallic. Some hung from the ceiling, heavily; others hung from the walls. Great massive hulks—not defined enough to be shapes— squatted on the floor. People drifted around the sculpture, sometimes bumping into it. A woman stooped to disentangle her skirt from some wire, a thick ball of wire that had been sprayed with white paint.

What were these strange forms? They were oppressive to Lawrence. But no one else seemed to be uneasy. He went to examine the wire—it looked like chicken wire—and he could make no sense of it. Elsewhere in the crowded room there were balls of metal that were distorted, like planets wrenched out of shape. Their shiny surfaces relected a galaxy of human faces, but the faces were not really human. They were cheerful and blatant and flat, as if there were no private depths to them. . . . How they were all chattering away, those faces! No privacy at all, nothing but the facial mask of flesh; no private depths of anguish or darkness or sweetness, nothing. The faces are all talking earnestly to one another.

Lawrence looked for his wife. He saw her across the room, talking to a tall man with silvery hair. It was the man he had seen downtown! Astonished, Lawrence could not move. He stood with his drink in his hand, as metallic and fixed as the pieces of sculpture. These columns punctuated the gallery, each reaching to the ceiling, with flat, shiny surfaces and edges that appeared razor-sharp. They made him think suddenly of the furniture in his parents' house that he had stood up on end as a child—allowed by his mother to play with the furniture of certain rooms, up-ending tables and chairs so that he could crawl under them and pretend they were small houses, huts. He had crouched under them, peering out past the legs of tables and chairs. Sometimes his mother had given him a blanket to drape over the piece of furniture.

The man with silver hair turned and Lawrence saw that it was not the stranger from downtown after all—it was someone he'd known for years. Yet he felt no relief. He was still paralyzed. Beverly, not seeing him, was looking around cautiously, nervously. The man was about to drift into another conversation and leave her. He had a big, heavy, handsome head, his silver-gray hair curly and bunched, his face florid and generous and a little too aggressive—too sure of itself. Lawrence felt a sudden dislike for him. And yet he was grateful that he had not become that man—grateful that, in the moment of paralysis and panic, his soul had not flown out of him and into that man, into that other body.

● He went out. He walked quickly out of his building and into the midday crowd, in a hurry, and once on the sidewalk he stayed near the curb so that he could walk fast. The day was cold and overcast. He walked several blocks to the end of the street and across the street to the riverfront. There were few people down here, only the most hardy of tourists. No shoppers bothered to come this far. There were no stores here, only concrete and walls and a ferry landing and the water, the grim cold water. He leaned over a railing. He stared down at the lapping water. It was not very clean; there were long streaks of foam in it, as long as six or eight feet, bobbing and curling and twisting like snakes.

The discontent of the past two weeks rose in his mind. What was wrong? What had happened? It had begun on that sunlit day when he'd seen his wife from a distance. His wife. His mother arrived the following morning; they picked her up at the airport as always. And his daughter—there had been something about his daughter as well—but he could not remember. In the dirty, bouncy water he saw Edie's face, grinning up at him. But she did not really see him. There was nothing there. He was alone.

He thought in a panic of himself and the river: the fact of being alone like this, with the river a few yards beneath him.

There was a sensation of deadness around his eyes. His eyes had become hardened, crusted over; like crusts of blood; the wounds where eyes had once been. And now they might fall off...?Another face was pushing its way through. He must scratch at the scabs of his eyes and scratch them off, to make way for the new face, digging the crusts of blood away with his nails. He must tear at himself. He must do it now, this minute...for at this minute his body could no longer contain itself; it was like a wrestler with superbly developed muscles bursting through his clothing, tearing his clothing with anger and impatience and joy—

He saw, suddenly, that the river beneath him was a river of souls: the souls of all the children he had been meant to father, flowing out of him and helplessly, ferociously downstream. He stared at the water. All of these his children! Sons and daughters of his body! He had been meant to father these thousands, these thousands of millions of souls, and yet he was on the concrete walk, leaning against the guard rail, and the children of his body were flowing by him, lapping noisily against the abutment, becoming lost.

For some time he stood in silence. His eyes ached. He tried to think of what he must do—had he planned something? Why had he come down here? If he were to drown, perhaps scenes of his past life would flash to him. He would see the up-ended furniture again—the clumsy gold-covered chair with its curved legs and its gauzy bottom, the springs visible through the dark gauze—he would crawl between the legs again, drawing his knees up to his chest, hiding there, sly and safe. He would see the big house, he would see the piles of magazines and he would smell the acrid, lovely odor of loneliness on the third floor of that house; he would pass into that room and live out his life there chastely and silently.

But perhaps he would fall into the water screaming. He would thresh his arms and legs—he would sink at once, screaming—and no one could save him. People might come to gawk, but they could not save him. And perhaps he would see nothing at all, no visions, no memories; perhaps it was only a lie about a drowning man living his life again and he would see nothing, nothing; he would drown in agony and be washed downstream, lost.

He glanced at his watch. After one.

He hurried back to his office. The receptionist, a pretty black woman, chided him for walking in the rain. She took his trench coat from him, shook it, hung it up. In the waiting room—he could see through two partly opened doors—a few people were sitting and had been sitting for a while. He went into his private office. In a few minutes his nurse showed in his first patient of the afternoon: Herb Altman.

"I'm back a little faster this time, but everything is the usual. Diagnosis the usual," Altman said flatly. He wore a stylish, wide green tie, mint green. There were tiny white streaks in it that bothered Lawrence's vision.

Shaking of hands.

"Maybe somebody should just shoot me. I should croak, eh?" Altman laughed. "Anyway I still can't sleep, Larry. The same damn thing. Give me something strong to help me sleep, eh? And did you hear about that bastard, that investigator I got to follow Evie? He was a friend of hers! It turned out he was a friend of hers! He told her everything, he tipped her off. I fired him and I'm dumping her, believe you me, I think even she and my wife are comparing notes on me and laughing and it's no goddam wonder I can't sleep. Maybe I should just drop over, eh? Make things easier for everybody? What is your opinion?"

"Let me do just a routine examination," Lawrence said carefully. "You do look a little agitated."

Exile

September 21. ...Watched him again this morning. Hidden behind a sumac bush. I was hidden, he was exposed. *He:* that doomed syllable. *He:* that fool. An elderly man, fishing on the river hour after hour, day after day, tireless, brainless. Is there nothing else for him to do, nothing else they will allow him to do? To touch?...Two or three times this summer another old man accompanied him, but most of the time he is alone. Out on the river as early as seven o'clock...drifting downriver until noon...then rowing back up to wherever he lives ...reappearing again between four and five in the afternoon. In the drowsy heat-haze of early autumn he wears a new-looking greenish straw hat, stiff and noble and only slightly absurd. Sometimes he fishes, sometimes he trolls, leaning over the side of the rowboat, humpbacked, patient. Old man, old fool! Is there nothing else...?

September 24. ...In the midst of struggle I awoke too early, too early; five o'clock; the birds are feverish in this wild place. Too early!...and now the day will be enormous, a craterlike expanse. To traverse this gigantic sky: an epic!...In the midst of strain, beat, pulse, wheezing, groaning, grinding of teeth I awoke, awoke, ah!...a sharp pain, a series of pains, jabs, running up the left side of my body, across my chest, I awoke snatching at them thinking *Rats! rats!* (For there are rats here, in this rented house; I believe they are river rats, astonishingly large, supple, and arrogant.) ... I had no intentions of dying. I am far too young: hardly past the midpoint of my life.

September 25.   ... Dark-soured molluscs, flesh drooping from flesh, my cheeks, my lips? ... jowls? Eyes naked, blinking innocently. I cannot see. I cannot *see*. Born partly blind; operations at the ages of five, eight, twelve, then again at twenty-two; they said I was brave who did not know my fury, my despair. And then, what a miracle! That one so afflicted should be so brilliant; that, out of the crevices of pain, one can manage to bleat a few Life-Affirming Percussive Notes. ...

Then again, the miracle of technology, lenses so finely ground, instruments so delicately forged, even the near-blind can be restored to the near-normal. Now, aging, my eyes deteriorate according to a scheme I cannot comprehend: on some mornings my vision is as close to perfect as one might wish and I can see clearly across the river to the peninsula, to the stand of tall straight lovely pine, can see (almost!) each tree distinct from the others; on other mornings there are shimmering soiled halos close about everything, noisy fluttering blurs in the elderberry bushes outside my bedroom window, a malevolent spillage of too-white light in the immense sky, toes so far away they writhe in comic helplessness. ...

Had I a pair of binoculars, I could spy upon the old man in the rowboat with more comfort, more sympathy. I suspect he is very old—in his late seventies, early eighties. He has a small potbelly, but his chest is sunken, his arms are thin, especially the upper arms; his hair, what I have seen of it, seems to be white. But of course I would never buy binoculars, of course I am only joking. I have no interest in my neighbors. I know none of them, not even their names; and they don't know me. Thank God they have no idea of who I am.

Thank God!

September 25 (evening).   ... About to go to bed, suffered an attack of breathlessness. Suffocation. Why is the air so thin? Suck at it, suck at it! Harder! ... Afterward, sat up half the night. Afraid to lie down, afraid to sink back into that vulnerable position. Angry, I was, and impatient with myself, and embarrassed. Still, I sat in that broken, sagging, soiled, oddly

comfortable old chair, leafing through a gardening handbook in
which I had no interest; one of the half-dozen books left behind
by my predecessor. When to start plants from seedlings, under
glass; when to till the soil; when to set the plants gently in the
earth; when to fertilize; when to dust against insects. Buds,
blossoms, vegetables. Food. Soil. Food. No other...? None.

Went to bed, finally, at four-thirty. Breathing quite normal. I
have no intentions of dying for quite a while.

September 26. ...No one wishes me to write my memoirs; no
one close to me. Fearful of my truth-telling. My reputation for
"ruthless" honesty. Ha, ha!—why so apprehensive? At the
Institute I reigned modestly, with little interest in demonstrating
my power. Thirty-seven years. *Thirty-seven years.* A small
provincial hospital with less than one hundred beds when I came;
a world-famous clinic when I departed. Certain grateful patients
did, it's true, beg me to set down a history of my work, to "leave
for posterity" an account of my life. The mystery of genius...the
convoluted ways by which a great achievement is brought into
being...the small ironies, reversals, bitter consequences,
betrayals...the inestimable satisfactions. You can't let your life
die with you! You owe it to us!...But my colleagues, my
associates, my friends, my family: they would like everything to
die with me. They are terrified of what I might reveal about
them. Petty creatures! Cowards!...Shall I be merciful, or
merciless?

September 28. ...No appetite today. In fact, no appetite for
the past four or five days. Even the thought of food upsets me.
Nausea that comes and goes, light-headedness, quirky vision,
finally a peculiar sort of euphoria that left me feeling quite
strong, convinced I have done the right thing. Farewell, Dr.
Zweifel, the voices chant. Farewell, farewell!...Even God must
be released, finally. Surrendered. Would you gobble Him up
whole, you greedy beasts?

September 29. ...A small single-bedroom house built by
strangers on a grassy knoll above the river. Hemmed in by trees,
overgrown bushes, weeds. Little room for breath. The summer's
heat is over, thank God. Mornings, noons, afternoons, the river,
the river's strenuous discordant music, evenings; nights, loons;
mornings, birds that flutter noisily in the bushes, black squirrels

that scamper across the roof; noons and afternoons, hazy slanted
sunshine, the rowboat drifting downstream, evenings, nights,
night. There are ungainly birds on the river, larger than mallards,
wide wings flapping: a certain charming clumsiness to them.
Possibly geese. Canada geese? If I were lonely I would buy a pair
of binoculars in order to watch these creatures more closely.

Fritz, where are you? Fritz? Do you hear me? . . . Woke from a
nap, woke without knowing I had been asleep, astounded by the
nearness of her voice. How had she found me? Who had told her
where I was? . . . Then, in the next instant, I realized it was only a
dream, a waking dream. I was alone. Safe. Safe still. In exile, and
safe. Ah, what terror! But in an instant it passed, it passed. I was
master of my mood. I was master of myself once again. *Fritz,
Fritz!*—her baffled angry voice. But no: no. And again, no. I am
alone.

September 30. . . ? October 1. . . ? A chilly breeze, damp, despite
the gusty patches of sunlight blown in all directions; wore my
coarse-knit sweater buttoned up, and an old tweed golfing cap;
found myself shivering anyway. That wind on the river!—a
continual assault. So long as I rowed downstream, however, I
had no difficulties. The rowboat was large, large enough for five
or six people, and rather awkward, and the oars were
surprisingly heavy; the splinters hurt my hands, which are
shamefully unaccustomed to work of this sort; but I made good
time, I began to enjoy myself despite the chill. The river is so
different from the land! How can you guess at the river, when
you stand on shore, shaking your eyes, staring, blinking painfully
and blindly into this turbulence . . . ? Bouncing slapping capricious ceaseless waves. Shapes darting beneath the surface of the
greeny-dark water: could make out a school of minnows, each as
small as my little finger, silvery-green, astonishing, held in
suspension for brief moments and then waking to life, waking to
quick brainless impeccable movement; and other, larger shapes,
what might they be?—the river is said to contain pike, bullheads,
perch, rock bass, and carp. The river bore me downstream,
waves rolled against the side of the boat, the sun beat against my
head through the tweed cap; the winds came from many
directions, fresh, piercing, moaning, whispering, accusing,
soothing, deafening me, bearing me onward; something was
caught in my right oar, a mass of seaweed or debris. I struggled
with it, suddenly aware of my shortened breath. I managed to get

the oar free; I raised it, dripping, held it in the air with some effort; but when I looked over the side I saw nothing in the water.

At that moment there was a bump against the bottom of the boat. What—? Must have been a sizable piece of debris, maybe a tree limb floating just beneath the surface. I lowered the oar cautiously and began to row, panting, and felt the oar gripped again, seized, there was a hand in the water, two hands that seized the oar as I stared, astonished, unable to act, not knowing what to do— What is it? Who is it? What do you want? A face in the water, contorted, white, drained bloodless and puckered: the forehead deeply furrowed, the eyebrows shaggy and bushy, protruding over the eyes so that the eyes were partly hidden; a narrow chin, narrow strained jaws covered with a week's stubble; grotesquely wattled throat, dead-white flesh hanging in small clumps. No! Impossible! Horrible! ... I leaned over the side of the boat, whimpering, trying to take hold of him; my fingers brushed against his, brushed against his thinly streaming white hair, I cried out for him to take hold of my hands, to release the oar; now I could see his eyes and they were almost without color, a grayish-pearlish-phosphorescent white, a blank soiled featureless white, blind?—staring and blind and hideous. No! Not this! Impossible! His fingers were gripped so hard upon the oar they could not be pried loose. What could I do? How could I haul him into the boat without capsizing myself? I was whimpering with distress, I was groaning aloud with the urgency of it, would he not look at me, would he not *see* ... ? How could I save him otherwise? I tried to maneuver the boat around, tried to get closer to him; tried to take hold of him by the shoulders; but there was no life in him, only weight, a colossal watery heaviness; what could I do?—what could I have done?

October. ... Several days of rain. Leaves blown from trees, slapped against windows all night long. Sleep? Never again. Something scuttling across the roof, then again along the side of the house, a series of high-pitched but muted shrieks—then silence again, then wind and rain again, again. Sat in the old chair but was unable to read, unable even to distract myself by turning pages; spent most of the night in the ugly drafty alcove that serves as a kitchen, the oven on and the door open, trying to get warm.... But never, never again.

October. Morning. Rain. ... Once shining, an exquisite auburn, her hair was now drab and lifeless, so thin on top I could see the poor woman's scalp. The Institute is failing without you, she tells me in her soft, quick voice; you must come back to us. Her fingers are stained with nicotine. She smokes one cigarette after another, a habit she got from me, one of my accursed legacies. Her costume is dark gray, almost black. Perhaps it is black? Old-style clothes, a suit of coarse wool, rather mannish, with plain black buttons and no ornamentation, the skirt at mid-calf. Her voice is muffled rather than soft. She clears her throat several times, as if very nervous. Fuss, fuss!—the needless pretentions of sorrow. Shaking ashes onto her own skirt. Her eyes darting about this wreck of a place, finding nowhere to stick, shying away from my own gaze—ravaged, am I, and not quite handsome enough these days?—not handsome enough to feed a woman's colossal vanity?—the eyelids appear to be reddened and grainy. Dr. Zweifel, she whispers. Fritz. . . . Please.

October. God slumbers and we live; when God awakes we die. The awakening of one is the death of the other.

How do I know? I know.

I *know*.

They said I had overtaxed myself and I countered by saying have I overtoxed *you*? A sly joke not everyone caught, though that sandy-haired sandy-bearded lout, that oaf with the Jaguar rumored to have cost so many thousands of dollars, resplendent there in the parking lot beside my own modest rust-edged car, that Dr. Cahill or Clayton, I had never bothered to be properly introduced to him, he stiffened with the precision of my charge: toxemia was of course their natural condition. In their perverse systems Truth itself is pathogenic.

. . . Perhaps, then, I should write my memoirs. Perhaps I should transcribe the Truth as separate truths, building to an overwhelming vision: for am I not the sole curator of Dr. Fritz Zweifel? Their eulogies have been, let us say, *somewhat premature*.

October. Midday. . . . Sunshine, twittering and chattering of birds, the world restored, the old man in the straw hat again on the river, drifting lazily downstream, totally absorbed in his fishing and unaware of me. If I walked boldly to the very edge of the scrubby beach and shouted to him and waved, he wouldn't glance around. The river is too noisy and anyway he is under a spell. Old fool, to be content with such small mindless pleasures!

But I suppose it is all they allow him. His grown-up children, his guardians. Really, I feel sympathetic toward him; I do not hold him in contempt. Simple pity is not contempt, though I myself, in the past, have perhaps mistaken the two.... Old man, I want to shout, old fool, wake up! Hey! Don't you know what they are doing to you, what they are cheating you of, don't you know they are your murderers and must be destroyed? Wake up! Wake up!

Of course he would hear nothing. The rowboat drifts downstream, riding the more rigorous waves, sliding effortlessly with the others. God slumbers, God slumbers, God slumbers.

Next day. ... Plunged ahead into winter, it seems. Stinging icy rain. The oars are surprisingly heavy, the water has thickened, toughened. So quickly has the sky changed, the weather changed, I am most pitifully caught a half-mile from my own beach, can barely see the big poplar on the riverbank that is my landmark.... Should have dressed more warmly. You know better, Fritz! You know better! How women fuss, how they scold, their fingers gleeful as they poke and pry and jab, their astonished concern only a mask to hide their true desire: to humiliate, to destroy. But it's true, it is true, I should have dressed more warmly this morning. My old coat-sweater, my black trousers worn so thin at the seat, and these cotton socks: not very helpful in a freezing rain. The rowboat is bouncing wickedly, as if eager to spin out of control. It could happen, it could—! Unless I grip the oars tight. Unless I refuse to heed *him*, snatching so futilely at the side of the boat, his clawlike fingers scooping the water, hopeless. No you don't—no. No no no. That face dipping and bobbing beneath the surface of the water, flung away by a wave, slapped back again, that bloodless eyeless face, there is no room for you, no room, the boat would capsize if I tried to pull you in, I can't help you, no one can help you, no—

Evening. ... The significance of matter has been greatly exaggerated, I told the young woman; everything points to the probability that existence is a mental phenomenon and that matter is a "trick" of consciousness. She pretended to understand. As they all do. In Dr. Zweifel's memoirs there will be many liars, some evil but most of them quite innocent.... How do I know? I know. After all, I was born in the nineteenth century, the century that *knew*.... Yes, I am joking. But my jokes contain truths; at the core of every joke there is a harsh, bitter, irrefutable truth, otherwise the joke would be a mere assemblage of words.... My dear, I began as a scientist of matter, a priest of matter, I wanted only to measure and weigh and dissect and categorize and explain the universe; surely I, of all people, who have gazed upon and slipped into the Void, and reappeared shaking my untidy hair out of my face, surely *I* know whereof I speak...?

You say I have overtaxed my system. This is often said of women whose pregnancies have gone wrong, who will give birth to stone-dead infants. It does not apply to me. Nothing that has been said about anyone else applies to me.... My dear, you must not interrupt! You *must* not interrupt!

The significance of matter has been greatly exaggerated. As our century closes, matter itself will begin to lighten, to become more obviously porous, hollow; enormous redwoods, seventy-floor buildings, concrete structures of all kinds, the human skeleton, enamel and gold and the earth's crust itself, all will become light-riddled, frail, subject to sudden breakage and most certainly to a gradual erosion. All, all will succumb to Spirit. It is inevitable. As God slumbers we dwell in our overheated busy consciousness; as God stirs, beginning to wake, we will fall one by one into the oblivion of that sacred sleep.... How do I know?

Woke straining for breath. What day? What month? Bedclothes sweaty, the air of this tiny room cold, cold. Must be very early morning. Before dawn. A curse, waking so early; I wish I could sleep until eight-thirty or even nine o'clock. The pain is lessening, the pinched sensation behind the eyes is now only a dull blur, a kind of dazzlement. Who had been with me, struggling in these filthy sheets? At first I was alone, then she came to my bedside and began to question me, as they all did, as they still do, without regard for my sorrow, my exasperation; then she leaned over me so that her hair brushed my face; she offered to hold me, to cradle me in her arms. The warmth of her body, her breath...! I could anticipate the pleasure of being held, my eyes closed, my face pressed gently against her breasts, but I resisted, I had more to say, much more. They cannot bribe me so easily!—cannot lure me into a premature silence. So I maintained my soul and awoke gasping for breath, weak and frightened and anxious but triumphant: triumphant. And now the pain is lessening, and now as minutes pass and I lie very still, cautiously still, the weight on my chest lightens; I am able to breathe again.

Afternoon. October...? Possibly November. ...A memoir is not a confession. In my life there is little to confess. A memoir should begin perhaps with the present situation, the writer sitting at his kitchen table, writing with an old-fashioned fountain pen, in dark-blue ink, on lined paper, sheets and sheets of grammar-school paper, the writer alone in a small wood-frame house he has rented, three rooms in addition to a small bathroom, a nondescript lot on the river, the nearest city nineteen miles to the south...though there are neighbors on one side, a quarter-mile away: a family with several small children. On the other side of the house is a kind of jungle, trees grown too close to one another and therefore stunted, many bushes, shrubs, weeds. It rains here often. Then the sun appears. It is quiet here, except for the river. One wave after another after another slapping against the beach all night long! Still, it is quiet. The quiet is indecipherable. In such quiet one must always be on guard: she came upon me stealthily, after all, taking advantage of my unsuspicious nature.

Fritz, she said, *Dr. Zweifel,* they said, *Father: please come back to us.*

Evening. ...In my life there was little to confess. The woman in the dark, old-fashioned clothes, fingernails bitten to the quick, one cigarette after another until she coughed so violently I shouted for her to leave: must I witness her death again? We were not truly lovers. It was not in us to give ourselves that thoroughly. There was always, there is always, a certain margin of irony necessary in love: otherwise they crowd you too close, there isn't room to breathe.... Come back to the Institute, she begged, they can't manage without you, none of us can manage without you; we study your records, your notes, your reports, but it isn't the same thing as having you near. There is only one Dr. Zweifel in all of history.... Please forgive us!

But I will not listen, I will not be tempted. The woman is a stranger to me now. Before her death she remarried, moved to the West Coast, went into private practice as a child psychiatrist, until illness made it impossible for her to continue. I know her name but will not record it. No melodrama in my life, no scandal. No record. *Fritz,* she whispers. *Fritz, please. Haven't we loved each other?*

No.

I don't know.

I don't wish to think about it.

Morning. Overcast day. ...Geese honking, flying overhead. I went out into the backyard to see, but was too slow; they were nearly out of sight. A surprisingly mild day, little wind from the river. Autumn again: fragrance of damp leaves, pine needles. If the sun appears, it will almost be too warm.

Father, she begs, please be reasonable. Don't do this to us.

Father, I echo, mimicking her distress. Father Father Father!—As if I had not earned my freedom by now!

Father, you aren't well enough to live alone, you know what happened last winter, if I hadn't telephoned when I did—

Honk honk honk, another magnificent squadron of geese overhead, just look at them! Look! My heart sinks. I have spent most of my life in buildings, in laboratories, in civilization, I have spent most of my life toiling in the service of others, and all along the river has been here, this old house has been here, the geese—

Father, please listen—Can't you hear—

Dr. Zweifel, your essay is certainly interesting, all the editors have read it and discussed it at considerable length, our problem is, as you must know, that the journal has always limited itself to scientific pieces, as you must know we've steered clear of controversies, your essay is certainly interesting and we're all very grateful to have seen it, though naturally we are somewhat baffled and one or two of us are, it must be said, rather offended—but we're certainly grateful to have seen it. Thank you so much!

Yes, that's my father, I heard her say. Then the weeping, the obligatory demonstration of kinship. I had packed no suitcase, had merely taken the fifty-dollar bills her husband keeps in one of the innumerable unread books on his shelves, took them without counting them, dressed, scribbled a note (they said it was unintelligible—is it my fault, that they are so ignorant!), left it on the dining-room table beneath the empty cut-glass fruit bowl, walked out to the corner and got a city bus and.... That's him, yes, my God yes, is he all right? *Is he all right?*

Why don't you leave me alone!

Later. ...My first extensive research was completed in 1921, I mean the first research that was truly valuable, the first body of work I wasn't ashamed of immediately afterward. Speech defects related to brain damage: speech "defects." Never had it crossed my young combative mind that I was forcing an education upon men and women who were, because of their unique disorders, free of the burdens that complex speech necessitates. A half-century later I wrote a parable entitled "Zweifel's Orthogenetics" in which I developed the proposition that the activation of ever-new and ever-more ingenious talents stimulates larger and larger and ultimately tragic areas of miscomprehension . . . the more subtle the means of communication, the more possibility that communication will not take place at all. *But no one believes this.* Each person believes that he is perfectly understood by everyone he addresses. Always and forever. For that is part of the tragedy, that very delusion. Those who read my essay denied its application to them and in any case they denied its value as a contribution to neuropsychiatric studies. For it is not possible, is it, that language itself in the primary obstacle to communication? No! Never! They denied it all!

Dr. Zweifel, they said, you have over-taxed your system. You must rest.

Must rest, rest, rest.

And again I addressed them, in my capacity as Director of the Institute I addressed them, a murmurous incredulous alarmed group, wondering why they had been summoned to the amphitheater in the middle of the workday, fearful of what accusations I might make: for they knew how they were disappointing me, they knew how inadequate their contributions were. And they were overpaid, of course. . . . *As one approaches the completion of a cycle of experience, he loops back upon his earlier self (or selves); what we call "time" is demolished and the soul is revealed as transcendent, though it is also physiologically viable. Do I make myself understood? Research must be done to determine exactly what chemical changes take place in the brain during these brief but intense durations. The visual apparatus seems temporarily inoperative, and though there is eye movement the individual is "blind"—or, rather, his vision turns inward, into the brain itself, where connections of an undeter-mined nature are made between earlier and more mature segments of the soul. . . . Did I say segments? No, no, "aspects" is a more precise term. Of course a great deal of research must be done on these matters, especially if it develops, as I believe it will, that "aspects" of the soul that exist ostensibly in what we know as future time are contemporaneous with us at the present time. Much, much work will be involved . . . our ordinary projects will*

*have to be set aside temporarily . . . it will be necessary to form
small teams . . . coordinated by . . . under the general supervision
of. . . . I foresee our Institute becoming the world's center for
electroencephalographic and neurophysiological studies of the
relationship between the brain mechanisms and consciousness. . . .*

That was many months ago. Perhaps I foresaw, at that time,
the clownish faces that would soon surround me, perhaps I
already heard the twittering and chattering and babbling, Dr.
Zweifel this, Dr. Zweifel that, please, if you don't mind, how
awkward for us, you leave us no alternative, chatter chatter
chatter, words looping back upon words, shameless formulae,
word-formulae, "we regret that," we profoundly regret that,"
Dr. Zweifel, please don't interrupt—please listen—*Please listen.*

The fey sounds of birds, the hoarse and almost comic honking
of the geese, the wind, the winds, the ceaseless waves, something
scuttling noisily through the bushes alongside the house,
squirrels, mice, raccoons, rats?—I am listening, I am listening
with awe and respect and something close to affection. What had
I done with my life until now!

Still, they lied. And I knew. Even the attorney I hired lied: it is
believed he was in their pay. Of course nothing can be proved.
Nothing. An old man's dawning sense of betrayal, gradual
awakening to the lie-riddled nature of the material world. And
yet—can I take these creatures seriously? Now that I am in
possession of my own savings once again, now that I am
economically independent—what connection have I with my
enemies?

They
came for me one autumn day, but I managed to hide in the
underbrush, lying flat behind a fallen log. *Father,* came the cry,
Father, Father. . . . My heart stormed, I wanted to seize it in both
hands to quiet it. But no one heard. After a while they left, but I
was wise enough to stay hidden. I lay on my side, the tweed cap
for a pillow; I slept. Naps are good for you at any age. . . . When I
woke it was sunset. Orange-red clouds of an astonishing beauty,
multilayered and yet translucent. My vision throbbed, confronted with such beauty. Ah, what a sight!

I shaded my eyes and I looked upriver where a helicopter was
suspended above the water. Blue lights flashing, it must have

been a police helicopter. An accident! A boating accident! . . . I walked along the beach, to the very edge of my property. Someone was shouting through a bullhorn. There were people on the riverbank, I could see a number of children; now a police boat appeared, slowed, rocking on the waves. . . . Must have been a boating accident. Bathed in warm lovely orange-red light!

Such beauty, how have we earned it? How can we even comprehend it?

Saw my neighbors for the first time. A boy of about eleven, two younger boys, running to the river. Hey, somebody drowned! Somebody drowned! The father appeared, carrying a can of beer. He wore work trousers and a checked shirt and bedroom slippers. Behind him, his wife in a dress, a sweater draped over her shoulders, bare-legged despite the growing chill. Their voices rose and fell; urgent, excited. What is it, what happened, who did it happen to . . . ? Somebody drowned . . . ?

The police boat, the throbbing motor; the helicopter's noisy propellers; the rescue team's shouts. Flashing blue lights as the sun faded, blue noise, blue beating, pulsing, rocking. Dusk. Then night. Blue flashing blue in the darkness, whipping round and round. No! Stop! So ugly! So awful!

I hid. They could not find me.

Grab hold, grab hold of my hand, I cried, nearly sobbing, leaning far over the edge of the boat, reaching for him; but his poor skeletal fingers scooped and closed upon the water and opened again, helpless. Here! Here I am! Grab hold! He surfaced once or twice, the dead-white face now eyeless—had something pecked the sockets clean, or were his eyes simply in shadow?—the lips stretched in an arduous grin. My feet were wet, there was a puddle of water in the bottom of the boat, waves hit the prow and splashed over, the wind sucked at my breath but still I shouted to him, my arm extended, my fingers outstretched a mere inch from his, Here I am! Grab hold of my hand! Here! I won't let you die—

Here—

The Giant Woman

"Get away! Get away! Get out of here!"

She came at us, swinging something. It struck the side of the shed—there was a metallic sound—and then her screaming again.

"—out of here—I'll kill—"

The others were ahead of me. I ran, whimpering with fear.

Behind us she stood at the end of the dirt path, screaming. Her words had lost their separate, distinct shapes; they were all one furious uncontrollable sound.

I ran panting and whimpering with fear. The others were in the cornfield—nearly at the creek bank—I could hear them laughing and squealing. I nearly fell, the cornstalks caught and tore at my face, I could hear her still screaming behind me and it was mixed with my own sobbing. I knew she had stopped at the edge of the path, on the hill. I knew she was not chasing me. But I could not control my terror.

At the steep creek bank they had stopped for breath. They were not waiting for me, they had forgotten me, they were gasping, laughing, Donna was doubled over with laughter, Albert was poking and jabbing her; it was all a joke, the whole thing was a joke.

Donna stared at me. "Look at her, look, the baby's

177

crying.—Hey, don't cry, she isn't going to get you. She isn't going to do anything, she's too old."

Albert was still laughing.

"Shut up, stop crying," Donna said.

"I'm not crying—"

"Just be quiet."

"She was so goddam mad—" Albert said.

They descended the steep hill, sliding down, grabbing at bushes and exposed tree roots. I couldn't go down that way because it was too steep. I went the long way around, on a path the fishermen used, but even so I stepped on loose dry pebbles and fell; I cried out in surprise more than pain, and at the bottom of the hill I was on my hands and knees in the rough stones when Donna ran to get me.

"Oh for Christ's sake!—Did you cut yourself? Are you bleeding?"

She examined me, making a face. She touched my knee where it was bleeding.

"It isn't anything," she said.

I wasn't crying.

"It's just a little scratch," she said angrily. "You're always falling down, stupid little goddam baby, why can't you keep from falling down— She fell down, she cut her knee," Donna told Albert, disgusted.

"I'm all right," I said.

I was still trembling, the giant woman had frightened me so that nothing else mattered.

"Are you going to tell?" Albert asked.

"She won't tell," Donna said.

"Are you—?"

"No."

"She won't tell, she wouldn't dare," Donna said.

"Old Mrs. Mueller will call the police on you," Albert said to me. "You heard her, huh? She's going to call the police on you, you're the one she saw, she knows your name and—"

"Oh shut up," Donna said. "She doesn't know anybody's name. She's crazy. Don't get the baby started."

"—really mad, wasn't she? Said something about killing us! The old bag! The old witch! Must have been hiding in there, in the coal shed. She must have been waiting for us. She's crazy, isn't she?"

"She isn't the only one," Donna sang out.

Many years ago, in the foothills of the Chautauqua Mountains, where the north fork of the Eden River flows into the wide, flat, shallow Yew Creek, there lived a giant woman.

A wide face, brown and leathery, wrinkled as an old glove. A head that seemed enormous, too heavy for her thin neck; and the gray hair wild and frizzed about it. Shoulders broad as a man's. The chest sunken with age but the stomach and hips mammoth, flabby, and the thin, dead-white legs still muscular. ...Sometimes she was seen walking along the road, as far away as Rockland, fifteen miles to the south; a few times we saw her in the little town of Derby, eighteen miles away, walking quickly along, her head down, muttering to herself. She usually carried bundles of some kind, and a satchel that seemed to be made of canvas. At such times she might glance up as ordinary people do—quizzical, attentive—and the eyes in that broad, big face were shiny-black, round, slightly protruding. Her expression would shift into a look of wonder and expectation. But then, for some reason, the eyes narrowed to slits, the face closed, stiffened, the line of the mouth became contemptuous and jeering, and she would mutter something inaudible.

"She hates us. She's always yelling at us. Why does she hate us?" I asked.

"She's no harm, is she?" my father said. He helped my mother with the wash, hanging the heavy things on the line, careful that the sheets and quilts did not touch the ground. My mother was pregnant. That was the summer she was pregnant for the fifth time. The baby was to be Jordan, the last child in the family. "She's no harm to you, is she, just stay away from her, let her be, she's older than your grandmother—she won't hurt any of you."

"Why does she hate us?"

"She hates everyone," he said indifferently. "She can't help it."

She lived alone in a decaying farmhouse. She had sold off most of her land, had only a few acres now, kept to herself and rejected any of her neighbors' offers of help. She never spoke to anyone; she simply signaled angry dismissal. No shouting at adults. Only her big arms folded across her breasts, her head jerking from side to side, an inaudible mutter that might have been in a foreign language or in no language at all.

"Why does she live alone? Isn't she afraid to live alone?"

"Why does she live back there, so far from the road?"

"Why does she hate us ...?"

None of the roads in our part of the country were paved then.

But the road she lived on dwindled into a mere lane, a cow path, that was muddy in spring and, in winter, impassable for weeks at a time. The snow could drift as high as twelve feet, blown into odd, slanted mountains and valleys, fanning out from the oaks and sycamores that lined the lane, and no snowplows bothered with it. The road hadn't even a name, people referred to it as the "Mueller Road," but it had no name, no signpost.

"Why won't she let us cross her property?"

"She's old, she's sick, she's not like other people, don't ask so many questions," they said.

I did not tell them about Donna and Albert and me.

"What if she dies, way back there? Wouldn't she be afraid, all alone? How could there be a funeral for her, how would people know about it...?"

"That's nobody's business, what she wants to do."

"Wouldn't she be afraid...?"

"She isn't afraid of anything."

People told stories about her; there were people who knew more than my parents, even my grandmother knew more. They said she had let someone die. They said she was like a murderer. It was the same as murder, wasn't it, what she had done...? Donna said it was her little boy, just my age; the old woman had let him die somehow and hadn't even told people about it, the way you are supposed to notify the doctor and the sheriff and other people in town when something bad happens... she had let the little boy die, a five-year-old boy, and then she had buried him herself. Dug the grave at the edge of the cornfield, down the hill from the back of her house, and put the little boy in it and covered him up with dirt.... "That's what she'll do to you, if she catches you," Donna said suddenly. "She'll dig a grave and push you in and fill it up again with that nasty dried-up old dirt—"

But I didn't cry, I wasn't going to cry. I wasn't afraid.

They said other things, different things. The little boy had not been Mrs. Mueller's own son. Donna was wrong—she hadn't even been born yet, she had heard the story wrong, had mixed things up. Twelve years old and big for her age, noisy and tough as any of the boys, but not too bright—so people in the family said, behind my parents' backs—she forgot important things and remembered small things, mixed up names, became red-faced and angry when mistakes were pointed out to her. I pretended to agree with her so that she wouldn't slap me or pinch my arm. I tried not to cry if she ignored me. But I didn't trust her to tell the truth, to know how the truth really went.

No, the little boy had been Mrs. Mueller's daughter's son. And Mr. Mueller had been alive then. It was true that they had let the boy die—and Mrs. Mueller had tried to bury him, had carried him down to the cornfield and was digging a grave for him, but the ground was too hard, it was still frozen, and she couldn't get the scoop of the shovel into it very deep.

But no: evidently that was just a rumor. A lie. There had been digging of a kind in the field, but it had nothing to do with the child, it hadn't been intended for a grave. There was no grave. Mrs. Mueller had not tried to bury him. He had died in late winter, in March, and they hadn't known what to do with him—with the body—so they carried it out to a corncrib and left it there, under some tarpaulin. Where had the story come from, about the grave? And Mrs. Mueller carrying the boy out to bury him?

After the boy died, the old couple were afraid to call a doctor. They believed they would be arrested and put in jail over in Rockland, where there was a state prison. Mr. Mueller couldn't speak English—knew only a few words—had been always shy of going to town, of dealing with suppliers and shopkeepers. Mrs. Mueller had done all the shopping. People laughed at them both. But they were intimidated by Mrs. Mueller because she was so big, at least six feet five inches tall, must have weighed nearly two hundred fifty pounds at her heaviest, so people said, before she started to waste away.... The old man, when had he died? Six years ago? Seven? No, at least ten. He had died working his team of horses, only a few months after the little boy's death. Heat exhaustion, people said. Or a stroke. Or a heart attack.

People whispered: "She let her little boy die because they were too cheap to call a doctor."

They said: "She worked her husband to death."

And: "They didn't put her in jail—just why was that?"

Sometimes they tapped their foreheads, meaning the old woman was crazy. Sometimes they said she wasn't crazy, but very shrewd, very cunning, only pretending to be crazy so that people would leave her alone. She had money hidden back there—no doubt about it. People like her, dressed in rags, always filthy, too cheap to keep up their houses and outbuildings, too cheap even to buy medicine when it was needed—why, people like that always had money hidden away. They were shrewd, cunning, evil.

What about the daughter?

People were less certain about her. She was "no good," of course. She had run away from home many years ago—many, many years ago. No one really remembered her. It was said that she ran away with a farm worker, a seasonal worker at one of the big farms, but it was sometimes said that Mrs. Mueller had kicked her out—had beaten her with a broom—had blackened one of her eyes. She had been a bad girl, she'd been "no good," "wild," "lazy." But no one remembered her, only the old people, and they disagreed with one another. My grandmother and her friends sat on the porch and plucked memories out of the past with a strange myopic intensity, really indifferent to one another. They needed one another's company, there was a hunger for company, and yet when they began to talk each seemed to speak to herself, unaware of the others. I sat on the steps playing with the kittens, listening. Or flicking pebbles toward the chickens, to make them think it was feeding time, to get their attention. Sometimes I sat with my arms tight around my knees, listening, not quite understanding what the old women were saying, just sitting there and listening, as if there were a truth that might suddenly become illuminated, though the old women themselves would not have realized it.

"...was working up at the train depot, they said. In the restaurant, so she could meet all kinds of men. They said she was married...."

"She was never married! Who said—!"

"...but that was a lie, she just came back here on Sunday with the baby and left him with her parents, and that was that. Mrs. Mueller had to keep him—what could she do? I never talked with her myself, I never visited with her myself but...."

"They hid away back there. They were both crazy."

"How much money do you think she's got?"

"...then the little boy got sick. And they wouldn't call a doctor, of course. They didn't want to spend the money."

"It was in the lungs, what do you call it—"

"Pneumonia."

"They said it was just a bad cold. It was the end of winter, the snow was melting, they could have gotten a doctor without any trouble...could have come to us and we'd gotten him...but they were too cheap, cheap and nasty and mean. So the little boy died."

"Blond curls all over his head, a beautiful little boy."

"He was *not*. A little dark-faced wizened thing, like a monkey. They never fed him right—they were too cheap. Somebody said he was just skin and bones, and his teeth were all rotted, so young. Baby teeth all rotted in his head."

"...had some Negro blood in him, maybe. That was the reason for...."

"They said it was just a bad cold, just a touch of the flu. It was in his lungs, then went to his stomach and bowels, and food wouldn't stay in him, he just emptied himself out, was passing blood too, they said there wasn't time enough for a doctor. But they were too cheap anyway: they saved every penny they could."

"It was pneumonia. He just choked to death, couldn't breathe."

"...just to save money!"

"Or maybe to get rid of him, to have one less mouth to feed. I wouldn't put it past them."

"*Her*, you mean."

"Do you think...? Do...?"

"Why, you said that yourself! More than once!"

"I never...."

Our property bordered her property in a swampy place. There was a marsh that dried out in summer, so that you could walk across it. I remember that rich sour stench; I remember getting dizzy from the stench, and being afraid of the marsh and liking it at the same time. I remember a special place inside a tall patch of cattails where I could crawl to hide; I remember crouching there and Mother running along the path only a few yards away, calling my name. "Oh, where are you? Hon? Are you hiding around here? Are you all right?— Nothing's going to happen."

Dragonflies. Frogs. Small yellow birds. The cicadas in the trees. The heat of August mixed in with the smell of the marsh. There might have been garter snakes but I tried not to think about them. Sometimes I was afraid of the snakes, sometimes I wasn't.

I was afraid of the old woman.

I was afraid of her catching me by the hair—shaking me

hard—the way they said she had grabbed a boy once.

Then there was Bobbie Orkin, who claimed she had crept up behind him, had grabbed him and screamed at him, said she would slit his throat like a chicken's, but he had kicked at her legs and gotten free ... had picked up hunks of dried mud and thrown them at her and yelled back at her, saying he wasn't afraid. He had been exploring the Muellers' old hay barn, the big barn that had been hit by lightning a long time ago and wasn't used for anything now, not even storage, like other old, big barns on other farms in the area; he'd just been walking around in there, hadn't been doing anything wrong, and she had tried to kill him. So he said. But he'd thrown mud and stones at her, and shouted that he wasn't afraid of an ugly old warthog like her, and she'd better watch out or he'd come back at night and set fires. . . . He was thirteen years old but small for his age, wiry and fidgeting all the time, and you couldn't believe him; sometimes he lied and sometimes he told the truth and sometimes he got things mixed up in his own mind, and didn't know what he was saying.

No one would talk about her for months at a time. She was forgotten—just forgotten. Then they would happen to see her somewhere. They would say: She looks meaner than ever! She doesn't even look like a woman now! Then they would forget about her. But then, later, someone might say: How much money do you think she has, hidden away under her bed . . . ?

Past the marsh was an old apple orchard. The Muellers had sold apples to a cider mill not far away, on the river, but that had been a long time ago—now the orchard was overgrown, the trees had not been pruned for years, the apples were tiny and hard and sour and worm-riddled. But we tried to eat them anyway—bit into them, then spat the pieces out in disgust. We picked up windfallen pears, turning them round and round to see how badly rotted they were or if there were worm- or insect-holes. And there were red currants, and huckleberries, and grapes that looked plump and sweet but were really bitter, so that we picked handfuls and threw them at one another. Everything had gone wild, like a jungle, like the banks of the creek where willow trees and bushes of all kinds grew so thick no one could keep a path clear for very long. There were flies and bees everywhere. And yellow jackets and wasps and hornets. And occasionally big birds, jays and grackles and starlings, even a few enormous crows, that hovered near us, tried to frighten us into leaving, shrieking and razzing us with their cries that were almost human.

But we played in the orchard anyway. We tried to climb the trees, even the old, rotting pear trees, with no low branches to grab hold of, and sometimes part of an entire tree trunk would break off, the wood black and soft as flesh, running with tiny ants.

Once, we crept through the orchard...we approached the old woman's house...we hid behind an old woodpile where weeds had grown...we whispered together, frightened, excited, not knowing what would happen.

It was August. An afternoon in August.

I had not been near the house for a long time, no nearer than the orchard. Albert and Donna had gone exploring once, so they said, and had peeked into the old woman's kitchen window and even stepped into the shed, but I had not been with them. She hadn't been anywhere around, they said; nothing had happened, no one knew. That scrawny, ugly tiger-striped tom cat that had been bothering our cats and chickens was sleeping in the shed on a pile of rags—evidently *her* cat! Albert had clapped his hands to wake it, Donna had kicked at it, but the creature hadn't even been afraid—it hissed at them, ears laid back, eyes slits, it awoke immediately and in the same instant was ready to fight, a dirty nasty thing, Donna said, that should be killed. But it had escaped, it had run right past them and out the door.

They had run home, frightened by the cat.

No, Albert hadn't been frightened; he denied it. Donna had been the one. But she denied it too. She had heard something in the house—she thought—it might have been the old woman—sneaking up on them—maybe with a butcher knife or a hammer or a hand-scythe—you couldn't tell, she was crazy. So the two of them had run home, all the way home along the creek bank, panting and terrified, and afterward Donna had told me about it, because of the secret of whose cat that nasty cat was, but she said I mustn't tell anyone else, or I would get into trouble.

If they teased me when I followed them, if they pulled my hair and told me to go back home, I didn't cry. I hid in certain places like the cattails and stayed by myself for a long time, sitting still, listening to the birds and insects, until I forgot about them and couldn't even remember what they had said or how delicate and painful the moment was when Donna could either grin and reach for my hand, and say I could come with them, or make a face at me and tell me to get back home where I belonged—I hid in the marsh or in one of the junked cars in the

Wreszins' orchard and stayed by myself, sometimes crying a little, but most of the time just quiet, listening to the sounds outside me that were not Donna and Albert or anything human at all, until I felt very happy, and everything seemed all right again, and easy to live, and there was no problem or worry or fear, nothing at all, nothing bad that would last for very long—these things just went away, just vanished. They couldn't last.

But when I was with them again, I forgot and something changed in me, I wanted to follow them, I wanted to play with them, I forgot about being alone and being safe and quiet. I did things to make them tease me. Albert would pull my hair and tickle me so that it hurt; Donna would say I was fresh and wanted spanking, and was going to grow up worse than Ronnie—one of our grown-up cousins—who had been in trouble with the sheriff and had had to join the navy to keep from going to jail.... But they liked me better then. "Can I come with you? Can I come with you?" I was always begging.

The shed stank.

They said it was spoiled food, maybe. Or maybe the cat had been bad in all those rags and papers.

"It smells like something dead," Albert whispered.

"It does not! There's nothing dead in here!"

"A raccoon could have crawled in here and died ... a rabbit or a woodchuck or something...."

Now the door to the kitchen, two steps up from the earthen floor of the shed.

There was a rusted screen door, the screen ripped and useless, and then a regular door. The spring of the screen door had broken. Donna opened the inner door slowly. She stood on her toes, on the step, and peered through the window of the door.

"You won't go in there," Albert said. "I bet you won't go in there."

"If I go in, are you coming...?"

"*You* won't go in. You won't dare."

"What about you?"

"Is the door locked? If it's locked...."

But of course it wasn't locked. No one locked doors around here.

The kitchen: a surprise because it was bigger than ours at home. But it was an ugly place, the walls and ceiling dingy, the wood-burning stove blocking out light from one of the two narrow windows, big and black and ugly, made of iron. It was an old stove, my grandmother had had one like it, but my father had bought her a new one. We stood in the kitchen and were afraid to go forward or backward. "What if she comes in from the shed...?" Albert whispered.

"She's out for all day," Donna whispered. "She was supposed to go to town, wasn't she...."

"What if she comes back early?"

"Ma said she was due at the courthouse, something about taxes. She'd be in town for all day, she'd have to walk.... She won't be back early. You're just afraid."

"I'm not afraid."

They opened the cupboard doors but there was nothing interesting there—stacks of dishware, kettles, a platter made of white glass with scalloped edges, canisters like the ones we had at home, with *Flour* and *Sugar* and *Tea* on their fronts. The kitchen table had heavy legs with carved flowers on them, the kind of table you would expect to see in a living room, and its surface was all scratches and burn marks. There were two chairs, one with a filthy cushion, the other used to set things on—cups, dishcloths or rags, a few knives and forks and spoons that seemed to be made of some dark, heavy, tarnished material, not like ours at home that were lightweight and stainless. These things were carved too and very grimy. The floor had no tile or linoleum, it was just bare floorboards, and could smell the earth through them—the house had no cellar, just a crawl space.

They worked the hand pump at the sink. The first water that came out was tinged with rust.

I opened one of the doors on the stove—but it was just the place where wood and old newspapers were kept. Then I saw a spider. I slammed the door shut.

"How big a spider was it?" Donna asked. Her face crinkled; she hugged herself. Spiders frightened everyone in the family except the men—spiders even more than snakes.

"I closed the door on it," I said. "It can't get out."

Albert and Donna went into the next room. It was a parlor, but very small. The shades were drawn, it was very hot and dusty. I was thinking of spiders and could feel things touching my bare legs, little pinpricks and itches. They went only a few steps into the room, then stopped. Albert glanced back over his shoulder and his face was pale and tight, a stranger's face. He looked at me almost without recognizing me. Donna giggled nervously.

"Jesus, it's hot in here.... What is that smell? Just dirt? Dust?" She
punched one of the cushioned chairs and a cloud of dust
exploded out of it. We all laughed.

They went into the last room, at the back of the house. I
followed them, I was afraid to stay by myself. There were
cobwebs everywhere, most of them broken and hanging in
threads, blowing this way and that. Even on the globe of a
kerosene lamp, where it would have been easy to wipe it away,
there was part of a cobweb. Everything was silent except for us.

"So there are only three rooms in the house...."

"It's bigger on the outside. It looks bigger on the outside."

"There's no stairway. It must just be an attic up there and no
way to get to it.... It's a sad, nasty place, isn't it?"

"I suppose you want to leave already!"

The back room was Mrs. Mueller's bedroom. Blinds were
drawn here, too, but it wasn't so dusty, you could see that
someone lived in it. There was even a mirror with an
old-fashioned ornate frame that could be tilted back and forth,
however you wanted. Albert moved it a little and Donna poked
him. "Stop that! Don't you touch anything!"

"Go to hell," Albert whispered. "I'll do anything I want."

"Don't you touch anything, I said!"

But he was already opening the drawers of a bureau—yanking
them open one by one. The top drawer was filled with women's
things, underclothes.

Donna was examining the bedspread. She didn't even notice
what Albert had done. "Hey, this is a fancy thing. She must have
done this herself. It's all crochetwork, all these squares sewn
together. It's pretty, it's nicer than Grandma's. But it's so old...."

"Is this real gold?"

Albert held up a hairbrush.

"It wouldn't be gold, it wouldn't be real," Donna said.

There were things draped over chairs, pushed back in a
corner. Clothes and sheets and towels. I couldn't tell if they were
dirty or not. I lifted a blanket and found a black leather purse
under it. "Look what she found!" Albert said. But the purse was
empty. It was very old, the catch was broken, it was empty
except for a few hairpins and a rolled-up handkerchief.

"Look here," Donna said.

She was squatting by the bed, had found a cardboard box
under it. When she dragged it out, Albert said: "Be careful!"
because she almost ripped the sides. There were all sorts of

papers in the box—letters still in envelopes—a book that must have been a Bible, with red-edged pages—but they were afraid to touch it, because of all the dustballs on top. She would know someone had been in her house.

"It's just some written stuff," Albert said.

"There might be money...."

"Yeah, but...."

"You think she's got it hidden here, in here? Underneath this stuff?"

"Let me look."

His hands were trembling. We all started to giggle.

It was too nervous for me, I couldn't watch him, I went to the window and peeked out—and it was a surprise, to see the Muellers' lane from here, from the inside of the house. I wondered if the old woman stood here sometimes, peeking around the shade, when people drove up the lane or when kids played out there. The lane looked so empty—someone could come at any time.

They were still looking through the box. They had found some old pictures, in frames, but didn't bother with them. "This one's sort of cute," Donna said indifferently. Brown-tinted, stiffly posed, a young couple with a baby—the man standing behind the woman, who sat on a straight-back chair, in a garden, holding an infant thickly wrapped in a long flowing white shawl. The man and the woman were young, very young, but the picture itself looked so old—their clothes were so old-fashioned—and it was strange, the stiffness of the pose, the dining-room chair out in a garden, the baby nearly lost in its blanket. I didn't want to look at it. I was very nervous; I started to giggle, though nothing was funny; I knew something bad might happen. Albert told me to shut up. His face was pale, so that his red-blond hair looked too bright. The way his mouth moved, the lips twitching while the teeth stayed clenched, was something I had never seen before.

"Go look through that bureau, get busy. We haven't got all day."

I giggled. Then I stopped giggling. "I want to go home," I whispered.

"You heard me, get busy."

"I want to go home.... I'm going home...."

"You wait for us!" Donna said sharply.

Her voice was louder than Albert's, so loud it frightened us all.

I went to the bureau. It was a big piece of furniture, made o
dark wood, not bright and polished like some of our furniture a
home. On top was a soiled white cloth and the hairbrush an
mirror and a few loose hairpins. They were the same kind m
grandmother wore, made of thin wire, U-shaped, not the kind o
pins my mother and sisters used. The bureau had carve
drawers, but the designs were grimy—you couldn't tell wha
they were meant to be—and one of the cut-glass knobs wa
missing I could see that the top drawer was filled with women'
things, like my grandmother's underwear. I didn't want to loo
through it. I was afraid to look through it. So I eased the drawe
shut, and Donna and Albert didn't notice. In the next drawe
were linens. Pillowcases. They had yellowed, but the em
broidered flowers and leaves on them were still white, smoot
like satin or silk. I ran my thumb over them—it was strange to fee
how smooth and clean they were.

A drop of water fell on the top pillowcase—it must have bee
sweat from my forehead. I wasn't crying.

I closed that drawer because there was nothing in it. I didn'
need to look. The bottom drawer was jammed with woollens,
couldn't tell if they were large things like afghans or quilts, o
shawls or sweaters. They were mostly dull colors—brown, olive
green, black. It was a shame, how the moths had gotten them.
poked around in the bottom of the drawer and felt something
hard. It was a book—a religious book—in a foreign language. It
must have been in German. There were tiny gold crosses on the
cover; the pages were very thin, almost transparent; in front there
was a picture of Christ with a halo around his head and his heart
flaming on the outside of his body. In back— In back there was
money, slipped in sideways.

The bills were new, not like the dollar bills I was used to
seeing, all wrinkled and dirty. These were stiff, they smelled
new, though the other things in the drawer smelled so musty. I
saw the numbers on the bills and my eyesight seemed to come
and go, I blinked to get the sweat out of my eyes, I started to
giggle and then stopped. I looked up, but there was nothing to
see. The shade was drawn. Around the edges of the shade the
sunlight was very bright, but I couldn't see out the window.

"What's this?" Albert was saying to Donna. "Can you read
this?"

"...goddam junk."

"What kind of stamps are these? A picture of a boat...."

I couldn't make my eyes stay right. When I looked back at
Albert and Donna, they were wavy, wobbly; they didn't seem
like anyone I knew. They were squatting over the box, pawing
through the things, panting, acting as if they were angry about
something. They seemed to shift in and out of focus.... I felt very
strange, the way I sometimes felt when I was alone, hiding, away
from everyone else. I could see them, but they couldn't see me.
Even when Donna glanced up to look at me, I felt that way.

"You done looking through that drawer...? Didn't you find
anything either?"

I told her no. I closed the drawer, I told her no.

"Damn stupid waste of time, look, my hands are all dirty, I
told you Mrs. Mueller wouldn't have anything...."

"You did not: it was your idea."

"It wasn't! I said right away—what if we got caught? What if
he came home?"

"You wanted to look around, you're always nosy. Probably
stole something when nobody was looking...."

"I did not!...Didn't want any of her old junk."

They were still excited. Their voices were low and sharp at the
same time; they didn't pay any attention to me.

"It's just as well...." Donna said.

"She might have walked in the door and had a gun or
something, she might have killed us. She's crazy. She could do
anything.... It was your idea first of all."

"I hope she doesn't figure out that somebody was in there. She
might call the police and there'd be hell to pay and.... It really
stunk in there, didn't it?"

They giggled nervously.

They looked at me.

"...not going to tell, are you?"

I shook my head *no*.

"She won't tell," Donna said. "She isn't a tattle-tale."

"She hadn't better tell," Albert said.

"Oh leave her alone!...You aren't going to tell, are you?
Anyway, nothing happened. We didn't find anything and there's
nothing to tell."

They started running through the marsh. I let them run away, I
fell behind, my face was burning and my eyes were sore and
strange, as if I had been awake for a long time. I was very happy.
I didn't know why: I was tired, I wanted to crawl on my mother's

lap, I wanted to sleep or cry or. . . . I didn't know what I wanted or why I felt so happy.

They were by the creek bank now and their voices were too faint for me to hear. Suddenly I didn't care about them, I wasn't afraid of them, nothing would happen to me, nothing bad: their voices were so faint now that I hardly knew whose voices they were.

Daisy

Daisy,
> Daisy,
> Give us your answer, sweet!
> We're half-crazy
> Wondering what you'll eat....

Purse-lipped, she would not speak to the young waiter but pointed at the items on the menu, one two three. And to drink? Tea, coffee—? No. Nothing. Milk? No. Nothing.

"The June bugs have arrived, not quite on schedule," he announced. "It's July. Shall we send them back, Daisy?"

She laughed. She snickered.

"Those bugs aren't going to listen to *you*," she said.

Defiant. But shivering. She was frightened of certain insects and so it was best to speak openly of them, to jest, to ridicule. Where laughter prevailed, he thought, there shall terror quaver and die.

"Ah but maybe they will," he said lightly. "I know their secret name—*Phyllophaga. Phylloflyofleeophagohgaga!*—An ancient curse."

She laughed in delight. She was his girl, his sweetheart, his pet, his nuisance, his little one, his angel, his wanton, his scrabble-dabble, his kitten, his flibbertigibbet of old. And a genius. No

193

small part of the riddle that she was a genius.

When they walked out along the sprinkled graveled path, between the banks of flowers, it was noted by all how attentive he was to her, how courtly; and wouldn't she try your patience, that one? When they walked above the sea cliff, fast-paced, never minding the strident northeast wind, it was noted how frequently he glanced at her in amazement, as if she uttered remarkable things and then turned defiantly and mischievously away. Her dark eyes gleamed. Glowed. Glittered. She was a hobgoblin, a fairy. At the age of four she had been the loveliest of the fairies in a production of *Midsummer Night's Dream*, staged by friends of her father's in Majorca, summer friends, a summer fantasy, the raising of funds for a cause now forgotten. She walked with her weight thrust forward, on the balls of her feet, as if ready to run or even to fly—to spring in the air. Once out of the sight of the hotel, she often ran. And circled back to him. And ran ahead again, teasing for him to join her. "Old scarecrow! Old bag of bones! You're just pretending you can't run because you're *lazy*."

"I own that I am lazy, bone-aching lazy," he sighed.

Often he fumbled in his pocket for the small black notebook he carried everywhere. And paused to record, in his tiny near-microscopic hand, certain treasures that skittered into his mind. It might be a word of Daisy's or a phrase evoked by her or a sudden explosive memory that came from nowhere, though probably he could trace it—as he often did when he was in that mood—back to Daisy. He wrote in abbreviations, almost in code. Perhaps he did write in code. He was fairly certain that no one could break that code, for it changed from day to day and sometimes even from hour to hour. Music, it was, the act of memory and of recording memory a kind of music, enigmatic and fluid.

"Father, what did I say?" Daisy sometimes asked. She would peer at him with her head held back, eyes half closed, so that she could look at him across her cheekbones. She was haughty. But a little anxious. Lovely girl with dark, dark eyes and windblown dark hair, a thick brush of hair she feared the spiders might someday seize for a home if she wasn't vigilant. "What did I say? It was something that surprised you, wasn't it, something you will put in a poem, wasn't it, something you'll boast about when people come to visit you, wasn't it? And you'll tell them about me, won't you?"

It made him uncomfortable when anyone watched him write. Even she. He would close the little notebook and slip it back in his pocket as negligently as if it were a crumpled handkerchief.

"I always tell them about you," he said.

He carried an umbrella. Never bothered to open it—had it ever been unsnapped? Used it as a cane sometimes. The steep path, the wind, the frequent euphoria of these walks, and the nearly as frequent jumps of his heart when he sensed danger: exhausting. But a cane would have embarrassed them both.

His little girl did not mind if they were caught in the rain. She would sometimes raise her arms, sometimes hold her face up and her tongue far out, to receive the raindrops. Like a communicant, he realized. And his eyes misted over with love.

"I always tell them about you," he murmured.

Tall and scarecrow-thin, he was; but did not mind. Did not pay much attention to his appearance. Which was ironic, people had noted, since he paid such scrupulous attention to the appearance of others and of things . . . to a universe of detail, beautiful clamorous inexhaustible detail. He was in love with surfaces, he claimed. Meaning by surfaces everything there was: layer upon layer upon layer. But his own physical existence did not interest him. It was a means, a medium. A vehicle. At times a burden: because he could not trust it. Suddenly tired, so bone-weary he believed himself on the brink of utter extinction, he would laugh nervously and berate himself for being lazy or "out of condition." No, the physical being was untrustworthy, an inferior Siamese twin stuck to the soul, a clownish Doppelgänger one could not—unfortunately—do without. He clothed this creature in matching trousers and vests and coats, he shod its bunion-prone feet in custom-made shoes that soon became muddy and scuffed, he jammed a shapeless hat upon its head, and sometimes added fey decorative touches: an ascot tie of flamboyant purple, a marigold in his buttonhole, one or two or even three of his famous big rings. For the past several years he had worn a copper bracelet to ward off the evil spirits that bring rheumatism, and it gave to his bony wrist a certain dash he rather liked.

Daisy dressed carefully. Not quite with style but with care, elaborate care. It had begun as a game between them, years ago, that she would have to ask her father permission for various things, and have to stand inspection by him before going out; gradually it had become a ritual and though Bonham did not care what the girl wore, so long as it was decent and appropriate to the season, he was unable to extricate himself from the ritual without upsetting her. He had tried, he had tried. God knows. *He* knew. But once imprinted in Daisy's imagination, the clothing-inspection ritual, like a number of other rituals, had become a permanent feature of their life together.

"Do I look all right, Father?" she would ask anxiously. "Are the colors right? They aren't too daring, are they? You won't be ashamed of me, will you? Is the blouse too big? Are the trousers baggy? Will people laugh? Will *you* laugh?"

"If you don't laugh at me, I vow not to laugh at you," he said gravely.

And they smiled happily at each other, in perfect understanding.

For their hikes out along the sea cliff Daisy wore sports clothes, attractive outfits that were nevertheless sturdy, so that she would not be hurt by briars or thorns, or if she happened to fall on the path. Bonham liked her dusky-rose slacks, though they were rather loose on her, and the caftanlike beige top she usually wore with them; he did not at all like a certain pair of trousers that were black and shiny with age and comically baggy, which Daisy would have worn most of the time if he hadn't expressed disapproval. On her feet were tennis shoes, once white but now dark with age. They were the most practical shoes for these walks because, from time to time, Daisy felt the compulsion to scramble down the bank to the water and wade out in it. Like Bonham she wore a hat, but her hat, unlike his, was wide-brimmed and tied beneath the chin, a pretty maidenish sun hat to protect her delicate complexion: she had two, one of a gauzelike white with a bright yellow ribbon band, and the other of new, greenish straw with a white band. When she ran, the hat would slip off and bounce behind her head, secured by the tie around her neck. One morning Bonham, watching her, had the involuntary and really quite silly vision of a girl running with part of her head fallen back, into two pieces. He had not liked the idea but, dutifully, religiously, had noted it in his little book. It had eventually found its way into one of his poems.

Father and daughter both favored rings. All her rings were gifts from him, and she wore them in rotation, except for the antique ring on her left hand that had belonged to his mother. It was not so precious as it looked—in fact, Bonham had pawned it in one of the squalid epochs of his earlier life, quite astonished at

how little money he had been able to get for it—but it was very
beautiful. Small diamonds arranged around an oval amethyst, in
a setting of gold. It was her special ring, her sacred ring. It could
never, never be taken off. Not even to be cleaned. Not even for a
moment! No! If he had commanded her to take it off, he
supposed she would have done so, but he could not bear to use
his power so arbitrarily and so cruelly; and the gesture would
have been futile anyway.

"What if a thief comes into my room and takes the ring while
I'm asleep?" Daisy asked. "What if he slips it off my finger?"

"That won't happen, dear. You know it won't happen."

"But what if it *does*? There was a burglary in town the other
day, I read about it, I read about it in the newspaper. Thieves like
hotels. Don't they? You know they do!"

Bonham whistled and shrugged his shoulders languidly.

"That time in Istanbul thieves got into Uncle Eli's room, didn't
they? They took something of his, didn't they? So they could get
into our ugly old hotel—they could get in anywhere—*and take
whatever they want.*"

"Sweet my girl," Bonham said, showing not a quiver of the
surprise he felt that Daisy should remember an event that had
happened so long ago, and which was nearly forgotten by
everyone concerned, "it just isn't going to happen. I have spoken.
V*oilà*."

"Do you *know* it isn't going to happen?"

It was a serious question. She squinted at him, her expression
childlike with interest.

"Do I *know* . . . ? Well, dear, am I omnipotent? Am I God? Am
I the author of creation? Not quite. Not *quite*. You'll grant me a
little marginal humanity, a little leeway to err now and then?
Daisy, please! Don't look so anxious. You know very well no one
can get into your room once you've locked it from inside."

"People do, though," she said.

"But they're dreams."

She shrugged her shoulders in imitation of him.

"They're only dreams," he said, still smiling.

But the anxiety in her eyes was fading, as if she had simply
forgotten it. That often happened when he distracted her or
when he spoke in his light, bantering, rather musical voice, and
reached out to tap her beneath the chin.

She whirled and ran, and the straw hat was blown from her
head and fluttered at the nape of her neck. Wind! Sunshine! The

wild gray Atlantic! Rocks thistles clouds gulls waist-high weeds with tiny blue flowers and behind her Father musing, staring, brooding. Poor Father! She knew his fear. She knew his dread. That she might fall and hurt herself or suddenly feel the need to wade in the surf, and what if the bank was too steep for her to clamber down? Daisy might be hurt—might be very, very badly hurt.

One terrible night he had wept, had wept. Had wiped at his nose with his fingers. Francis Bonham! Bonham himself! He who quivered at bad manners, who could not bear Daisy to sniffle in his earshot—he had wiped at his nose with his fingers. Daisy had seen and had wanted to giggle. So funny! Shivering fearful broken whisky-smelling Father, wordless for once as he wept, not even noticing—he with his keen cruel eye—the uniformed people exchanging glances. Ah hah, they were thinking, *Ah hah*. He crouched above her and wept that she was his life, his soul, his dear one, his most precious girl, his only baby, and she must never never do this again—never—*never*—otherwise he would be destroyed and they would take her away and she would be theirs.

She did not giggle. There was nothing funny. She saw the others approaching. She saw her father's blue eyes washed pale with tears. What had happened? Did she remember? No. Yes. There was a movie and people had been screaming. Ugly, ugly. Someone caught in quicksand. Sucked down. Screaming. In the movie there was screaming and in the theater there was screaming and Daisy had tried to get away but was fixed to her seat. So there was nothing to do but scream and scream and scream.

But maybe she had mixed that with something else. Or maybe she had dreamed it. Or painted it. Or one of those nasty children had told her about it, to confuse her. Only her father knew what was real and what was error.

"You won't ever do this again, Daisy? Won't ever run away again?"

She shook her head, mute. Why did he ask her when he already knew? He knew what she would do, and what would be done to her, so why did he pretend not to know—why did he pretend to be so frightened?

"We'd love to see you, of course," he said, "but at the moment we're still not quite settled into a routine. The trouble in March, you know. . . . No, no, she's nearly recovered now. She's made quite a comeback. Back to her drawing again, even a few paintings, though nothing too ambitious. Has to guard against excitement. . . . Yes, like her father; yes. That's right. I've always said that, since the start, haven't I?—she's no different from me. Our temperaments are identical. If anything, Daisy is more sensitive, possibly more original. . . . Yes, we'd love to see you, but maybe Christmas would be the best time. Christmas. That isn't too distant, really. You see, for one thing, I've had some difficulty getting back to work. I *work*, yes, I labor away, my usual eight hours, but I'm not at all satisfied with the results. Another problem is your girls. Daisy loves them, of course, she feels very close to her cousins, but at the same time she's a little . . . she's a little uneasy in their presence. I think; a little jealous. It's quite natural. Her life has been so eccentric and theirs have been so beautifully, formidably *normal*; and too much conversation, too much stimulation, you know how it excites her and she's back on the pill routine again, which is repulsive to me. . . . Yes, we're fine, really. Our move to this hotel was a good idea, in spite of the cost. . . . The strangest thing, today on our walk Daisy began speaking of you, of that theft in your hotel room in Istanbul, so many years ago—isn't that odd?—it must have been in connection with your call tonight . . . she must have sensed you were going to call. Really. Really! It's more than just a coincidence, obviously. With Daisy these odd little things happen constantly. We make light of them, she and I, it's best to skim the surface of such things, otherwise one grows frightened. . . . For instance, she has an astonishing memory. It seems to be growing sharper. The other evening at dinner we could hear a string quartet in another part of the hotel, where there was a wedding party, and Daisy suddenly began telling me how vividly she could remember the little pieces I had played on the violin for her, when she was in her crib . . . only an infant, think of it! . . . in her crib. So long ago. I used to entertain her and her mother, just nonsense tunes, nursery tunes . . . and now, three decades later, my daughter claims she can remember. . . . And there have been even more remarkable things, Eli, almost unbelievable things. . . ." But he was speaking rapidly. Too rapidly. He stood in his shabby dressing gown by a mirror, turned away from his reflection so that he need not look at himself. At the same time, he was conscious of himself twinned in the mirror, the telephone receiver clutched tightly in his left hand. He forced himself to speak in a more normal voice. "Of course I'll make all the arrangements, Eli, and you and Florence and the girls will be my guests for Christmas. . . . No, please. Don't argue. Please. I'm not that seriously in debt, don't believe the rumors, and in any case I'm your elder brother and your host and I insist, I *insist*. We'll have a fine Christmas. By then Daisy should be settled down and I should, I fully expect, have my interminable poem finished and ready for publication. Yes. . . . Yes. Of course I'm telling the truth: Daisy and I are both in excellent health."

"Did you dream, Daisy?"

"Did I dream? He wants to know did I dream. . . . Yes, I did but I won't tell you," she says smugly.

Arm in arm along the corridor. Soft muffling rugs. Hands that emerge from the pale wallpaper, lace at cuffs, holding aloft torches that are really electric lights with small salmon-colored shades. So silly. Silly. The elevator is too dangerous so they take the stairs. Seven flights. Daisy's dark bright-gleaming bush of hair has been tied back from her face with a velvet ribbon. She is pretty. Her complexion is almost clear again. She is sprightly. Sly. She is the Day's Eye. The Night's Eye as well. She sleeps, but her eyes are open all night, stony and merciless. The night air burns her eyes. The ceiling is crowded with lights. People appear—sometimes her mother appears—and instruct her; hour after hour she stares at them, unable to look away. They show her what to draw. They take her hand and guide it through the secret patterns so that, in the morning, she can repeat these patterns. Father never appears; that is because he controls everything. He is the author. He controls the night and he controls the day. Only lesser beings appear at his bidding.

"The telephone rang last night in your study," Daisy says. "Was it Uncle Eli?"

"No, Not at all," Bonham says. "It was no one important."

"It wasn't Uncle Eli?" she asks, squinting at him.

"A young man who had gotten my number from an editor, an arrogant little soul, wanting to come up here for an interview—no one important, as I said. No, it wasn't your uncle."

Daisy smiles. Daisy is relieved. Daisy thinks it didn't happen that time.

At the age of three Daisy Bonham had drawn a remarkably detailed picture of hundreds of butterflies. Her first poem accompanied it, as a caption: *The Butterflies lick Butter from the Buttercups*. The words were childlike, but the drawing had not seemed childlike. The butterflies were not laboriously drawn, as a child might draw them, but were mere sketches, thin and insubstantial, as if in motion; they were a cloud narrow at one end and swollen at the other, and there had been something disturbing about them. When she was finished with the drawing, Daisy had no interest in it, not even any pride; she told her mother it was Daddy's—it belonged to him.

She recited his poetry. She made up little melodies and accompanied herself on the piano, singing his words. Friends and visitors were amazed, charmed. They were eager to praise her. They noted how Francis Bonham stared at her, his expression rapt, his customary restlessness gone. He loved her, did he?—loved her. Doted on her. An artist-friend painted their portrait together. A fellow poet, once close to Bonham and then banished, inexplicably, sought to regain Bonham's favor by writing a dense little lyric about the two of them. Bonham's wife retained her position in his household for years simply because she was the mother of his daughter and he was absurdly and sentimentally grateful; had she not chosen to leave, he would never have expelled her—it would have been impossible. Even after their quarrels. Even after their celebrated fights.

But that lovely little girl! How was it possible, Bonham asked everyone, that *he* had fathered so exquisite a child?

She had a private tutor. He refused to send her to school, even to a private school. What did it matter, the expense? The debts? People came along and helped him out, people were always appearing to help him out, magically, as if by an act of his will. He might be destitute—the three of them literally hungry—but someone came along, or a grant or an award came through, and all was well. Money spent on Daisy did not really count to Bonham, just as money spent on drinking or restaurants or house-guests or books did not really count; he never considered himself extravagant and was always rather hurt when people criticized him for certain expenses. Daisy loved costumes, loved to put on little shows, dancing and singing and acting in dramas she had written; her mother took her to theatrical supply shops and old clothes shops in New York, to outfit her, and sometimes

Bonham himself accompanied them. What did the expense matter? It did not matter at all.

At the age of six Daisy put on a puppet show for the children of Bonham's friends and for children in the apartment building they were living in, having made the puppets herself, and the puppets' costumes, and the small portable stage. She did the voices beautifully, with an almost eerie, adult precision. Afterward one of Bonham's friends told him that his daughter was the most precocious, gifted child he had ever encountered—and that she would go beyond Bonham himself. He had been delighted. He had been wonderfully moved. It annoyed him that the other children could not appreciate her and that she hadn't any friends her own age—but that was to be expected, after all. Other children were so clearly her inferiors. Bonham, as a boy, had been very much alone, usually in frail health, and he had had few friends. It was the burden of a certain sort of genius, the genius that develops early, flooding the child personality with another, more complex, less easily accommodated personality. But where Bonham had been lonely, his daughter did not seem to be lonely at all. Throughout her childhood she expressed quite emphatically her preference for the company of adults rather than children; she mocked other children, imitated their voices and behavior and silly little repetitive routines. She provoked quarrels, even provoked fights. And she never cried, not even if her hair was pulled or her face slapped. She glared at her small enemies, flushed and victorious. "I despise you," she sometimes shouted. If their parents were friends of the Bonhams, it was necessary for them to apologize, explaining always that Daisy was high-strung and sensitive; if the children were insignificant, or the children of people Bonham disliked, he often winked at Daisy and gave her the old Roman sign of approval.

Ah, the secrets between them! The pantomimes, the parodies, the burlesques of fools they knew; the ingenious mimicry of affectations, mannerisms, voices, patterns of speech. Years later, when the first of Daisy's troubles began, a psychiatrist suggested that he had spent too much time with her. But that struck Bonham as preposterous. The children of many of his friends and acquaintances had been miserable because their fathers had neglected them, or had moved out of their households altogether; he, Bonham, had made every effort to be an attentive, loving father. He had been enchanted by her drawings and paintings more than by anything else, for it seemed to him that in these she was not merely talented, but genuinely gifted; hadn't it been wise of him, as her father, to recognize her genius and to encourage it? His wife had been enthusiastic as well, but her praise had often seemed forced and unconvincing, and, as her drinking increased, the quarrels between mother and daughter increased, and Daisy was all the more dependent upon her father. And he had not really spent that much time with her, not in actual hours. Most of his life was his poetry. He worked alone, in absolute sacred solitude, and no one—not even Daisy—ever dared to disturb him.

"She's like me. She has a temper," he said.

After her mother's death Daisy's tantrums became more protracted, and more physical. She smashed things. She tore at one of her most beautiful paintings—an intricately detailed forest of leaves and animals' eyes and feathers and what might have been human organs—with a scissors in one hand and a kitchen knife in the other. She could no longer work with clay—the feel of the clay seemed to enrage her. Bonham had taken his wife's death hard, though they had been separated for years. He had had a kind of breakdown, in spite of his resolution to remain completely calm, and it was thought that his mourning for his wife infuriated Daisy. "*Him?* That idiot?" she would say over the telephone if someone called to ask after her father. "*He's* playing games."

In her fourteenth year she often refused to eat, to bathe, to undress for bed, to leave the house even on special outings Bonham arranged for her to theaters and museums. It was clear to him that she wasn't sick but merely stubborn. "I won't. I won't," she said, her voice inflectionless. Even when she refused to speak and lay there unmoving in her rumpled, dirty bed, arms and legs rigid, eyes stony-cold, it seemed to Bonham that her soul cried out *I won't.*

Stubborn, she was. And capricious. And sly. Pretending to be in a heavy, unstirring sleep, she would nevertheless be aware of his every movement, and if he left the apartment—if he met friends at a tavern nearby, or simply went out for a night walk—she was waiting for him when he returned, angry and babbling. At such times she often destroyed work of her own or ripped her clothing. Her senses were so keen, she could even hear him dial the telephone in his study, though she was rooms away. She accused him of meeting with her mother, of making plans to go away and leave her. She accused him of listening to her thoughts. She accused him of not loving her.

Bonham drank, forgot to eat, couldn't afford a housekeeper, so the apartment grew shabby and filthy. He quarreled with his family, who offered unwanted advice. He emptied a glass of wine into his brother's face and ordered him out—out of the apartment and out of his life. His friends knew enough to stay away. He had no friends. They were all opportunists, all out to betray him. They were delighted that he was finished as a poet: he could imagine their jubilant conversations about him. The sons of bitches! But he knew they were right, he knew he was finished. For nearly two years he didn't write a single good line.

Instead, his energies went into coaxing Daisy out of bed, or encouraging her to eat, or to take a bath. He composed rollicking little songs and limericks in her honor, some of which remained in his repertoire permanently, sung to Daisy at appropriate times. She wasn't ill, only stubborn. And hot-tempered. If he could make her laugh, she usually gave in, seemed to melt, suddenly tractable and sweet as a little girl.

The psychiatrists and psychotherapists enraged him with their jargon, their fixed imaginations, their relatively unexceptional minds. It astounded him to realize that these people were—quite ordinary. Some of them were personally charming and could no doubt help troubled people simply by seeming to know what they were doing, but Daisy was too sharp for them; afterward she mimicked them savagely. And there were the magical therapies, seized hopefully and then rejected, one by one: bio-energetics, the Alexander technique, music therapy, light-and-color therapy, eurythmy, massage, desensitization, hypnosis, a high-protein diet, a low-protein diet, a vegetarian diet, a diet of fruits and grain, a diet that required the drinking of ten glasses of water daily. Exercises. Regulated breathing. A form of meditation taught by a disciple of Krishnamurti.

"She isn't ill," Bonham said sullenly. "No more than I am ill. No more than any exceptional human being is ill."

She was the only person he trusted. He spoke to her of the books he wanted to write—read aloud to her from journals and notebooks, or from old crumbling books he delighted in, for their sheer irrelevance to his own life. His first book of poems had celebrated the austere madness of Cotton Mather; it had contained an ingenious five-hundred-line journey to Hades, praised by some critics as one of the most remarkable things ever

written by an American. His second book had been a free
improvisation on the theme of *succubi*, with a long, gorgeous,
highly allusive passage about Saint Anthony in the desert. His
third book would not write itself—would not emerge. One
evening, reading animatedly to Daisy from an old, eccentric
book on Egyptian mythology by Sir Gaston Camille Charles
Maspero, he had happened to glance up—saw a curious
half-smile on his daughter's face, and a glassy, utterly entranced
look to her eyes—and it struck him, with the ease of a knife-blade
slipping into his heart, that his subject was there: was Daisy
herself.

Many years later she fixes the napkin about her left hand, as if
it were a skirt, and walks two fingers comically across the table
toward him.

"Silly," he murmurs.

"How small it's all! How cruel, you fool! How silly, you dilly!"

"Daisy, hush."

"*You* hush. You're the one."

Sunday brunch. Leisurely lazy luxurious Sunday. The terrace
a little crowded but pleasant, sunny, warm. Daisy's eyes sparkle.
Daisy's tempo is faster than his. He hopes she won't suggest a
walk along the sea-cliff until he feels better. Slight indigestion—
mild hangover—a headache concentrated in the area above his
left eye. He never tells her when he's unwell because it alarms
and excites her to a peculiar scoffing amusement. "Hugger-
mugger!" she will say, shaking her forefinger, as if he were a
naughty deceiving child.

Day's Eye, his Daisy. His girl. His Princess. His Eye of Night
as well.

"Mother was bothering me last night," she says suddenly.

"Oh? Yes?"

His interest is so quick and unguarded that she naturally turns
aside, smiling smugly. He knows better—should have replied in a
light bantering tone if he really wanted to explore the
subject—but she caught him napping.

"You don't want to walk, do you?" she says flatly, accusingly.
"You just want to sit here."

"It's lovely here, isn't it? You said you liked it out on the
terrace. Why don't you sketch something, Daisy? Sit in the sun
and relax. . . . Daisy? Why are you frowning? That's better. That's
a good sweetling. *For looks kill love and love by looks reviveth.*"

She is wearing his mother's dainty ring on her left hand and a large, ungainly, "good luck" ring of inexpensive garnet on her right hand. He sees it is too large for her finger—she has put a turn or two of adhesive tape through it. Because it is Sunday he is wearing the ring of hammered gold that is his own good-luck charm—for certain occasions at least—which he bought one day many years ago in another seaside town. That day there had come to him, almost perfectly arranged, line after line of one of his poems; the one about Hermes, Mercurius, he of the prankish double nature. One of his forms is a lion and, by chance, Bonham happened upon a ring with a lion's head on it, rather nicely done. He bought it without hesitation, though he had only enough money in his pockets for a down payment and had to borrow the rest.

"What did your mother have to say?" he asks lightly.

But she snubs him. She is sketching in the sketchbook, frowning, completely absorbed. A droplet of saliva in the corner of her mouth. She is his girl, his baby, and so it sometimes startles him to see that she is no longer young—no longer girlish. A woman of thirty-six. Slight coarsening of her features, around the mouth especially. But charming. Charming. Thank God the skin eruptions are nearly gone. He wishes she would not frown so, as if she were in agony, but he knows better than to scold.

Sometimes she draws her dream-visions and they are elaborate, knotty things, curlicues like thought itself, hopelessly snarled. Sometimes she draws faces, strangers' faces. Sometimes she draws stark, mysterious designs. Bonham feels he can almost interpret them. But in the end he cannot—he merely stares at them, feeling the prick of excitement, of wonder. He knows he is in the presence of something remarkable, but he does not know what it is. Must be careful. Very careful. As if in a god's presence, must give no sign of being moved by an emotion.

It occasionally happens that Daisy cannot get the drawing right. This morning she is having trouble. Again and again she draws a small, fairly simple design, stares at it, then crosses it out violently or turns the page of the sketchbook. She is becoming overheated. He wishes she would sketch their surroundings—the clouds, which she does so beautifully, or the other diners, whom she can render in realistic or in parodistic tones. Sometimes the two of them play a game. Bonham, who can draw with a fine amateur flair, will begin a caricature, and Daisy will finish it, laughing excitedly. Over the years they have drawn wicked caricatures of everyone they know and of many strangers who happen to be in the vicinity. The other day, at this very table, they immortalized the pathetic obese women with the Southern accent, who often sits as long as they do at breakfast, sipping coffee thick with sugar; they have immortalized most of the waiters, the hotel manager, the black wide-hipped woman who cleans their suite; a few of the more obnoxious children staying at the hotel; Bonham's editor and long-suffering champion, named Stanton, a man with a horse's face and morose droopy eyes; and Bonham's brother Eli and his smiley gat-toothed wife Florence—Eli as a befuddled pelican, his wife as a pig with plump cheeks and lots of lipstick. Gay as children they have done hundreds of these drawings and saved each one. It chills Bonham, however, to see how quickly—almost instantaneously—Daisy guesses whom he is caricaturing. Sometimes he draws no more than one or two lines before she snatches the sketchbook away. And she is never wrong: never.

"Don't push yourself, Daisy," he says uneasily. So far as he can see, she is drawing utterly simple designs, hardly more than lines and circles. Yet none is quite right. She crosses it out and begins again, her lips pressed tight together. At the next table a woman is eying her, a bitch with a crusty made-up face, and Bonham begins to tremble with irritation. "We could go for a walk now if you'd rather...."

As she draws she mutters half-audibly. Then purses her lips shut. Then mutters again, as if the words come unbidden from her, without her consent. "Always. Allggoes. Butterfly. But/Or Fly. Draggingfly. Firefly. Jewelfly. Diamond Eye. Day's Eye. Ose Eoseye. Eee eee eee. Earth's Eee. June bug. June flood. June mud. Bud. Bed. Slug. Sweet."

Bonham's head trembles on his thin stalk of a neck. He remembers—remembers— Suddenly he remembers— Himself a young man, joyous with love, teasing his bride on a sunny lost morning because she slept late and he had been up for hours, prowling about some long-forgotten street, impatient for her, teasing her with these lines of Herrick's, which he knew by heart:

> Get up, get up for shame! The blooming morn
> Upon her wings presents the god unshorn.
> See how Aurora throws her fair,
> Fresh-quilted flowers through the air.

> *Get up, sweet slug-a-bed, and see*
> *The dew bespangling herb and tree!*

But of course, Bonham thinks carefully, the memory is only an accident. It has nothing to do with Daisy or with her frantic drawings.

Something terrible had happened once. And he was to blame.

Without telling Daisy he had slipped from the apartment—they had lived in New York at the time—and gone to a ceremonial dinner in his honor. Bonham scorned such awards, and certainly scorned the people who presumed to hand them out to their betters; but this particular award carried with it an extraordinary prize—fifteen thousand dollars. He had not wanted to take Daisy with him. So he had gone, had told her he would be in his study all evening, and since his study was the one room she never entered, out of a superstitious awe he had done his best to evoke, he had presumed he would be safe. But of course she sensed his absence, sensed fraud.

She ran out into the winter street. Coatless, with thin bedroom slippers on her feet, unwashed hair wild about her face. Ran on the icy pavement. Darted through traffic. Eluded people who tried to stop her. Babbling, weeping angrily. His daughter! His dear one! She had run and run like a maddened animal and a patrolman chased her and another joined him and people on the sidewalk stared and smirked and giggled and she tried to hide in an alley, a filthy alley, whimpering, crouched behind garbage cans, hugging herself and rocking from side to side. It took both policemen and another man to subdue her. "I'm going to punish you!" she screamed. "I'm going to slay you all! You'll see! Give me one hundred years! I'll slay you—I can't be stopped—I am the greatest genius of the century—"

Bonham was forced to commit her to a hospital. They had not allowed him to take her back home.

"She isn't crazy," he protested. Nevertheless they forced him to commit her. In his weakened state he signed a certain paper. And, in the hospital, where he could not watch over her, they did terrible things.

Pills and injections. Electro-convulsive treatment. Solitary confinement. Torture. By the time of Bonham's first visit the powerful drugs had dulled her eyes, thickened her speech, caused her delicate skin to break out in ugly boil-like eruptions.

Of course he had not known at once what was wrong. Gradually she grew worse: double vision, constant headaches, nausea. When she reported her symptoms, the staff retaliated by subjecting her to a series of brutal tests, including a spinal tap which was evidently poorly administered by a young resident. For several days she was partly paralyzed. He was going to sue them, was in the process of suing them, the bastards, the crude ignorant sadistic incompetent bastards! He would avenge himself and his daughter, he would punish them if it took every penny of his and all his energy. How she had suffered, and for what crime? Seeing her, he had burst into tears and demanded that she be released in his custody at once. No more of this!—no more. "From this day forward," he had shouted at them, "let everyone be free of pain! Let there be no more agony inflicted on human beings by human beings—do you hear? Do you hear? I'll make you hear!"

So he had taken her from the hospital in New York City to a small rented frame house in Springfield, Massachusetts, aspiring to an absolute anonymity, an obliteration of *Bonham* in any public sense; from there they had moved to the enormous estate of an acquaintance, who provided them with a handsome guest cottage and fine, private meals, near Lake Placid, New York; and from there to Cambridge, Massachusetts, to an apartment sublet by an old friend. Under threat of imprisonment and torture Daisy maintained a remarkably alert and responsible sanity, edged with cynicism, and Bonham believed she had never been more lucid in her life—capable of lengthy, sustained conversations, devoted to his work and to her "play," as she called her art, and rarely compulsive or manic. He took her to the seashore. He took her to a small resort town in northern Massachusetts, a once-fashionable watering place, and there they rented by the month a suite with a balcony in an old, attractive hotel with Gothic pretensions. There they were happy. Are happy. "The sea," Bonham says, "is a place for the birth of visions. Thus Venus rises from the sea: the Eternal Feminine rising in a man's carnal mind. Thus the eagle in *Esdras* rises from the sea, and the vision of Man himself comes up 'from the midst of the sea.' And so we are here, at the edge of the great American continent, looking out."

Daisy has failed to reproduce the design. She lays down her pencil carefully on the table; she does not throw it down. She allows her father to take the sketchbook from her. In the old days she would have ripped its pages but now she surrenders it sullenly.

As he examines the torturous, inconclusive, and seemingly inconsequential marks on the paper, his girl mutters, "Nought. Rien. Zed. Zed. Zed." She begins to mimic his voice, fluttering all ten fingers in what must be a parody of his paternal concern. "*She isn't ill but in the process of discovering the fount of creativity! She isn't sick, she's a genius! The world isn't yet ready for her! Not crazy, our Daisy! Not—*"

"Hush," Bonham says. "People are listening. You and I are not public entertainers."

"Passencore," says Daisy. "...My life, Mother says, was invisible. That's why she clutches at me in the night. She. She wants to be born again, she says. This time she would escape you, she says, she would live and live and live and live."

Bonham forces himself to continue examining the little drawings. He does not dare show his daughter the sick apprehension he feels, nor does he dare ask her what she means. Her mother? In the night? The dead come back to suck at the vitality of the living? Wishing to be born again? But of course it is nonsense: an ugly dream merely. Very ugly. In life he had easily won the struggle between himself and his wife for the rare Daisy, he had scarcely thought of it as a struggle, his opponent was so readily flummoxed and dismissed.

Daisy is singing under her breath in a gross guttural mockery of Bonham: "*Not crazy over Daisy, not ill our Jill, not dross our ghost, not Daisy our lazy....Gentlemen I forbid you to touch her! Nay, not a hair on her head! Nay, not even a tick on her scalp! She isn't ill, gentlemen, no more than I am ill....* Oh, I hate her! I hate her. She crawls under the covers with me and whispers in my ear. Wants to turn me against you. Tear up his little notebook, she says. Snatch his glasses from his face and break them in two. Run out into the street at noon and tell everyone what he has done. I hate her, I don't want her back, I don't know what to do, I said I would show you what she wanted," Daisy says, striking the sketchbook, "and maybe she would let me alone . . . but I failed. I don't know how to draw it. What she wants. I tried but I failed," she says, rolling her eyes comically. "Bad Daisy! Hazy Daisy! Big fat lazy! She said for me to ask you, she said, give me your big big hand for my tiny one, Daddy, don't shut the door against me, don't leave me ever again. She wants to be born—she held me in both arms last night—strapped me in so that I couldn't move. Crossed my arms in front of me and held them tight. She is strong now, very strong. Stronger than before. O very strong! But you are stronger. You are always stronger. Will you kill her again . . . ?"

"Hush, Daisy, for God's sake," Bonham mutters.

"*We are not public entertainers*. But are you? Are you?"

"Leave the table. I forbid you to speak to me in this fashion."

She throws her napkin down with a snort of angry triumph and rises from her chair, unsprung, all arms and legs, spidery, energized and frantic and gleeful. Boldly she strides across the terrace, blind, glowing, her countenance so terrible that the staring multitudes are forced to look aside. Bonham sits frozen, his ringed hand to his face, watching to see which direction his daughter will take:

LEFT to the hotel and the cloistered safety of the room
RIGHT to the path high above the tumultuous sea

Left. Right. Left? To the path, to the sea, to death? *Daisy*, he commands, his eyes shut tightly and every atom of his spirit reaching out to her, *Daisy, I order you to turn left, I order you to turn left, go up to your room and go to bed and sleep and no more of this no more of this no more of this ever.*

He opens his eyes to see his gangling galloping daughter turn abruptly to the left, nearly colliding with one of the waiters.

She will be safe. Is safe.

She will sleep, and forget. And awake. And all will be as it was.

Bonham gives the impression of relaxing. He is being watched, he is acutely conscious of being watched, and so he turns the pages of the sketchbook slowly and languidly. He will not satisfy the gawking fools of the world by showing the distress he feels, or by wetting a napkin and pressing it against his forehead to ease the alarming pain. Not at all. Not he. He finishes his coffee without hurrying, he signs the check with his usual gay flourish, rises from the table with an ironic little smile. "What do you know of *us*?" he seems to say. "You know nothing. 'Like as thou canst neither seek out nor know the things that are in the deep of the sea, even so can no man on earth see my daughter. . . .'"

Later that afternoon they are strolling along the sea cliff and Bonham scribbles in his tiny notebook, held up close to his eyes, and Daisy pauses to gather buttercups in great clumsy charming bunches and all is well is well.

The Murder

A gunshot.

The crowd scrambles to its feet, turmoil at the front of the room, a man lies dying.

The smell of gunpowder is everywhere.

It has not happened. He stands there, alive, living. His shoulders loom up thick and square: the cut of his dark suit is jaunty. He is perfect. He shuffles a stack of papers and leans forward confidently against the podium. Those hands are big as lobster claws. He adjusts the microphone, bending it up to him. He is six and a half feet tall, my father, much taller than the man who has just introduced him, and this gesture—abrupt and a little comic—calls our attention to the fact.

Mr. Chairman, I want to point out no less than five irregularities in this morning's session.

That voice. It is in my head. I am leaning forward, anxious not to miss anything. What color is his suit exactly? I don't know. I am not in Washington with him; I am watching this on television. It is important that I know the color of his suit, of his necktie, across the distance. That voice! It is enough to paralyze me, safe here, safe here at home.

It is evident that the Sawyer report was not taken seriously by this committee . . . we wish to question the integrity of these

213

proceedings.... A ripple of applause. His voice continues, gaining strength. Nothing has really begun yet—the men are jockeying for position, preparing themselves with stacks of papers, words, definitions. It has the air of a play in rehearsal, not yet ready to be viewed by the public, the dialogue only partly memorized, the actors fumbling to get hold of the story, the plot.

Look at him standing there. He speaks without hesitation, as if his role is written and he possesses it utterly. So sizable a man, my father!—the very soles of his shoes are enough to stamp out ordinary people. His voice is aristocratic. His voice is savage. Listen to that voice. *I request a definition of your curious phrase "creeping internationalism of American institutions"*—

Laughter. The camera shifts to show the audience in the gallery, a crowd of faces. I am one of those faces.

—*most respectfully request a definition of "bleeding-heart humanists"*—

Scattered laughter, the laughter of individuals. It is mocking, dangerous. The distinguished men of the committee sit gravely, unsmiling, and their counterparts in the audience are silent. Who are the people, like my father, who dare to laugh? They are dangerous men.

He was almost shot, some months ago. The man was apprehended at once. He had wanted to kill my father, to warn my father. But the shot had gone wild; the future was untouched.

His voice continues. The session continues. When the camera scans the audience I lean forward, here in Milwaukee. I need to see, to *see*. Is his murderer there in the audience?

My father is a man who will be murdered.

There are reasons for his murder. Look. Look at my mother: she is striding towards this room, her face flushed and grim. She is seeking me out. Her hair is in crazy tufts, uncombed, gray hair with streaks of red.

She jerks the door open. "What the hell?" she cries. "Are you still watching that?"

She stands in the doorway of my room and will not enter. It is one of her eccentricities—not to enter my room.

"Have you been watching that all day?" she says.

"It's—it's a very important hearing—"

"Turn it off! You need to go out and get some air."

I get to my feet.

My fingers on the knob—my head bowed—I stand above my father. He is a handsome man, but he cannot help me. He is a very handsome man. People stare after him. In the street, in a hotel lobby, anywhere people stare.

He was born to be stared at by women.

I am prepared to take my place in this story.

I am twenty-three and I have a life somewhere ahead of me, I believe. As I brush my long black hair I think about this life ahead of me, waiting. You see my fresh, unlined face, these two enormous strands of black hair, the white part in the center of my skull, the eyes. Dark eyes, like his. You see the pale, rather plain face, the ears pierced with tiny golden dots, almost invisible. You are dismayed as I walk across the room because my shoulders are slumped as if in weariness. I am round-shouldered, and I have grown to an unwomanly height. Deep inside me is a spirit that is also round-shouldered. Smaller women dart ahead of me, through doors or into waiting arms. I lumber along after them, a smile on my face, perspiring inside my dark, plain clothes. I am weighed down by something sinister that gathers in my face, a kind of glower, a knowledge perhaps.

I wake suddenly, as always. I sit up in bed. I remember the hearings and wonder if anything has happened to him overnight. There are no sessions scheduled for today. I dress slowly and brush my hair. I am preparing myself for anything, and it may be to review the clippings on my bureau—articles on him or by him, some with photographs.

He has moved away permanently.

Always, he has traveled. I remember him carrying a single suitcase, backing away, saying good-by. His hearty, happy good-bys! I would follow him on the globe in his old study, so many times, pressing my forefinger against the shape of the country. There, there he was. Precisely there.

He is going to visit. I know this. He is nearby. This morning he is nearby.

My mother: nearly as tall as I, in slacks and an old sweater, in old bedroom slippers, a cigarette in her mouth. She smokes perpetually, squinting against the smoke irritably; right now she is arguing on the telephone, one of her sisters. They are both going on a trip around the world, leaving in August. She doesn't really want me to join her, but she keeps after me, nagging me, trying to make me give in. Her sturdy legs are too much for me, her thick thighs, her robust face, her pocketbooks and hats and shoes. She is on the telephone in the kitchen, hunched over, barking with sudden laughter, one side of her face squinting violently against the smoke.

The house: three floors, too large for my mother and me. You could drift through the downstairs and never find anything to sit on. A statue from Ceylon—a ram with sharp, cruel horns—canvases on the walls, like exclamations. A crystal chandelier hangs from the ceiling, large and dangerous. Over the parquet floor there is an immense Oriental rug, rich as a universe. On the mantel there are more statues, smaller ones, figures of human beings and sacred animals, and a large ornamental dagger in its fur sheath, everything filmed over lightly with dust. Everything is pushed together: there is hardly room to walk through it. We live in the back rooms. My mother strides out occasionally to add another table or lamp to the debris, her cigarette smartly in her mouth, the shrewd cold eye of a collector taking in everything, adding it up, dismissing it. We enter the house through the back door.

The street: a city street, town houses and apartment buildings and enormous old homes. On a weekday morning like today you expect to see a face high at one of the windows of these homes, an attic window maybe. You expect to hear a faint scream. We watch television along this street and read the newspapers, staring at the pictures of men in public life.

The water: Lake Michigan frosted and pointed at the shore, a look of polar calm, absolute cold, absolute zero. It is zero here. I can hear the waves beneath the ice. I can hear the waves at the back of my head, always. We who live on the edge of the lake never leave the lake: we carry it around with us in our heads. My father lived in this house for fifteen years, and so he must carry the sound of the waves in his head too.

I was conceived, of course, to the rhythm of Lake Michigan.

He is approaching this house, driving a large car. He eyes the house from a block away, respectful of the enemy. He brakes the car suddenly, because he sees a tall figure appear, coming around the side of the house, her shoulders hunched against the wind. She walks with the hard stride of a soldier getting from one point to another, wanting only to get from one point to another.

A car slows at the curb, and I stare at it, amazed. At such times I may be pretty. But the glower returns, the doubt.

"Audrey! Don't be alarmed, just get in . . . can you talk with me for a few minutes?"

We stare at each other. His face is melancholy for a moment, as if my flat stare has disappointed him. But then he smiles. He smiles and says, "Please get in! You must be freezing!"

"I didn't—I didn't know you were in town—"

"Yes, I am in town. I am here. Have you had breakfast yet?"

"No. Yes. I mean—"

"Get in. Or are you afraid your mother is watching?"

I cannot believe that he is here, that I am so close to him. "But what—what do you want?" I hear myself stammering. He gets out of the car, impatient with me, and seizes my hands. He kisses me, and I recoil from his fierce good humor.

"Forget about your unfortunate mother and come take a ride with me," he says. "Surely you can spare your father ten minutes?" And he gives me a shake, he grips my elbow in the palm of his big hand. There is nothing to do but give in. We drive off, two giant people in a giant automobile.

He says, "And now, my dear, tell me everything!—what you are doing with your life, what your expectations are, whether you can spare your father a month or so of your company—"

I begin to talk. My life: what is there to say about it? I have written him. I imagine him ripping open the envelopes with a big fatherly smile, scanning the first few lines, and then being distracted by a telephone, some person. In one hand he holds my letters. In the other hand he holds the letters from his women. He loses these letters. He crumples them and sticks them in his pockets or thrusts them into drawers, but he loses them in the end.

"And Mother is planning—"

"No, never mind your mother. I am not interested in morbid personalities!" he cries.

His sideways grin, his face, his thick dark hair. I laugh at his words. They are not funny, and yet they win me to laughter.

"Audrey, I've moved into another dimension. You know that. You understand me, don't you?"

He squeezes my hand.

"I woke up missing you the other day," he says.

I stare at the dashboard of the car. My eyes are dazzled by the gauges, the dials. I can think of nothing to say. My body is large and heavy and cunning.

"Why are you looking away from me? You won't even look at me!" he says. "And that peculiar little smile—what is that?" He turns the rearview mirror above the windshield so that I can see myself.

"Do you hate me very much?" he says gently.

When I packed to leave that afternoon, my mother stood in the doorway and said in a level, unalarmed voice: "So you're going to live the high life with that bastard? So you're going to move out of here, eh? Please don't plan on coming back, then."

She was amused and cynical, smoking her cigarettes. I was opening and closing drawers.

"I don't mean... I don't want to hurt you..." I stammered.

"What?"

My suitcases are packed. I am making an end of one part of my life. In the background, beneath my mother's voice, there is the sound of water, waves.

"Women are such fools. I hate women," my mother says.

Some time ago a woman came to visit my mother. I was about fifteen then, and I had just come home from school; I remember that my feet were wet and my hair frizzy and bedraggled, an embarrassment as I opened the door. The woman stared at me. She had a long, powdered face, the lips drawn up sharply into a look of tired festivity. Something had gone on too long. She had been smiling too long. The eyes were bright and beautiful, the lashes black, the hair black but pulled sharply back from her face, almost hidden by a dark mink hat. Though it was winter, she looked warm. Her cheeks were reddened. The lips were coated with lipstick that had formed a kind of crust. She was glittering and lovely, and she reached out to take hold of my wrist.

"Audrey. You're Audrey..."

Her eyelids were pinkened, a dark dim pink. I smelled a strange fruity odor about her—not perfume, not powder—something sweet and overdone. Her bare fingers squeezed mine in a kind of spasm.

Then my mother hurried downstairs. The two women looked at each other gravely, as if recognizing each other, but for several seconds they said nothing. They moved forward, both with a slow, almost drugged air: they might have been hurrying to meet, and only now, at the last moment, were they held back. "Am I too early?" the woman said.

"No. No. Of course not," my mother said.

The woman took off her coat and let it fall across a sofa—the bronze of her dress clashed with the things in the room. This woman was a surprise a holiday, a treat.

"I can't seem to stop shivering," the woman laughed.

That evening my mother drank too much. She told me bitterly, "Women are such fools! I hate women."

We take a private care from the airport to the hotel. It is Washington, and yet my father doesn't telephone to say that he is back. "Tomorrow it all begins again," he says. "I want us to have a few hours alone." But he is energetic and eager for it to begin, and I am eager to be present, to watch him. I am scanning the crowds on the sidewalk, for he is in danger, someone could rush up to him at any moment.

He is in an excellent mood. He is bringing me into his life, checking me into the hotel, into a room next to his; he is my father, taking care of me, solicitous and exaggerated. The hotel reminds me of my mother's home—so much ornamentation, rugs thick and muffling, furniture with delicate curved legs.

"Well, this is my home. I live here most of the year," he declares.

We have drinks in the lounge. We chat. I ask him, "Has anyone ever tried to shoot you again?" He laughs—of course not! Who would want to shoot him? He smiles indulgently, as if I've said the wrong thing, and he turns to call the waitress over to him. Another martini, please. There is joy in the way he eats, the way he drinks.

It occurs to me that he is a man with many enemies.

"Why do you look so somber?" he asks me.

"I was worried—I was thinking—"

"Don't worry over me, please, I assure you I don't need it!" he laughs. He pats my hand with a hand that is just like it, though larger. "You sound like a—" and he pauses, his smile tightening as he tries to think of the right word. He is a man who knows words, he knows how to choose the right words, always, but he cannot think of the right word now. And so finally he says, strangely, "—like a woman."

Who is watching us?

Some distance away I see a woman...she is standing unnaturally still, alone, watching us. She stands solidly, her feet in low-heeled shoes, and she wears a dark coat buttoned up to the neck, very trim and spare. I find myself thinking in disappointment, *She isn't very pretty.* But really, I can't see her face across the crowded lobby. I feel dizzy with her presence. I would like to point her out to my father.

But he doesn't seem to notice her. He looks everywhere; it is a habit of his to scan everyone's face, to keep an eye on the entrance; but his gaze doesn't settle upon that woman.

We get into a taxi and ride off. It is a suspension of myself, this drifting along in the cab, between the hotel and the chamber where the hearings are taking place. From time to time my father asks me something, as if to keep me attached to him. Or he squeezes my hand.

Photographers move forward to take his picture. They maneuver to get my father and to exclude other people. My father, accustomed to attention, waves genially but does not slow down. He has somewhere to get to: he is a man who has somewhere to be, people waiting for him. I look around the sidewalk to see who is watching us here. I expect to see the woman again, but of course she could not have gotten here so quickly. Is his murderer in this crowd, the man who will leap forward someday and kill my father? Even my father's face, behind its bright mask, is a face of fear.

He too is looking for his murderer.

In the gallery one of his associates sits with me. *Your father is a wonderful man,* he tells me. The proceedings begin. People talk at great length. There is continual movement, spectators in and out, attorneys rising to consult with one another, committee members leaving and returning. I understand nothing will be decided. I understand that no one is here for a decision.

"Mr. Chairman," my father says, barely bothering to stand, "I wish to disagree..."

I look around the room, and there she is. She is standing at the very back. She is alone, listening to my father's words, standing very still. She is my secret, this woman! I watch her: her attention never moves from him.

She is staring at *him*. She doesn't notice anyone in the room except him. Her eyes are large, fawnish, very bright.

"Do you hate me very much?" he must ask them all.

Over the weekend we go to one party after another. My father is handsome and noisy with success. I sit and listen to him talking about the terrible, unfathomable future of the United States. I listen to his friends, their agreement. *Everything is accelerated, a totally new style evolves every four or five years now, it's seized upon, mastered, and discarded—a continual revolution,* he says. These conversations are important, they determine the condition of the world.

"But do you think things are really so bad?" I ask my father when we are alone.

"Have you been listening to all that?" he teases.

I am dragged into taxis, out of taxis. The ceilings of the hotel corridors are very high. The menu for room service lists a bag of potato chips for one dollar. Always there is the sound of a machine whirring, a mechanism to clear the air. We meet in the coffee shop, and eventually we go out to the street, to get in a cab. Once I looked over the roof of the car and saw that woman again—I saw her clearly. She was staring at us. Her purse was large, and she carried it under her arm.

"There is someone—"

"What?" says my father.

"Someone is—"

But the taxi driver needs directions, and I really have nothing to say.

I am silent.

Evening: we are shown into a crowded room, a penthouse apartment. The height is apparent; everyone seems elongated, dizzy, walking on the tips of their toes. I watch my father closely; he stands in a circle of people. In this room, awaiting him, there is a woman, and she will look at him in a certain way. They will approach each other, their eyes locking. His elbows move as he gestures; he bumps into someone and apologizes with a laugh.

I find a place to sit. The evening passes slowly. I am sitting alone, and people move around me. I sit quietly, waiting. From time to time my father checks on me, my hair plaited and smooth, my face chaste, innocent.

"Not bored, are you, sweetheart?" he says.

Women are placed strategically in this room: one here, one there, one in a corner, one advancing from the left, one already at his side, leaning against him, her hand on his wrist, the little lips, the dainty nostrils.

I will go to my father and take his arm and tell him quite gently, *You are going to die*.

My face is silent, fixed, my lips frozen into a kind of smile learned from watching other women.

No, I will say nothing. I will not tell him. I am silent. The shot will be precise and as near to silence as a gunshot can be. It will tear into his heart from the corner of a crowded room.

It is a way of making an end.

Fatal Woman

The first, the very first time, I became aware of my power over men, I was only twelve years old.

I remember distinctly. Because that was the year of the terrible fire downtown, the old Tate Hotel, where eleven people were burned to death and there was such a scandal. The hotel owner was charged with negligence and there was a trial and a lot of excitement. Anyway, I was walking downtown with one of my girl friends, Holly Turnbull, and there was a boardwalk or something by the hotel, which was just a ruin, what was left of it, and you could smell the smoke, such an ugly smell, and I was looking at the burnt building and I said to Holly: "My God do you smell *that*?" Thinking it was burnt flesh. I swear it was. But Holly pulled my arm and said, "Peggy, there's somebody watching us!"

Well, this man was maybe my father's age. He was just standing there a few yards away, watching me. He wore a dark suit, a white shirt, but no tie. His face was wrinkled on one side, he was squinting at me so hard his left eye was almost closed. You'd think he was going to smile or say something funny, grimacing like that. But no. He just stared. Stared and stared and stared. His lips moved but I couldn't hear what he said—it was just a mumble. It wasn't meant for me to hear.

My hair came to my waist. It was light brown, always shiny and well-brushed. I had nice skin: no blemishes. Big brown eyes.

A pretty mouth. Figure just starting to be what it is today. I didn't know it, but that man was the first, the very first, to look at me in that special way.

He scared me, though. He smelled like something black and scorched and ugly. Holly and I both ran away giggling, and didn't look back.

As I grew older my attractiveness to men increased and sometimes I almost wished I was an elderly woman!—free at last from the eyes and the winks and the whistles and the remarks and sometimes even the nudges. But that won't be for a while, so I suppose I must live with it. Sometimes I want to laugh, it seems so silly. It seems so crazy. I study myself in the mirror from all angles and I'm not being modest when I say that, in my opinion, I don't *seem* that much prettier than many women I know. Yet I've been in the presence of these women and it always happens if a man or a boy comes along he just skims over the others and when he notices me he stares. There must be something about me, an aura of some kind, that I don't know about.

Only a man would know.

I got so exasperated once, I asked: What is it? Why are you bothering *me*? But it came out more or less humorously.

Gerry Swanson was the first man who really dedicated himself to me—didn't just ogle me or whistle or make fresh remarks—but really fell in love and followed me around and ignored his friends' teasing. He walked by our house and stood across the street, waiting, just waiting for a glimpse of me, and he kept meeting me by accident downtown or outside the high school, no matter if I was with my girl friends and they all giggled like crazy at the sight of him. Poor Gerry Swanson, everybody laughed. I blushed so, I couldn't help it. It made me happy that he was in love with me, but it frightened me too, because he was out of school a few years and seemed a lot older than the boys I knew. (I had a number of boy friends in high school—I didn't want to limit myself to just one. I was very popular; it interfered with my schoolwork to some extent, but I didn't care. For instance, I was the lead in the Spring Play when I was only a sophomore, and I was on the cheerleading squad for three years, and I was First Maid-in-Waiting to the Senior Queen. I wasn't voted Senior Queen because, as my boy friends said, all the girls were jealous of me and deliberately voted against me, but *all* the boys voted for me. I didn't exactly believe them. I think some of the girls probably voted for me—I had lots of friends—and naturally some of the boys would have voted for other candidates. That's only realistic.) When Gerry came along, I was sixteen. He was working for his father's construction company and I was surprised he would like a girl still in high school, but he did; he telephoned all the time and took me out, on Sundays mainly, to the matinée downtown, because my father didn't trust him, and he tried to buy me things, and wrote letters, and made such a fool of himself everybody laughed at him, and I couldn't help laughing myself. I asked him once what it was: *Why* did he love me so much?

He just swallowed and stared at me and couldn't say a word.

As I've grown older this attractiveness has gradually increased, and in recent weeks it has become something of a nuisance. Maybe I dress provocatively—I don't know. Certainly I don't amble about with my bare midriff showing and my legs bare up to the buttocks, like many other girls, and I've recently had my hair cut quite short, for the warm weather. I have noticed, though, that my navy-blue dress seems to attract attention; possibly it fits my body too tightly. I don't know. I wish certain men would just ignore me. For instance, a black man on the street the other day—a black *police*man, who should know better—was staring at me from behind his sunglasses with the boldest look you could imagine. It was shocking. It was really rude. I gave him a cold look and kept right on walking, but I was trembling inside. Later, I wondered if maybe I should have pretended not to notice. I wondered if he might think I had snubbed him because of the color of his skin—but that had nothing to do with it, not a thing! I'm not prejudiced in any way and never have been.

At the hospital there are young attendants, college-age boys, at the very time of life when they are most susceptible to visual stimulation; they can't help noticing me, and staring and staring. When I took the elevator on Monday to the tenth floor, where Harold's room is, one of the attendants hurried to get on with me. The elevator was empty except for us two. The boy blushed so his face went beet-red. I tried to make things casual by remarking on the weather and the pretty petunias out front by the sidewalk, but the boy was too nervous and he didn't say a word until the door opened on the tenth floor and I stepped out. "You're so beautiful!"—he said. But I just stepped out and pretended not to hear and walked down the corridor.

Eddie telephoned the other evening, Wednesday. He asked

about Harold and I told him everything I knew, but then he didn't say good-by, he just kept chattering and chattering—then he asked suddenly if he could come over to see me. That very night. His voice quavered and I was just so shocked!—but I should have seen it coming over the years. I should have seen it coming. I told him it was too late, I was going to bed, but could he please put my daughter on the phone for a minute? That seemed to subdue him.

In church I have noticed our minister watching me, sometimes out of the corner of his eye, as he gives his sermon. He is a few years younger than I am, and really should know better. But I've had this certain effect all my life—when I'm sitting in an audience and there are men addressing the group. I first noticed it, of course, in junior and senior high school, but it didn't seem to be so powerful then. Maybe I wasn't so attractive then. It's always the same: the man addressing us looks around the room, smiling, talking more or less to everyone, and then his eye happens to touch upon me and his expression changes abruptly and sometimes he even loses the thread of what he is saying, and stammers, and has to repeat himself. After that he keeps staring helplessly at me and addresses his words only to me, as if the rest of the audience didn't exist. It's the strangest thing. . . . If I take pity on him I can somehow "release" him, and allow him to look away and talk to the others; it's hard to explain how I do this—I give a nearly imperceptible nod and a little smile and I *will* him to be released, and it works, and the poor man is free.

I take pity on men, most of the time.

Sometimes I've been a little daring, I admit it. A little flirtatious. Once at Mirror Lake there were some young Italian men on the beach, and Harold saw them looking at me, and heard one of them whistle, and there was an unpleasant scene. . . . Harold said I encouraged them by the way I walked. I don't know: I just don't know. It seems a woman's body sometimes might be flirtatious by itself, without the woman herself exactly knowing.

The telephone rang tonight and when I picked up the receiver no one answered.

"Eddie," I said, "is this Eddie? I know it's you, dear, and you shouldn't do this—you know better—what if Barbara finds out, or one of the children? My daughter would be heartbroken to know her own husband is making telephone calls like this— You know better, dear!"

He didn't say a word, but he didn't hang up. I was the one to break the connection.

When I turned off the lights downstairs just now, and checked the windows, and checked the doors to make sure they were locked, I peeked out from behind the living-room shade and I could see someone standing across the street, on the sidewalk. It was that black policeman! But he wasn't in his uniform. I don't think he was in his uniform. He's out there right now, standing there, waiting, watching this house. Just like Gerry Swanson used to.

I'm starting to get frightened.

Everyone tells me to be strong, not to break down—about Harold, they mean; about the way the operation turned out. Isn't it a pity? they say. But he's had a full life, a rich life. You've been married how long—? Happily married. Of course. And your children, and the grandchildren. "A full, rich life." And they look at me with that stupid pity, never seeing me, not *me*, never understanding anything. What do I have to do with an old man, I want to scream at them. What do I have to do with an old dying man?

One of them stood on the sidewalk that day, staring at me. No, it was on a boardwalk. The air stank with something heavy and queer and dark. I giggled, I ran away and never looked back. Now one of them is outside the house at this very moment. He's waiting, watching for me. If I move the blind, he will see me. If I snap on the light and raise the blind even a few inches, he will see me. What has he to do with that old man in the hospital, what have I to do with that old man . . . ? But I can't help being frightened.

For the first time in my life I wonder—what is going to happen?

The Sacrifice

There was once a man who had guided his life perfectly. At the age of sixty-one he had been happily married for over three decades; he had many friends and acquaintances and respectful associates; and he knew himself to be at the peak of his intellectual powers, which had always been considerable. Still he worked hard, harder than ever. He did not plan to retire for another decade. Ten hours a day in his office, at his desk; sometimes twelve hours a day. He worked hard and he loved his work.

Dr. Reaume, people said, *how remarkable you are! What would we do without you?*

He listened politely, but their praise embarrassed him. He knew they were not lying—they were not consciously flattering him. But it was embarrassing, their gratitude and their adulation; there was no possible way for him to reply to it. When people wrote to him, however, he found it less awkward to reply. He could always begin by thanking them for their thoughtful, generous letters, and then he could adroitly shift attention from himself and his own work to something larger—to earlier, little-known books in his field or to work being published by young colleagues. Over the years he had received thousands of letters, most of which he kept in his files without looking at them a second time. *Dr. Reaume,* the strangers cried, *Dr. Reaume,* they cried aggressively, *how remarkable a man you are . . . !*

But he did not look remarkable. He did not strike himself as remarkable. Slight, almost elfin—no more than five feet three inches tall, never more than one hundred and twenty-five pounds at his heaviest—he had a round, almost babyish face, and now that his hair had turned white and had thinned to feathery, fluttering wisps, his skull resembled an eggshell in its delicate coloring. His arms and legs were thin, almost skinny; almost like a child's limbs. But he was not weak; far from it. There was a quick, alert wiriness to his body and he was nearly always in excellent health. From boyhood onward he had played hard and exercised faithfully, had even taken boxing lessons in college, and lifted weights; he had trained himself to withstand and even to be exhilarated by physical stress—loving the sensation of strain, in his leg muscles especially, as if this were a part of the life-contest he might have missed otherwise, left to himself and his studies, his predilection for solitude. In his early fifties, after a mild heart attack, he had joined an indoor tennis club in Georgetown, and, though he no longer played tennis as often as he wished, he was still in quite good shape—in surprisingly good shape. And his eyes were still good. He wore glasses, of course, but his vision had stopped deteriorating many years before. His eyes, a pale, bright, innocent blue behind his rimless lenses, sometimes gleamed with sly good humor or irony that others failed to get. They took him so seriously, after all . . . ! But he was not remarkable, not to himself. He had always felt perfectly and exquisitely ordinary.

One mild April day, shortly after noon, Dr. Reaume was stopped on the sidewalk a block or two from his home by a woman he had never seen before. She seemed to know him, however. She called him by name and clutched at the sleeve of his old tweed jacket, begging him to listen. She wanted only five minutes of his time.

"Of course— Yes— What is it?" he said, startled. He had thought she must be a former patient. She must be someone he knew, someone for whom he was responsible.

"Something terrible is happening to me," the woman said. "I have terrible dreams—unbearable dreams—I'm afraid of going insane—I don't know what to do, there's nothing wrong with me, no reason for—no explanation for— Yesterday I had a dream while I was awake—I wasn't asleep—I had a dream while I was awake—a hallucination— But there's nothing wrong with me, I've always been in good health—in excellent health—"

He managed to calm her. He showed none of the alarm he felt, of course; it was second nature with him, after so many years, to absorb into himself the agitation of others, to soothe them with respectful but unexcited attention. He smiled encouragingly. He nodded sympathetically. He was infinitely patient, and was transformed at once into the role of the healer, though in fact he had been rudely accosted by a stranger on his way home from the German delicatessen where he had bought some rye bread and skim-milk cheese and garlic pickles for his lunch. And he had an appointment at one, a patient coming to see him at one. But he was calm, courteous, gazing up at the distraught woman as she told him her complicated story, still clutching at his jacket sleeve.

He did not know her. Did not recognize her. Her gray, colorless eyes were bright with emotion and the self-importance of emotion; her voice was rapid, unnaturally low as if she were fighting the need to scream. A young woman, in her early thirties. Perhaps younger. Her fine pale skin was unevenly flushed; her coppery-red hair was disheveled; she had neglected to tie the bow of her cream-colored silk blouse and so, though her suit was of a rich beige fabric with suede-covered buttons, obviously expensive, and her shoes looked custom-made, she gave the impression of being slovenly, even intoxicated. But there was no odor of alcohol about her: Dr. Reaume smelled only a faint dusty pleasant scent, as of lily of the valley.

"... never anything wrong with me, never anything serious," the woman was saying. "I've had some unhappy times, of course, but nothing unusual ... nothing to be alarmed about ... when I was married a few years and we moved here and I had a miscarriage, I was twenty-five then, I had a miscarriage and was very depressed afterward, for six months afterward, then I got pregnant again, you know, and it was all right, but ... but when I was depressed, during that time I was just tired and I didn't want to leave the apartment and I cried a lot but I never had bad dreams or hallucinations, you know, it was never like that, it was never anything that serious. I went to a psychiatrist then—I mean a psychoanalyst—my husband thought maybe I should go and so I did but the psychoanalyst hadn't much to say and I got better by myself after a few months, after I got pregnant again; it was never anything very serious. But now.... Yesterday.... It began last week, these dreams and then thinking about them while I was awake and worrying about what they mean and if I will have another one and if I am going insane.... You don't think I am going insane, Dr. Reaume, do you?"

"Of course not," he said. "Of course not."

"... I was in our bedroom going through one of the closets, just the linen closet, I was rearranging the towels ... just rearranging some things in the closet, on the shelves ... and suddenly I had a dream, I had a dream that was over in a few seconds, I was fully awake and my eyes were open and ... and yet I had a dream, a dream came to me, it seemed to push its way through my vision, it crowded out what I had been looking at and everything else faded as if it had never existed ... as if the world itself wasn't real and could be pushed aside at any time.... One moment I was checking the towels and sheets and the next moment I was trying to carry someone, a man or a child, someone small and wizened and hurt, slippery with blood ... bleeding ... screaming and sobbing and clutching at me.... It was horrible! ... horrible. He was naked, his body was slippery from the blood, his face was all wrinkled, screwed up, he was in terrible pain and so afraid, so afraid, I wanted to comfort him, I wanted to help him but I didn't know how.... It was so horrible, so pathetic ... I didn't know what to do ... couldn't even keep him in my arms, he kept falling, clutching at me.... His face was like a baby's, all wrinkled and red and damp. I knew it was my duty to save him but I didn't know how. I would have to telephone for an ambulance or for the police but there was no telephone, and I could have driven him to the hospital myself but ... but there was no car ... I didn't know where the car was ... I didn't know where I was. The man was crying so, he was in such pain, he was dying, shriveling, there was blood all over me and I couldn't comfort him, couldn't do anything, and ... and ... and that was it. That was it. The dream ended. It lasted only a few seconds, it wasn't a real dream, I was on my feet all the while and fully conscious and aware of myself.... Dr. Reaume, am I going insane? Does it mean I am going insane? ... Afterward, all night long and this morning, afterward I felt such sorrow ... disgust with myself ... I can't explain it to anyone, wouldn't dare talk about it to my husband, because he would just be upset and would want me to make an appointment with our doctor and they would make a fuss, they wouldn't understand, they aren't like you.... Afterward I felt so horrible, as if I had failed at something entrusted to me; I felt as if someone had really died and I was to blame even though there was nothing I could do.... I must be going insane," she said, laughing suddenly. "There's no other explanation."

"But would insanity be an explanation?" Dr. Reaume said. The woman was calmer now and he could appeal to her, smiling his slight, ironic smile, raising his eyebrows quizzically. He had her attention; he sensed that it had shifted from herself, from her own subdued hysteria, to him. And so he spoke to her frankly and courteously, telling her what he knew of "hallucinations"—what experience he had had with them—patients of his who had had similar dreams or visions while awake, always at a time in their lives when unconscious psychic contents were unusually powerful, when a crisis of some kind was developing which, in consciousness, was being denied. He spoke to her as if to an equal. That was his style, a style he practiced intuitively, knowing that it was an error to accept a disturbed person's estimation of himself; even the emotionally unbalanced possessed a margin of rationality, of intelligence, which must be addressed. So he spoke to the woman calmly, rather professorially. He even mentioned the names of books she might acquire to gain insight into her experience. "By no means is it necessarily pathological," he said. "In fact, I have gradually come to see, in my long career, how the *pathological* is a mere catchall—a term to explain away what is mysterious and stubborn. Like saying that God is responsible, eh?—God or the Devil is responsible, as in the old days. It tells us nothing. It explains nothing. It is our own honest ignorance and befuddlement mirrored to us...nothing more."

Her eyes half closed with relief. For a moment her mouth went slack. He saw, with a small thrill of pleasure, that he had really comforted her—she believed him, she had been instructed by him. She was an excellent patient. He was the healer, she the wounded one, bringing her mysterious wound to him for his magic, alert to every nuance in his voice, every subtle shifting of his facial expression. Though they were strangers, the relationship between them suddenly felt as if it were very old. Dr. Reaume felt he had known the woman for centuries.

Several weeks later, when they met again, she was to explain to him the circumstances behind her having sought him out—and having recognized him on the street. "You're a famous man," she said softly, shyly. "Your books...your photograph a few months ago in the *Post*....But I had always known about you anyway;

since I was a young girl, I've been hearing about you. My mother's maiden name is...." And here she told him a name that was distinctly familiar. Dr. Reaume frowned, trying to recall. "...her older sister, my Aunt Rachel, you were...the two of you...for a while, wasn't it," she said, blushing, "when you were both living in Boston? My Aunt Rachel," she said. Dr. Reaume nodded slowly, still frowning. He had crossed his short legs and his hands were clasped atop his knee, a small round knob of a knee; he gave his foot a shake suddenly. A girl...a woman...someone named Rachel...and now someone watching him closely, a stranger, face painted a warm flesh color and eyes intense, feverish, bright.... He nodded slowly, slowly. She said, apologetically, that her aunt wasn't...was no longer...had died some years ago, at least ten years ago...had never married, had remained in Boston and had become one of the leading...."I'm sorry to hear she died," Dr. Reaume said quietly. He could not recall a face: could not, in all honesty, recall anything about the woman. It was obviously a case of exaggeration, one of many, a distant friend or casual acquaintance of years ago making claims, contriving memories; perhaps even believing them, as people do. It was quite human. It was certainly forgivable in a woman dead ten years. "My aunt became one of the leading neurologists in the area," his patient said. "And so...and so I had always heard about you, Dr. Reaume, your name alluded to or mentioned in a mysterious way...and then of course you became famous; now everyone knows your name. I recognized you at once on the street. I would have recognized you anywhere."

But that first day, he had not known this; he had felt, returning home, a curious mixture of elation and apprehension—as if, everywhere he walked, he drew strangers' eyes to him, compelling them to pay him homage. It was ridiculous, of course. And even if people did know him—in this neighborhood many did, of course; and the shopkeepers certainly did since his wife would have told them, could not have resisted—it meant nothing; being known in a public sense, having had his photograph in the papers, having appeared several times on television, even though he detested the medium, really meant nothing in his profession. If he was distinguished, it was in the eyes of his colleagues; what other people thought did not matter, though of course it could be distressing or exciting—Dr. Reaume was, after all, quite human.

Because of his appointment at one o'clock, he had been unable to talk with the woman for very long. Ten or fifteen minutes. He gave her the name of a lay analyst in the city who would, if she explained the circumstances, and if she told him that Dr. Reaume had referred her, probably be able to see her that afternoon; a fine person, a naturalized Belgian who had trained with Dr. Reaume himself some years ago. He was certain she would like this man. He would not treat her perfunctorily, nor would he attempt to reduce her dreams to cruel psychoanalytic jargon. The woman had wanted to see Dr. Reaume instead, but he interrupted her, laughing, explaining that it was not necessary to see *him*, to be treated by *him*—in person; a desire of that kind indicated exaggeration, inflation, a predetermined transference that would only muddle things badly.... If, however, the other analyst did not seem quite right for her, Dr. Reaume would naturally be happy to see her. But she must give the other man a chance—did she understand?

She looked so disappointed!—like a young girl. Her feelings exposed, no shame, innocence of the kind that always moved Dr. Reaume, since he encountered it so rarely. But she must be disappointed. It was for the best.... She saw his point of view, she agreed with him, though her expression was still rather lifeless. Behind her, in the butchershop window, one of the butcher's assistants, in his red-stained white outfit, leaned to get a heavy slab of meat; he glanced out at Dr. Reaume and the woman.

"...but if...if I really need you.... You will give me an appointment, won't you?" the woman begged.

"Of course," Dr. Reaume said. He tried to chuckle, to make light of her solemnity. "...What else are we human beings for, except to be of service to one another?"

His brownstone house consisted of four floors; his office was on the ground floor and had its own entrance, a few steps down from the sidewalk, behind a wrought-iron gate that had been painted a smart, gleaming black just recently. Dr. Reaume loved his home, though the rooms were rather small and the backyard was only a courtyard with a few square yards for flowers and a single tree. He had bought the house nearly thirty years ago; he would never sell it.

That day, he had time for a hurried lunch in the courtyard—eating alone, as he usually did, sitting at the handsome glass-topped table beneath the ginkgo tree. How agitated he was!—it was unlike him, really. His routine upset, his schedule interrupted, a stranger stopping him on the street like that; and the fact, which distracted him, that his one-o'clock patient would arrive all too soon and her recitation of the past week, and the dreams of the past week, would probably drive the young woman's presence out of his mind.... Birds were fluttering at the rear of the garden. The air was mild, almost hazy. Sunshine, spring, temperatures already in the high sixties; no wonder he felt so oddly pleased, almost triumphant. And excited. He was sorry that his wife was gone for the day—she was visiting in Bethesda with her younger sister, whose husband had died eighteen months ago. He was alone except for his grandson, with whom it was difficult to talk; alone except for his secretary and his procession of patients. One o'clock, two o'clock, three.... And all so desperate for him, so grateful. It was tiring, of course. Draining. But he loved his work, loved the clinical practice as well as the research, the small inconsequential satisfactions as well as the larger, more public victories. *Dr. Reaume, how do you manage? ...a man half your age would be exhausted by....*

He ate quickly, without tasting his food. Two cups of tea, no sugar allowed. An orange, which he peeled with his small, finely shaped fingers; then a thin cigar, five minutes of a partly forbidden pleasure. Then time to brush his teeth, wash up, prepare for the afternoon's obligations. He felt calmer, more composed. What had been upsetting him? Could not recall.... Was settled in behind his enormous desk, studying his notes, comfortable and composed and altogether his customary self, when his one-o'clock patient rang the outer bell.

In the small guest bathroom adjacent to his office, Dr. Reaume combed his filmy wisps of hair, which he had wetted so that they might lie close against his head. Exasperating! And comic also, he knew. On the inside, in his soul, he knew himself to be a certain person; but the outside world looked upon a slight, fey creature, an elderly man who was dapper rather than distinguished, whose clothes never quite seemed to fit him. He studied himself with ironic detachment: *Dr. Reaume, how small you are ... l What a small vehicle for so grand a soul!*

The woman had telephoned him to make an appointment. On the street, by the butcher's shop, he had known she would call;

but then she hadn't called; days and weeks had passed . . . and she had not called. By May first he had forgotten her. He had forgotten the incident. A trivial but vexing matter had arisen concerning his son—and his son's eleven-year-old boy, who was living temporarily with Dr. Reaume and his wife—and this had necessitated telephone calls to lawyers and even several visits to the lawyers' offices in downtown Washington; so Dr. Reaume forgot the distraught woman who had stopped him on the street. And then she had called. Had made an appointment to see him as soon as possible.

The first several minutes were wasted on apologies. She seemed to think it necessary to explain herself at length. Dr. Reaume tried to interrupt her, but she continued—she might have rehearsed her words beforehand. ". . . would never have bothered you except. . . . I've been quite well, perfectly normal. . . . After I talked with you that day the trouble lifted . . . I didn't feel the need to call the other analyst . . . I felt so relieved, so normal once again. I started a half-dozen letters to you, thanking you, but wasn't satisfied with any of them . . . they all sounded so. . . . It's difficult to be. . . . Difficult to speak clearly and coherently about . . . about such matters. Sanity and insanity. What it means to know you are sane," she said slowly, "and to know that it can slip from you at any time . . . that it isn't in your keeping after all. It isn't in your control."

She spoke gravely, like a schoolgirl. A lovely woman, her face shaped like that of Botticelli's Flora. Not so disheveled as before, dressed simply in a white-linen sheath, her face prepared, painted, the lips rouged, the eyelids pearlish green, hair fixed in an elegant bun at the nape of her neck. She had taken pains to prepare herself for their meeting. But he could see, beneath her composure, the distress and bewilderment and odd, confused shame he had sensed at their first meeting.

"Theoretically you are perhaps correct," Dr. Reaume said in his low, rasping voice, "but in fact . . . in practice . . . in the living of one's life. . . . The center of consciousness that is your ego has much more volition, much more freedom, hasn't it? . . . and the balance of conscious and unconscious forces is not so difficult to maintain. In practice, that is. In theory—who can tell?"

He sat behind his desk, in his leather chair; the woman faced him across the desk, leaning forward a little in her anxiety, her hands clasped together and raised so that her rings glinted. Yes, she was quite lovely. And younger than he had calculated. The

lamplight flattered her fine, delicate features. Because Dr.
Reaume's office was relatively dark, it was necessary to have a
lamp burning even during the day. It was a handsome room,
walnut-paneled, with many books and a few works of art—a
small, perfect watercolor by Dufy, a series of frieze-rubbings
from a Buddhist temple in Ceylon—and a thick tufted
hand-loomed rug from Turkey. Shadowy, cavelike, utterly
private. He had worked here for years, for decades. He loved the
quietness of this place, the sanctity, the very texture of the
atmosphere, which was entirely his own, his own creation. The
temperature was just right, controlled by a nearly inaudible
air-conditioner; outside, on the street, it was a too-warm May
afternoon, muggy and overcast.

"Yes," the woman said. "Yes. I believe you. I know you are
right, yes." She paused. And then she began again, cringing
slightly, her rather incoherent, time-wasting apologies, and Dr.
Reaume saw there was nothing to do but allow her to speak as she
wished. He crossed his legs and clasped his hands on his knee and
smiled patiently and paternally and simply waited, giving the
impression of being willing to wait forever. She had had another
disturbing experience, she said. A far more disturbing one this
time. . . . Then she paused awkwardly and told him of the fact
that she had been aware of him for many years; she mentioned
the feature story in a recent issue of the *Post*, a very kind,
generous, and surprisingly well-informed article about Dr.
Reaume on the occasion of his having been given a special
citation from the American Academy of Humanistic Science . . . she mentioned the aunt, a woman named Rachel, whom
Dr. Reaume had purportedly known in Boston, a lifetime
ago . . . and again apologized for having troubled him. ". . . so
afraid you'll be angry with me . . . disgusted. . . . There's no one
else I can talk to, no one else I dare to. . . . And if you are offended
and disgusted with me, something terrible will happen, to both
of us; I feel that we are both . . . both of us . . . we are both. . . ." She
was staring at him. Dr. Reaume, watching her benignly, did not
show the alarm he felt; in a sense he was prepared for a radical
shift in the woman's behavior. He could sense such shifts ahead
of time. But of course he showed nothing, only that calm,
paternal sympathy.

It turned out that she had had another dream while awake. But
it was not a dream of her own, she claimed; it had nothing to do
with her personally. It had simply come out of nowhere. She

hesitated to tell the dream to Dr. Reaume because it was so ugly, so horrible...because she was afraid it would offend him irreparably.... "Ah, really!" Dr. Reame sighed. "Really! Do you think I am that shallow? Have the men in your life been so fickle, so childish, that you project into me such disappointing qualities? I am really not so bad as you may think," he said. He smiled. He was intrigued now, rather excited. Though he had been told literally thousands of dreams in his lifetime, he was always intrigued by the prospect of a new adventure; what extraordinary good fortune, that so many thousands of dreams and visions and yearning, questing, incomplete people had come his way.... They were broken, bewildered, panicked, wounded; they were desperate for help, desperate for him. And so he gave himself. Again and again he gave himself, without restraint. The wounded were so childishly grateful for anything he did, however minimal it might be: and Dr. Reaume did not delude himself, as other analysts did, knowing very well that he sometimes helped his patients only slightly, and sometimes not at all. He tried to be as honest as possible with them. He could not be their savior, after all—not at all. He was only a human being, quite ordinary, humble, exquisitely humble. This must be understood. But they needed him so passionately that their need often stimulated in him a keener, sharper, inspired Dr. Reaume, a genius of a healer, disguised in this inappropriately undersized body. And so he loved them, almost against his will. They gave birth to his genius and he loved them, loved it. Loved the experience.... Loved even this woman's clumsy presentation of a rather melodramatic nightmare. How real it was to her! How real such psychic experiences were, to the sufferer! No one else could understand as Dr. Reaume understood.

A man had been beheaded. Priests had beheaded him, men in women's clothing; long blood-splattered gowns. Or perhaps the priests were women. She could not be certain. Perhaps she had been one of them, herself.... But she was a foreigner, unable to understand the language of the ceremony, the ritualistic chanting; she had been terrified at what was being done. She tried to scream but could not. Wanted to stop them but could not. Paralyzed. Frightened as she had never been frightened in real life. She was an observer, helpless; but had she been able to run away, still the knowledge would have remained with her that the ceremony continued.... It continued and could not be stopped. *It could not be stopped: it was perpetual.*

Evidently the dream had really frightened her, for even now she looked upset. She covered her face with her hands. Rubbed at her eyes. Had she been crying? Unfortunately, there was now a black smear just below her left eye.... "The dream came to me from somewhere outside myself," she said faintly. Her mouth, trembling, was rather ugly for a moment; but only for a moment. She stared at him with that look of vacuous, pitiable yearning he knew so well. "I'm so afraid you will be angry with me or think I'm insane and want to have me hospitalized.... I'm afraid you will be disgusted with me, hate me...."

"But why?" Dr. Reaume asked.

"...the man in the dream was you, the man who was beheaded," she said. Her voice was so weak, he had to ask her to repeat herself. She was cringing, coquettish. "...it was you, but you were much smaller, and older, you were shriveled...slippery with blood...you had no strength, your legs couldn't support you, the others grabbed hold of you and held you up to a...a kind of sink or basin or trough.... They were so cruel! They were so rough, so indifferent to you. You screamed and pleaded with them and pleaded with me but I couldn't...I couldn't move.... I was paralyzed, I didn't understand, I was a stranger, it wasn't my fault.... Then, afterward, there was so much blood...running into a tub...something like a tub...and there was just the body and the head, there was no life to it now, and the others didn't care, didn't notice, hadn't noticed all along...I was the only one who realized.... The body was wearing a dress too, a long robe like the others. But nobody cared. I wanted to save you but I couldn't, and now I feel so horrible, so filthy, I feel filthy with it, splattered with blood and so filthy I couldn't help you or anyone: I'm guilty but it isn't my fault; it isn't my life, is it?...and so it can't be my fault."

Dr. Reaume gave his leg a small shake. He was perky, wiry, very alert; the dream made near-perfect sense to him, but he suppressed the glow of pleasure he felt, and told the woman gently that of course he did not feel disgust and of course he was not offended. The dream was a sacred experience of her own, of hers, and he and she would proceed cautiously, and thoroughly, and with as much frankness as possible, to relate it to her troubled life.

"Who was that hag with the black stuff running down her face?"

"What? Who are you—?"

"Some ugly old dame I met out front," Timmy said. "... She almost walked into me like she was drunk and I told her to watch it, to watch the hell where she was going, and she just looked at me, a real nut. One of your people, Grandpa, huh?" he said, yawning. "... reason I'm late is I missed the bus and the next one was jammed and I said what the hell, I'll walk home...."

"You walked home? Walked nine miles home?"

He shrugged his thin shoulders and yawned again.

The boy had his mother's platinum-blond hair, worn in bangs cut straight across his forehead, skimming his eyebrows. He had his father's prim, rather insolent features: the small clever mouth, the pointed nose, the near-colorless blue eyes. He wore rimless square-cut glasses, in imitation or parody of glasses worn by Benjamin Franklin; his eyes were very weak and even with corrective lenses his vision was poor. He was eleven years old and already as tall as his grandfather.

"... yeuh, my feet hurt like hell ... gonna swell up, maybe," he mumbled. "... I'm not hungry; I already ate. I'm going upstairs."

"You walked *nine miles* ... ?"

The boy walked past him. It was not that he was rude: he was indifferent, vacuous, even puppetlike in his movements. Dr. Reaume knew he was lying; he suspected the boy had not gone to school that day at all, since he had no books with him; but their clashes, their confrontations, their spasmodic little arguments always left Dr. Reaume exhausted and perplexed, never enlightened, and seemed to have no effect on his grandson at all. So he called up the narrow, circular stairs to the boy, "... but you must be hungry, Timmy? ... aren't you? ..." and waited for the boy to shout back something unintelligible but there was no reply, no response at all.

Dr. Reaume stood in the tiny foyer of the town house, his hand on the wrought-iron railing, lost in thought. His half-smile was frozen in place....An eleven-year-old child, a grandson. His only grandchild. Timmy. Timmy, his son's boy. His son was no more than a boy himself, but he had a child who was now eleven years old and who would never be any older. Dr. Reaume knew, as his son would never be any older than he was, would never grow; had stopped, stubbornly, spitefully, at about the age of nineteen.... But of course he was brilliant. He was brilliant. Dr. Reaume had always believed his son superior to himself, in terms of raw intellect; he remembered how incredibly hard he had had to work in school and at the university and in his post-doctoral studies.... Wisdom had not come easily to Dr. Reaume. He had struggled for it. His son, willowy, charming, with that melodic ironic voice of his, had been brilliant even in boyhood, had never had to work hard in school, and perhaps the confusion of his life in recent years . . . the bad luck with his first marriage, the worse luck with his second . . . and, at the present time, the complications arising out of his involvement with a quite young Lebanese girl, in Beirut. . . . Perhaps these snarls were somehow due to the fact that the young man was simply too sharp, a raw, undisciplined genius, who might sometime in the future make a contribution to society, but was at the moment. . . . Dr. Reaume shook his head, bewildered. He loved his son and he loved his grandson. He loved them without understanding them.

". . . the temptation is to judge, to judge hastily from one's own prejudice," he said aloud. He stood for a while at the foot of the stairs. Then, when the pounding began on the fourth floor, the downbeat of heavy rock music that Timmy played hour after hour, the doctor moved slowly into the living room and to the rear of the house. He would have a glass of dry sherry and relax before dinner. He would sit on the flagstone terrace he loved so well, in the tiny courtyard, and think back over the day's work and relax while the cook prepared dinner. He could smell something frying in butter, probably mushrooms.

If Timmy declined to join him, he would be eating alone that night. His wife was visiting with elderly relatives in Cambridge, Massachusetts; she would be gone another four or five days. Of course he would not force Timmy to join him. He really did not mind eating alone, since he enjoyed reading at such times, leafing through magazines of a nonprofessional nature like the *Atlantic* or *The New Yorker*, and if he did not care to read he simply liked to think, to rethink his work and prepare for the next day. He was never lonely. Never. He did not even know, exactly, what the average person meant by the word *lonely*.... No, he did not mind eating alone. Timmy's company was not always pleasant when he was cajoled into doing something against his will; that sleepy, easygoing, indolent nature of his could change in a second to something quite vicious, and Dr. Reaume was repelled by emotional scenes.... Well, people had a right to their eccentricities. The boy, the boy's father, Mrs. Reaume herself. Nearly everyone he knew, Dr. Reaume thought, sighing. At times they disappointed him. But that was only human, after all; other people could not be controlled. Dr. Reaume had always been able to accept this fact of life. He believed he was strong enough to absorb it into himself. At the age of sixty-one he had had to absorb into himself a considerable number of painful disappointments, not only in the realm of the personal—what peculiar, quirky people had crossed his path, disguised as well-meaning friends!—but in the larger, impersonal world as well. Many of his professional colleagues were strange people. Not disappointing so much as simply strange, possessed by willful, bizarre theories of the psyche, which they could not discuss rationally. Dr. Reaume knew enough to back away from such creatures, who might attack if they were excited . . . who would not even respect him, should he challenge their ideas. And he had lived through wars, through many domestic and international crises and catastrophes; the ongoing malaise of the twentieth century was a condition of life he was able to accept, now, in his old age, having found a way to fit it into the structure of the universe without undue bitterness or melodrama. If only his son had been capable of such maturity! . . . but his son was still relatively young. Dr. Reaume must not judge him.

He watched the fan-shaped leaves of the ginkgo take the frail, saffron-tinted sunlight, absolutely immobile, beautiful as a work of art. The sherry was excellent. The odor of frying mushrooms was delicious. And what had gone so well today, what had pleased him so . . . ? He felt quietly pleased, gratified. Hours of work, a morning of research and an afternoon of patients, climaxing with that extraordinary young woman and her remarkable dream. . . . Yes, the day had gone well. He had worked very hard, had been perplexed and challenged, invigorated. *I'm afraid you will be disgusted with me, hate me,* the poor woman had said, before he worked through her dream with her, explaining how the psyche had utilized certain personal and impersonal symbols to present to her an objectification of the dilemma of her life. She had resisted the personal—had insisted her own life was not troubled, there was nothing wrong with her marriage, no disappointments, no residue of conflict with her parents, or resentment over the fact that she had buried herself in her husband—her masculine self sacrificed, in fact *beheaded*, so that she could maintain a perfectly ordinary Washington marriage, performing a role, acting as a priestess in the ritual sacrifice of her own spirit. She had resisted, had tried feebly to argue with him; however, since Dr. Reaume did not argue, but merely set forth tentative, hypothetical suggestions, her emotion soon subsided. At the end of their session she had not quite come round to understanding the crucial importance of the dream in her own psychic development, but she had agreed with him that the dream's images probably related to her and to her alone, since the dream was, of course, a spontaneous creation of her own. He believed she was able to see how her imagination had seized upon him as a symbol, in order to present to her the dramatic nature of her inner struggle; she was an intelligent woman, after all. She was far superior to most of the patients he worked with.

She made an appointment to see him on Monday, and then again on Thursday. They had a great deal of personal material to work through. Her husband was an attorney associated with the State Department, evidently quite successful, and her daughter was enrolled in a small private school in Virginia. There would be no problem about Dr. Reaume's fees, she told him several times; it seemed important to her that he understand. He waved aside such remarks, as if embarrassed. Money! Of course one must eat, one must lower oneself occasionally and think of economic matters. . . . But it was not the primary concern, certainly. He hoped she knew that. Her concern was touching, however, since it contrasted so sharply with the attitude of a woman who had given Dr. Reaume a hard time recently; the middle-aged wife of a wealthy Washington internist, she had paid Dr. Reaume with a worthless check, some six hundred dollars for past accounts. And had been so sincere, so "grateful" at their last meeting, had even managed a few dramatic tears. . . .

But he did not want to think of anything disturbing, just before dinner. His day had been challenging but rewarding also, and now he deserved to relax. He deserved this small measure of happiness.

A harsh ringing woke him. He did not know what day it was or why he lay on his bed, fully clothed. Who had put him here? Where were his glasses?—his shoes?

The telephone was ringing. He had been dreaming of something ugly—an infant—an infant with a mean, withered face—sitting in its own excrement—the filth smeared onto its bare arms and legs and chest. He woke, confused. He sat up. He answered the telephone on the third or fourth ring.

"Dr. Reaume? Is this Dr. Reaume?"

He recognized her voice at once.

She had telephoned earlier, to cancel the two appointments she had made. Since she spoke only with Dr. Reaume's secretary, he had not been able to ask what was wrong: he had been profoundly disappointed. Hurt. The look on the woman's face when she said good-by...the almost ecstatic expression, mingled with fear and awe, as if she had been in the presence of something extraordinary....Unless Dr. Reaume had been deceived, the young woman had certainly benefited from that single session. Her anxiety had lessened. He had helped her so much, had given her so much of himself! Inspired, excited, with a lover's graceful spontaneity, selfless in his zeal, he had been at the peak of his powers. Yet the call came that Monday morning, shortly after nine o'clock, and the woman slipped out of his life once again.

Of course he had been disappointed, but he had managed to forget. Did the woman matter, really? Not really. He had his own life, his long marriage and his family and his career. No stranger could disturb the harmony of his world. He had been hurt, but not deeply. He had forgotten.

The call came one Sunday afternoon in mid-August. He recognized her voice at once: childish, plaintive, a catch in it that was perversely coquettish. "Dr. Reaume? Is this...?"

Yes, yes? What did she want with him?

"Dr. Reaume, please come to me. Come to me here. I can't leave this place...I don't dare leave....I'm not well. You must come to me. Something will happen to both of us if you don't come...."

Sick, was she? Too sick to leave her home?

"You must come to me," she whispered.

He tried to explain that he did not make house calls. It was out of the question. On this hot summer afternoon he was certainly not going to venture across town; her request was impossible.

"Dr. Reaume!" she begged.

He began to shiver, hearing the woman's low, urgent, familiar voice. It was mixed in somehow with the dream he had had: something to do with an infant crying furiously, smeared with its own excrement. The strident ringing of the phone had wakened him. He was still rather confused, disoriented. What did she want, after so many months? Why was she persecuting him?

"Dr. Reaume...?"

He listened. He sat on the edge of his rumpled bed and listened. It was obvious that the woman needed him and that he must go. Her need was raw, pitiless. No matter that his poor heart was pounding and his senses were in a swirl and his wise, pragmatic soul was saying *No, no you don't, absolutely not. Impossible.*

Yes, he would go to her.

That morning he had showered and shaved and patted his face with a fine mild lotion that smelled of mint. Now he had only to change his shirt, which was damp with perspiration. A pale-blue shirt, short-sleeved. And his handsome white summer suit. In the floor-length bedroom mirror a trim, compact little man stood, studying himself. Pale blue on white. And his skin fairly ruddy, almost tan. Tan on white, white on tan. White against blue. And his smile. And that look about his eyes of impish but serene wisdom. She would be impressed by him, as she had been impressed before. "You must come to me, to help me," she had whispered.

Sixty-one years old, was he? He looked much younger. He looked ageless.

Or was he seventy-one now . . . ? He remembered a recent birthday, a mailbox of cards, he remembered checking a date in *Who's Who in America*, bemused, faintly astonished. Seventy-one, seventy-two? It was impossible.

The midday heat was oppressive. He called for a cab but none came. He waited on the sidewalk, he walked to the corner and back, but the cab did not come. A bus? He would go over to the Avenue and catch a crosstown bus, though it had been years since he'd traveled by bus. . . . She had disappointed him, had wounded him deeply. But he had forgiven her. Long ago. In the end she was returning to him, as he had hoped. He remembered her lovely face, that bronze hair of hers, that cringing, coquettish, frightened manner; he remembered her, though he forgot the exact circumstances of their meeting. It was necessary to forget as much as possible, in Dr. Reaume's profession.

After fifteen or twenty minutes a bus came along and Dr. Reaume boarded it.

. . . Necessary to forget as much as possible. He had made an excellent joke along those lines just recently. The young people laughed, grateful for an old man's honesty. A small auditorium of people, men and woman both. An empty seat in the front row, reserved for Mrs. Reaume. She had been ill that evening. He would not miss her, she said. Never missed her. Another award,

nother citation, another honor in the dense procession of honors.
A plaque, a scroll nearly a yard high, handshakes, enthusiastic
miles. *Dr. Reaume, may I . . . ?* A photographer. Two photographers. Explosions of light. Dr. Reaume the noted psychologist,
he distinguished scholar, the author of many books and
hundreds of articles and reviews. *Dr. Reaume? Will you come to
me?* The great achievement of his life was an immense
encyclopedic work with the simple title *Psychologies*. It was in
three volumes, over fifteen hundred pages, an exhaustive,
infinitely detailed historical and analytical and speculative study
of various theories of the psyche, including even those of
witchcraft and the occult and other discredited systems of folk
psychology; including, in a chapter over one hundred pages long,
observations on the often-violent reaction against these psychologies, by governments, churches, professional groups, and other
establishments throughout history. His major work, heroic and
tireless. Monumental. Enthusiastically received even by those
reviewers who admitted they were unable to read much of it.
Psychologies. A lifetime had gone into it and yet the creator still
lived at the peak of his powers. Every year there were new
editions and translations and paperback reprints; most recently,
Yale University Press had brought out an abridged version, in a
handsome paperback with a glossy cover. He was grateful, of
course. What else? He grinned impishly. He shook hands all
around until his frail hands ached. And he made his appreciative
audience laugh by telling them that he, too, had difficulties with
he book. So many pages, so much information! It was more than
mortal man could bear. In preparing it for publication, a lifetime
ago, he had often been unable to decipher his own handwriting.
Who had scribbled so many brilliant, inspired ideas? Who had
guided his hand? Who was responsible? Now he used
Psychologies as a handy reference book, paging through it
impatiently, recognizing very little as his own. Someone had
written the book and that someone was Dr. Reaume, but who Dr.
Reaume was he himself did not know.

"... please come to me," the woman had begged. "Before it's
too late."

And so he had changed his damp shirt and hurried out into the
midsummer heat, trembling with excitement and apprehension
and dread. Genius, they cried. Healer. Come to us. But he was a
humble, ordinary man. He had no pride, no egotism. He differed
from other people only in that he was not fragmented: he was

complete. The burden of his completeness was a painful one, however. He had felt it all his life. Unlike common people he could not project out into the world those conflicts that were inner facts, originating in his own soul; he could not confuse the world with himself, as others did. He was sane. Always had been. In his long lifetime he had witnessed the gradual disintegration of the world, even the "civilized" world, but he himself had always been sane and his sanity had been, at times, a burden. His wife and his family and his friends and his associates and those confused, ignorant people he read of in the daily press—some of them the nation's leaders here in Washington—saw evil in the outside world, always at a distance, always threatening, deathly. They did not know how they participated in it, helped to create it. Like the young woman he was going to save, they were not entirely sane. They were not mad, yet not really sane. And so they turned to him, they called to him, begging for help.

But they sometimes neglected to pay their bills. They moved away or died or broke appointments at the last minute. Sometimes they gave up and killed themselves to spite him. Dr. Reaume offered them a vision of wholeness and they recoiled in fear or in childish pride, like his own son. Like his grandson, now living in San Francisco—no, in Vancouver—thousands of miles away. They hurt him, they wounded him deeply, but he forgave them. He showed no anger. Very little emotion at all. A normal, ordinary man, he was, moving among ordinary people, not distinguished from them except perhaps by the quizzical, intelligent expression that was characteristic of Dr. Reaume; and his almost European courtliness. His concern for others. On this humid August afternoon he was trembling with fatigue and apprehension, astonished that the bus was carrying him into so run-down a section of the city, and yet he did not betray any distress and he would not turn back.... Did he want acclaim for his courage, his heroism? Did he want recognition? But no one was here to observe; he was alone. He sat alone, just behind the black bus driver, his hands clasped on his knees. No one knew him. No one witnessed.... His wife had telephoned from Baltimore. Her voice was lusty, overloud. "It's Margaret I'm concerned about," she said. "The poor woman dwells too much in the past. She drinks too much. I told her I would stay with her as long as necessary, until she was herself again. I told her you wouldn't miss me...." It had been snowing that day, a rare November blizzard. Dr. Reaume had stood at the bedroom window on the third floor of the empty townhouse, listening to a woman's distant voice, watching the idle snow flurries, thinking: What do these things mean? This woman's voice, the nuances in it, the code in which she speaks? Who am I, that everything converges in me? What or whom do these things serve?

A street of brownstone buildings. Black children playing freely in the street, on the sidewalks. Garbage cans. Sacks and cartons of trash, some of them broken open. Why am I here? Dr. Reaume wondered, stepping from the bus. What is going to happen?

His neighborhood lay miles to the northwest. He could not remember. Sunlight blinded his eyes, he was late, very late, the woman had perhaps despaired of him, had gone on without him, had done something irreparable. That was it, you see!—the irreparable nature of sudden, violent acts, the irreversible nature of time. It was not his fault. He was not to blame. The world tottered, the world stank with corruption, how was it his fault?—he had made his journey in the heat, in the dense swarming air, as quickly as possible. But he was an elderly man now: seventy-two years old. Seventy-three. Seventy-five? It was not his fault.

Someone yelled from a second-story window to one of the children in the street. Come in! Get in here! Dr. Reaume squinted through his fingers, blinded by the sun. They were no one he knew. No one he was responsible for. At the curb a young white boy was repairing a car, its hood raised, the boy's long pale hair breaking stiffly about his face; he glanced up at Dr. Reaume but did not seem to see him. Dr. Reaume considered asking him where he might locate the address the woman had given him, but something in the boy's manner was discouraging. . . . He had never been in this part of the city before. Had never been driven through it. Hadn't known, really, that it existed. Such poverty! Such closed-in lives! Half the numbers were missing on the buildings, how could he find her, how could anyone find anyone in this maze? He walked slowly through the waves of heat, half expecting to see the woman leaning from a window, an infant in her arms. . . . *Dr. Reaume,* she would cry, *here! Here I am.* Had to force himself not to hurry. Even when he saw her, he must not run. Since his second heart attack, at the age of seventy-two, he carried himself slowly, slowly. The world had to be incorporated into the soul; otherwise there would be no harmony. Shadowy patches of madness would grow like cancer. More than one trusted friend had betrayed him—had turned against him, either out of envy or because of psychological problems of their own, and of course Mrs. Reaume had disappointed him throughout their marriage. Dying, she had disappointed him. Had turned from him altogether. Men had betrayed him, and women; his son and now his grandson, lost to him, lost by him. He was not to blame. There were those who valued him, like this woman: he lived for them now, he devoted himself to them exclusively. Wounded and incomplete they craved him, called for him, drew him to their sides. *Hello, he would cry in triumph, when she opened the door to him, did you think I wouldn't come?—had you lost faith in me?*

Black children were playing in the street, screaming with excitement. Something struck him—must have been a ball, but it felt very hard. Suddenly a half-dozen children were swarming around him, yelling. What were they saying? Their words were incomprehensible. What, what? Stop, he wanted to plead, don't you know who I am . . . ? One of the boys gave Dr. Reaume a push, for no reason, and he nearly fell to the sidewalk.

The street tilted crazily and for an instant he believed he would slip off and be lost.

He started across the street to escape. Noise! Shouts! Giggles! Words Dr. Reaume had never heard before. He had been too sane all his life and now they were turning against him. They had lured him out into the bright, dazed air, giving him a false address, begging him to come to them, to heal them, and for what—? The woman had lied, she had not wanted to be healed; she had loved her sickness all along.

A black boy appeared before him, looming up. His face glowed with sweat. His eyes bulged. His hair was a dark glimmering aureole, terrible to see. Hello, Dr. Reaume stammered, offering his frail hand, didn't you call me, don't you need me, can't I be of service to you . . . ?

The Thaw

Shortly after noon on their second day at Baylis Lake they encountered the girl: she passed them swiftly, headed in the direction of the lake, accompanied by a large sleek gray-furred dog. She was about eighteen years old, with loose, thick shoulder-length hair of a striking dark gold, quite tall, nearly as tall as Scott. They were on their way to the village, to buy a newspaper and a few supplies. It was a mile's hike and the wind was rather chilly from the northeast, but they did not want to drive; they had come to the lake to get some exercise. When they saw the girl approaching, striding along the hard, frozen path, Ellen could sense her husband's surprise and then his interest and she could almost have said, to the instant, when he would raise a gloved hand and call out a greeting. He was a reticent man and so he sometimes forced himself at such times to be friendly; to behave in a friendly manner. She knew how vulnerable he was and she hoped the girl would respond.

At first she was not going to notice them. She walked hurriedly, eyes lowered, hands thrust into the pockets of her oversized wool jacket; she was very much alone, even with the dog beside her. But it really would have been impossible for her to ignore them. The lake was deserted at this time of year. Apart from the caretaker who lived in one of the smaller cabins on the far side of the lake, the three of them were probably the only people in the immediate vicinity. So it was quite natural for Scott to speak to her as they passed. His greeting was casual, cheerful. She glanced up at him and at Ellen, unsmiling, and murmured a few words, and continued on. Yet she had not been unfriendly. She had managed the encounter gracefully enough.

"What a pretty girl!" Ellen said warmly. "She didn't look familiar, though. Whose cabin do you suppose she's staying in?"

"She looked familiar," Scott said.

"Did she? Do you know her?"

"No."

"I wonder if she's here alone. We didn't notice anyone yesterday, there weren't any cars around yesterday....It would be odd, wouldn't it, for her to be here alone?"

Her hair was so rich a color: her eyes deep-set and blue and thickly lashed, like a child's. Like a child she had had an open, frank, disingenuous stare, raised to them and then lowered, with that timid, clever grace, acknowledging them in one instant and in the next dismissing them.

"She looked familiar," Scott said. "Someone's daughter. Someone's daughter grown up, since we last saw her."

"A very pretty girl," Ellen said.

Scott said nothing.

They had driven up the day before, a Sunday, four hundred miles to the upper peninsula of the state, into the lake country. The roads had been nearly deserted. The drive had been long and exhausting and when they got to their cabin, it had seemed rather shabby and smaller than they remembered—hadn't it been more attractive last summer?—the summer before last? They had not been to Baylis Lake for a year and a half. As soon as they unlocked the door and went inside the cabin Scott said the trip had been a mistake. "Obviously we shouldn't have come. It's wrong. It feels wrong."

"But we thought...."

"I didn't. I wasn't the one. You were the one who insisted."

"But...."

"It's freezing in here," he said, his voice rising shrilly. "What are we going to do until it warms up? It might take hours...."

"We could sit in the car."

"In the car! And risk being asphyxiated...."

"We could drive around the lake. We could drive back to the village and stop somewhere...at the hotel, or the pub...."

"It wasn't my idea to come here," he said.

It had been his idea from the first. But she would not challenge him.

"Everything seems so ugly, so muted at this time of year," he said helplessly. "Easter Sunday...Easter....And the lake is icebound and there's snow everywhere and it's so cold in here in this ugly cabin, what are we going to do?"

"Would you like to go back home?"

"It's out of the question to go back home."

Dismay and anger had enlivened him. His cheeks were flushed, the very tip of his nose had reddened, his dark, almost black eyes were bright and glistening. He knew she was watching him and so he refused to look at her. He went to stand by the floor-to-ceiling plate-glass window that faced the lake, fifty yards away; even in his bulky, coarse-knit sweater he looked frail. His red-brown hair seemed to move, however, even to breathe, wisps of it stirring as if with his emotion. Ellen said, softly, "If you want to go back, I don't mind. I don't mind driving."

"You're being ridiculous."

"I don't mind. We could start out and stay in a motel."

"You're exhausted. You don't know what you're talking about," he said tonelessly. "We might as well stay."

After they unpacked and the cabin heated and Ellen fixed a light, warm meal—scrambled eggs with ham and cheese, and thick dark bread—the tension between them lessened. It had been a good idea to come north, after all. The stillness, the isolation, the view of the lake—the cold, harsh, fresh air—the occasional honking of mallards or geese and the sound of the wind in the pines: Ellen felt moved by these things, reassured. When the sun set, the sky and part of the lake were transformed, subtly, richly, a pale red-orange that accentuated the division between the open, choppy water and the jagged line of ice that edged the beach. They sat in silence, watching. "It's so beautiful here," Ellen whispered. "People can never imagine...can never remember, in that other life...."

"Yes," Scott said. "It's beautiful. It always is."

The cabin belonged to Scott's uncle, now an elderly man in a nursing home in Ft. Lauderdale; it, and the fairly large lot that came with it, would go to Scott when the old man died. Scott had always liked their brief vacations here, though he had not liked the presence of other people, and had detested the noise of outboard motors on the lake. But now it was late winter and no one was around.

"Then you're happy we came? You don't think it was a mistake?" Ellen asked.

" . . . as good a place as any to die," Scott said lightly.

"But you're not going to die," Ellen said. "That's ridiculous."

"I know. I know it is."

"It's ridiculous to talk like that," she said, blinking rapidly.

"I know. . . . But death is ridiculous in itself. It's ridiculous anywhere."

"Scott, please. . . ."

"I know, I know," he said quickly. "I *know*."

In the distance, the soft wheezy cry of an owl. A barn owl, probably. Closer, the calls of mourning doves, light, eerie, melodic, blending with the wind; and the abrupt, raucous cries of the mallards; and the chattering of smaller birds, primarily sparrows and juncos and cardinals. Ellen heard a red-winged blackbird, far away: so it was spring, it was going to turn warmer, it was going to thaw.

One day he had said to her: "I'm not what I appear to be." She had laughed nervously. She had not understood.

"I appear to be well, don't I? In good health? Eh? I appear to resemble anybody, any normal man? Don't I? . . . But that's not the case. That's an illusion."

"I don't understand," she had said.

They had been married for many years. She would not have hesitated to say that they were happily married; she believed they were "happily married." But when he sat with her that day, holding both her hands in his, grave, decorous, faintly mocking, when he spoke in a deliberately casual voice of certain physical symptoms and a visit he had made to their doctor without telling her and the need for a few days' hospitalization in order for tests to be made, she had thought, suddenly, that she did not know him at all; she was terrified not to know him. The prospect of his being seriously ill, even the prospect of his death, did not seem so terrible to her at that moment as the realization that she hardly knew him.

"I appear to be absolutely normal," he said, chuckling. "I'm not much different—only a few pounds heavier—than the man you married, eh? I could fool anyone. I do. But not for much longer."

Now, eighteen months later, the pale skin stretched tight over his prominent cheekbones and there were bruiselike pockets beneath his eyes and faint, vexed lines on his face and throat; but he was still attractive. His brown hair was fine and silky, his eyes were sharp, alert, bright. He walked stiffly, carrying himself almost with a kind of awe or dread; sometimes he leaned upon Ellen involuntarily. He did look older now. He had lost weight. But he had triumphed; by his thirty-ninth birthday they were reasonably sure he had triumphed.

"I love you so much," he had said, weeping in her arms. "Without you I couldn't ... I couldn't have...."

"It's all right," she said. "It's over."

They met the girl again, on the beach. This time they stopped to talk, self-consciously, as the dog sniffed at them and circled them in silence and then trotted away. At first they spoke of the weather—a record cold for this time of the year, according to the news broadcast that morning—the coldest Easter Sunday in twenty-three years—and light snow flurries predicted for today. But it would thaw soon, it *must* thaw soon. Unless of course the North American climate were really changing, as some people claimed, and a new Ice Age was imminent.... "I believe that," the girl said. "I think that makes sense.... We deserve it, I mean, don't we? I think that makes sense." But she smiled. And her manner was rather gay, almost flippant. "I don't mind at all. I really don't. I came here on purpose because I knew it would be cold, I love it up here when the lake's frozen and no one's around and you can hear your footsteps crunching in the snow, breaking through the crust of the snow...."

Then the dog trotted back and the girl bent to hug him and they complimented her on the dog: a Russian wolfhound, long-legged, silky, aristocratic, with a head so small and narrow as to seem unnatural. A handsome dog, though. Both Ellen and Scott patted him. The girl seemed pleased by their attention, still bent over the dog, fussing with him, even kissing his head. She was extraordinarily pretty, Ellen saw, with her wide, expressive blue gaze and her loose blond hair and her manner of bright, agreeable insouciance, her sense of being the center of attention, childlike and even innocent in her vanity. She chattered and they listened, warmed by her. Ellen felt a pang of emotion; nothing so simple or crude as jealousy, not even envy....

"I'm here because I want to be alone," the girl announced. "I need to be alone. I need to think my life through ... need to assess certain things that have happened to me recently ... certain involvements I can't handle. I love to be alone. I don't mind at all. I could live alone for years like this, with Randy, without any human beings at all.... Why are you here? Just for a change?"

"For a change, yes," Scott said quickly. "A change in the pattern of our lives."

The girl looked from Scott to Ellen, smiling. The whites of her eyes were very white. Her skin glowed, her teeth were perfect. Strands of hair were blown into her face and she brushed them away, with a graceful flicking of her long fingers.

"For a change in the pattern of your lives," she repeated. "I think that's wonderful."

"She's very pretty," Ellen said.

"Very young and thinks awfully well of herself," Scott said.

"...She's confident. She's evidently able to take control of her own life, her own feelings. It's confidence."

"It's arrogance," Scott said.

"But—don't you like her?" Ellen said, as if hurt. "I thought you liked her. We had a pleasant conversation."

"She's only a child," Scott said irritably.

"Do you know who she is? She's that Carlisle's daughter—the doctor—you remember, the doctor?—with the blue-striped sail? I saw her going into his cabin. I'm sure it's his. I remember his children being so young!—I'm sure I remember her, from years ago, as a skinny little girl."

"Does it matter?" Scott said evasively. "I don't think it matters."

Ellen stared at him, uncomprehending.

"Why do you hate me?" she whispered.

During the difficult time of his illness she had read many books and articles; most were on the subject of his illness, but some were by poets and mystics; even by saints—Saint John of the Cross, Saint Teresa. There seemed to be a great deal of time, once he was home from the hospital. There were many hours,

ne following another. A long stretch of hours broken only by
ighttime and the possibility of sleep, hour following hour,
ndless. Sometimes she read aloud to her husband, in a girlish,
uavering voice; almost at random she read to him—*Near is
:od, and hard to apprehend, but where danger is there arises
alvation also*—grateful when he was struck by the wisdom or
eauty of her offering. She searched through her college
nthologies, discovered poems she had not read or recalled for
ifteen years, some of them minutely annotated in her schoolgirl's
and; she came upon a poem she had loved and had forgotten,
Iopkin's "As Kingfishers Catch Fire," and read it to Scott, deeply
noved, almost euphoric, transported. He had not understood it,
ut had seemed to like it. Reserved, always a little secretive, he
ad become almost mute since the operation . . . though at times
e would speak effusively, chattering of inconsequential
natters.

He had triumphed and would continue to triumph.

"How wonderful to be alive!" he said often. And then again:
How queer, to be alive—how unreal it seems!—and not very
mportant."

There were days of relative normality, peace, contentment.
And then, unaccountably, a bad day. Two or three bad days. But
e had triumphed and would continue to triumph, had endured a
eries of seven cobalt treatments, headaches and indigestion and
emporary blindness the only side effects. He grew stronger.
Gained a few pounds. Seemed to enjoy her reading to him when
e was lying down, not quite in the mood to read for himself.

"There are times when your voice is so bell-like and reverent,"
e said. "You must love me . . . ?"

"Of course I love you."

"But it doesn't change anything, does it? It doesn't change
ne."

"Doesn't it?"

"Does it?"

"I wish you wouldn't joke, Scott."

"You're such a good, reverent wife," he murmured, taking her
ands. "How could I joke with you? That would be cruel."

They walked to the village a second time, in jeans and boots
ind heavy belted sweaters bought in Scotland years ago. The air
vas wet, cold, sharply pleasant. The smells of spruce and yew
vere strong and Ellen would have liked to wander, alone, back

into the woods; the trees were more impressive at this time of year than in the summer. Everything was strange, unsettling. There were patches and fingers of snow on the ground and yet the earth's axis had shifted and the days were noticeably longer, the pale sunlight more intense, concentrated. It was April. Snowflakes fell while the sun shone and vast areas of the sky were clear, so that the open waters of the lake were a deep, vivid blue, violent in motion. A small flock of mallards, males and females, rode the choppy waves placidly; Scott called her attention to them. He squeezed her hand. He mumbled something about being sorry for certain remarks he had made—being sorry he was an invalid, in ways he could not always control.

"You're not an invalid," Ellen said flatly.

They saw a deer several hundred feet away, motionless in a grove of yew trees, watching them. They saw rabbit tracks and what must have been raccoon tracks. They stood for several minutes watching three black squirrels high in an oak tree, involved in a noisy skirmish of some kind, agitated, manic. They held hands, laughing at the squirrels.

"Yes, it was a good idea to come here," Scott said.

In the village they went to Vic's Drugs, with its new mock-colonial façade, to buy a newspaper. A radio played rock music. Then there was a five-minute news break: an arms build-up somewhere in the Mideast, the first several indictments handed down by a grand jury investigating conflict of interest in the state legislature, a fourteen-year-old girl found dead in a field near Ypsilanti, having been raped and stabbed repeatedly. They paid for their newspaper and a bottle of hand lotion and left. The little town was fairly busy; the parking lot adjacent to the A&P was filled. Children rode bicycles, squealing, as if delighted with the snow flurries. They went to the Wellington Hotel, where there was a pleasant English-style pub, but it struck them as different from what they remembered—not so charming, rather chilly, shabby. And a television set was on above the bar. They did no more than glance in. "Just as well," Scott said. "I don't want to start drinking this early in the day."

They walked back down to the lake, both rather tired. From time to time Scott leaned against Ellen, his arm through hers. He was panting slightly and his breath steamed. There was an odd attentiveness in him, a tension she could not comprehend; he seemed expectant, apprehensive. When he spoke, it was absently, as if he were thinking of something else, not attending to his own words. When she spoke, she knew he wasn't listening. She knew from the past that there were reserves of blind, baffled rage in him, as if a complex story were working itself out inside him and only its outbursts were known to her; and she did not dare interrupt that story.

Nearing the path that led to the cabin both spoke at once, at the same moment. Ellen asked what he would like for dinner that night and Scott murmured: "...Carlisle place, did you say? Which one is that?"

Entering, she wore a crocheted cap of red wool and a long red scarf, wound about her neck; and a navy-blue jacket, sheepskin-lined, shapeless. Beneath it she wore rather soiled jeans and an inexpensive jersey blouse, pale blue, which fitted her tightly. Her breasts were surprisingly full; her thighs and hips well-developed. Her name was Abigail. Her father was indeed Dr. Carlisle, of Grosse Pointe Farms, but she did not care to speak of her parents at the moment. "I came here for solitude," she said. "I came here to assess my life."

Her pronouncements were solemn and yet audacious, almost coquettish. She laughed quite a bit. The white wine went to her head and she laughed superbly, tilting her shoulders, showing her beautiful teeth. She complimented Ellen on the dinner several times; she wished she had the ability to cook but it was hopeless—she had no patience for that sort of thing. "Sometimes I wish, y'know what I wish?—that I was just like anyone else, that I would marry someone I loved and stay in one place and be content, you know, and live out my life like that."

There was a half-moon. Ellen stared at the lake, at the icy glinting waves, wondering why she felt so indifferent. The dinner had gone well and Scott was in an excellent mood, the happiest she had seen him in weeks, and Abigail was charming, really very sweet; but Ellen could not concentrate on their conversation. Scott was asking questions and the girl replied evasively, hinting of some disappointment, then laughing again, like a child eager to escape adult surveillance. Was she in love?—had she ever been in love? Scott did not quite ask this, and the girl managed to not quite answer. Ellen watched the moonlight on the water, hypnotized by its constant agitation. She had had only one glass of wine but she felt numbed. Abigail's dog lay asleep at Ellen's feet. The weight of its head was warm and pleasant, rather heavy.

Scott and the girl talked. They drank and talked. They
laughed together, companionably. Ellen heard again her
husband's young, vigorous voice and she did not dare look at
him—did not dare see, again, the bold flush of youth in his
wasted face. She remembered having seen him that morning, by
accident, as she was about to leave the bedroom and he was
crossing from the kitchen area to the side door: thinking himself
alone, unobserved, he had been frowning, his face tight and
pursed, his lips slightly moving as if he were whispering to
himself, arguing. At such times his eyes narrowed and his jaw
tensed, as if he were confronting an enemy. Who was the enemy?
What was it?—But now he was transformed, now he was another
man entirely. And she did not dare look.

It turned out that Abigail sang; that she took voice lessons. But
she had no talent, she insisted. Her voice was weak. —Would she
sing for them? No, no, her voice was weak, her breathing wasn't
right, she hated herself. —Please, wouldn't she sing? It would be
lovely to hear her sing!

She laughed in embarrassment. No, really she couldn't. She
couldn't.

But it would mean so much, Scott insisted.

Abigail managed to change the subject and they talked for a
while of the northern woods, and Scott gave Abigail a book to
read or to keep if she liked—*The Great Lakes: From
Pre-Historical Times to the Present*. It was one of the many old
battered books Scott's uncle kept here in the cabin. Then they
spoke of the weather again and Abigail thanked them once more
for having invited her to dinner and then, adroitly, Scott shifted
back to the subject of her singing; wouldn't she sing one song for
them? Please?

So she sang. And it was quite a surprise: not a popular song,
not even a ballad, but an art-song a friend of hers had composed,
setting the words of a Höderlin poem to music. She sang the
German words in a strong, deep, thrilling voice, a woman's voice
and not a girl's, not a child's. The effect was so startling that Ellen
and Scott glanced at each other. Her shyness had misled them;
they were really not prepared for the deep-voiced, mysterious
power of what they were hearing, these incomprehensible and
yet utterly convincing words—

> *Gröbers wolltest auch du, aber die Liebe zwingt*
> *All uns nieder, das Leid beuget gewaltiger,*

>*Doch es kehret umsonst nicht*
>>*Unser Bogen, woher er kommt!*
>*Aufwärts oder hinab....*

When she stopped, they were silent for a moment; then Scott began to clap and Ellen joined in, self-consciously. The girl flicked her hair out of her face and grinned, with a curious reluctance, as if the song and their admiration had really given her no pleasure.

"Amazing," Scott said, staring at her. "I wouldn't have thought.... Yes, it's amazing. And very beautiful."

She shrugged her shoulders. "Thank you. You're very nice. A friend of mine set the poem to music, a close friend, someone who was a close friend at one time.... It has a private meaning to me and I wouldn't have sung it except it's the best thing I know, I feel closer to it than to anything else...."

"What do the words mean? Ellen and I don't know German."

But the girl had turned away and was preparing to leave. She ignored Scott's question. He jumped to his feet, helped her with her chair, fussed over her. "Very nice of you to come... your voice is haunting, isn't it, Ellen? ... and beautiful ... powerful ... you shouldn't underestimate yourself; modesty isn't always becoming.... Wait, I'll get my sweater. I can't allow you to walk back alone."

"It isn't far. There's no one around."

"Really, must you leave so soon? It's still early."

But she was waking the dog, hauling him playfully to his feet. "Randy is all the protection I need, aren't you? Hey? Wake up!"

"It's early, Ellen, isn't it! Tell Abigail she shouldn't leave so early...."

Ellen forced herself to speak. She was still transfixed by the girl's voice and by the mysterious authority of the German words, only a few of which she recognized; the sudden intrusion of her husband's voice and the bustle of leave-taking disturbed her. "Yes? ... Yes, it's early, it's still early ... won't you stay a little longer? Shall I make coffee?"

But the evening was over; the girl was clearly anxious to leave. She slipped on her heavy jacket and wound the scarf about her neck and folded the red cap, not wanting to wear it, and slipped it into one of her pockets. Scott was muttering to himself, getting his sweater from the closet. "I really must leave," the girl said, edging toward the door. "Thank you very much. You were very kind to invite me over...."

"I hope we'll see you again soon," Ellen said politely. "How long will you be staying here?"

"I can walk back alone," the girl said to Scott. She smiled brightly, showing her lovely teeth. "Really. Randy is all the protection I need. And no one's around, no one is staying here except us...."

"Don't be silly, Abigail," Scott said shortly. "I'm certainly not going to let you walk a half-mile in this dark, even with your elegant wolfhound. Don't you agree, Ellen? ... Of course."

Ellen agreed. She rose, watched them from the door, her arms folded across her thin chest. The girl, Scott, the slow-trotting dog; that mysterious song, the simple, almost plain melody, the precise progression of words. What did it mean? What did they mean? She was numb, as if her spirit had been drained from her. Not indifferent but numb, stricken. The girl's voice had been such a surprise, so beautiful, so compelling....

She watched the three figures until they were out of sight, then she stood in the open doorway for a while longer, staring at the lake and the broken border of ice and the opaque line of trees on the opposite shore. She wondered how long her husband would be gone.

She had learned to nurse him many months ago. She had learned not to weep or to show exhaustion in his presence. Had she lied to him?—perhaps, but only occasionally. Never about anything serious. She lied about herself, about her own feelings; not about him.

She had followed him a great distance, along endless low-ceilinged corridors, between windowless walls. Her voice had echoed monstrously as she spoke his name, assured him he would not die, citing statistics, summarizing case histories, reporting doctors' pronouncements in her small clear voice. White-clad attendants, faceless, pushed the dying man on a hospital cart and she followed behind him, murmuring his name, trying not to scream. There were walls of antiseptic tile, doors that swung heavily to and fro, stairs that led into the cavernous earth or up into the shadows, out of the range of her vision. Except for her sobbing and the squeaking of the cart's wheels, all was silent. Perhaps he had already died: he lay on the cart motionless, beneath a thin white cloth.

There were enormous humming machines. There were unwinking lights. Transparent tubes fed him, by way of his blood-rimmed nostrils and the vein on the inside of his left arm. He groaned, stirred, breathed laboriously. He had not died. She watched over him, miraculously clearheaded, not at all afraid. It was a shock to see how wasted his arms and legs were and how pale his flesh, the papery-thin flesh of his face. But she withstood it. She had no choice. She learned to nurse him: how to sponge his body with warm water and a gentle, fragrant soap, how to help him with the bedpan and, later, how to walk with him to the bathroom, how exactly to hold him so that he would not bruise.

She was with him, always. When she was in another part of the house or outside, she was still with him—her mind circled him, always, absorbed by him. He had not died. He was not going to die. She read to him and brought the phonograph into his room and played records, the volume turned low. She measured out his capsules; she brought him food on a tray; she helped him exercise. Later, he would claim that he owed his life to her. She had always loved him and now she loved him more than ever. She did not speak of love, nor did he. But it was obvious that they loved each other very much, having come so close to death.

"It's been a year and a half," Scott said one day. "I'm not going to die, am I?" His voice was toneless.

"Of course you're not going to die."

"Am I going to live, though . . . ?"

He lay back on his pillows, watching her. He was the man she had married and yet a man she did not know, had never met. Her own husband had died and another man had slipped into his body. . . . But that was a ridiculous thought. She loved him just the same. Tears edged into her eyes, provoked by his rude stare. "Why do you hate me, Scott?" she whispered.

"You know too much," he said.

The day dawned like the others, dark and cold. But shortly after nine o'clock the sun shone and after an hour or so the eaves began dripping and there was the sense of change, of melting, of a thaw—though it was still quite cold and there was a northeastern wind so strong that tiny whitecaps appeared in the open water. Scott tossed down the book he had been trying to read and picked up yesterday's newspaper and, after a few seconds, tossed that down as well. "My mind is wrecked. My mind is broken," he said. "I can no longer concentrate on words."

He was slouched in the leather chair that faced the window and the lake, and Ellen was in the second bedroom, going through a pile of old books and magazines, and though she heard him clearly enough she pretended she had not.

"Ellen? I think I'll go out for a while."

"Yes?"

"I think I'll go out for a while."

He had no need to tell her, as if he were a child and she his mother, but it was an odd habit they had gotten into since his illness. Sometimes he made such announcements ironically, as if he were aware of what he did, aware that it was not really necessary, yet resentful that he must do it. Ellen murmured a reply.

He was going to the girl, of course.

But she did not mind. She was not going to mind. She continued working in the bedroom, listening to the dripping of the eaves and the excited chattering of birds close by, in the pines. The day was sunny and windy. There was excitement in it, an almost tangible sense of motion, change. Scott went out, wearing the handsome beige sweater she had bought him in Inverness and a cloth cap with earflaps, because of the wind. "Do you think I look ridiculous in this cap?" he said doubtfully. "I do. I look ridiculous. But I can't help it."

He did not head for the girl's cabin, however; surprisingly, he got a rake from the toolshed and began clearing the grassy patch and the stretch of sloping beach before the cabin, working briskly. Ellen watched him. He appeared to be absorbed in what he did. A tall, touchingly thin figure, rather awkward with the rake, but industrious. Ellen wondered if she should help him. She wondered if it might be too tiring for him, or too cold; he was susceptible to chest colds and the wind from the lake was strong. But she did not dare disturb him. When she looked out, after fifteen minutes, he had slowed considerably and she could see that his face was closed, pursed, his lips moving again in that ceaseless argument, his body stiff with antagonism. A story of some kind was telling itself in him, below his level of consciousness, erupting only occasionally into the world he shared with others. Sometimes he burst out, unaccountably, against members of his family or friends or business associates—sharp bitter denunciations, really inexplicable—and it seemed to Ellen that these remarks made reference to a level of discourse totally alien to her, coming from nowhere, fitting into no prior scheme of his. After the outburst he would seem to catch himself and say he hadn't meant it—hadn't even known what he was saying. The night before, returning from walking Abigail back to her cabin, he had said suddenly, undressing, "Do you think that was intentional, the German song? The German words?" and Ellen had not known what he meant, so he went on to say, with a peculiar anger that was half-apologetic, that maybe the girl had deliberately sung a song they wouldn't know, maybe she had wanted to put them in their place, let them *know*. "Know? Know what?" Ellen had asked. But Scott could not explain. "Let us know...who she is, who we are," he said vaguely. "The differences between us."

He had been gone no more than ten minutes, walking with Abigail and the dog. Probably less. Ellen had had time only to clear the table and rinse the dishes; time only to play back in her imagination the scene at the table—her husband's rapt gaze, the girl's smile and her paradoxical manner and her strong, deep, thrilling voice. Ellen hated the girl. She hated the girl and Scott both. Her heart seemed to stab at her, with the realization of her hatred. She was excluded from their pleasure in each other, from the easy intimacy that had grown between them...she would be excluded forever, set aside. Yet she worked mechanically at the sink, and when Scott returned, so soon, she felt an indefinable disappointment. He had seemed rather tired. He had remarked on the persistent cold—unnatural, freakish, maddening for April. Ellen said nothing, thinking of the girl singing, and of the dog at her own feet, and of her husband's transfixed face. She did hate them, hated even that elegant, comely dog, but it gave her pleasure to think of them. *Did you kiss her?* she wanted to ask, bitterly.

At the long walnut table they sat in silence, eating, facing the window as always. The sun was still shining. The water shone coldly, broken and agitated, hypnotic. On the far side of the lake the pines appeared to be of a uniform, rigid height. Everything was still except for the sound of dripping and the birds' cries and the wind, which had not died down. At the rear of the cabin something was scraping irritably against the roof.

"This is the edge of the world," Scott said in a queer hollow voice. "It was like this before we lived."

Ellen turned to him. "*We...?*"

"Our species."

She laughed. The sound surprised her, it was so joyless.

"Why don't you go to her?" she said softly after a moment. "That's what you want, isn't it?"

"It's beautiful here but it hurts. The air hurts. The sun. The water. It isn't human here," he said in the same hollow, bewildered voice.

"Go to her, why don't you? The girl. *Her*. She's waiting for you."

Her mouth twisted as she spoke. Her voice was ugly, not her own.

"She's waiting for me . . . ?" Scott said.

"I know what you want, what you've been thinking of. I know how you've been thinking of her."

"You do?"

His voice raised lightly, scornfully.

"I hate you both," Ellen whispered.

She rose blindly from the table and went into the bedroom.

At the window she half closed her eyes. She saw a man's figure on the beach, a man's figure cutting across the edge of the lake, risking the ice. He walked quickly, knowing his destination. Quickly. Confidently. He was young, energetic, shameless. She hated him. Yet she would watch: she would stand at the window and watch until he was out of sight.

She could hear again the girl's lovely calm mysterious voice. It had issued from her as if it were not her own possession, as if it were a bodiless sound, excruciatingly beautiful, indescribable, not hers, not even human. She could hear that voice, and she could see, again, her husband's face: the intensity of his emotion, the shameless blunt power of his lust.

"Why don't you go to her . . . ?" she whispered aloud.

It was horrible, hideous, that he should not, that he should remain in this place, fixed and helpless; merely her husband. That he should be himself and none other. That he should someday die.

They listened to the rhythmic dripping of the eaves. Harsh rude joyful dripping melting thawing: the entire world was thawing.

"Look at that sun!" Scott said.

Ellen shaded her eyes and squinted. It was true, the sun was enormous, powerful, almost intimidating. The thaw had begun. Something in her responded to it, some feeling too subtle, too deep, to be called an emotion. She wanted to cry, then again she wanted to laugh. She wanted to exclaim in vexation.

"She has a visitor anyway," Scott said. "Someone drove over there around noon."

"A visitor?"

"It looked like a man. A young man."

"Then we won't see her again...?" Ellen said slowly.

Scott was lying on a sofa, facing the windows, propped against a pillow. He had pulled an old afghan of green and brown squares up to his chin. In the painful clarity of the sunshine he looked aged and yet peaceful, serene; for the first time Ellen saw him as an old man and realized that he would be—he would be beautiful. She stared at him, struck by her knowledge, and he must have felt her surprise because he turned to her, trying to smile. Yet he misunderstood. He said, "Do you forgive me?"

"Forgive you?"

"For the girl—for all that."

"Of course I forgive you," Ellen said, still in a slow, stricken voice. She took his hand and squeezed his cold fingers.

"If I had gone, I might never have come back...."

"Yes, I know."

"...you wouldn't have wanted me back, and I couldn't have come back...."

"Of course I forgive you," she said.

She bent to kiss him. She hoped neither of them would draw away.

"I love you," one whispered.

And the other replied at once, "I love *you*."

Further Confessions

I

On the morning of October third I boarded the *Cap Arcona* and, in my opulent stateroom, where my steamer trunk and my innumerable pieces of luggage were already waiting, I chanced to look out one of the portholes and saw a hellish sight.

A half-dozen gulls were fighting. Their wings flapping, their beaks furious, their cries demented and alarming—they were fighting over something that floated in the water, bobbing and plunging with the waves. Though I knew better, I could not resist staring. I threw the porthole window open and actually leaned forward to take in that ugly sight.

(It will be sufficient for my purposes to report that the thing that floated in the harbor, eyeless and trailing its guts, was not human: was not of our species.)

Shocked, sickened, I slammed the window shut.

And then a vision came upon me, seemed to open within my affrighted head. I lost all awareness of my surroundings—lost my interest in the other estimable passengers—in the identity of a particularly handsome woman who had boarded the ship unaccompanied—and I found myself, inspired by the ungainly splashing and cries of the gulls just outside my window, recalling with disturbing vividness a dream I had had shortly before dawn.

I am not one to linger in the realm of dreams. If I may speak of myself frankly, I must say that I am, far more than most, *attuned* to the world—to its splendid demands and its even more splendid rewards. *He who really loves the world shapes himself to please it*—so I have known from earliest adolescence, though it is only in the past few years that I have felt confident enough in my own destiny to articulate that truth. As one loves the world and serves it, by being, not least of all, one of its more graceful creations, so the world will respond in kind—will offer evidence of its respect; will offer evidence, upon occasion, of its adulation. And so the world of dreams, claustrophobic and overheated, has never interested me. I sleep well—like all healthy animals I sleep intensely—and I have always enjoyed sleep, as a physiological pleasure; but dreams have struck me as merely distracting and in any case indecipherable.

Very early in the morning of October third, however, I had been visited by a ghastly dream that could not so easily be brushed aside. It was utterly silent—except for the stray, seemingly accidental, and very faint cries of seabirds: a dream of my own death, my own corpse, laid in state in an enormous coffin that was at the same time a kind of boat, pushing out to sea. Hideous . . . ! At each of the four corners of the darkly gleaming coffin was a bird of death which flapped its wings solemnly; its eyes were agates, cloudy and opaque. The corpse—my corpse—lay with its head resting upon a pillow of white satin, eyes shut, lips firmly closed, an expression of sorrow giving the face a grayish cast: aging it by ten years at least. But the face showed not merely sorrow; it showed, as well, a certain resentment, a look of vexation, almost, as if the death that had come was really a most unpleasant surprise. I stared and stared upon that extraordinary sight. I awaited a flicker of life, a movement of the eyelids—a glance of recognition. Could I really be dead? I, Felix, so young, so handsome, hardly across the threshold of a life that promised great riches of all kinds? Incredible that the adventure might be so abruptly halted: yet the corpse was my own. Those fair brown curls arranged about the waxen, peevish face were my own, "arranged" just as artificially as they would be, no doubt, if a stranger were given license to dress them for the grave.

The horror of gazing upon one's own corpse can well be imagined. I stared, sickened with a sense of outrage as well—a sense that something had gone wrong, some mistake had occurred. But the corpse did not stir. The eyelids did not flutter.

There was no sound except that of the ugly, ungainly birds of death, their high-pitched, random cries that blended with the sounds of the sea and the wind, and the vast indifferent spaces of the world itself—the "world" as it exists emptied of the human and of all human values.

I cried aloud, stricken with anguish. It was not simply "my" death I mourned but the fact of death itself—and most egregious of all, the fact that so graceful, so very nearly beautiful a creature as I might be brought to a premature end. I cried aloud and turned away and awoke, heart pounding; and the vision came to a merciful conclusion.

Of course I managed to forget it almost at once. After a few agitated minutes I fell asleep again, and did not wake until seven-thirty. From that point on I was exceptionally busy— settling my accounts with the Savoy Palace, bestowing generous though not lavish tips on its employees (for, having been a hotel employee myself at one time, I can well testify to the demoralizing consequences of unreasonably lavish tips), arranging for my considerable amount of luggage to be transported to the *Cap Arcona*. I did note that the day was overcast and humid. There is something melancholy about white, impassive skies— they are like ceilings that press too closely upon us, from which we cannot escape.

Once at the harbor I was, of course, distracted by the general atmosphere of festivity, busyness, and anticipation. I have always rejoiced in ceremonial occasions—in those occasions, at least, when the more attractive aspects of human nature are called forth. All about me my fellow passengers were saying good-by to relatives and friends. I halfway regretted my decision to leave Lisbon without informing certain acquaintances of mine (of whom I do not choose to speak at the moment); at the same time, being alone in the midst of so much commotion gave me the opportunity to study the others closely. I took notice of the very attractive woman of whom I spoke—took notice first of all of the phaeton from which she alighted; it was elegant, upholstered in dove-gray silk, almost too luxurious for my taste. And the woman herself!—beautifully dressed in scarlet and creamy-white and black. She must have been about thirty-five years old, with a pale, narrow face, very dark eyes and hair; seeing her off were an older couple, no doubt her parents, and an elderly white-haired woman, probably her grandmother. I could not overhear their conversation yet I seemed to sense, or to actually know, that the woman was a widow. (I knew also that we would become acquainted, well before the ship docked in Buenos Aires.) And there were other fascinating passengers boarding the ship: twin boys of about eight, strikingly beautiful, dark-complexioned, almost swarthy, accompanied by an older woman who must have been a governess, and by an enormous whippetlike dog; and a couple in their forties, the gentleman in earnest conversation with his rather plain but agreeable wife—I was certain I had seen him a few days ago in the Museu Sciências Naturaes in the Rua da Prata, studying with great interest a display of fossil remains; and an elderly white-haired gentleman with a fine Spanish face who leaned heavily on the arm of a smartly dressed young man about my age; and . . . and also. . . .

But it is pointless to recount these sights and to record the excited impressions I received that morning. For I was fated not to sail on the the *Cap Arcona* after all.

As soon as my vision cleared I left my stateroom. I took no luggage with me, not even a handbag; in my panic I thought of nothing except escape. No doubt people stared—I did not see—my eyes were blinded with tears—I could not remain on the ship another moment—I had to get back to land. It did not occur to me at the time that I might be acting unwisely, or crazily, or that I would regret my impulsive behavior once the ship sailed.

The death warning could not be ignored. Its vividness, its incredible authenticity could not be ignored. And so I fled . . . I fled . . . leaving behind my handsome leather suitcases filled with clothes and costly possessions, and my detailed plans for an itinerary that was to have included South America, North America, the South Seas, Japan, India, Egypt, Constantinople, Greece, Italy, and France. I fled like a frightened child, unashamed, unself-conscious; knowing only the necessity of immediate flight. I did not want to die. I did not want to be transformed into that corpse! And so there was nothing to do but escape, carrying only the money I had in my wallet, and sacrificing forever the small fortune I would have acquired had I been in a position to draw upon the letters of credit awaiting me in banks in the principal ports of call around the world. . . .

What good is the promise of wealth, if one has gazed upon the face of his own corpse? Life calls to life, wishing only to sustain itself. And so I made a rather ungracious exit and thwarted my destiny.

II

I spent the rest of that day and the night in a nondescript hotel near the Tagus, where no one knew me, and then, with the aid of my halting Portuguese, I managed to secure a small but altogether charming, and very clean, apartment along the side of the Praça de São Pedro de Alcántara. The steep street pleased me; I seemed to feel that I might be safer on a hillside. Fate could not so easily approach me.

For some days I was not really aware of the apartment's modest furnishings, or the heavy tolling of a cathedral's bells every quarter hour, or the fine, warm autumnal rain that fell every morning. I was still in a dazed condition. The dream-vision had shaken me as violently as if I had, in my own person, only barely escaped death. (Indeed a death of some sort had taken place in my soul. From that morning on I could no longer think of myself as a young man: not as *young*. My features grew more serious, more somber; I even discovered a few bone-white hairs at my temples. Sleep, which had always been so pleasurable, and so effortless, became now an uncertain venture from which I might wake at any time, disturbed and perspiring. Life itself became an uncertain venture.) Never a religious person, and certainly not superstitious, I nevertheless found myself in the habit of closing my eyes at odd, incidental moments of the day, and offering thanks that my life was saved. I did not know to whom or to what I offered thanks, but the compulsion had to be honored; it was an instinct as direct as that which forced me to leave the doomed ship.

(For the *Cap Arcona* did indeed meet with disaster, five days out. A hurricane struck, most of the passengers and seamen were killed, the battered ship itself sank. A horrible tragedy that shocked all of Europe, but especially Lisbon. I read again and again news articles about the disaster, my eyes welling with tears at the thought of the passengers who had died so senselessly. The woman in the handsome scarlet dress, the elderly white-haired gentleman, the twins with the dog— It had been in my power to save them but I had done nothing: I had been concerned only with my own safety.)

The days became a week, the week two weeks, and then a month. It was now November. Not only because I wished to make my money stretch as far as possible but also because I wished to disguise my appearance, I bought quite ordinary clothes, a dark woollen overcoat for the winter, cotton shirts in place of linen. I made a conscious effort to minimize my German accent; my speech became less impassioned and flowery and self-consciously poetic; fortunately there had always been a Mediterranean cast to my features. While I did not exactly disappear into the populace, I did not stand out as remarkably foreign.

(I have no intention of going into my personal history—for it belongs not only to the past, but to the past beyond my "death"—it should be remarked, however, that I have always had the ability to adapt myself to my environment. I share the talent of certain species of plants and animals for achieving, almost without design, a protective coloration, a cunning camouflage.)

Daily I walked about the many hills of the city, meditating upon my own survival and the tragedy of the others' deaths; tormenting myself with the thought that perhaps I could have saved them, had I had more faith in the validity of my own premonition; absolving myself, at last, of all guilt—for certainly my warnings would have had no effect. I read newspapers in four or five languages. I ate only twice a day, always at different cafés; I was perhaps unnecessarily careful about patronizing the same café more than once a week. If anyone spoke to me, I was courteous but said little, and of course I never approached anyone, even those occasional tourists—many of them American—who struck me as being particularly attractive. I fled from Germans, I fled from the French. Why? There was no need, surely. There was no need that I could determine. I sensed only a vague, primitive urgency that I keep my distance from everyone—even obvious strangers who would not know me. It seemed to me that someone or something (Death itself?) was hunting me; unless I was very prudent I would not thwart my destiny after all.

And so the weeks passed. Something stirred in my soul: a premonition of the design my life might take. But I did not feel any impatience; the impatience of youth was gone forever. It might be that I would take up another disguise . . . it might be that I would be a poet, or a writer, or an artist . . . or a musician . . . or a

man of God, should I come to believe in God. . . . It might be that
I would remain quite anonymous, living a placid and eventless
life from day to day, utterly alone; or I might marry; or I might
suddenly leave Portugal for another part of the world—for
Rome, perhaps, or Tangiers. But in the meantime it was
imperative that I live quietly, exulting simply in the fact that I had
escaped, at least temporarily, the fate that had been intended for
me.

It was in early December, I believe, that I saw, in the
Cathedral of Santa Maria, my former mistress—her large, stern,
melancholy face nearly hidden by a dark veil. She was alone,
unaccompanied by either her husband or her charming
daughter. My senses leapt; I wanted, of course, to approach her
or to signal her; for a delirious instant it was as if no time at all had
passed—only a day or two since we had declared our passionate
love for each other, and stepped into our first embrace. But of
course a great deal of time had passed. And I had not thought of
her—had forgotten her entirely. And I was "dead" so far as she
knew: the Marquis de Venosta who had been her feverish lover
was dead, killed at sea. (The "Marquis de Venosta" was the
identity I had had while in Lisbon; so far as I was concerned the
young marquis was dead and there was no need to resurrect him
now.)

I did not, therefore, approach her; I forced myself to look
away from her stern, grieving figure. In the past the interiors of
cathedrals had offended me with their ornate altars and statues
and rose windows, but today the Cathedral of Santa Maria struck
me as beautiful indeed, very nearly mesmerizing. If my northern,
Protestant soul had been irritated previously by the South's
shameless delight in the senses, and its random mixture of
styles—pagan and Christian, Moorish and Greek—today I found
the display splendid; I slipped forward onto my knees to pay it
homage. My lips moved in prayer—a wordless prayer. As usual I
offered thanks to the Presence that had saved my life, and in
addition inquired about the purpose of my having been
saved—what was I to do with the rest of my life?

By the time the answer suggested itself to me, my former
mistress had left the Cathedral without my having been noticed.
So unobtrusive was I in my dark, inexpensive clothes, so
commonplace was my posture of unquestioning adoration, that
had she paused to look at me I very much doubt that she would
have recognized me. She had loved me—true enough; and I had

felt a fierce, loving passion for her. But such matters come to seem insignificant once one has looked upon Death.

III

It was not until some months later—in late March—that another apparition from the past appeared, this time my father. And it was quite evident that he had come searching for me, his only son; that he had stirred from his place of repose in the Rhine Valley in order to seek me out and lay claim about me. A curious, frightful figure!—almost comic in his rumpled, tight-fitting clothes—and heavier than I remembered him—his eyes ringed with fatigue and desperation and a peculiar *spitefulness* that alarmed me almost as much as the mere fact of his appearance in Lisbon.

By this time I had engaged a housekeeper and had settled into an almost bourgeois routine of work. The conviction that I was destined to be an artist, which had come to me in the Cathedral as I knelt with my hands pressed reverently against my eyes, had never left me—had been strengthened, in fact, by subsequent reflection; and not least by the initial and surprising success of my efforts. In order to make a little money (for my savings were running low) I did quick sketches of the kinds of sights tourists find pleasing—the market at its busiest; the baroque and rather ponderous monuments in the Anglican cemetery; small churches, monasteries, ruined cloisters; stone walls; fig trees; cypresses; sailing barges; ferries; Black Horse Square; priests and nuns and peasants and fishermen and fishwives and black-eyed charming urchins. These I managed without much difficulty to sell to tourists whom I was careful never to approach—instead, I allowed them to approach me as I stood in the open air, my easel before me. By now my disguise as an artist was complete: I did not need to take pains to disarray my hair or clothing. I *was* an artist. My little sketches were signed *Felix Krouveia*—a nonsensical polyglot name that served its purpose well enough. To the English and American and French and German tourists I was a Portuguese; to the Portuguese I was a foreigner, possibly French, more likely Italian. Though I often frequented cafés, I was careful to avoid the society of fellow artists—of whom there were a few in Lisbon—but I foresaw the time when my need for sympathetic and stimulating colleagues would outweigh my need for privacy. (In *Le Figaro* I had read a most astonishing

manifesto by one Filippo Tommaso Marinetti, a name entirely
new to me; with what bold, uncompromising energy did this
poet set down the foundation of a revolutionary art!—
remarkable, enviable—making my own customary amiability
appear, by contrast, to be merely diffidence.)

It was in a small square near Coimbra that my father
appeared—the apparition of my father, that is; for the poor man
had been dead for years. I wore my dark overcoat and a cloth cap
that had lost its shape and I was doing a very rough charcoal
sketch of a bewhiskered Portuguese hero—a general on
horseback—as a kind of exercise, simply to develop my skill;
with one part of my mind I knew, and had known even before
reading of the Futurists, that the sort of pleasant, innocuous work
I was doing was no more than provisional and pragmatic: my
true genius lay elsewhere. It was an unusually mild, sunny day, in
mid-week, the square was by no means deserted, yet I picked out
at once the awkward, ungainly figure of my father. For some
seconds I stared at him, frozen. I could not believe what I saw.
(And afterward, in reflecting upon the extraordinary visitation, I
came to wonder if perhaps my poor eating habits—I often went
without breakfast in my haste to get to work—had not caused me
to hallucinate.) That obese, slow-moving man in the expensive,
custom-made, but rather rumpled cashmere coat—that pale,
solemn, peevish German who stopped passers-by frequently to
ask them questions that (so I gathered) they could not
comprehend: my poor father, dead by his own hand in my
eighteenth year.

My surprise was such that, for several long minutes, I was not
even terrified; I experienced a peculiar light-headedness, an
almost euphoric sensation, as if the apparition—or the man
himself, for he certainly appeared solid—were proof of what I
had suspected since early boyhood, *The world if a fathomless
mystery.* My weeks of intensive artistic activity had also taught
me to honor the unique, the odd, the surprising, even the
perverse—for it is the unexpected that excites the artistic
temperament. And here, not one hundred yards from the stately
buildings and walls of Coimbra University, making his way
along a wide graveled path in my general direction, was my poor
father himself.

He had shot himself through the heart, one of the very few
successful ventures he had ever undertaken. (Having inherited
the firm of Engelbert Krull, makers of *Loreley extra cuvée*

champagne, he had seen the business slide into bankruptcy and had been totally unable to alter the course of events.) The end of his life had, therefore, been especially unhappy, and perhaps it was for this reason that he did not resemble the father I knew so much as a vexed, fussing stranger. Of course it was the same man—there was no mistaking his fair, silken, thinning hair and his large morose features and his unconscious habit of stroking his round belly (which he did now though he was wearing an overcoat); I recognized him at once.

But, though he was obviously searching for me, he did not recognize *me*.

After I recovered from my astonishment I continued to work at the sketch, despite my shaking fingers. The equestrian statue took shape; I then spent time trying to suggest, with soft feathery strokes, the lovely delicacy of the cypress trees in the background. At the same time I was well aware of my father, who stopped a middle-aged gentleman on the path and asked him a faltering question—in Spanish, I believe—and, receiving for reply a half-humorous gesture of total incomprehension, took out an already-soiled white handkerchief and passed it rapidly over his face and beneath his drooping chin. What must it mean, that my father had left his place of repose in order to seek me out ... ? My inclination was to step forward and identify myself; for after all the man *was* my father, or had been. Yet for some reason I hesitated. I stood close to my easel, frowning, fussing over the sketch, even muttering to myself, for all the world like a self-absorbed, eccentric artist who would not welcome any interruption.

My father wandered near, still dabbing at his face. I saw that he was weary, perplexed, a little resentful. For a dead man he certainly perspired (as he had in life); his complexion was ruddy and flushed and quite damp. "Excuse me, sir," he would call out as someone passed near, and then, in his courteous but strained voice he would make inquiries about his son Felix who had been scheduled to meet with him some months ago but who had disappeared ... had disappeared, evidently, somewhere in this city. He switched from Spanish to French and then to German, and then to a kind of French-English, always without success. Indeed it was kind of people not to laugh at him. I continued working at the sketch, able to control my trembling by supporting the wrist of my right hand with the fingers of my left; it seemed to me very important that I continue work, that I refuse to be frightened or even distracted by my poor father's presence. Was he a temptation that I betray my new calling by answering to my old name...? That I thoughtlessly align myself with the dead...?

Afterward I came to believe that the situation was more sinister. My father was searching for me in order to draw me into the other world with him; he didn't want to express his love for me but only his authority, his paternal right. A soft, slovenly, lazy, good-hearted man in life, he had become, in death, a malevolent figure—there was something mythically Teutonic about his manner, that perverse blend of cruelty and formality, as he made inquiries about his beloved son who had failed to meet with him on schedule.

By what power he was able to disengage himself from the Land of the Dead I cannot imagine. I do not wish to think of it, or of him—transformed as he is. Our fathers inspire our love only when they are truly fatherly; when they become *other*, greedy creatures from the night-side of the earth, we must stand fast against them. Teutonic, Germanic, an ostensibly life-affirming and life-honoring son of the fertile Rhine Valley, my father was nevertheless a ghoul—and I did right to resist him.

Sighing he passed near me. He paused to watch my fingers; he even bent close to the paper. "Very good, very good," he mumbled. "If only I had time... the luxury of time... to begin again, to see as you see... to *see* at all.... If only.... But...."

Though I made no encouraging response, he continued, now in German, speaking irritably of his renegade son who had betrayed him. It seems the son had simply disappeared—on the morning of October eighth—had not shown up where he was expected. "He was always a capricious boy," my father complained, "but I would not have thought he would go against *me*."

I nodded brusquely.

And he wandered away, he disappeared into the city; I never saw him again.

IV

Nor did I think of him again.

And, freed of him, of that mysterious "father" whose biological presence weighed heavily upon me, without my quite acknowledging it, I found myself thinking more and more seriously of leaving Lisbon. The kind of art I did was satisfactory on its own level, that of the picturesque representational; but more and more there crept into my paintings, and even into the most innocent of sketches, a certain impatience with the decorative, with familiar surfaces and textures. Was I, as an artist, to remain forever a *servant* of both the gullible public and the visual, three-dimensional world . . . ? I dreamed of locomotives rushing through exquisite gardens, of aeroplanes soaring above the golden crosses of cathedrals. I dreamed of Borghese Park crossed with ugly trenches and, in the background, immense buildings of granite and glass, of a kind never seen before on earth, rising into the smutty sky. Often, while awake, I had only to blink my eyes to see familiar streets and shops and people transformed into writhing patterns of energy, fairly pulsing with the angry joy of existence.

I yearned to visit Paris; and Rome; and perhaps Milan, where I might meet with the Futurist painters Boccioni and Carrà and Balla, whose work excited me more—perversely, perhaps—than that of the Parisians, whose fractured and cubed studies struck me as being oppressively intellectual, and in any case static. Even Picasso, whom I was to admire so fiercely in later life, did not much intrigue me at this time. My soul was stirred by what little I had seen of the Futurists: I was hungry to experience again and again the vertigo of Boccioni's *The City Rises*, to see it in person, to stand before it in homage.

Never had I been so wedded to life, never had my expectations been so various. My former existence faded and fell away; the old Felix seemed to me no more than a foolish child, intoxicated with the lush surfaces of the world and drawn away by them from his deepest self. Or was it the world that had enchanted me, really? I often thought it might have been my father's poor example; or the example of other adults; or a mysterious Presence that sought to guide me along pathways I would not have chosen for myself. (There were, I recalled in astonishment, several incidents in my life that were not characteristic of my life—I mean by that the half-dozen thefts I committed as if in obedience to a force outside my will. Thieving is base, dishonest, stupid, and degrading; I swear that it is not, and has never been, natural to my temperament. On the other hand, my artistic yearnings were never given adequate expression: were never taken seriously enough by myself and others. I was destroying my creative genius by performing in various masquerades, none of which expressed my own nature.)

In later years the conflicts within my soul were to be better understood by me, but at this time—during those bizarre months in Lisbon following my failure to "meet with my father on schedule"—I was often confused and discouraged. Only when I worked did I feel *myself*; only when I plunged into hours of activity, oblivious of my personal being, and of any dangers it might encounter, did I feel I moved with the pulse of life. This was the case despite the fact that my efforts at that time were crudely experimental—studies of raw undifferentiated motion, of blurred and frenzied moments not convincingly transcribed from the mind to the canvas.

And so I prepared to leave Lisbon in the spring. My fears about leaving were greater than I had supposed—like a child who has been terrified by an experience outside the home, I really wished to hide in my apartment on the Praça de São Pedro de Alcántara forever. (And it was out of the question for me to travel by water. Though in later years, airplane travel did not worry me in the slightest, but seemed, in fact, quite pleasant, crossing any body of water wider than a river was impossible.)

It was on a warm afternoon in April on the day before I was scheduled to leave, by train, for Madrid, that the most sinister of all imaginable apparitions appeared to me. For days I had been anticipating something of the sort—my dreams had been turbulent, filled with images of a formal, ritualistic death—my soul oppressed by the invisible weight of a Presence I could not fathom. Yet I never hesitated in my plans to leave. (It was as if I sensed, beyond the chill authority of that Presence, the warm, congenial, combative circle of fellow artists I was to meet in subsequent years.)

I was saying farewell to certain sights I supposed I would never visit again: squares, churches, marketplaces, the view of the Tagus from one of the hills, the Anglican cemetery. I wandered for some time in the cemetery, lost in thought, gazing at the tombstones, the broken columns, urns, crosses and spires and crude winged creatures squatting atop mausoleums. How lovely the April sunshine, after the damp, cold persistent winter!...I rejoiced simply in the familiar fact that nature had again revived and that all was well. (I have never been ashamed of sentiment and of expressing it.) Even the inscription on a time-darkened vault did not depress me: *We, the bones who are already here, wait patiently for yours.*

Is it possible to elude death?—if one is conscious of the imminent struggle? Or is it only possible when one has firmly envisioned in his soul a fate, a necessary destiny, that forbids premature extinction?

In the leafy sunshine of that mild spring day Death approached me. I glanced up, saw, stared. I realized that it was no accident, my wandering into the cemetery; it had been *his* design. . . . Death approached me in the figure of a distinguished elderly gentleman of about eighty. He wore a black topcoat and very white, blindingly white, linen; he was leaning heavily upon a gleaming black cane. Something about the austerity of his bearing, despite the difficulty with which he walked, made me think for a moment that he was English. As he drew nearer, however, I saw that he was of my own nationality—though, like me, he exhibited none of the more obvious characteristics of that nationality. His expression was dignified and stern, even severe. He wore glasses; he was clean-shaven and fastidiously groomed; his gunmetal-gray hair lay combed across his impressive skull in several damp strands. He had fixed his gaze upon me from the first and though I had the idea that his vision was badly deteriorated, I could not turn away. My impulse, of course, was to run like a terrified child—to rush past him and make my way frantically back to the street.

"Felix . . . ?"

The word was terrible: I had not heard it pronounced for so long.

"Felix?"

Death's voice was both curt and gentle; unlike my poor father, this gentleman knew exactly who I was, and what he wished of me. He could not be deceived.

"You *are* my Felix, my own child, are you not . . . ?"

"I . . . . I don't. . . ."

"Why do you shrink away like that?"

"I don't know you. . . ."

"Don't know me? My own Felix, my child, my most cherished son?"

He drew nearer; he leaned heavily on the cane. Through the thick lenses of his glasses he blinked at me, making an effort to smile. I was trembling violently. I wondered if he saw—if he could sense. My terror was his strength; in my malleability had been his authority.

"You must believe me when I say that you are my most

cherished son," the gentleman said in his formal, ponderous voice. His narrow lips performed a smile; I could see now that he was very old—his face, though still handsome, was a mass of fine wrinkles. "...my most cherished creation. Though you have changed somewhat in the past few months, Felix, though you are no longer quite the...the work of art I had imagined...nevertheless you are...you are the child closest to my heart. You have been careless of your beauty, haven't you? The beauty with which I entrusted you? And your clothes...."

"But I don't know you," I said quickly. "My dear sir, you must be mistaken. I don't know you at all."

"Felix, that voice is my own!...it is yours, and mine. That marvelous soft voice I heard first in my imaginings, long before *you* drew breath. And your eyes, and your lean, graceful bearing, your beautiful lips, fingers...your soul itself."

"I don't know you. I have nothing to do with you," I said.

"Why are you trembling? Why are you frightened of me? You have everything to do with me," the gentleman laughed. "By which I mean—*everything*. You came into existence through my efforts, which should be perfectly obvious. And it should be perfectly obvious, as well, that your existence is bound up irrevocably with my own: that you must obey me in all matters. Therefore...."

I was shaking my head like an obstinate child.

"Therefore you had better surrender yourself to me, Felix. This latest disguise of yours is, I admit, a splendid one: the pretense of being an artist...an artist, moreover, with a curious bond of sympathy with a handful of barbaric Italians who have been (as you possibly don't know) a mere exercise in public relations. It is quite amazing, and quite unprecedented...rather ingenious, in fact. But contrary to nature. Contrary to the nature I have bestowed upon you."

"I reject that nature," I whispered.

"What are you saying?—I can't hear."

"I reject that nature," I said. Again I experienced the sickening desire to push my way past this old man, to rush headlong from the cemetery. We were alone; no one was watching. "I....I reject it and you...and everything you have planned for me....I reject everything of yours," I said.

"That is not possible," he said curtly.

The effort of speaking with me was obviously tiring; he paused for a moment to regain his breath. Then he repeated in a softer tone, "*That is not possible.*"

"My dear sir," I said, trembling now with a mixture of emotions—anger and frustration as well as fear—"I insist upon the fact that you and I are strangers. We share a common language, perhaps, and a common ancestry; but that hardly makes us kin, and it hardly gives you any authority over me. Moreover.... In addition...."

"My dear child, you are beginning to sound exactly like my Felix! Sweet and histrionic and bold, with all the hyperbole of a favored son, not restrained by timidity from making the most stilted of speeches.... You have the self-consciousness of beauty, Felix; why do you want to betray your destiny, which is bound up with my own, and which will protect you from the vicissitudes of the world? Even if it were possible for you to have your own life, apart from my gentle nurturing, *why* should you wish it? You will grow old and decrepit, as I am now. You will never succeed in being more than a third-rate painter—of that I am certain. In fact I very much doubt whether anyone living in this era of ruins will be more than third-rate—"

"You don't understand them," I said. "You don't understand us."

"Felix, did not your Creator smile upon you, at your birth? Were you not destined for—for pleasures of the flesh, for boyish raptures—for adventures of the kind that I, burdened by the weight of my own genius, had to forgo? ... What do you mean by *us*, who is this *us*? You belong to no one else; you know very well that you're mine."

"I know very well that I am not yours: I am my own person."

He adjusted his glasses and peered at me, smiling faintly. I was beginning to feel the injustice of it—the colossal injustice. That this elderly man should wish to claim the life he had created, that he should wish to draw *me* back into his head: what right had he? Simply because I had grown into an extraordinarily attractive young man and, for a while, mesmerized by *his* fantasies, had led a stupid, vain, frivolous life, trying on one costume after another like a monkey, performing in order to dazzle ignorant audiences—simply because I loved women solely in order to satisfy *his* base lusts, and his even baser desire to imagine himself as a successful lover: what right had he to appear now, on the eve of my departure, and make his claim? Granted he was an elderly man; granted, also, that he had labored to bring me to life, and might not be blamed, perhaps, for wishing to bring me to death—wishing me to accompany him to the Land of the Dead: I had achieved my own soul, nevertheless, during

those months when I was freed of his authority. I was no longer
his Felix—I was no longer that person at all. I belonged solely to
myself.

As if sensing my thoughts, he began to speak. His manner was
artificially genial; his fatherly smile did not call forth a smile from
me. He spoke of the travails of artistic creation...of the artist's
suffering, which is not unrelated to the suffering of a woman in
childbirth. He spoke of the paradox that lies in the fact that the
artist must create living beings, beings fully capable of drawing
breath, and yet he must control them always: he *must* not allow
them to escape the structure his imagination has created to
sustain them. He spoke of the artist's altogether human desire to
unleash, in his creations, those characteristics he does not possess,
or does not dare acknowledge....

"I have nothing to do with that," I cried. "I don't exist merely
to fulfill *you*—to act out fantasies of yours you all but admit are
infantile and unworthy of serious consideration—"

He stared at me, perplexed. It was obvious that my stubborn
opposition was tiring him, yet he seemed unaware of his own
quickened breath. Instead he stepped closer, now bent forward.
I had to resist the desire to strike him. (What an imp Death is,
taking on those forms that most intimidate us—stifling the
natural impulse to lash out against what threatens to overwhelm
and destroy!) Again he spoke: sadly, gravely. He spoke of the
artist's necessary cruelty in bringing his creations to a finish, no
matter how they might beg for life, no matter how boldly and
prettily they might demand their freedom. It is an imitation of
nature, no more and no less, and cannot be denied. The artist, far
from transcending the sprawling drama of nature, is in fact a
cunning servant of nature, and wishes merely to impose *his*
design upon the larger, untidy design—and so the artist's
authority must be obeyed, the life he brings into being must
acquiesce to the death he ordains. It is unthinkable that a creature
might rise up against his creator and demand his own
autonomy....

"I have nothing to do with this," I interrupted. I had taken a
few steps forward; it was my intention to brush past him. "Even
if I do acknowledge that there is a bond of some kind between us,
a feeble sort of connection—frail as a cobweb; even if I do
acknowledge that I am, of course, most grateful for your—for
your perhaps involuntary generosity in giving me life: nevertheless I have forgotten most of my past; what I do remember I

reject impatiently and irritably, having judged it to be a
not-very-worthy prelude to my real life. And now if you will
excuse me—"

"Felix, it simply isn't possible— What you are attempting is
not possible—"

"You are going to die! You are an old man, and you are going
to die! Can't you see that you want nothing more than to drag me
with you?—there's nothing noble about it, nothing inevitable! It's
selfishness! Vanity! I refuse—"

"Felix—"

He reached for me and, without thinking, I shoved him away.
I shouted into his astonished face. "No! Never! I am not yours!
Not yours!." Blinded with anger I shoved him again—I was only
dimly aware of his having staggered backward. "I refuse to go
with you—*I am not yours.*"

"But my boy, my dear— My dear one—"

"*No.*"

He stared at me and a terrible, stricken look manifested itself
slowly in his eyes and in the slack flesh about his mouth. It was a
look of recognition, of realization: I understood afterward that it
was the old man's acknowledgment of my being, my ferocious
and indomitable life. And that acknowledgment carried with it
the necessity of his own death.

He collapsed in the cemetery but I ran away. Death
blossomed in him, a void opening in his brain; but I ran, I
escaped, I left Portugal that very evening.

V

Years passed and no one pursued me. No apparitions
approached me, no "fate" claimed me; yet I was cautious still.
(Of my life at the present time I will not speak—it is too
complicated, too improbable; in many ways it is more
astonishing than the story of my Portuguese adventure.)
Someday, no doubt, I *shall* die: but I and I alone will determine
when. My work draws me forward, teasing me with its enigmatic
complexity. I cannot quite understand it. And so I am drawn
forward, year after year, decade after decade. . . . I seem to know
that so long as I am caught up in my work, I will not die; I am
immortal.

The world is emptied now of all apparitions. No Presence directs me away from my truest self. Moment by moment, heartbeat by heartbeat, I live out the drama of my own life. Is this another masquerade? I grasp my brush, I plunge forward. Where I once questioned everything I now question nothing. I am supremely myself: the only immortality allotted to mankind.

The Blessing

The Blessing—advertised for months—was two hundred seventy-five miles north of the city, up the Coast, and Roy lay awake most of the night listening to the rain, angry with himself for not getting everybody started earlier; he'd had months to plan the trip, now the rain might make some roads muddy and the highways might be crowded and, though he had tickets, something might go wrong and it would be a disaster to miss The Blessing, and though he seemed to be awake and muttering to himself and anxious all night, in fact his wife woke him at six o'clock, said everybody else was up and dressed and anxious to get started, what was wrong with him...? Sleeping so hard, twisting the bedclothes, grinding his teeth together. What was wrong?

A rebuilt U.S. mail truck, bought back in February; a bargain, but it might break down and it used a lot of gas. Roy liked the truck—was even proud of it and the flowery tendrils painted on it—but he worried about it and about the complex route, the expressway then the highway then the smaller roads; he had had months to master this journey, of course the responsibility was all his: always was. Husband. Father of a two-year-old son. Older brother to his wife's fourteen-year-old sister Bunny since her mother died and the father was lost somewhere or in hiding or maybe hospitalized under a fake name. He did not mind Bunny living with them: he liked her. He liked everyone. He liked being the young straw-haired sun-burned smiling man behind the wheel of the truck, a pal to Frankie—a neighbor's boy—patient enough to answer Frankie's questions through the cheerful babble and singing of his wife and Bunny and the noise of the transistor radio; he liked it all, was excited and pleased and anxious about everything, did not mind the responsibility that had come upon him at the age of twenty-nine, so fast it seemed as if he had woken one morning and there it was. He was Roy and that was Roy. And he puzzled over it in his dreams sometimes then woke to everything being turned around and completely different, like a landscape he had never seen before though he lived in it. For instance—it had not rained at all.

Frankie asked him questions but Frankie already knew the answers. Roy had to admit it, the boy was wise, shrewd, even clairvoyant—only ten years old—more mature than Bunny with her gum-chewing and short red shorts of the kind girls didn't wear now, sometimes sharper than his wife Micheline—who talked baby talk to the little boy, a bad habit Roy couldn't break her of—and though he got distracted from time to time, almost exasperated by the boy's questions, he liked Frankie very much. Enjoyed talking with him. Enjoyed trying to answer the questions. Frankie sat beside him, squeezed between him and Micheline in the front seat of the truck, and sometimes he twitched with excitement that was almost like an electric current going through him—only ten years old, undersized, said proudly of himself that the social welfare people had him in a file called *Genius*—which Roy doubted; he had never heard of anything like that, an actual file with the title *Genius*. But the boy was clever. Asked Roy if he knew Radio YTK's astrological weather forecast for the day. (Roy didn't.) Asked Roy if he knew that Bercholz County had, just the night before, reversed their earlier ruling on the sheriff's jurisdiction issue. (Roy didn't know much about this, except there had always been the promise—the vow—that no police, sheriff's men, or state troopers would be stationed inside the fairgrounds: The Blessing—a People's Experience.) Asked Roy if he knew The Shining One's primal name. (Viràj.) And what about The Shining One's mother, did Roy know *her* primal name?

Roy had to admit he didn't.

They left the house at six forty-five and by eight were out of the city, passing DeRamus; by nine they had driven about one hundred and twenty miles, making good time on the wide, dry expressway; by ten, when they stopped at a roadside park on the outskirts of the Duntrine Valley, Roy had driven one hundred and seventy-five miles according to the speedometer. The day was clear now that they were in the country. Sunny, hot, dry; even dusty. Mountains in the distance: a few filmy vaporous clouds broken against them, as usual. Scrub jays in the pines behind the rest rooms. Noisy, happy. A sparrow hawk overhead. Micheline and Bunny passing out peanut-butter cookies, the honey jar, the spoons. Frankie spread out the map of the northern part of the state on a picnic table and crouched over it, dwarf-like, muttering to himself. He was a wonderful boy: Roy had taken him on as a little brother, had befriended him, since Frankie's family lived in a broken-down trailer up the street, a father who was laid off from the aircraft factory (where he worked in the machine shop, anyway), a mother who supposedly had multiple sclerosis (though she looked all right to Roy), two little sisters and one brother, fifteen years old, all crowded together in that trailer, where the sun beat on the tin roof. The social welfare people were out all the time. The truant officer came around. Roy's household was so much more stable, he had so much to offer a little boy like Frankie, and didn't mind at all the extra trouble.... Except it was strange: Roy and Micheline and Bunny had more or less introduced Frankie to the music and the message of The Shining One, a few months ago; and now Frankie seemed to know more about him than they did.

It meant something, Frankie declared, pointing at the map: it meant something that the Abeignos Fairgrounds was located where it was. That particular spot on the map. You could draw two interesting circles ... could transcribe a triangle ... you could figure out the ultimate circumference and probably it would reveal its meaning. But he hadn't his instruments with him: his compass, his ruler. So he would have to do it when they returned home.

By noon they were passing through the Kokanee Highlands, only five or six miles from the ocean; but the ocean was out of sight. Frankie was still chattering away. In the back of the truck, stretched out on the pile of sleeping bags, Bunny was switching the radio from station to station. Micheline and little Alistair were sleeping. Roy was less worried about the truck now: they were

making good time and it was reassuring, all the other cars and
made-over school buses and trucks like his own, and kids on
motorcycles, and even a long string of people—shoulders
hunched, heads down, legs working hard on the steep hills—on
bicycles, heading for the fairgrounds. It was obvious they were
all heading in the same direction when you contrasted them with
people who were not: people in new model cars or in commercial
trucks, who stared over at Roy as they passed him, curious and
contemptuous. Roy smiled back.

Frankie stuck his tongue out at a boy his own age who was
grinning at them—his daddy roaring past Roy's truck in what
appeared to be a Cadillac—and Roy said, shocked, "Why,
Frankie, what are you doing? Those people are no different from
us. They're not enemies. *What are you doing?*"

So he got the best of Frankie that time. Because Frankie had to
admit he'd done wrong.

They left the main highway just north of the Abeignos River,
around one in the afternoon. Now traffic was slowed: hundreds
of cars, trucks, trailers, buses, motorcycles, bicycles, men and
women and even children and even pregnant girls on foot,
knapsacks and occasionally staves, dogs trotting along with that
merry, frightened look of dogs who seem to be smiling and
panting at the same time . . . some of them loping ahead of their
owners, some of them already trailing behind, exhausted.

"My God, look at all the people!" Micheline cried. "Why, isn't
it wonderful? Why, I can't believe it. It's just the way everyone
predicted." Atop a hill they could see, strung out before them, a
line of traffic that snaked out of sight, miles away into the
burnt-out glowing-gold foothills. Roy's wife reached over to
squeeze his thigh, she was so excited. He felt reassured now: they
were making good time, the gates to the fairground would not
open anyway until the next morning at eight, all these pilgrims
were headed in the same direction and that was reassuring in
itself. The prediction was coming true. A prediction of seven
hundred thousand and unbelievers had scoffed and yet it was
coming true. . . .

Some boys in a stripped-down car, no fenders no bumpers no
tires—only the bare raw rims of the wheels—rattled past Roy,
their horn honking in good cheer. What a rattling clanking noise!
Roy had to laugh at them, though he wondered what they
thought they were doing: that pile of junk might disintegrate at

any minute. But the boys were waving and shouting to everyone as they passed, careless of oncoming traffic.

The little town of *Chillicothe unincorporated pop. 675:* a sheriff's blue and white car parked in the waist-high grass at the side of the road, the sheriff and his men sitting inside—car must be air-conditioned—watching as the pilgrims slowed down to 25 mph speed limit. One of the officers was a boy with straw-colored hair, younger even than Roy, smoking a cigarette, staring at him, nose wrinkling and twitching like a rabbit's: Roy just smiled in return.

Chillicothe must have been no more than a mile long. A few of the hikers were sitting by the Post Office, resting, their knapsacks off; a few more were lounging on the small, burnt-out lawn of the Court House; a girl no older than Bunny, her belly enormous, was hitchhiking right out in the road, grinning, her squaw-black hair hanging in her face, while a young man stood beside her evidently arguing with her. Jesus, was that girl pregnant!—Roy couldn't help staring at her, just staring. Micheline had not been that size, not even the day before the baby was born; it didn't seem possible that a girl that young, out hitchhiking in the midday heat, should be so swollen, so enormous.... But they couldn't give her a ride: not enough room. Roy was sorry about that. And the boy would want to climb in as well.... Not enough room.

There were sheriff's men scattered throughout town, and another blue and white car parked at the outskirts: a deep-tanned brawny man, six foot seven and maybe weighing two hundred eighty pounds, jammed in a sheriff's outfit, stood leaning against the car watching the procession, pleasant-faced, almost featureless behind his oversized metallic sunglasses. He wore a straw hat pushed back from his forehead. As Roy drove by a small group of hikers—it looked like a family, someone was carrying a baby on his back—came along and seemed to be engaging the sheriff in conversation; but Roy couldn't see what happened.

"There was a good feeling in that town," Micheline said. "I sensed a . . . a good feeling in that town . . . not, you know, not any hostility. I think that's a good sign."

But after Chillicothe the road became narrower. The turns were sharper. Traffic slowed: the speedometer registered 15 miles mph then 10 mph then 5 mph and occasionally dipped down to 0. Going uphill was the worst, of course. Stalled cars parked halfway in the grass, halfway on the road. Hitchhikers.

According to the map they were only a few miles from the fairgrounds. But Frankie estimated, his voice a whine, that it would take them hours to get there: why the hell hadn't they got on the road earlier? *He* had told Roy, hadn't he? He had argued they should leave a day earlier. The tent-city was probably filled by now.... He had told Roy—hadn't he?—and now look.

Roy had to admit that maybe he'd made a mistake.

But they were only a few miles away and it was early afternoon and there was a good feeling, even among those who had abandoned their cars or bicycles: they hitchhiked, trudging backward good-natured and smiling and forgiving when they could see there was no room for them. Micheline leaned out the window and Bunny was leaning out the back, carrying on conversations, waving, touching hands.... There was only trouble from time to time: a boy of about seventeen climbed on the hood of the truck and wouldn't get off and began bouncing up and down, giggling, waving his arms, while Roy leaned out one window and Micheline out the other begging him, and he seemed to hear them after a while, turned, startled, to stare at them through the windshield, his hair out around his face...squatted down, approached the windshield, staring at them or at something.... He picked a mangled insect off the windshield and parts of another and parts of a yellow butterfly's wings...tried to fit them together.... Perplexed, his face a hot-looking pink, newly sunburned, he tried to fit the parts together while Roy pleaded with him to please get off the hood....

Cars parked on either side of the narrow dirt road. The jalopy without tires abandoned, probably left in the middle of the road and pushed over to the side by someone else, partway in a ditch. More and more hitchhikers, more people trudging by, some of them singing, some very good-natured, leaning in the window on Micheline's side and asking if there was any room for another passenger?...no?... but God bless you anyway. A girl tickled Roy's face with a long feathery white-thistled weed. Some husky young men wearing sun visors, white-teethed like handsome young men in advertisements, bicycled by in a long procession—at least fifteen of them—chanting a mantra of some kind. They were able to weave in and out of the stalled traffic. Roy envied them. He envied also the people at the very head of the line: he could no longer see them but he could imagine them. Already at the camping grounds, already setting up their tents outside the gates of the fairgrounds....

But if he worried, Micheline always cheered him up. And Bunny. Even little Alistair seemed happy enough. Frankie kept muttering that they should have started out the night before but nobody paid attention to him. He was a restless, wiry child, his legs appeared too short for the rest of his body, Roy had the freaky idea for a moment that the boy was really a stunted adult, an evil creature, but of course it was wrong to think that.... Still, when Roy had trouble getting the truck started again, after a long wait by a single-lane bridge, Frankie threatened to get out and walk and nobody begged him to stay.

"If you feel you must, then you must," Roy said neutrally.

So Frankie got out and ran ahead and got in with a group of boys not much older than he, able to squeeze between the cars and the bridge's railings, and Roy forgot about him in the vexation and near-panic of trying to get the motor going: What if it stalled? What would happen?... Behind him, someone was honking angrily. Bunny tried to quiet him down. Roy turned the ignition off and then on again, carefully, reverently. What if. What. In the back, Bunny was saying *Have patience! Have love!* and the horn-honking stopped for a while and Roy tried again, turning the ignition again, pumping the gas pedal, his eyes half closed and lips muttering a prayer... and thank God, thank God and The Shining One, thank all the powers in the universe... the motor caught and held and the truck gave a small leap forward.

An open area: two or three farmhouses, not very prosperous, set back from the road in dusty grassless plots of ground, the outbuildings a uniform weathered gray. Horses in a corral, eying the road. A small boy on a front porch. On another porch, a small crowd of hikers had gathered—for what reason, Roy couldn't tell—and a collie was barking at them. The farmhouse looked abandoned. But no: somebody must be living there, a line of wash out back, white sheets drooping close to the ground.... The other house was just a shanty, abandoned; you could look right through it—doorway and windows like cutouts—scrub land in the back.

Rumors that the celebration had been canceled: a girl with a dirty, streaked face tried to tell them that, limping back from somewhere up ahead, but someone else said that was a lie—a falsehood—a deliberate fabrication by the Shining One's enemies. But the rumor turned up again, a few minutes later. A bearded man of about fifty, so deeply tanned he seemed to be made of dark-stained wood, paused to lean in Roy's window and say, "It's over. The celebration was held and it's over. The cycle has to begin again—back to zero and through all the phases once again—it's hopeless for us now. It's too late." But these must have been no more than rumors, because the radio station friendliest to the event, YTK, was playing music most of the time and the announcer only interrupted to say that all was well out in Abeignos County and to repeat the things that had been said many times. There would be a Blessing...a community celebration...a period during which certain questions would be answered (*Where is the lost continent of Atlantis?*—for one)...and the gates would be opened at eight in the morning, no sooner. Only ticket holders would be admitted, of course. Tickets to The Blessing had been sold weeks ago, completely sold out. Fantastic. Unprecedented....Word had come to the station that there were rumors circulating, which would not be repeated because they were false and subversive. The temperature was eighty degrees; the barometer was steady; it was now 2:10 p.m. and all was well.

"I'm so afraid," Micheline whispered suddenly. "What if...."

But she was wrong to be afraid. When Roy saw the fairgrounds up ahead, when he saw the tents and camping sites and all the people, all the people, he reached over to squeeze her arm in pure joy.

"You shouldn't have doubted!" he said.

Somewhere to the east of them, behind them, was a fire, or at any rate a lot of smoke. Field grass burning...? A brush fire...? Roy hoped it wasn't anyone's car or one of the big buses. Or anyone's house or barn. Overhead, several helicopters flew past. Maybe they were state police, maybe they were FBI, in violation of the agreement with The Blessing's managers...but they didn't seem to be bothering anyone...and Roy was too relieved now, too happy, to pay much attention to them. But how noisy, the roaring of those motors!...and it was startling to see the helicopter's shadow spring out of nowhere and glide by....But he had too much to be grateful for to worry about anything like that. *Law-enforcement officers will have no jurisdiction over The Blessing because it will be held on grounds rented by a private party....*

So they found a place to park, about a half-mile from the gates. If you could get around the selfish people who had set up camp right in front, near the road, you had plenty of free space out back. Scrub land. A few trees. But they found a good place between a young couple who had a new-looking tent, with side flaps and screens, and a noisy cheerful group in an old school bus painted blue.... Roy was tired from the drive. Too tired to eat. The others ate and he stretched out in the back of the truck and pulled a towel over his face and fell asleep and began to dream almost immediately....

Near sunset he was still looking for Frankie. But he used the opportunity to meet people. Shake hands, exchange greetings. Everyone was so friendly!...but it was confusing, this many people and all of them strangers. Roy kept imagining that people he saw at a distance were people he knew, but when he approached them they turned out to be other people; he chased after a half dozen boys with brown curly hair and blue pullover shirts, certain that each was Frankie.

He liked to wander freely. Always had. Micheline and Bunny were back at the campsite, cleaning up after supper...the baby was asleep...Roy was well rested now from his nap and excited about tomorrow morning and excited about the acres and acres of people all around him, friends in the temporary guise of strangers.... No trouble about finding his way back to the truck. There were several balloons in the air, dirigible-size. One was scarlet and one was jade green and one was a crazy-quilt of oranges and pinks and one was sky-blue—which was the sacred color—and one was yellow-and-black-striped and it was this balloon, anchored with a real anchor, that was fairly near his campsite. Evidently the balloons were meant to be landmarks. They could be seen from great distances. It was lovely to see them, the bobbing brightly colored balloons....

Someone threw a rock at one of the balloons. It fell back to earth, a loud crash. Landed on the roof of a Volkswagen, left quite a dent; Roy was only a few feet away and was startled by the noise.

...A girl was passing out apples, gumdrops, chocolates. Roy watched her for a while, knowing she was a stranger, yet curious, enticed, almost annoyed by the fact that she resembled a girl he had known some years ago...a friend of an ex-friend whom he had roomed with at college...many years ago. But that girl would be older than this girl, who looked about sixteen. Anyway, he could not have pushed his way to her.

Odors of food. Smoke. How friendly everyone was, and how Roy loved being among them! ... just as it had been prophesied. A blessing.. The Blessing. Guitar music. Drums. Singing and chanting. Someone screamed; or was it a horn.... The wide throbbing blades of a helicopter chopping the air, and again a shadow gliding by.... Roy stared at the helicopter until it was out of sight. He had to shade his eyes, gazing into the sun.

A small brush fire: half-nude boys and girls were trying to put it out. They were beating it out with towels and blankets. Screams, giggles. A girl with waist-long red hair danced around. What if her hair exploded into flames? Roy would have helped them, but the fire was already out. There were too many people anyway; they didn't need him. The fire was beaten out, thuds and thumps, then the sharp acrid stink.

Nearer the gates of the fairground there was a different feeling: people were crowded closer together, they seemed more energetic, more talkative. There was more noise here. Transistor radios were turned up high but not to the same station—why not?—so it got to be quite a din before Roy became accustomed to it. The balloon above the gates was the scarlet one. It looked satiny. A sign floated in the air: *The Blessing—A People's Celebration*. Firecrackers were being set off, but Roy couldn't see who was doing it. A happy, festive atmosphere. Maybe a little high-pitched. A woman in her thirties, a stranger, approached Roy and began to complain, as if she knew him, of the fact that there was a private airfield inside the fairgrounds. Special people, specially invited people, were being flown in. By helicopter, by single-propeller plane. That accounted for all the air traffic, all the noise overhead. Roy had never seen the woman before. But he was polite. She wore a man's shirt; her hair hung straggly down her back. She kept blinking tears out of her eyes. She was angry. It was not fair, she claimed, that some people were being airlifted and housed in dormitories and treated like royalty, while the rest of them, "the rest of us," had to camp outside, all night long, like rabble. Roy tried to tell her that those were probably people connected with The Shining One and his family, people who were organizing the celebration. As his words came out, they sounded strange: ... *Shining One?*

She interrupted him to say that wasn't true.

Specially invited privileged people like film stars and millionaires and maybe even politicians; maybe even foreign aristocracy. It happened at every celebration. But she couldn't stay away, she couldn't live without The Blessing. "You get to be hungry for it, then ravenous for it, then you can't go a minute of your life without seeking it," she said. "That's why he's so cruel...to favor other people and to airlift them into the...." Roy said the people in the planes must be workers to set up the stage or maybe bodyguards and when she tried to contradict him he pushed her aside. Walked fast, not looking back.... Why did people want to ruin everything! He never listened to negative spiteful earth-despising people if he could help it.

Everywhere, crowded close together, were cars and buses and trucks and sleeping bags and tents; everywhere, people. Roy stepped on someone—a silly accident!—stooped over to shake hands and apologize and then moved on. He liked to keep free. Hands in his jeans pockets, wandering where he liked. Not far from the gates now. He could see the walls, which seemed to be made of pale-green stucco, topped with barbed wire and shards of broken glass...and the thick arch at the entrance...the letters spelling out *Abeignos Fairgrounds*. Yes, he was close to it now. A hum of excitement here. Almost tangible—you could breathe it in. His heart was beating faster here. So much life!—so many people. He could feel his heartbeat accelerate and then it was mixed with the beating of a helicopter's propellers. People nearby were yelling. Someone threw another rock, but it missed the helicopter—landed out of sight. Much noise. Music from radios jarring, blaring.... A young man of about twenty was sitting on the ground, his feet bare, bleeding. He was dabbing at the blood. Must be painful, but he didn't wince. When he looked up at Roy, it was amazing how sunburned the upper half of his face was: glowing pink.

Oxycodone, he whispered.

What?

Oxycodone. Nothing else, the boy murmured, shaking his head.

Roy backed away. *Oxycodone*...?

Selling. Or buying.

Half the boy's nose was going to peel off, by morning. Hot-pink, burnt flesh. Roy walked away, moving with a stream of people. *Oxycodone*. He didn't know what it was or whether it was anything at all—could be a lie—could be a narcotics officer's trick. Anyway Roy had not squatted down there in the mess with him, he had escaped and was now almost beneath the scarlet balloon. What did he know or care about *oxycodone* or *The*

Blessing or someone a mile away, his wife and baby and sister-in-law, it was too difficult to keep so many things in his head at the same time.

Just a moment before it had been daylight: now it was dusk. Torchlights. Flashlights. Floodlights.... Roy was walking with a number of people, strangers, all of them pressing forward, flowing slowly forward, while overhead a man's voice floated warning them to get back...to go back...a bullhorn from one of the helicopters. The gates to The Blessing will not be open until 8 A.M. in the morning. The gates to The Blessing will not be open until 8 A.M. in the morning. The gates.... But Roy could see the gates, he could see the archway not far ahead. Everyone was leaping. It was to get a better view. The gates were opening...? Someone said they were going to be opened ahead of time; it was a special surprise. There was always at least one surprise, one unmerited act of grace, one gift that could not be anticipated.... Still, the man's voice warned them to go back, to go back to their campsites.

But why?...The din around Roy was so joyful now. The gates were open: he understood they had been open all along. Men and women at the very front of the crowd had managed to get them open. Or maybe they had been broken down: Roy heard something being smashed. A cry went up. Sheer joy. He was sorry that Micheline wasn't here but it would be impossible to get back to her—everybody pushing from behind—a man right behind him, pushing him, urging him *Go on, go on! Hurry*—giving him a hard jab in the small of the back. *Hurry!*

Behind him, beside him, on all sides. Beneath the shouts and cries, he could hear a single sigh. It was bliss, it was unimaginable, it was the sigh of rain, of rain loosening mud, of a mudflow, of lava, of earth itself coming alive and making its claim. The gates were smashed. The walls were being attacked.... Beneath the cries and screams and shouts, a single long shudder of exquisite relief, a sigh. Crowds on small knolls rose to join one another. Crowds leaped to their feet and rushed together, into this central crowd, this flow through the broken gates. Roy was frightened, but only on the outside of his body. He felt the trembling on the outside; the clammy skin, on the outside. *Micheline*...? And the baby, and the sister-in-law, what was her name...and the neighbors' boy...what was his name? No, it was too difficult. Couldn't keep so much in the imagination. Moment by moment, so swiftly changing, one moment it was daylight and the next it was dusk, swiftly changing to dusk here in the mountains, it was impossible to get back to the truck and take the little boy from Micheline's arms and put him on his shoulders where he couldn't be trampled. . . .

Loudspeakers. The voices of strangers. Some cried *Get back!* and others cried *Keep going! Hurry*! A helicopter flew low over the wall, its blades chopping the air, drawing gulps of precious air up to it while somebody shouted down at Roy until he could hardly bear it. *Get back! Warning! Get back* ! But others pushed him forward; others were stamping on his feet, shoving him, their fingers entangled in his hair. Cheers. Shouts. . . . About five hundred yards away was the stage itself, but it was unlit. What was wrong? . . . Up on a platform, on posts. And unlit. Floodlights played over the people but the stage was not lit and nobody was on it, nothing was happening, until a man tried to climb up one of the posts and fell backward and disappeared from Roy's sight and somebody brushed past Roy, so violently that Roy was knocked to one knee, protesting; but his voice could not be heard. What was happening? Who had taken over the stage? . . . Roy managed to get to his feet. Somebody fell against him and Roy pushed the man away. He managed to get to his feet again, but the scene had changed or perhaps he had been turned around and was now facing another direction. . . .

People were screaming: an earthquake! Tremors! But Roy knew better, he wasn't going to panic. If the earth was trembling, it was because of the excitement on all sides. So many voices, so many pounding feet. . . . And those maddening threats: The Blessing will not be held. Will not be administered if. The Shining One will withhold himself from The People, unless order is restored. . . . But there were threats from all sides, not just from the air. At the rear more people were pressing forward, pressing through the entrance. Word had gone out everywhere and all the groups had sprung forward and moved together into this central flow of voices and feet and legs and arms. . . . Of course there was room for all. It was promised, it had always been promised. Room for all, for everyone. Of course. But it was necessary to spread out more carefully, to move out to the sides. Roy knew that. No need for panic. No need to keep pushing. . . . Roy caught a glimpse of the stage, now overrun with people. How quickly they had climbed up and taken possession! And more were trying to climb up. But there wasn't enough room: some fell back, some were kicked back. The stage was lopsided. From beneath, it was being dismantled. The shouts from the sky were now incomprehensible, in this miraculous din from the earth....

It must have been a drainage pipe. Smelly but dry. Someone else crawled in, sobbing. Roy was hunched over, his arms wrapped around his legs, sunburned forehead pressed against his knees. Shivering. Sighing.... Thinking of The Shining One whom he had contemplated for so long, images of that radiant face, the ankle-length saffron robe, the outspread arms and many-ringed fingers, The Blessing itself at last proclaimed.... His teeth chattered. As soon as the sun set in this part of the world, it got chilly. He was exhausted, he could not stop shivering. He was too tired to lift his head from his knees. There were thousands of Michelines, thousands of wives and two-year-old boys. Millions of them. And the girl, the girl named Bunny. And the boy. And Roy ... Roy-the-father. That had been Roy-the-father, driving the truck for so many hours. Well, that was past. He could not hope to piece together so many broken things.... Outside it was still noisy; it was very noisy. The earth rocked. Shuddered. He was exhausted and he was not going to think of them, so many thousands of them: the girls, the women, the men, the children, the helicopters, the flailing arms and legs, the procession of silent people in his mind's eye, led by The Shining One in his gleaming saffron robe who had promised them a blessing but must first lead them into despair. Why was he sobbing? Why was someone sobbing near him? ... First they must be led into despair; then into salvation. Roy knew that. He wasn't going to panic. Already he had dismissed the rest of them and he was free of them and their identities and his own identity. Roy-the-husband, Roy-the-father, Roy-the-registered-owner-of-the-truck, Roy-the-son, Roy-that-was. Already he had dismissed it all. He was free. Perhaps that had been the blessing, that alone. The Blessing. Perhaps he already had been liberated from the bondage of himself, and this purity of detachment, this shivering peace, separated his old life from ... from whatever lay before him.

But he was too tired to think about it at the moment.

A Theory of Knowledge

A shadow moved silently through the grass. Professor Weber looked up from his work, startled, and saw a child approaching him.

"Yes? Who are...?"

The boy was four or five years old, a stranger. He was barefoot; there were innumerable reddened marks on his feet and legs; his short pants were ripped and filthy, and his shirt was partly unbuttoned. Professor Weber stared. Should he know whose child this was? The boy carried himself oddly, as if one side of his body were higher than the other. He was unusually quiet, timid, not like Professor Weber's grandsons, who ran anywhere they liked around the old farm, noisily, in robust good health, whenever his married daughter came to visit. "Yes? Hello? Are you a neighbor of mine?" Professor Weber said. He smiled; he did not want to frighten the boy.

The boy smiled shyly and came no closer.

It was a shock—seeing the boy's teeth. They were greenish, that thin, near-transparent look of poverty, ill health, malnutrition. The boy had wild curly hair, blue-black as an Indian's; his face was thin, too pale for this time of year, but Professor Weber thought him strangely beautiful—the eyes especially, large dark eyes that seemed entirely pupil. And so intense! The boy licked his lips. His mouth moved in a kind of convulsion, shaping words that could not be given sound. Professor Weber stared, pitying; his own lips moved in sympathy with the boy's. *Hel— Hel— Hello.* It cost the child some effort to pronounce this word.

"Can you tell me your name?" Professor Weber asked softly. "Where do you live?"

The boy was older than he had appeared at first. Professor Weber judged him to be seven or eight years old, severely undernourished. His eyes were so dark, so intense!—the intensity of his gaze deepened by an obscure shame, a despair that was almost adult. He reminded Professor Weber of a misshapen, dwarfish man who had lived in a hut beyond the village dumping ground in Katauga...but that had been many years ago, a half-century or more.

"Have we met, little boy? I'm notoriously forgetful about names, faces...you'll have to forgive me if...."

Embarrassed at such attention, the boy squatted in the grass and pretended an interest in something there—it was Professor Weber's journal, which must have slipped from his lap. Had he dozed off again? And where was his pen?—he was holding his pen, clutching it tightly. The boy turned pages slowly, frowning. A convulsive tic began at the corner of his mouth and worked gradually up into his cheek, as if the effort needed for concentration on Professor Weber's writing was painful. His lips moved soundlessly, shaping ghost-words. But of course the tight, slanted handwriting would have been too difficult for him, even if he could read; it was doubtful that he could read. "You wouldn't be interested in that, I'm afraid. Just jottings...labored whims...propositions that float of their own accord and lead nowhere. You wouldn't be interested in Reuben Weber's theory of knowledge, little boy; no one else is. Could you hand my book here, please?" The boy did not seem to hear. He was imitating or perhaps mocking the effort of reading: his head bowed, his chin creasing toward his chest, his child's forehead furrowed like an old man's. Professor Weber thought suddenly: What if he rips the pages? What if he runs off with it maliciously? The child must have wandered over from a neighboring farm. Probably the Brydons'. But Professor Weber had not known they had a grandson. Had their son married? The child did not resemble anyone in the area; but of course Professor Weber knew few people, he had kept to himself all along, it was his daughter Maude who took an interest in local news and had a fair number of acquaintances in the area.... Professor Weber's legs were thin as sticks, but the muscles of his calves and thighs had tensed like those of a much younger man, preparing to get him to his feet if necessary. "Little boy, could you hand that to me? This lap-desk is so awkward to set down, and this blanket...."

"Go away, please!" someone called, behind him.

It was his daughter Maude, down from the house.

The boy lifted his head; but not quickly; rather slowly, as if he had not heard the words, had only sensed someone else's presence. At once his dark eyes widened with fear. Professor Weber was sorry his daughter had discovered them, after all; the boy was a sweet, docile child, obviously not malicious. "He isn't harming anything," Professor Weber said curtly. "He doesn't seem to be ... isn't any.... Just a little visit...."

"Please go home, little boy," Maude said. She spoke calmly and flatly, as she sometimes spoke to Professor Weber himself. "Can't you hear? Can't you understand? I said...."

The boy straightened cautiously, as if he were afraid of being struck. He began to scratch at himself—his neck, his shoulders, his ribs. The dark eyes, fixed upon Maude, were now narrowed.

"I believe he came from that direction, from the creek," Professor Weber said, embarrassed. His voice was kindly; he wanted the boy to look at him again, as if this were a social occasion of some kind, swerving into error. It required the human element, an intelligent restoration of balance. "He evidently cut himself on the bushes, or fell on the rocks—do you see his legs? I don't think it's anything serious, he isn't crying, but perhaps we could ... it might be a good idea to wash him and...."

"Do you want me to tell your parents on you?" Maude asked the child.

He turned and ran away.

They watched him until he was out of sight—across the creek, through a field of wild shrubs and saplings. He seemed to be headed in the direction of the Brydon farm.

Professor Weber was drained by the excitement but wanted very much to talk. "Did the Brydon boy marry, after all? Is that his son?... and I didn't know about it until now? Could it be possible that...."

"The Brydons have been gone for years," Maude said flatly. "You know that." She stooped to pick up his journal. And his pen, too, which had just fallen into the grass. "*That* certainly isn't any Brydon—did you see him scratching himself? Lice. That's the kind of people living there now and I don't want anything to do with them. Nobody does. The things people say about that family, the woman especially...." She broke off, sighing angrily. "Imagine, a child with lice! Letting him go like that, running wild!"

"But who are they?" Professor Weber asked. He was confused; as always, his daughter seemed to know far more than he did; the variety of things she knew, and the emotional discharges they allowed her, seemed remarkable. He was contemptuous of the gossip she repeated—yet he wanted very much to know about the boy. "He didn't seem.... I really don't think he has lice.... Who told you that? What kind of people are his parents?"

"Never mind," Maude said. "I won't let him bother you again.... The sun has moved behind that tree, hasn't it? Are you still warm enough?"

Professor Weber was staring down toward the creek, at the tangle of trees, saplings, and bushes. A marvelous thick-bodied white willow—three enormous poplars in a row—birds fluttering in their leaves. He could not see the creek from here, but he could make out its sound; he was very happy here, no matter what people might whisper about him, and he did not want to be moved. He had not exactly heard his daughter's question. "Yes, yes," he said firmly. "Yes. That's so."

June, 1893. No: it was 1897. Professor Weber kept mixing those dates together, and he did not know why. There was nothing important about 1893 that he could recall. His wife had died a few years earlier.... No, there was nothing special about that date. The perplexing, humiliating tricks of the mind.... He had spent the greater part of his life trying to cut through obscurity, murkiness, the self-indulgent metaphysics of the past. *Of laws logically contingent the most universal are of such a kind that they must be true provided every form by which logical necessity must be thought of a given subject is also a form of its real being. If this is "metaphysical" necessity we may divide laws logically contingent into laws metaphysically necessary and laws metaphysically contingent.* But his hands trembled, it was so difficult to write, to keep pace with his thoughts. They sped forward, youthful as always, darting ahead into sub-propositions, into qualifications, refinements, hypothetical objections put forth by his enemies . . . his thoughts seemed, at times, not his

at all, but the brilliant, tireless, relentless thoughts of a stranger.
And his hands trembled, unable to keep pace. He had to steady
one hand with the other. He bit his lower lip with the effort,
impatient at how long it took him to scribble into his journal a
thought that had sprung fully matured into his mind: *Humanism
was feeble in its mental powers...incapable of subtlety. The
acceptance of nominalist beliefs has poisoned all of Western
thinking. As if a reality that has no representation could be other
than one without relation and quality....*

He had waited so long for summer. Winter here, in the
foothills of the Chautauqua Mountains, was interminable...spring was unpredictable, heartbreaking for an old man
who craved the open air, release at last from the stuffy rooms of
the house and from his absurd dependency upon the wood-
burning stove in the kitchen. From time to time he had been
actually frightened at the prospect of a chilly spring. Why had he
come here to this dismal place? Several miles north of the small
town of Rockland, on the Alder River...a full day's drive to a
decent library, at the seminary in Albany; and of course that
library was always disappointing. Twelve years ago, was it, since
his retirement? His "retirement"? Everyone had urged him not to
move away from Philadelphia, even his enemies had hypocritically urged him to reconsider his decision; there were vague airy
insincere promises...the possibility of lecturing, tutoring,
independent work with advanced post-doctoral students who
required more logic and mathematics. James Emmett Morgan
had said...Charles Lewis had said....But he had moved away
just the same.

And he did not regret it, really. The foothills were
beautiful—the poplars, willows, blue spruce, elms surrounding
his house—the many birds, including pine grosbeaks and
dark-headed juncos—the fragrance of open air, solitude—
freedom at last to compose his book on the foundations of human
knowledge—freedom to sit in the sun for hours, brooding,
dozing. He half hoped the curly-haired boy would appear again,
to interrupt his work. Though he had lived in the old farmhouse
for years now, he knew no one in the neighborhood; he could
count the number of times he had bothered to go into
Rockland....Insignificant, the affairs of most men. Monstrous
economic snarls, shortsighted passions, the ignorance of which
Socrates spoke with a good humor perhaps ill-advised. So no one
came to interrupt him; it had been years now since he'd really

talked with anyone, argued with anyone about matters of importance; he half hoped the neighbor boy might.... But Maude said they were no better than gypsies. She said it was a "scandal," the things that went on ... as bad as living on the outskirts of Rockland itself, where there was a paper mill and mill-workers' hovels ... unspeakable crimes that went ignored. But the child had seemed to Professor Weber remarkably well-behaved, especially in contrast with his own grandsons.

What was that sound?—high-pitched vibrating racket? Ah, the flicker in that big poplar. Professor Weber strained to listen.

No, he did not regret his move. Not once had he indicated to anyone, in his correspondence, that he regretted it—or any decision of his life. He was stubborn, flamboyant as in his prime, immensely certain of himself. He *knew* what was right; he had an instinct for the truth. The stone farmhouse with the rotting roof, originally built in 1749, the three acres of land, the several decaying outbuildings his grandchildren played in when they came ... these were pleasant, agreeable things, hardly a mistake. What had been needed so sorely, his defenders told him, was a single work, a work that set forth his system; had he had time, while teaching, to bring together the thousands of pages of notes, sketches, hypothetical problems ... the essence of "Weber's Epistemology" ... he and his disciples could hold their own against the outrageously popular William James and the equally insupportable ideas that were coming in from Germany, like an infection Anglo-Saxons seemed eager to catch every half-century or so. Had he the time.... Had he the energy.... What he kept secret from everyone, even his closest colleagues, was the perplexing fact that ideas stormed his brain with such violence that he was capable even at the best of times of doing no more than jotting down five or six pages of continuous discovery. If only he were content with being superficial like James! ... but that was unfair, he supposed, since James had written several very perceptive and kindly letters to him, and had even arranged for a lecture series ... unfair, unfair ... his thinking was muddled because of the tranquility of this place, the seductive qualities of.... Was William James still alive? Were Lewes and Wrightson still alive? Why had it never been offered him, that position at Harvard everyone knew he deserved ...? The jealousy of his colleagues at Philadelphia had been quite a surprise. That they should gossip behind his back ... refer to him in the presence of graduate students and young faculty as a crank ... laugh and jeer and ridicule his oratorical method of teaching. ... Or had he imagined it? Bursting into the Common Room, hearing laughter, had he misinterpreted the silence, the guilty looks, the uneasy smiles? Of course he had always intimidated them. Always. His attacks upon their complacency, upon their beloved "areas of specialization," his pronouncement that all philosophical speculation must flow through the rigorously narrow channel of logic and linguistic analysis—he had intimidated them all! He had frightened them all!

"Father. *Father*."

Maude was speaking. He awoke: was astonished to see that it was no longer daylight, that he was in the old leather chair by the fireplace, a book on his lap. What day was this? Where was the little boy? He checked the book—yes, it was Euclid—so he did remember something of what was going on. He had been dictating to Maude and she had allowed him to fall asleep, as usual. Now she was asking him, in the kind of impertinent tone one hears in the nursery or the sickroom, if he was all right? "You seemed to be having a nightmare ... you were twitching all over ... talking in your sleep. ..."

"Leave me alone," he said. "... persecuting me. All of you."

"Father, did you have a nightmare?"

"It was because I frightened them ... outraged them, wasn't it," he muttered. It seemed to him obvious that an injustice had been committed against him; a series of injustices had been committed, in fact; and why was Maude staring at him so uncomprehendingly? "What I must live to establish, when I finish the book I'm doing, is a science of a newer sort ... a Science of the Unique ... a respect for ... awareness of. ... Let the Hegelians rage, let the Platonists ... let them band against me. ... It wasn't fair, you know. I was never taken seriously ... I had anticipated in the fifties the methodology of 'pragmatism' ... if not the term, that despicable misleading term! ... they could not forgive me that I valued Truth over social pieties and religious nonsense ... that my first marriage was ... was not ... did not prove stable. ... Cowards, all of them."

"Yes, Father," Maude said.

"Is not belief 'that upon which a man is prepared to act'?—and is not anything man will not *act* upon likely to be fraudulent belief—hypocrisy—lies—sheer rubbish? And so, because I valued my search for Truth over—over—"

"Yes."

"Philosophy must be cleansed, harshly. Without mercy. Are you writing this down, dear? Or am I speaking too fast?...Philosophy must be cleansed...purified...must keep aloof of the myriad sordid political skirmishes of the day...must keep aloof of the historical world altogether. And the church in any form. That goes without saying.... Without saying. What is dead will sink, what is vital and living will rise to the surface. The future...the future...."

"Yes, Father?" Maude said flatly.

But for a moment he could not think: could not even seem to comprehend the meaning of that term.

Future. *Future*?

Time itself had betrayed him.

"I was born before my time, you see. A premature birth. Graduated from Harvard at the age of eighteen, my Master's at twenty...considered abrasive and insolent simply because...because others resented my youth. Did I tell you that as early as the fifties I had formulated the concept of 'pragmatism'...without using that word, of course...but the methodology, the...the aura of...the reliance upon phenomenological procedure.... According to my notes it was in 1859. No longer young then, no longer a rebellious 'upstart'...thirty-nine years old, in fact...yet no one listened to me. No one."

Ah, but it was dangerous, to allow his body such nervous excitement! He knew very well that it was dangerous; he had no need for an ignorant backwoods general practitioner to tell him...a man with tobacco-stained hands and teeth...a medical degree from a school probably unrecognized in the East. He had no need for his wife or Maude or Clara or.... His heartbeat accelerated until his entire body seemed to rock. His face grew heated, flushed. His muscles twitched with the need to act, to break free of these idiotic restraints...to assert himself as his will demanded he must. But time had betrayed him. Time: an abstract term, a mere condition of the human mind...a condition dependent upon perception, grammar, the logical assumption of...of finitude. Time had betrayed him, had leaped from the early decade of his young manhood to this decade of exile...had confused every issue...splashing him with blobs of color, emotion, noise, tears.... that hideous time

when, after his first stroke, he had had to watch a scrawny stray
cat systematically torture a chipmunk out in the yard ... fifteen
minutes of it ... *fifteen minutes* ... and Maude hadn't heard his
cries, his shouts of anger and despair. Time had rushed him
along, too hurriedly for him to organize his thoughts, set down an
outline for A *Theory of Human Knowledge* ... he had been a
rather fashionably dressed young man with a full blond beard, a
penetrating voice, a frame that had been solid, muscular ... rather short legs, and slightly bowed, but of undeniable
strength. And purpose. He had been too young for his elders to
take seriously; now he was too old for anyone to take seriously.
His elders: enemies. They were dead now. He did not want
revenge on them. Truly, he did not want to hurt them. He wanted
only justice. Recognition. Acceptance of his ideas. He did not ask
to be loved or even liked, but simply tolerated. Was it too much
to ask? ... Incredible, that he, Reuben, his father's most
promising son, a boy who had absorbed all there was to know of
mathematical theory before the age of thirteen, was now so
altered that his own mirrored face repulsed him!

"... but you must draw your ideas together, Professor Weber.
You must construct a system, Professor Weber. Your ideas will be
lost ... will be misunderstood ... will be appropriated by lesser
men or by your enemies. You must compose a rebuttal to
Professor Madison's shameless neo-nominalism. You must
compose a letter explaining your own actions in regard to your
absence from the university community for those years. You
must withdraw from this atmosphere ... purify your
thoughts ... draw your ideas together before it is too late."

He began to laugh.

He opened his eyes: the boy was laughing with him.

It was July now. The boy had visited only twice, but they
were on quite friendly, comfortable terms. Professor Weber
wrote in his journal, or fussed and sighed with his notes, or called
the boy's attention to certain birds' songs—the flicker, some
cardinals, some warblers—while the boy usually sat in the grass,
silently, listening with great concentration. He did not speak;
even trying to speak was too much of an effort. But from time to
time he laughed, which delighted Professor Weber. He had not
tried hard enough, as a teacher, to be amusing ...
witty ... playful. He would have liked, perhaps, to have been
more entertaining. A robust lecturer, yes, but too driven by

a sense of urgent points to be made during a lecture period, too nervously abrupt.... It pleased him when the boy laughed. "Yes, that's right," he said. "That's the proper judgment."

The boy's eyes were immense. Gypsy blood, perhaps. But no, that was Maude's nonsense.... Too pale to have gypsy blood. Looked more like the child of a mill-worker or one of those luckless children Professor Weber had seen occasionally, in Boston, sickly pale, staggering with weariness, workers at one of the factories along the river. A pity, a pity. The young blond-bearded man walking along so quickly, lost in abstract thought, and the scrawny pale children, unnaturally quiet for children... an adult or two, probably their parents or an older brother or sister, herding them along. A pity. Couldn't something be... ? But he would forget them in a few minutes; would forget whatever had been upsetting him. "People haven't anything to do out here except gossip," Professor Weber told the boy, shaking his head. "My own daughter is one of the worst offenders. I don't listen any longer, I press my hands over my ears and refuse to listen!... But you evidently don't go to school? You can't read? A pity, a pity. Why don't they send you to school?... Perhaps I could teach you. If we could work out some way of.... Of course without offending your...."

He was staring at the boy's forehead. The skin was discolored near his left temple, as if he had banged his head against something. A very pale violet-orange. As Professor Weber spoke, the boy stared and smiled and then half closed his eyes, basking in the sun. Marvelous, this peace. The two of them. Maude did not like the child but would not dare interrupt. No need to talk, of course. The wind in the poplars... the cicadas... the sun. July now; midsummer. A pile of notes on Professor Weber's lap, an outline in faded ink that he had discovered the evening before... which would save him the labor of writing an outline... hadn't known he had already gotten so far with A Theory of Human Knowledge or Knowing, as it was to be tentatively called... really, the outline was excellent; it would do. "Platonic Realism: must be defended against its own excesses. The extremities of Realism touch Nominalism itself. How could Plato not know... ? How could he fail to see... ? A tragedy, that Plato never consolidated his system but presented it piecemeal... gave in to the performer in Socrates.... No," Professor Weber said suddenly, "it's really too late. Plato is lost, he can't be resuscitated. Shameless. That he could allow one of his characters to tease us by saying *Not-being is a sort of being*....Spinoza. You will fall under his spell, like children. Adulthood cannot be approached except by way of the...the mastery of...submitting of oneself to....Discipline, rigor, tautological propositions...language...beauty. Ah, what beauty! It cannot be denied. But he lacked humanity, he lacked a sense of terror. As for Kant....Why are you startled? Why are you no longer taking notes? I suppose you will report me to the dean of the college, who imagines himself a Kantian!...without possessing even the rudiments (I know: I have quizzed him personally) of a mind. As for Emerson....It was an insult, and yet I nearly accepted. 1869. 1870. Reuben Weber to follow Emerson's lecture series: a disciplined philosopher to follow a scatterbrain! No evidence of mental powers at all. Baffling, that he could be so shameless, arrogant. And yet successful. Cambridge infected with it . . . monstrosity, parody . . . fragments of ideas from Hegel, Schelling, Plotinus, even from Boehm; and from the East, of course. The unsightly pantheism of the East. Undifferentiated. Evil. And now offered to the New World. What an insult!" Professor Weber laughed.

The convulsive twisting of his mouth woke him.

A woman was dragging the boy away, screaming at him.

No. He opened his eyes and the boy was still there, lying in the grass at his feet, asleep.

"Why, Matthew and Tim are grown up," Maude said slowly. "Matthew is at West Point and Tim is....You know that. Whyever are you saying such things?"

"I thought they might...might like to come visit," Professor Weber said in an agony of shame. "Boys, farms, the country...playmates...that sort of thing. They used to like the big hay barn so much."

"They're grown up now and you know it."

"Why do you persecute me?" Professor Weber whispered, bringing his hands to his face. "Why do you lead me into traps, and laugh at me?"

One humid afternoon, when the sky had suddenly darkened over, Professor Weber heard quite clearly the boy's screams.

They were beating him over there. Abusing him.

He knew, he knew. Maude would not tell him what the neighborhood rumor was—said it was none of his concern. The boy was not "right in his head." He was sickly, he was always dirty. Those people . . . ! No better than gypsies. Trash that had moved out of Rockland. Had probably been forced to move. The man drank. The woman drank. They were no good, were only renting the old Brydon place, would probably be moving out once cold weather set in . . . so there was no need to get involved with them. Or even to talk about them.

"Maude, help me! Maude!"

He got to his feet unaided. He was on his feet. But his legs were so weak; there was a sensation of tingling, harsh fleshless vibration; he knew he was going to fall.

"Maude—"

She denied hearing the screams.

"I don't hear anything," she said.

To prove it, she went down to the creek—to the very edge of their property. He watched her: watched her stand with one hand cupped to her ear, in a pretense of listening.

"No, I don't hear anything," she told him flatly, looking into his eyes. He saw a middle-aged woman, stout, graying, her hair wispy, her expression a curious blend of insolence and melancholy. ". . . Now we'd better get you back to the house; it looks like a thunderstorm. . . ."

"There—do you hear it?"

But it was only a jay.

There are an infinite number of logics; of structures into which sense experience can be put; there are an infinite number of mathematical systems and geometries. We have no reason to believe that only one system is valid for Nature, since Nature is infinite. When our myopic systems intrude upon Nature, Nature takes revenge simply by retreating. We reach out—but the object of our inquiry eludes us. Philosophy falters because it must use words. Philosophy is words. Still, it is noble, it points to the reality beyond itself, reverently, if it cannot chart the wonders of a multi-dimensional universe but must remain in the three-dimensional, it can at least . . . it can at least. . . .

Early August. But the starlings and red-winged blackbirds were already flocking . . . ! It must be some mistake. Early August according to the calendar. Hot, humid, shadowless days. Still summer, surely. And yet certain species were already flocking. . . . Professor Weber mentioned it to Maude and she said that she'd seen quite a number on her way to town, in a burnt-out field. Yes, they seemed to be flocking early this year. But certainly they knew what they were doing.

It frightened Professor Weber, and rather angered him, the birds' perverse behavior.

When the boy came to visit that week, ascending the hill shyly as always, furtively, not responding to Professor Weber's enthusiastic greeting...when the boy came to visit...when he came to sit in the grass a few yards away, wiping at his nose, sniffing, Professor Weber complained to him about the birds; it did not seem quite right. Then he heard his voice complaining about the trickery of time, which philosophy had not adequately explored. It was subjective, of course: the worst kind of idealism. And yet.... During his absence from teaching, his self-imposed retreat from both teaching and marriage (ah, how they had persecuted him afterward!), as a man still young in his ideas, he had seemed to slip into another dimension of time: working as a shiploader in New Orleans, later working on a freighter on the West Coast...one year in a lumbering camp in Alberta, Canada.... Ah, he had experienced a different sort of time. He had gazed back upon his earlier self and upon his colleagues and saw them sluggish-slow, elephantine, trapped by their own theories of numbers and knowledge and love and God. But his intellect had not surrendered. It had struggled, had fought bitterly. Nominalism would not triumph. The sleazy sordid Sophistic relativism of the *Republic* would not triumph over *him*.... And it did not. Even while he worked with his hands, a laboring man among laboring men, his mind had held itself detached, it had continued to operate with the same rigor and purity as before...though now he felt himself strengthened with an additional wisdom. He had slipped out of the dimension of language and had entered the dimension of brute reality, in which time is so ruthless a tyrant. And he had gazed back upon his earlier life—upon what he had imagined to be all of life—and found it anemic, self-deceiving, and vain. Still, he had not rejected it. He had assimilated it into himself, had somehow grown into it once again, from another direction, no longer his father's son or his professors' most promising student, but Reuben Weber, and no other. Physical labor had come to seem, during the last weeks of his obligation to the lumbering company, as phantasmal as any idea or proposition. And gradually he had come to see that ultimately only the mental processes were real, since only the mental processes activated and recorded the other processes.... "I don't mind dying," he whispered to the boy. The boy slept, breathing noisily through his mouth. There was a raspy, hoarse sound to his breathing. "But I must tell people what I have discovered. Before I die, I must consolidate these notes ... these thousands of.... Otherwise.... They will shake their heads and say, *He failed, he was only a crank. Look at the unreadable mess he has bequeathed! Fifty-five years of brooding ... fifty-five years of notes ... into the fire with them, hurry, before we're infected with his madness!* They will laugh at me, I know. They will pass the cruelest judgment on me. They have no mercy, no mercy. I don't mind dying, if only...." He stared at the sleeping boy. Hideous irony, that his salvation lay in the twentieth century, that the child—the child would live into that century—wouldn't he?—one of them must! His salvation lay in the future, for only future logicians and philosophers could begin to comprehend his work; and yet the future would exclude him. It would vindicate him, redeem him, bless him—and yet exclude him. "Little boy, are you ill? You shouldn't sleep so long ... your mother will be angry with you, she'll wonder where you are ... she'll come get you and be very, very angry.... Little boy?"

No one visited him now: no one wrote. He had been careless about writing to people, even to Professor James, who had been so kind and had meant well, hadn't intended to be so patronizing. No one visited, and the boy came so infrequently, limping up the hill from the creek ... shy, smiling guiltily, fearful. He must call Maude. The boy might be ill; his breath sounded so labored. And he must insist that Maude notify the authorities. He would insist. He would write a letter himself if she refused to tell the sheriff. He would.... "Lewes. Charles Lewes," he said suddenly, just remembering. The boy opened his eyes groggily. "Yes, it was Charles Lewes—my last visitor. I don't suppose it mattered, the favor he did.... Or perhaps he never did it, how could I know?"

The boy was awake now. In a moment he would leave.

"... must have been eighty years ago, at least," Professor Weber said sadly. "If only I could teach you to read! That would be so very, very rewarding.... But you don't come close enough, do you? ... shy and frightened as a wild animal ... as if I would hurt you.... Yes, you'd better hurry home; it's late. Can you come visit tomorrow? Tomorrow? ... I want to tell you about Professor Hockings, Myron Hockings ... that wonderful old man.... Will you come back tomorrow?"

The boy looked over his shoulder, hurrying away.

"... wonderful, brave old man.... A head of white hair, snow white. At least eight years old and still teaching, though it was, I believe, his last year of teaching. And so gentle! ... I barged into his office and for two hours I told him the implications of Holub's work on numbers theory ... how it totally superceded his own work.... A young man no more than twenty-one at the time and yet I saw in a flash all that Holub was up to, the most extraordinary demolition work since Hume! ... and it totally, totally superceded Professor Hockings' own work in the field. An incredible intellect, Holub. Professor Hockings as well. So much learning, so much ... and courage as well ... nobility ... that he argued with me dispassionately for two hours and then, at last comprehending the superior strategy of Holub ... that he should do no more than close his eyes for a moment or two ... and then whisper *I see*. Only that: *I see*. That he had been eighty years old and had dedicated the last twenty years of his life to ... to a spirited but wrong-headed defense of.... And the genuine nobility with which he admitted defeat, finally, holding no resentment against me for having been so impertinent or against Holub for having ... having superceded him. Eighty years old, a renowned teacher, so patient with young argumentative men like me, so very kindly, though intense discussions obviously exhausted him, his hands would tremble and his eyelids flutter...."

The jays were squawking. Probably a squirrel. They were unusually active at this time of day: very late afternoon.

Professor Hockings was dead, was he? Probably. Yes, certainly. He had lived a long, full life, eminently respectable, perhaps rather cagey in terms of Harvard and Boston society: had endured somehow one of the usual marriages to one of the usual well-bred young ladies. Odd, that Professor Weber should remember that gentleman so clearly, as if it were only a few weeks ago that their exciting conversation had taken place; as if many years had not intervened ... decades ... in fact, more than half a century, incredible though it was. He was now seventy-seven years old, had been twenty-one at the time, just beginning to assemble various theories, hypotheses, "flexible foundations" as he came to call them, and of course numerous notebooks and journals, none of which he had ever really rejected, though as time went on he realized that his continually developing and continually skeptical intellect had long moved beyond the scribblings of his youth. Remarkable, the restless

movements of the human intellect! Not to be contained within
the sober, somber, all-too-proper restraints of a mere article for
Journal of Metaphysics or *Monist* or ... what was that other
periodical, the one edited by James Morgan ... in which
Professor Weber's first, iconoclastic, and rather famous little
piece had appeared, "Recent Fallacies in Epistemological
Methodologies" ... ? Ah yes: *Transactions of the American
Hegelian Society*. Well, nothing could restrain the intellect. That
was a triumph, of a kind, was it not? In one sense he had failed,
had not even managed to put anything together between hard
covers, anything to be set defiantly on the shelf beside the
others ... but in another sense he had ... someone had ... *it* had
triumphed, however improbably, however difficult it would be
to explain to any of his enemies or jealous, spiteful colleagues or
even to his sympathetic associates ... or ... or to anyone who
cared to know. "Difficult to explain," he whispered, watching
where the boy had gone. "Impossible. They would say I had
gone insane or had become senile, they would dismiss whatever
wisdom I had to offer, thinking it was simply that of a deluded
old man who had never quite succeeded in ... in ... doing
whatever it was. ... Maude? Maude?" He managed to get to his
feet, had even taken several steps down toward the creek,
walking slowly, his arms outstretched like a sleepwalker's,
before she came running to him.

"What are you doing? Why are you behaving like that? —Why
are you becoming so childish, Father!"

There it came again—that isolated, piercing cry.
There was no mistaking it.

He called for Maude, but she failed to come. He shouted for
her, banged on the floor of his bedroom with a shoe, and still she
refused to come. "I know what's happening ... I can hear ... I'm
not deaf, I'm not a deluded old man. ..." Finally his daughter did
come: anxious, drawn, her face thickened with something very
like terror. She told him it was very late, after 2 A.M. He had been
screaming in his sleep again. A bad dream. Would he like a
sleeping draught, would he like the window closed? She closed
the window before he could reply. "... nightmares," she
murmured. "... you must be working too hard during the day,
straining yourself. ..."

"I don't want that window closed," he said feebly.

Owls in the distance. Loons. The gathering force of the wind, as summer retreated. Noises of nighttime, so very different from those of the day—haunting, teasing, undifferentiated. Mysterious. Why were the peepers—the frogs—so noisy one night, and silent the next? Why did a single cricket take up residence just outside Professor Weber's bedroom window, so that its solitary singing became something irritating and rather monstrous? Professor Weber loved the crickets *en masse*. But this cricket kept him awake.... And yet, a day or two later, the cricket was gone and the night should have been harmonious again, why was it so turbulent and frightful?

He wrote a letter to the local authorities, explaining his suspicions as briefly as possible. *Have reason to believe that a child is being mistreated. Demand that you send investigators.* Maude promised to mail the letter; afterward, she claimed she had mailed it. It was late August now and autumnal, actually cold in the evenings, not always pleasant during the day. Days passed quickly. Daylight was abbreviated, unpredictable. "Why doesn't he come over again?" Professor Weber asked. "How long has it been since...?" He lay awake, listening. There were owls, loons, occasional dogs' cries and, well before dawn, the cries of roosters that must have been miles away. He could not sleep and no longer wanted to sleep. Thoughts raced and jammed together in his skull: colliding and then ricocheting away. *What if....If only....Have reason to believe....Demand....*

Then, one night, he could stand it no longer.

He rose and dressed as quietly as possible; he stood trembling before the door of his closet for some time, worrying that it would creak when he opened it, but finally he did open it, and the sight of the clothes inside somehow strengthened him, they were his, his own, and he would not need Maude to take them from the hangers and help him dress. Quiet, quiet. He found himself at the door to his room; he listened for some time, hearing only the ticking of a clock, and in the distance the usual night noises and, at irregular intervals, that peculiar human cry his daughter had refused to acknowledge. He heard it. He knew.... There it was again, there. It was unmistakable and he could not deny it though his entire body trembled with fear and with a sense of ... a sense of intelligent awareness that...that he was perhaps making a mistake: the parents would yell at him, would demand that he go away, would possibly punish the child even more cruelly than

before. Those welts on his bare, thin legs! The discoloration on
his forehead and upper arm! "Here, stop, what are you doing,
you don't know what you're doing, you don't know the pain you
are inflicting, you can't possibly know how it hurts, what agony
he is suffering. . . ."

He rehearsed his speech as he made his way along the
darkened corridor . . . to the kitchen, to the back door . . . and
breathing hard, pausing to get his bearings after every five or six
steps, outside into the moonlit night, onto the dew-wet lawn.
Quiet. Must be quiet. He was walking bent over, as if fearful of
straightening. A curious shuffling walk, an old man's walk.
Descending the hill, however, he discovered that it was not
necessary—such caution—he could breathe better by straightening his back—bringing his arms out at his sides, like a
sleepwalker.

At the bottom of the hill, the creek.

Ah, he had forgotten how shallow it was in late summer. So
there was no real difficulty in making his way across: he was able
to cross without getting his feet very wet, inching along a ridge of
gravel and rock. Then the creek bank. Fortunately there were
bushes, he seized branches in both hands and hauled himself up,
heart pounding but triumphant. Now it was necessary to rest for
a while; he forced himself to rest, to be prudent. "I hear you. I
hear you," he whispered. The child's cries were louder now. He
had to resist the temptation to run to the house and shout at them
with all the authority of his position. *Stop! You are criminals and I
have come to free your child—I will take him back home with
me—*

But the child was not in the house at all. There would be no
confrontation with the parents at all.

When he finally got to the end of the lane, and in sight of the
old Brydon farmhouse—distressingly decayed, even by moonlight—it was obvious that the cries and moans were coming from
one of the outbuildings. He whispered, "I hear you, I hear you,"
and crossed the grassy open space as quickly as possible. His legs
ached; his entire body was rocking with the effort of his heart;
but his thoughts were surprisingly calm, and in a sense he did not
seem to be thinking at all. His mind, the consciousness with
which he had been so familiar, had become wonderfully
calm . . . clear . . . a liquid purity he had never before experienced,
as if another person or another aspect of his own being had taken
over. They had locked the child in an old shed or rabbit hutch.

vidently. He seized the wooden handle of the door—was
urprised that it wasn't locked, after all—"Are you in here? What
as happened?" he said aloud. "Are you—?"

The boy was there, on the floor.

He had been tied to a weight of some kind, or perhaps it was
n old farm implement; bound cruelly and tightly with leather
traps; and they had even wound a rag around his mouth, which
ad come loose. He was sobbing. He saw Professor Weber and
is eyes widened in amazement. His mouth opened, soundless.
n the moonlight Professor Weber could see the welts and
leeding scratches on the child's bare chest, beneath the straps.
I'll untie you, it's all right, everything is all right," Professor
Veber whispered. He was agitated, even terrified. Such
rembling. . . . But he hid his alarm, he didn't want the boy to see.
n another minute or two, in another minute, as soon as he caught
is breath. . . .

He needed something to cut the straps with. A knife—a pair of
cissors—

The boy was whimpering.

What if the parents came—?

Isn't my love enough, Professor Weber thought, why isn't it
nough, no one understands me!—kneeling beside the boy,
ugging wildly at the straps. He too was whimpering. His breath
ad become shallow and ragged. What if the parents came! All
e needed was a knife or a pair of scissors or a file, something
harp enough to cut through these ugly straps—if only he had
nown before leaving the house, if only he had guessed what he
vould encounter—

"What have they done to you? Why—?"

His fingers were bleeding. His thumbnail was broken close to
he flesh. The surprise of pain—! But then, miraculously, one of
he straps broke. He worked his fingers desperately under
nother and tugged at it, panting. "Here. It's weak. It's rotten. I
hink I can get it. . . . Ah: there you are. It's going to be all right
ow, you're going to be all right now, those horrible people won't
urt you any longer. . . ."

The boy was staring up at him. His face was swollen, hardly a
hild's face now, puffy and bruised; his lips were twitching as he
ried to speak. Luminous, his poor skin. So pale. And his eyes so
lark. Professor Weber touched his cheek to comfort him—"No
eed to speak! You're safe with me!"—and suddenly the last
trap broke—the ordeal was over.

The boy laughed in delight.

"You see—? It's over. I've saved you," Professor Weber said.

They laughed quietly together, so that no one else could hear.